Critical acclaim

'Baldacci inhabits the skin of his creations –
tripping us up with unexpected empathy
and subtle identification'
Sunday Express

'Compelling . . . finely drawn . . .
a page-turner worth losing sleep over'
USA Today

'As expertly plotted as all Baldacci's work'
Sunday Times

'Baldacci cuts everyone's grass – Grisham's,
Ludlum's, even Patricia Cornwell's – and
more than gets away with it'
People

'A plot strong enough to make
the bath go cold around you'
Independent on Sunday

'Yet another winner . . . The excitement
builds . . . The plot's many planted
bombs explode unpredictably'
New York Times

'As usual, Baldacci delivers the goods in
fine style, with thrills and spills aplenty'
Independent on Sunday

The Whole Truth

David Baldacci is the internationally acclaimed
author of eighteen bestselling novels. With his books
published in at least 45 languages, and with over
90 million copies in print, he is one of the world's
favourite storytellers. His family foundation, the Wish
You Well Foundation, a non-profit organization, works
to eliminate illiteracy across America. Still a resident
of his native Virginia, he invites you to visit him at
www.DavidBaldacci.com, and his foundation at
www.WishYouWellFoundation.org, and to look into
its programme to spread books across America at
www.FeedingBodyandMind.com.

DAVID BALDACCI

The Whole Truth

PAN BOOKS

First published 2008 by Hachette Book Group, USA

First published in Great Britain 2008 by Macmillan

First published in paperback 2008 by Pan Books

This edition published 2012 by Pan Books
an imprint of Pan Macmillan, a division of Macmillan Publishers Limited
Pan Macmillan, 20 New Wharf Road, London N1 9RR
Basingstoke and Oxford
Associated companies throughout the world
www.panmacmillan.com

ISBN 978-1-4472-2685-7

Visit **www.panmacmillan.com** to read more about all our books
and to buy them. You will also find features, author interviews and
news of any author events, and you can sign up for e-newsletters
so that you're always first to hear about our new releases.

To Zoe and Luke

*Why waste time discovering the truth
when you can so easily create it?*

— The person quoted above requested anonymity
as he was not authorized to speak on the record
as to matters of truth.

PROLOGUE

"Dick, I need a war."

"Well, as always, you've come to the right place, Mr. Creel."

"It won't be a typical conflict."

"I never expect typical from you."

"But you have to sell it. You have to make them believe, Dick."

"I can make them believe anything."

1

At precisely zero hours UT, or midnight Universal Time, the image of the tortured man erupted onto the world's most popular Web site.

The first six words he spoke would be remembered forever by everyone who heard them.

"I am dead. I was murdered."

He was speaking Russian on the screen but at the bottom his tragic story was retold in virtually any language one desired with the press of a key. Secret Russian Federation police had beaten "confessions" of treason out of him and his family. He'd managed to escape and make this crude video.

Whoever held the camera had either been scared to death, drunk, or both, for the grainy film vibrated and shook every few seconds.

The man said if the video had been released that meant he'd been recaptured by government thugs and was already dead.

His crime? Simply wanting freedom.

"There are tens of thousands just like me," he told the world. "Their bones lie heavy on the frozen tundra of Siberia and in the deep waters of Lake Balkhash in Kazakhstan. You will see evidence of this soon. There are others who will take up the fight now that I am gone."

He warned that while the world had focused on the Osama bin Ladens of the world for so long, the old evil, with a destructive force a million times greater than the combined Islamic renegades, was clearly back, and deadlier than ever.

"It is time the world knew *the whole truth*," he shouted at the camera, then broke down in tears.

"My name is Konstantin. My name *was* Konstantin," he corrected. "It is too late for me and my family. We are all dead now. My wife, my three children, all gone. Do not forget me, and why I died. Do not let my family perish in vain."

As the man's image and voice faded from view, a mushroom cloud lit up the screen, and superimposed on the bottom of this horrifying visual was the ominous tagline: *First the Russian people, then the rest of the world. Can we afford to wait?*

The production values were rudimentary, the special effects amateurish, but no one cared about that. Konstantin and his poor family had made the ultimate sacrifice so that the rest of the world would have a chance to live.

The first person to see the video, a computer programmer in Houston, was stunned. He e-mailed the file to a list of twenty friends on his share list. The next person to view it seconds later lived in France and suffered from insomnia. In tears, she sent it to fifty friends. The third viewer was from South Africa and was so incensed at what he'd seen that he phoned the BBC and then did an e-mail blast to eight hundred of his "closest" mates on the Web. A teenage girl in Norway watched the video in horror and then forwarded it to every person she knew. The next thousand people to view it lived in nineteen different countries and shared it with thirty friends each, and they with dozens each. What had started as a digital raindrop in the Internet ocean quickly exploded into a pixel-and-byte tsunami the size of a continent.

Like a spreading pandemic, the video ignited a maelstrom worldwide. From blog to blog, chat room to chat room, e-mail to e-mail, the story passed. With each retelling it grew in proportion until the globe was in apparent jeopardy of being overrun at any moment by crazy, bloodthirsty Russians. Within three days after Konstantin's sad proclamation, the world rang with his name. Soon half the earth's population, including many who had no idea who the U.S. president or the pope was, knew all about the dead Russian.

And from the e-mail, blog, and chat room circuits the story was picked up by newspapers on the outskirts of the mainstream. And then the likes of the *New York Times*, the *Wall Street Journal*, and leading dailies around the world were sucked into the frenzy, if for no other reason than it was what everyone was talking about. From there, it hit the global TV circuit, with everyone from Channel One in Germany to the BBC to ABC News and CNN to government-run TV in China heralding a possible new doomsday era. And from there it became firmly planted in the world's collective mind, soul, and conscience, becoming the number one story to such an extent that there were no other stories anyone cared about.

The rallying cry of "Remember Konstantin" was heard on the lips of people on all seven continents.

The Russian government issued emphatic denials to all of it. Russian president Gorshkov even went on international television to denounce it as a complete and total lie and offered up what he called "slam dunk" evidence that no such person as Konstantin had ever even existed. Yet not many people believed him. Gorshkov was ex-KGB. From top to bottom, the Russian government was filled with fascist demons; journalists across the world had been informing people of that for years. It was just that up to this moment no one had really cared, because, well, it hadn't interfered with their lives. Now they had dead Konstantin and a mushroom cloud on the Internet telling them that it suddenly mattered very much.

There were certainly plenty of skeptical people out there who held serious doubts as to who and exactly what Konstantin and his video were actually supposed to represent. These same people would start to investigate the supposedly dead man and his story. Yet for many others they had heard and seen all they needed to unequivocally make up their minds.

But Russia and the rest of the world would never discover that Konstantin was actually a fledgling actor from Latvia, his "wounds," and "emaciation" the result of clever makeup and professional lighting. After shooting his piece he'd washed up, removed all elements of his disguise, and had a nice lunch at, of all places, the Russian Tea Room on 57th Street in New York, spending part of the $50,000 he'd been paid to do the shoot. Since he also spoke Spanish and possessed dark good looks and a chiseled body, his chief ambition now was to win a major role in a Latino soap opera.

Meanwhile, the world would never be the same.

2

Nicolas Creel leisurely finished his Bombay Sapphire and tonic and put on his jacket. He was going for a walk. Actually, normal people went for walks. Billionaire corporate chieftains traveled high above the rabble. As he looked out the chopper window on the short ride across the Hudson to Jersey the skyscrapers below reminded him of how far he'd come. Creel had been born in West Texas, an area so big and barren with a seemingly endless flatness that it was said many who called it home were unaware there was any other place to live, or at least any way to get there.

Creel had spent exactly one year of his life in the Lone Star State before moving to the Philippines along with his army sergeant daddy. From there seven other countries had followed bang-bang-bang until Creel's father was deployed to Korea and promptly blown to ash in what the army later described as an unfortunate logistical snafu. His widowed mother had remarried, and, years later, college followed for Creel, where he earned an engineering degree. After that, he cobbled together enough funds for an MBA run, but petered out after six months, choosing instead to learn the ropes in the real world.

The one valuable lesson his soldier daddy had taught him was that the Pentagon purchased more weapons than anyone and overpaid for every single one of them. And even better, when you needed more profit, you just asked for it and they gave it to you. It wasn't their money, after all. And there was nothing easier to give away than someone else's cash, especially since America had the biggest piggy bank in the world. It seemed a damn fine business to be in, because as Creel quickly found out, one really could sell the U.S. military $12,000 toilets and $9,000 hammers and actually get away with it under a mountain of legal trickery and congressional hearing mumbo-jumbo.

Creel had spent the next several decades building what was now the largest defense conglomerate in the world, the Ares Corporation. According to *Forbes* magazine he was the fourteenth richest person on the planet with over twenty billion dollars to his name.

His late mother had been a native Greek with a fiery temper and fierce ambition he'd inherited along with her dark good looks. After Creel's father had been logistically snafued in Korea, she'd remarried to a man higher up the socioeconomic scale who'd shunted Creel off to boarding schools and not very good ones at that. While the sons of other wealthy men had everything handed to them, the outsider

Creel endured their taunts and sweated and scraped for every nickel. Those experiences had given him armor for skin.

Naming his company after the Greek god of war was a tribute to the mother he'd loved above all others. And Creel was proud of what his company produced. The name stenciled on his four-hundred-foot motor yacht was *Shiloh*, one of the bloodiest battles in the American Civil War.

Though born on U.S. soil, Creel had never considered himself simply an American. Ares Corp. was based in the United States, but Creel was a citizen of the globe, having long ago renounced his U.S. citizenship. That suited his business well, for no country had a monopoly on war. Yet Creel spent as much time as he liked in the States because he had an army of lawyers and accountants who found every loophole in the stuttering linguistic morass called the U.S. tax code.

Creel had learned long ago that to protect his business he had to spread the wealth. Every major Ares weapon system contract was disseminated across all fifty states. His glossy, expensive ad campaigns touted that fact above all others.

"One thousand suppliers spread across America, keeping you safe," the Hollywood voice-over would proclaim in deeply resonant tones that made your skin tingle and your heart pound. It sounded very patriotic.

It had actually been done for only one reason. Now if some bureaucrat tried to cut any of the pork, 535 members of Congress would rise up and strike the person dead for having the audacity to try and take jobs from *their* people. Creel had successfully implemented this same strategy in a dozen other countries as well. Just like war, the Americans did not have a monopoly on self-serving politicians.

Ares-built military jets flew over every major sporting event in the world, including the World Series, the Super Bowl, and the World Cup. How could you not get goose bumps when a tight formation of space age warships costing $150 million a pop came roaring overhead with enough firepower to easily take out every man, woman, and child in the place with a single strike? It was near poetic in its frightful majesty.

Ares's global marketing and lobbying budget was three billion dollars per year. For that mammoth sum there wasn't a major country with defense dollars to spend that didn't hear the message over and over again: *We are strong. We stand by you. We keep you safe. We keep you free. We are the only thing standing between you and* them. And the pictures were just as compelling: barbecues and parades, flags waving, children saluting as tanks rolled by and planes soared overhead, and grim-faced soldiers with black-smudged faces threading through hostile territory.

There was no country on earth that could withstand

that sort of heart-pumping message, Creel had found. Well, perhaps the Germans, but that was about it.

The way the commercials were scripted it was like the mighty Ares Corporation was giving the weapons away out of patriotic fervor instead of eternally being over budget and behind schedule. Or convincing defense departments to buy expensive war toys that were never even used while ignoring the lesser-priced items, like body armor and night-vision goggles, that grunts on the ground actually relied on to survive. It had worked brilliantly for decades.

Yet things were changing. People, it seemed, were growing tired of war. The attendance at the enormous trade conventions Ares put on annually had fallen for five years in a row. Now Ares's marketing budget was bigger than its net income. That revealed only one truth: people weren't buying what Creel was selling.

So he was currently sitting in a nice room in a building owned by his company. The big man sitting opposite him was dressed in jeans and combat boots, looking like a grizzly bear minus the fur. His face was tanned and worn, with what looked like either a bullet crater or the mother of all measles pocks on one cheek. His shoulders were thick and his hands huge and somehow menacing.

Creel didn't shake hands.

"It's started," he said.

"I've seen comrade Konstantin." The man could

not resist a smirk when he said this. "They should just award him the Oscar now."

"*Sixty Minutes* is doing a story on it this weekend. Along with every other newsmagazine. The idiot Gorshkov's making it easy on us."

"What about the incident?"

"*You're* the incident," Creel pointed out.

"It worked before without boots on the ground."

"I'm not interested in wars that stop at a hundred days or devolve into glorified gangland street fights. That doesn't even pay the light bill, Caesar."

"Give me the plan and I'll execute it, Mr. Creel, like always."

"Just be ready to go."

"It's your dime," said Caesar.

"You bet it is."

On the chopper ride back to the Ares Building, Creel eyed the city's concrete, glass, and steel temples below. *You're not in West Texas anymore, Nick.*

This, of course, wasn't just about money. Or saving his company. Creel had enough money and regardless of what he did or didn't do, Ares Corp. would survive. No, this was really about putting the world back into its proper structure. Things had been misaligned for long enough. Creel had grown weary of watching the weak and savage dictate to the strong and civilized. He was about to set things right. Some might claim he was playing God. Well, in a way he was. But even a benign god used violence and destruction to make his point. Creel intended to follow that model to the letter.

Initially there would be pain.

There would be loss.

There always was. Indeed, his own father had been a victim of keeping the spectrum of world power on a firm footing, so Creel quite clearly understood the level of sacrifice required. But in the end it would all be worth it.

He settled back in his seat.

The creator of Konstantin knew a little.

Caesar knew a little.

Only Nicolas Creel knew all.

As gods always did.

3

"What's the 'A' stand for?" the man asked in fluent English with a Dutch accent layered over it.

Shaw looked at the gentleman standing opposite him at Passport Control in Schiphol Airport fifteen kilometers southwest of Amsterdam. One of the busiest airports in the world, it rested five meters below sea level with trillions of tons of swirling water nearby. Shaw had always considered this the height of engineering daring. Yet much of the entire country was below sea level, so they didn't really have much of a choice on where to park the planes.

"Excuse me?" Shaw said, though he well knew what the man was referring to.

The fellow stabbed the photo page of Shaw's passport with his finger.

"There. Your given name is just the initial 'A'. What does it stand for?"

Shaw gazed at his passport while the Dutchman looked on.

As befitted the tallest nation on earth, the passport man in his regulation uniform was six foot two, only one inch above a Dutchman's average height, but still coming in three inches under Shaw's imposing stature.

"It doesn't stand for anything," Shaw answered. "My mother never gave me a Christian name, so I named myself for what I am. *A* Shaw. Because that *is* my surname, or at least it was my mother's."

"And your father had no objection to his son not taking his name?"

"You don't need a father to deliver a baby, only to make one."

"And the hospital did not name you, then?"

"Are all babies born in hospitals?" Shaw jabbed back with a smile.

The Dutchman stiffened and then his tone became less adversarial.

"So Shaw. Irish, as in George Bernard?"

The Dutch were a wonderfully informed people, Shaw had found. Well educated and curious, loved to debate. He'd never had anyone before ask him about George Bernard Shaw.

"Could be, but I'm Scottish. The Highlands. At least my ancestors came from there," he added quickly, since he was holding an American passport, one of a dozen he actually possessed. "I was born in Connecticut. Perhaps you've been there?"

The man said eagerly, "No. But I would like very much to travel to America."

Shaw had seen that lustful look before. "Well, the streets aren't really paved with gold and the women aren't all movie stars, but there's a lot to do and lots of room to do it in."

"Maybe one day," the passport man said wistfully before reassuming his duties. "Are you here on business or pleasure?"

"Both. Why come all this way and have to choose?"

The man chuckled. "Anything to declare?"

"*Ik heb niets aan te geven.*"

"You speak Dutch?" he said in a surprised tone.

"Doesn't everyone?"

The man laughed and smacked Shaw's passport with an old-fashioned ink stamp instead of the high-tech devices some countries were using. These, Shaw had heard, implanted a digital tracking device on the paper. He'd always preferred ink to tracking devices.

"Enjoy your visit," said Shaw's new Dutch friend as he handed back the passport.

"I intend to," Shaw replied as he walked toward the exit and the train that would carry him to Centraal Station in Amsterdam in about twenty minutes.

From there it would only get more exciting. But first he had a role to play.

Because he had an audience.

In fact, they were watching him right now.

4

The cab Shaw took from the train station dropped him off at the grand Amstel Intercontinental Hotel. It housed seventy-nine rooms of great beauty, many with enviable views of the river Amstel, although Shaw was not here for the views.

Adhering to his role-playing over the next three days, Shaw was a tourist in town. There were few places more suited to that enterprise than Amsterdam, a city of 750,000 people, only half of them Dutch-born. He took a boat ride, enthusiastically snapping pictures of a city with more canals than Venice and nearly thirteen thousand bridges in a space of barely two hundred square kilometers, of which one-fourth was water.

Shaw was especially drawn to the houseboats, nearly three thousand of them, docked along the canals. They appealed to him because they represented roots. Even though they were floating on water, these boats never moved. They were handed down from one generation to the next or sold outright. What might that feel like, he wondered, to have such ties to one place?

He later donned shorts and running shoes and jogged across the wide-open spaces of Oosterpark near his hotel. In a very real sense Shaw had been running his whole life. Well, if things went according to plan that was going to end. Either that or he'd end up dead. He would gladly take the risk. In a way, he was dead already.

Sipping a coffee at the Bulldog, Amsterdam's most famous café chain, Shaw watched people go about their business. And he also eyed the men who were so very clearly watching him. It was pathetic, really, observing folks undertaking surveillance who didn't have the least clue as to how to do it properly.

The next day he lunched at one of his favorite restaurants in the city, run by an elderly Italian. The man's wife sat at one table reading the newspaper all day while her husband acted as maître d', waiter, chef, busboy, dishwasher, and cashier. The place only had four barstools and five tables, not counting the wife's domain, and prospective customers had to stand in the doorway and be scrutinized by the husband. If he nodded, you were allowed to eat. If he turned away, you found another place to dine.

Shaw had never been turned away. Perhaps it was his imposing physical stature, or his magnetic blue eyes that seemed to snatch one up in their powerful embrace. But most likely it was because the owner and he had once worked together, and it wasn't in the field of food and beverage.

That night Shaw put on a suit and attended the opera at the Muziektheater. After the performance was over he could've walked back to his hotel, but he chose instead to head in the opposite direction. Tonight was why he'd really come to Holland. He was a tourist no longer.

As he approached the red-light district he observed some activity down a dark and particularly narrow alleyway. A little boy stood there in the shadows. Next to him was a rough-looking man with his zipper down and one large hand stuffed in the boy's pants.

In an instant Shaw had changed direction. He slipped into the alley and placed a blow to the back of the man's head. It was a measured strike, designed to stun, not kill, though Shaw was sorely tempted to finish off the predator. As the man fell unconscious to the pavement Shaw crammed a hundred euros in the boy's hand and sent him off with a hard push and a dire warning in Dutch. As the child's frantic footfalls echoed away, Shaw knew the boy would at least not starve or die tonight.

As he resumed his original route he noted for the first time that the old stock exchange was directly across from the hookers in the red-light. This struck him as odd until he thought about it. Cash and prostitution had always been bedfellows. He wondered if some of the ladies accepted company shares in lieu of euros as payment.

Even more ironic than the exchange's close prox-
imity to the whores was that the red-light district
completely surrounded Oude Kerk, or Old Church,
the city's most ancient and largest house of worship.
Built in 1306 as a simple wooden chapel, it had been
constantly tinkered with and enlarged for the next
two centuries. One jokester had even inlaid a brass
pair of breasts into the pavement by the front entrance.
Shaw had been inside a few times. What had struck
him was the series of carvings on the choir benches
depicting men having massive bowel movements. He
could only assume that masses must have been *really*
long in those days.

Saints and sinners, God and hookers, mused Shaw
as he reached the middle of this strip of iniquity. The
Dutch called the area the Walletjes, or "Little Walls."
Presumably what happened behind the Walletjes stayed
there. Tonight he was counting on that.

The red-light district was not that large, perhaps
two canals long, but there was a lot packed into that
pair of blocks. At night the prostitutes on duty here
were the most beautiful. Many were stunning eastern
Europeans who'd been brought to the country under
false pretenses and then become "trapped in the
trade," as it was delicately termed. Ironically, the night
hookers were mostly for show. After all, who wanted
to step through the libidinous portals with thousands
watching? In the mornings and afternoons the district

was quieter and that's when the serious customers paid their visits to the far less comely but efficient ladies of the second and third eight-hour shifts.

The whores' rooms were difficult to miss, as they were all outlined in red neon tubing that was nearly blinding. The rooms also had fluorescent lighting such that the skimpy clothing the girls wore blazed like a summer sun. Shaw passed window after window where women stood, sometimes dancing, sometimes posing erotically. In truth most people who came here came to gawk, not fornicate, although the beds still racked up roughly half a billion euros in sales yearly.

Shaw kept his head down, his feet carrying him to one particular destination. He was almost there.

5

The lady in the window was young and beautiful with raven hair that swirled around her bare shoulders. She was wearing only a white thong, spiked heels, and a cheap necklace wedged between her large breasts, the nipples of which were covered with sunflower pasties. An interesting choice, Shaw thought.

He kept eye contact with her as he threaded through the masses. The woman met him at the door, where he confirmed his interest. Even in her heels she was a foot shorter than him. In the window she'd looked bigger. Things on display often did look bigger. And better. When you got your purchase home, it didn't seem nearly as special.

She shut the door and then closed the red curtains, the only sign one would get that the room and the lady were occupied now.

The space was small, with a sink, toilet, and, of course, a bed. Set next to the sink was a button. It was the one the hookers pushed in an emergency. Then the police would suddenly appear and drag away the customer who'd gone too far to satisfy himself.

This was one of the best-patrolled areas in the city—anything to keep the tax revenue coming. Shaw saw a second door in the back wall and then glanced away. In the next room the sounds of another happy customer were coming through loud and clear. Hooker digs were set side by side with cheap drywall or sometimes only a curtain in between. The business clearly did not require much space or frills in which to operate.

"You're very good-looking," she said in Dutch. "And large," she added, gazing up at him. "Are you as big all over? Because I am not so big down there," she added, now staring pointedly at his crotch.

"*Spreekt u Engels?*" Shaw said.

She nodded. "I speak English. It's thirty euros for twenty minutes. But I'll do an hour for seventy-five. It's a special, just for you," she added matter-of-factly. She handed him a list in Dutch but that was also repeated at the bottom of the page in ten different languages including English, French, Japanese, Chinese, and Arabic. It was entitled, "Things I Will and Won't Do."

Shaw passed her back the paper. "Is your friend here?" he asked. "I've been waiting a long time to meet him." He glanced toward the second door.

She appraised him in a different way now. "Yes, he is here."

She turned and led him to the door set in the back

wall. Her exposed butt cheeks, though firm, still quivered slightly as she performed an exaggerated model's sashay in front of him. He didn't know if she did that out of habit or because the stilettos were too unstable.

The woman opened the door and motioned Shaw in. She left him there facing the old man seated at a small table where a plain meal had been laid: a wedge of cheese, a piece of cod, a fist of bread, and a bottle of wine.

The man's face was a cache of wrinkles, the white beard scraggly and the small belly soft and round. The eyes peered out from under tufts of ramshackle snowy hair badly in need of pruning. The eyes caught on Shaw's and held.

The man motioned to the table. "Hungry? Thirsty?"

There was a second chair but Shaw chose not to use it. Indeed, if he had attempted to sit down, the man might have shot him, for there was a gun grasped in his left hand pointed right at Shaw and the pre-arranged instructions had been explicit. One did not sit. One did not eat or drink if one wanted to live.

Shaw's gaze had already swept the tiny room. The only entry was the doorway he'd come through. He'd positioned himself so that he could keep one eye on this portal and one eye on the man. And his gun.

He shook his head and said, "Thank you, but I

already ate at the De Groene Lanteerne." It was a cheap place with traditional Dutch food served in a room that was three hundred years old and looked it.

The dopey code words out of the way, the man rose, slid a piece of paper from his pocket, and handed it to Shaw.

Shaw glanced at the address and other information on the paper, ripped it up, and tossed the pieces into the toilet set against one wall and flushed it. Seemingly on cue the old man put on a beaten-up hat and patched coat and left.

Shaw could not leave yet. Sexual encounters typic-ally lasted a bit longer than two minutes even for the teenage first-timers. And you never knew who was watching. Well, actually, he did. There were several of them.

He stepped back into the main room where the lady was stretched out, catlike, on her cot. The curtain was still drawn; her meter was still running.

"Do you want to screw me now?" the woman asked in a slightly bored tone as she started to slide the thong down her legs. "It's been paid for," she added if he needed any inducement. "A full hour. And I will go *off* the list for another thirty euros."

"*Nee, dank u,*" he replied, smiling politely. If you were going to turn a lady down in the matter of sex, better you say it in her own language.

"Why not? Is there a problem?" she said, obviously offended.

"I'm married," he said simply.

"So are most of the men who see me."

"I'm sure."

"Where is your wedding ring?" she asked suspiciously.

"Never wear it at work."

"You're sure you don't want me?" Her tone of disbelief was as clearly etched as the look of incredulity on her face.

He hid his bemusement. She must be really new because her vanity was largely intact. The older whores would surely jump at the chance for full pay that included no humping.

"Absolutely sure."

She slid her thong back up. "Pity."

"Yes, pity," he said. Actually, if things went according to plan, in two days hence he'd be in Dublin with the only woman he'd ever really loved. And also the reason why he had to get out. Now.

Still, even Shaw had to acknowledge, it was a big if. In his line of work, tomorrow was just another day to die.

6

There is always a damn Tunisian, Moroccan, or Egyptian involved. Always. Shaw said this to himself. One slip with these gents and they'd rip your gonads off and force-feed them to you and say that Allah had told them to do it if they bothered to give you a reason at all. *See you in paradise, infidel. Serve me well for eternity, filthy pig.* He knew the speeches by heart.

He clenched the heavy suitcase in his right hand and held the left out from his side as the wiry Tunisian, eyes red, features grim, and teeth bared, patted him down.

Six men other than Shaw stood in the small upstairs room. It was a typical flat situated on a minor canal. High up, it was narrow as a snake hole, with knotted rope pulls in lieu of stair rails to enable the climber to make the near-vertical assault. One could easily become winded merely going from the first to the second floor of an Amsterdam canal residence.

The reason was historical, Shaw had learned. Centuries ago all these homes had been merchants' places of business. And back when they'd been constructed the only carpenters available were ship's carpenters. These men, logically, had decided that what was good for a boat was good for a house and had built the stairs nearly straight up as was the practice on space-challenged ships. That's also why most such homes had a steel beam like a ship's prow jutting out from the top floor. They once had been used to haul up goods for sale and now were employed to hoist in furniture because there was no way in hell you'd get even a modest-sized couch up the stairs.

The night before, Shaw had left the red-light district, returned to his hotel, and informed the front desk that he was checking out. The clerk on duty there was undoubtedly in the pay of people who wanted to keep tabs on his movements and would relay this intelligence to them. Men would be dispatched to follow him as soon as he left the Intercontinental.

Since Shaw didn't particularly want the extra company he left his bag and clothes behind and exited the hotel via the basement. That was why he'd stayed at the large Intercontinental, with its numerous exits; he needed to get away without being seen. Using the memorized information he'd gotten from the old man in the hooker's digs, he rode in the back of an old farm truck to a destination outside the city where the land was broad and green and there was no water for at least a good ten feet. He made a few phone calls and the next evening took possession of the suitcase that the Tunisian was now attempting feverishly to wrest from his grip.

The far bigger Shaw suddenly wrenched the satchel free, sending the smaller man tumbling headfirst to the floor. The Tunisian rose, blood dripping down his nose, a knife clasped in his muscular hand.

Shaw turned to the leader of the pack, an Iranian who sat in a chair—his miniature throne, Shaw could see—and was eyeing him steadily.

"Want me to show you the merchandise?" Shaw asked. "Then call off the hyena."

The slender Persian, clad in crisply pressed knit slacks and a loose-fitting white long-sleeved shirt, waved his hand and the Tunisian's knife disappeared, but the snarl remained.

"You managed to lose my men last night," he said to Shaw in a British accent.

"I don't like company."

He set the suitcase on the table, input two separate digital codes, slid his thumb through a scanner, and the titanium locks sprang free. Shaw closely observed the man from Tehran's reaction to the little present lurking inside. The Iranian's expression was clear: Christmas, ironically, had come early to Holland for the Allah worshiper from the Middle East.

Shaw announced, "Officially, this is an RDD, radiological dispersal device, otherwise known as a suitcase nuke or dirty bomb." He said all this in Farsi, which got an eyebrow hike from the Iranian.

The men gathered around. The Iranian gingerly touched the device with its wires, metal carcass, stainless steel tubes, and multiple LED readout screens.

"How dirty?" the Iranian asked.

"Gamma radiation core with a nice dynamite kicker."

"Enough to kill how many? An entire city?"

Shaw shook his head. "This isn't a weapon of mass destruction. It's what we call in the trade a weapon of mass *disruption*. It'll kill some folks near the detonation site. And the radiation will nail some people too. The farther away from ground zero, the less damage."

The Iranian looked displeased. "I was under the impression this device would kill thousands, knock down buildings."

"This is *not* a mushroom cloud boom-maker. If you want that you can go get plans off the Internet. But you'll find yourself stuck for necessary ingredients like highly enriched uranium. But what this baby will do is scare the shit out of an entire country, shut down the economy, and make people afraid to leave their homes. In a way, just as effective as the mushroom cloud, without all the mess. And a helluva lot cheaper to you."

This seemed to appease the Iranian. He turned to Shaw after giving the bomb one last affectionate pat. "The price?"

Shaw stood straighter towering over all of them. "The same as the one on the term sheet we sent."

"That was your opening offer, I assumed. I now want to negotiate."

"You *assumed* incorrectly. The price is firm. If you don't want it, there're a lot of other people who do."

The Iranian took a step forward. His men did likewise. "You *will* negotiate."

Shaw tapped the contents of the suitcase. "This is a gamma bomb, not a set of knives, not a diamond for the missus. I'm not running a special, no two-for-ones tonight."

"And the reason we cannot simply take it from you now? For nothing?"

The Tunisian must've been a mind reader because he already had his knife back out and his eyes were burning, no doubt with the thought of sticking the blade to the hilt in Shaw's thick neck.

"And kill you," the Iranian finished, quite un-necessarily, for Shaw had already gotten the point.

Shaw motioned to a slit on the side of the dirty bomb that resembled a DVD intake slot. "That's the import drive for the accompanying software package that has the automatic detonation codes and generally makes this thing go boom and the radiation go sizzle. You try to do it without the software the only thing that gets fried is your ass."

"And where is this package?"

"Nowhere near here, that's for damn sure."

The Iranian slapped the suitcase. "So this is useless to me!"

"As the term sheet clearly said," Shaw began in a weary voice, "you get the hardware with fifty percent down and the *software* when the other half is received in the designated account."

"And I must simply trust you?" the Iranian said, a nasty undertone to his words.

"Just like we have to trust you. We've been doing this a long time, and never had a disappointed customer yet. You know that or you wouldn't be here."

The Iranian hesitated.

Come on, you maggot. Sacrifice a little lost face in front of your boys to get the golden egg. You know you want it. Think about how many Americans you can zap with this shit.

"I will have to call someone first."

Shaw said in an annoyed tone, "I thought you had the authority to act."

The Iranian shot nervous glances at his men, the embarrassment clear on his finely cut features. "One call," he said quickly. He pulled out his phone.

Shaw held up a hand. "Hold it! Interpol crashing our little party does not figure into my vacation plans."

"I won't be on it long enough for anyone to trace."

"You've been watching too many *Dirty Harry* movies. That's not healthy in our line of business."

"What are you talking about?" snapped the Iranian.

"I know you guys are really into the ninth century and all, but you need to get with the *twenty-first* century if you want to stay off death row. They don't need you yakking on a rotary dial phone for two days to trace you. They need exactly three seconds for a satellite to track the digital fingerprint, run a triangulation, isolate the cell towers, burn a signal mark to within ten feet, and deploy the strike team." Shaw was speaking mostly crap but it sounded good. "Why do you think bin Laden lives in a cave and writes his orders down on frigging toilet paper?"

The Iranian glanced at his phone as though it had just stung him. Shaw reached slowly in his pocket, mindful of the bloodthirsty Tunisian, and withdrew his own cell phone, which he tossed to the terrorist leader.

"State-of-the-art scrambler and signal diffuser. That sucker even has photon light burst encoding capability, so not even a quantum computer, in the event anyone has actually invented one, can crack the bytes packet. So dial away, my friend. The minutes are on me."

The man made the call, facing the wall so Shaw could not hear him or read his lips.

Shaw turned his attention to the Tunisian. In a language he was reasonably sure neither the man nor any of the others spoke he said, "You like to hump little boys, don't you?"

The baffled Tunisian simply stared at him, unable to comprehend a Chinese dialect from a tiny province in the south of the communist country. Shaw had spent a year of his life there, almost died twice, and only managed to get out with the help of a peasant farmer and his ancient, belching Ford. With all that, he figured learning the language might come in handy, though he never saw himself going back there, at least voluntarily.

The Iranian handed the phone back to Shaw, who flipped it into his pocket.

"It is agreed," he said.

"Glad to hear it," Shaw replied as his fist crushed the nose of the Tunisian. In the same motion he swung the heavy suitcase around, catching two other men flush on the temples. They toppled to the floor either dead or damn near it.

An instant later the door burst open and a half dozen figures clad in body armor and hefting sub-machine guns crowded in, screaming at people to put their hands up and their weapons down and not necessarily in that order if they didn't want a new eye in the middle of their foreheads.

Then the Iranian did the unexpected. Hands over his face, he crashed through the window and flew out into space.

Shaw raced to the window, convinced he would see the man end his life as a bloody splat on the street below.

"Shit!" The man's momentum had carried him just far enough out that he'd landed right in the canal.

Shaw glanced at two of the armored men, who

stared back at him, stunned. "Somebody get a tetanus shot lined up. My last one was a long time ago."

He tossed his phone to one of the men, snatched up the Tunisian's knife, and muttered a curse. He perched on the windowsill for an instant, briefly mulled the insanity of what he was about to do, and then sprang out into nothing but fine Dutch air.

7

If there's a body of water outside of the former Soviet Union, or perhaps Venice, that one would not want to dive into, it would be one of the Amsterdam canals. They are famous, but not because of their clarity, cleanliness, or healthy circulation.

Shaw hit the water, cleaving it neatly in two. Still, the impact from four stories up was jarring to every nerve and bone in his body. He turned and propelled back up, breaking the surface and looking around for his man. Nothing!

Apparently the Iranian was a fast swimmer for a person hailing from a desert country. Shaw was also a strong swimmer, and when he finally spotted his quarry he shot across the narrow canal with a powerful stroke, nearly hooking the other man's foot as he climbed out of the water. Kicking out, the Iranian caught him painfully on the jaw with the heel of his boot. It did nothing to improve Shaw's mood.

The two men squared off near the base of the Magere Brug, its cheerful lights offering an odd backdrop to a pair of boiling furies looking to kill each other.

"You betrayed me!" screamed the Iranian.

"You'll get over it."

The Iranian assumed a sophisticated fighting stance. "I was trained as a mujahideen. I fought the devils in Iraq and Afghanistan for years. I look forward to killing you with my bare hands. Serve me well in death, filth."

Before he could attack, Shaw pulled his throwing knife and let it fly. It struck the other man in the foot, sliced through skin and bone, its point finally embedding in the wooden treads of the bridge underneath.

The Iranian screamed in pain and hurled obscenities at Shaw as he tried to pull his limb free.

Shaw used this moment of distraction to knock the Middle Easterner cold, his foot still pinned to the wood like a butterfly on a corkboard as he lay sprawled on the planks.

"You talk too much," he told the unconscious man.

An hour later, Shaw sat in the back of a white van with a blanket around his burly shoulders sipping a cup of hot Dutch coffee. Two men in uniforms that were conspicuous for not having a single identifying mark, along with a third fellow in an off-the-rack business suit, sat across from him.

"Diving out windows? Into the canal? At your age?" the suit said as he scratched at a patch of reddened skin on his bald, egg-shaped head.

"Did you trace the call?"

The man nodded. "Quick thinking giving him your phone. We nailed Mazloomi and his crew in Helsinki about ten minutes ago. Nasty group of people. Yeah, real tough." The man did a mock shiver and then laughed.

Shaw didn't crack a smile. "Good guys rarely try to nuke innocent people. That's why we have governments."

"You really believe that?"

"Yeah, and so do you, Frank, if you had the balls to admit it."

Frank looked at the twin uniforms and nodded at the door. They quickly got up and left. Frank edged closer to Shaw.

"What's this I hear about you wanting to hang it up?"

"How long did you expect me to keep doing this?"

"Didn't you read the fine print? Until you died. Like you almost did tonight."

"Tonight? Not even close. This was about as dangerous as taking on a nun in a ruler smackdown."

"Well, if you do ever get around to dying, don't let it be on my watch. I don't need the hassle."

"Thanks for caring."

"Where to now?"

"Dublin."

Frank said curiously, "Why?"

"Vacation. Maybe you don't think I deserve one after tonight."

"Oh, you can go, but you'll be back," Frank said confidently.

Shaw rose, let the blanket slide off his shoulders, and handed his empty cup to Frank. His skin was itchy as hell and it felt like his hair was falling out.

"Just as soon as you send me a picture of you swimming in the canal. Naked, of course."

"Right. Still glad you came over to our side?"

"I really didn't have a choice, now did I?"

"Have a nice time in Dublin, Shaw."

"You can see for yourself, can't you? Your boys will be right on my ass."

Frank lit up a Dutch cigar and gave Shaw a smirk through the curtain of smoke. "You think you're important enough for us to chase all over the world? My God, what an ego."

"May you never grow old, Frank."

8

"Remember Konstantin" had reached fever pitch. There were rallies against the Russians in fifty countries and the United Nations had formally asked a furious President Gorshkov for a more thorough response. And yet calmer, or at least more skeptical, minds were establishing a wall against this groundswell of anti-Russian sentiment.

A good number of political leaders, journalists, commentators, and think-tank types, stung in the past by rushes to judgment, urged caution and restraint in the wake of the "Remember Konstantin" outrage. More questions had been raised about the authenticity of the man and the video, particularly in the wake of detailed denials and unprecedented access to classified records provided by the Russian government to outside media. Soon after this measure of cooperation by Moscow, the worldwide sentiment that Russia was evil incarnate had begun to ebb a bit. And leaders around the globe began to breathe a little easier. However, this was merely the calm before the real eruption.

Two days later the world received another collective shock when digitally goose-stepping across servers around the globe came the names and photos of thousands of Russians allegedly slaughtered by their own government. They included men, women, children; young, old, pregnant, and disabled. And included with the faces and names were details as to each of their lives and gruesome, tragic deaths. More damaging still, these files all possessed the indicia of coming right from the classified files of the Russian government.

The "RE:" line of the accompanying blast was simple and devastating: "Remember More Than Konstantin." Soon everyone from so-called experts to expatriate Russians and people from former Soviet bloc countries went on TV, radio, and the Web to attack Russia for its obvious descent back into a maniacal, world-power-grabbing menace.

It was as though the image of poor, tortured Konstantin, bolstered by the indelible imprint of thousands of "new" dead, had given people the courage to finally speak out. On a bizarre note, coffee mugs, and T-shirts silkscreened with Konstantin's haunted image, apparently now the Che Guevara of his generation, flooded global markets. And the 1960s had suddenly returned with accompanying images of mushroom clouds alive in people's collective nightmare.

Folks claiming to be family or friends of Konstantin

appeared on news shows around the world, telling and retelling the plight of a man who had never existed. Yet they spun their yarns with gusto, having apparently convinced themselves that he was real and they had known him. He was a martyr, famous and beloved, and now they were too. Their poignant appearances captured the attention and the hearts of people around the world.

The talk show hosts and news anchors asked these folks many probing questions, like, "This is all very upsetting, isn't it?" and "If he were alive right now what message do you believe poor, murdered Konstantin would like to deliver to our millions of viewers?"

One man wisely intoned on a BBC channel, "In a world of scarce power, scarcer water, and new enemies cropping up every day, the Russians are clearly not content to play second fiddle to places like China and India, or even the United States." The fellow went on to add that the Russians had tried democracy and they did not care for it. The Russian Bear was about to assert itself once more and the world had better damn well take notice.

The world *had* taken notice, because the speaker of these words was none other than Sergei Petrov, the former number two man in the successor entity to the KGB, the Federal Security Service. He'd barely escaped his homeland with his life. Any day now he said he expected to be struck down by a bullet, bomb, or polonium-210-laced coffee for his candor. He'd also been well paid for his remarks from a source totally unknown to him. People were still trying to ferret out if all this was true or not. But they'd get no help from Petrov, for he had no love lost for his homeland.

Yet the real question on everyone's mind was, who was behind all this, and why were they doing it? And despite this being the information age, no one could find a definitive answer to that, for a very simple reason that most people overlooked: in the information age, there were not millions of places to hide, there were *trillions*.

The multiple crises in the Middle East were forgotten. Crazy Kim in North Korea was relegated to the back pages. Every U.S. presidential candidate in the upcoming election was asked the same question: "What do you intend to do about a country with almost as many nukes as the United States and a past full of world-domination-minded leaders?"

The American public, in particular, was furious. All this time, money, and lives wasted in the Middle East while the Russians secretly pursued their plans to crush the free world? Russia had thousands of fully realized nuclear warheads that it could deliver to any place on earth. It made bin Laden and al Qaeda look like petty criminals. How had all the smart people missed that one? And when the American public was upset, it let people in power know it.

The incumbent president, who was running for reelection, saw his poll position go from first to fifth as his opponents successfully painted him as soft on Russia. Every major magazine had Konstantin's picture on it. Every pundit show from *Hardball* to *Face the Nation* to *Meet the Press* and every blog, chat room, and cybercafé talked about nothing else other than the rise of Russia, the possibility of a return to the cold war, even the reemergence of a new Iron Curtain that some insensitive souls were already dubbing the Titanium Coffin.

The political talk show pundits were screaming the loudest from their billion-watt stages, claiming that they'd been voicing this potential danger all along when of course they'd been laser-fixed on the Middle East like everyone else. Still, they collectively roared, "I speak for the common man when I say, nuke the damn Reds before they nuke us. It's the only way."

The major television networks trotted out their enormous archives of grainy black-and-white images of nuclear bomb detonations. At least two generations of Americans for the first time saw pictures of wide-eyed 1960s-era schoolchildren huddled under desks as though a bit of laminated wood and flimsy glass could actually protect them from a thermonuclear blast. Along with this came film footage of the communists parading their military might in front of the Kremlin. And it scared the hell out of everybody.

As one op-ed piece candidly, if tastelessly, stated,

"If Moscow hits New York with nukes, it won't just be *two* buildings falling down. It'll be *all* of them."

The U.S. military, the only viable counter to Moscow's army other than perhaps China's three-million-man machine, was beaten up, its numbers and morale down and its equipment destroyed by Iraqi sand and jerry-rigged IEDs. While it was true that the American air force and navy were far more than a match for anything the Russians could cobble together, the United States and the rest of the world were still holding their collective breath. No one knew what the crazy Russians would do next. Yet the planet did seem to know one thing.

The Evil Empire was back.

Nicolas Creel put down his newspaper and his coffee. He was presently flying seven miles above the earth on his way to a very important event. He'd been filled in on all the latest developments. Things were going along nicely. In the parlance of the perception management field, the world had firmly entered the "gripper" stage, where the majority of people embraced as true everything they were told. It was far easier to accomplish this than most would care or dare to believe. It was easy to manipulate people. Folks had been doing it pretty much forever with results that had taken the world right to the edge of destruction.

The digital images flowing across global networks

right now, the faces of tens of thousands of supposedly murdered Russians looking pleadingly at the rest of humanity, was a tactical maneuver that Creel's perception manager liked to call a "Vesuvius," after the volcano that had erupted and destroyed the Roman cities of Pompeii and Herculaneum. Through sheer overwhelming bulk, it made whatever denials the government in Moscow was making seem absurd, even though it was the truth. It was part of a classic "mind manipulation maneuver," something Creel's man referred to as the "Triple M," and that had worked in this instance to perfection. Not only did the Russians look like liars, but they appeared to be *incompetent* liars on top of it.

Creel looked out the window of his 767 wide-body jumbo jet. Designed to hold over 250 ordinary people, it was amazing how one could make the ordinary extraordinary by reconfiguring the aircraft to accommodate twenty privileged individuals, wrapping them in the embrace of private bedrooms with en suite baths, a gym, full-time masseuse, dining room, conference room, and even a movie theater. And at his beck and call were three leggy flight attendants in tight skirts with "Ares" on the back of their blouses. Not that Creel noticed this. Well, perhaps a bit.

He was a married man. In fact, he had been married four times and counting, the latest to a Miss World Hottie or something like that; he couldn't exactly remember her title. It was absurd of course and wouldn't last. He'd have some fun, though, and she'd get enough from the divorce to live comfortably. His first two wives had been elegant, smart, and opinionated and driven him absolutely insane. He now opted for the arm candy, trading in for a new model every so often with the security of an ironclad prenup seriously limiting what the lady walked away with.

He looked out the window. Down below was China, a country with more potential and more problems than any land on earth. Yes, a complex place, perhaps the most complicated of all. And what a superb place to start a war, thought Creel. Yet it was actually far more complicated than something that simple.

Nicolas Creel had never sought out the easy. He always went for the seemingly impossible.

9

Katie James groaned as sunlight flooded the room. Apparently the three wake-up calls had failed to stir her, even though she'd specifically asked for them, naively believing perhaps that one of them would break through the fog of her brain. She was exhausted from travel, time zone changes, and lack of sleep, and anyway, who wanted to get out of a comfy bed to go to a funeral? Groggy, she finally sat up, tugging the sheet high up around her neck. She coughed, rubbed her throat, and glanced at the clock.

Oh shit! I'm really late. Hold the body, I'm coming.

She leapt up, dashed naked into the bathroom, and in the span of ten blurred minutes was showered, dressed, and slamming the hotel room door behind her, wet hair and all. The life of the globe-trotting journalist had at least prepared her to move fast when she absolutely had to. Fine, she was attending a funeral. What she really wanted was a mojito. In fact she wanted about three of them, just to start. Then the bourbon would kick in. Then the martinis followed by the gin and tonics. She didn't discriminate. She loved them all.

It had started with too much bar time trying to keep up with the boys covering the next big story overseas. Yet it was when she'd won her second Pulitzer, almost dying in the process, that the booze had gotten out of hand. Katie had very good reasons to drink after that near-death experience, but she kept them strictly to herself.

The alcohol had not become a career problem until her editor had noticed the slurred speech, the red eyes in the afternoon, and the occasional forgetting of places to go, stories to write, asses to kiss. He in turn had informed the managing editor, and up the line of command the lurid truth had galloped. They were all lushes themselves, having successfully extended the liquid lunch into the twenty-first century, yet the hammer had come down on her until she'd finally been reassigned to write about dead people. In Hollywood, going into rehab got you instant street cred. In journalism, she was damaged goods.

It'd been the talk of New York journalism circles for a few weeks and then everyone quit caring. Everyone except Katie.

So here she was covering a state funeral of a beloved Scottish leader who'd lived to be a hundred and four or some ridiculous age. To see a shriveled man with the face of a Shar-Pei dressed in a full kilt lying at the bottom of a gigantic coffin like a miniature doll in a massive toy chest made her want to laugh, not cry.

She'd tried AA, only because her editor had demanded it as a condition of her continued employment. He'd obviously forgotten the two Pulitzers she'd earned the damn newspaper or the wound in her left arm that had never really healed. Or the powerful stories she'd delivered, plumbing them over the years from every chaotic and wildly dangerous corner of the earth. This had been accomplished at enormous personal cost to herself, meaning, exactly, that she had no life outside of putting pen to paper. She'd been to eighty-four countries and experienced exactly one blind date, to a Pakistani who'd told her she reminded him of his favorite cow. *Bless him.* She wondered if his nose had ever healed from her fist colliding with it.

Then, three years shy of the big four-oh, she'd woken up in a room she didn't recognize with a man she didn't know, in a country she didn't know how she'd gotten to, covered in what appeared to be her own sick. That had propelled her back to AA, where she'd stood up and told a roomful of strangers that she was a totally screwed-up basket case who hoped to get better. Her last drink had been six months ago. Yet every morning, afternoon, and evening the monster was there, urging her to break her pledge, take that one little sip. And here she was in Scotland, home of the world's best whisky, or at least the most choices of it. Her lips quivered and her throat tightened at the thought.

It wasn't until she arrived at the funeral that she realized she'd mistakenly dressed all in white, frantically grabbing whatever clothes she could find in her hotel closet. She looked like a lily amid the sea of dreary black. Katie was tall and slim, with shoulder-length blonde hair that was still wet even after hanging it outside the taxi window on the ride over. She'd been mistaken more than once for Téa Leoni. There might have been a time when Téa Leoni would have been mistaken for *her*, especially after the second Pulitzer when her picture was plastered all over the world, because she'd come seconds and inches away from losing her life getting the damn story.

One older man had suggested that she was actually a dead ringer for Shirley Eaton, the *Goldfinger* girl from the Bond film. He'd intimated that he wouldn't mind seeing Katie in gold enamel paint and nothing else, even as his hand had slid to her rear end and squeezed tightly. She'd hurt her fist on his face too.

Hollywood of course had wanted to film her harrowing adventure in winning journalism's top prize, and had even suggested Leoni as a potential lead to play her. Yet Katie had said no to all such offers. It was not for reasons of vanity, or privacy. It was for reasons of shame. Of guilt.

There had been someone else involved, someone who had lost his life while she earned her short-lived fame. A child. A little boy. And it had been somewhat Katie's fault. No, perhaps mostly her fault. No one knew that part of the story. No one except Katie. That's when the only solace she could find anywhere in life was while staring at a full glass of liquor and then pouring it down her throat, letting it burn the hell out of her, grafting scars onto her soul on the way down one highball at a time.

The little Afghan boy's name had been Behnam. She'd been told the name meant goodness and honor. And he had possessed both qualities she'd found. Curly black hair, a smile that could melt the stoniest of hearts, full of life right up to the moment it was violently taken from him.

Her fault. He'd died. She'd lived. But not quite all of her had made it. A part of Katie had perished with the child. When she'd received the second Pulitzer her emotions had been such that no wordsmith, no matter how gifted, could have hoped to capture them in mere language. It was her night; everyone was telling her how brave, how wonderful, how talented she was. Her wounded arm bundled up in thick bandages and a brace, the really serious internal damage the bullet had done mostly hidden away in her emaciated, weakened body, had only seemed to emphasize in a dramatically visual way her unequivocal birthright to the prize. Yes, a deserving winner if ever there was one. She'd smiled, hugged them all with her one good wing, and generally given off the aura of someone perfectly at peace with herself and her exalted position in life.

She'd gone home alone that night to her apartment in New York and woken up the next morning in her underwear on her living room floor, an empty bottle of Jack on her gut, hating herself. Yes, perfectly at peace. Other than her very soul having been rent in two, she was doing fine.

10

Katie sat at the funeral and took copious notes that she would somehow fit into a story that people would read one minute and forget the next. Walking back from the gravesite she exchanged a few pleasantries with people she didn't know. Her reputation had suffered such shipwreck that no one there recognized her other than one old codger from the *Times* who shot her a condescending smile. He was eighty-four. He should be covering the death page, she felt; it was a great way for him to check up on his contemporaries. Yet it was also very plainly true that he was here because he wanted to be. Katie was here because she had nowhere else to go.

Back in her hotel room she typed up her piece. The official bio of the departed Scot had long since been archived, as were those of all persons with even a remote connection to celebrity. Her story was simply to add atmosphere, her take on the proceedings. Yet there were only a few ways to describe the event of someone's passing. People are sad; people cry. People go home and keep on living; the departed, out of necessity, stays behind.

Andrew MacDougal had enjoyed a long career in European politics but had been "retired" for over thirty years and thus he'd long since faded from the public eye. The whole story would encompass fewer than five hundred words and it would only be that long because the president of Katie's newspaper was Scottish. If there was a picture attached to the story, it would no doubt show the dead man in his prime kilting years.

She shook her head at the thought of it. A nearly seven-hour flight to London and a ratty connector to Glasgow, with the same on the way back. All that for a man who'd ended his political career when Katie was still a child. And all while the news story of the millennium was playing out right before her eyes.

She of course had been following closely the events of Konstantin and all the rest. She had even sent carefully worded e-mails to her editor suggesting that perhaps since she was over this way anyway, a trip to Moscow might be worthwhile. She took it as a bad sign that he never bothered to respond.

I write about dead people while the story that could resurrect my career rolls on. Lucky, lucky me.

After she e-mailed her obit masterpiece off, Katie had the rest of the day free. Hell, she might even extend her stay. It wasn't like she had anything to go back to. She could venture to the ancient city of Edinburgh, which was just a short hop to the east.

Glasgow was Scotland's largest city and not particularly inviting ground for a recovering alcoholic since it was filled with enticing pubs and clubs. By comparison, the capital of Edinburgh was a bit more sedate. And who knew, another hundred-year-old Scotsman worthy of obit page status might drop dead while she was here. She could bag two prone Scots with one roll of parchment. If she were lucky she might even get a bonus.

Katie made a wide detour around the hotel bar and hit the streets.

She'd never really spent much time in Scotland. Ireland was where all the news was, at least when the IRA was active. Very early in her career she'd once been caught in a crossfire in Belfast that had gone on for half a day. She'd phoned in the story while squatting behind a rusted Fiat and dodging bullets. After it was over, she'd made the bar rounds, and then taken a bath back at her hotel. It was only then that she'd found the flattened bullet stuck in her hair. It must have ricocheted off something. She'd kept that slug all these years; it was her lucky piece. Yes, she kept it, wore it around her neck in fact, despite it obviously having stopped working a long, long time ago.

She dropped by a café to eat. When the Earl Grey and blueberry scones came, she barely touched them. She paid her bill and left, her disinterested expression lingering behind somehow as though her weariness had the power to create solid mass from the shitty circumstances of her life.

She didn't like being depressed, or one binge away from destroying her life again, perhaps for good. She knew she had to take steps to turn herself around, and that included more than leaving the bottle alone. The alcohol was capable of crushing her, certainly. Yet Katie knew her real demons lay *within*, much of it emanating from the death of an innocent little boy. It was a guilty secret of devastating degree.

And every minute she could feel those demons trying to take her over. She walked down the crowded street in Glasgow feeling more alone than ever.

11

Dublin was one of Shaw's favorite cities. With a pub and bookstore on virtually every corner, what wasn't to love? Half the population was under thirty and the second most spoken language was Mandarin Chinese: young, diverse, and well-read pub dwellers, who often settled differences with a glib Irish tongue, speedy Irish fists, or sometimes both.

Shaw had gotten into two fights in Dublin pubs, both one-punch victories for him. He could have held back and made them suffer, but combat to him had always had one rule: when given the opening, deliver the haymaker and let somebody else sweat the eulogy.

When the opponents had regained consciousness they'd each asked the victor his name.

"Shaw."

"Scottish?"

"No." The truth was Shaw didn't really know his origins. For him, one past was often as good as another, when you needed it to be.

"Well, damn, that explains it," one of them had said in his brogue, with soft, truncated vowels and rock-hard consonants as he rubbed his smashed jaw. "You're bloody Irish!"

After tossing his bags in his hotel room and changing clothes, Shaw pounded along the 709 hectares of Phoenix Park, a green paradise over twice the size of Central Park. Along his run he passed the residences of the U.S. ambassador and the Irish president and failed to salute at either one, though at various times he'd worked for both as a freelancer. He covered five miles in half an hour. Not his personal best, but a good pace. He could run it faster and he knew the time would come when he would have to.

He returned to his hotel, took two showers, put on lotion and extra swipes of deodorant, and still swore he could smell the stink of the Amsterdam canal oozing from his every pore. He checked his watch. He still had some time to kill so he took a stroll, finally reaching the spot on the river Liffey where as recently as 1916 the Brits had sent a gunboat up and commenced lobbing shells into Dublin proper to quell the "Uprising." It was no wonder, Shaw thought, that the Irish were still a bit prickly with respect to their neighbors to the east.

Wars. They were the easiest things to start and hardest things to end. Shaw knew this, unfortunately, from experience.

He checked his watch again. It was time to go see Anna.

Anna Fischer. Born in Stuttgart, university-educated

in England and France, she was now currently living in London, except when she was giving a speech, which she was doing in Dublin. Hence Shaw was here too. He and Anna often hooked up around the world, yet this time was different. And the nerveless Shaw suddenly felt his heart rate quicken and his breathing grow more shallow. It really was time.

12

The walk to Trinity College took only about ten minutes with Shaw's long-gaited pace and pent-up anticipation. Her lecture nearly over, he waited for his lady across from a side entrance to the college close to Maggie's Bookshop, a favorite of theirs. He spent a few minutes chatting with the woman who ran the shop.

On one shelf he found a copy of a book that Anna had written on the subject of the origins of fascist governments entitled *A Historical Examination of Police States*. The love of his life was fun-loving in many ways, emotional and romantic, but she also possessed an IQ far to the north of genius level and the issues that dominated her professional life were serious ones indeed. Was there ever a more potent combination to win someone's heart than brains and beauty?

When Anna came out, the hug lingered. She pressed her long fingers directly into the small of his back, kneading as she moved up the spine. She could always sense pain in him and he was a man who hid such things extremely well.

"Tense?" she asked, her German accent virtually nonexistent. Anna Fischer could speak fifteen languages at last count and all of them like a native. After six years at Oxford writing brilliant research papers and books, she had joined the UN as a simultaneous translator. After that stint, she'd accepted a position at a think tank in London and did work on international policies and global issues of unfathomable complexity with not an easy answer in sight. She was certainly far smarter than Shaw, yet never made him feel it.

"A little."

"Bad flight from Holland?"

"Ride was great. Just an old rugby injury." Actually it was the free fall into the canal cesspool, but she didn't need to know that.

"Boys and their games," she said in a mock scolding tone. "Is that how you got that?" She pointed to the bruise on his face courtesy of the Iranian who would never see freedom again.

"Luggage came out of the plane bin faster than I thought it would. Looks worse than it is."

When they finally let go of each other, Anna stared up at him, but at five-eleven and wearing two-inch pumps she didn't have to crane her neck too much. Still, Shaw had never been more grateful for his imposing height.

"How was the speech?" he asked.

"It was fairly well attended. However, in the

interests of full disclosure I have to add that the heightened numbers were probably due largely to the catered food from the best Indian restaurant in town, and the open bar. I'm disappointed you missed it. I could have at least imagined you in your skivvies."

"Why imagine when you can see it for real?"

She kissed him and intertwined her long fingers through his thick ones.

He held out her book he'd purchased.

"You *paid* for it? I could've given you one for free. They sent me all the unsold copies. They were so numerous I used them as furniture in my office."

"Well, this one you're getting the full royalty on. Will you sign it for me?"

She took out her pen and wrote something in the book. When he tried to see what, she said, "Read it later. After Dublin."

"Thanks."

"You're interested in police states?" she asked.

"As much as I get around I'm usually in one at least once a month."

He'd literally run into her on a Berlin side street three years ago. She was in the process of being mugged by two men and he'd just finished a solo mission not unlike the one in Amsterdam and was not in a particularly good mood. When the thugs saw him they made a big mistake by thinking they'd rob two birds at the same time. The police showed up a few minutes after Shaw called them when he'd finished beating both men unconscious. He'd hit one of them so hard he had nearly broken his hand on the man's skull.

He'd walked Anna back to her hotel after she refused to go to a hospital. He held ice against her face for an hour and then slept on the floor of her hotel room because she was still so unnerved by the attack.

Shaw had never had a serious relationship with a woman before. That might have stemmed from his relationship with his mother, or rather his lack of one.

Abandonment did that to you.

Yet from the moment he saw Anna Fischer, bruised and bloodied though she was, on that dimly lit avenue in the German capital, Shaw knew that his heart was no longer his alone.

Nearly three years had now passed and her feelings had clearly deepened toward him. He knew that Anna loved him. Yet he could sense her growing bewilderment at his lack of commitment.

Well, that was about to end. Shaw was not yet free from Frank but he could wait no longer. He would make this work. Somehow.

"You're pensive," she said over dinner. At age thirty-eight she still wore her hair long. It curved seductively around her sculpted Germanic bones.

"No, just hungry. With men they carry the same

expression. I suppose they don't serve coddle here." It was a working-class meal of rashers, potatoes, onion, and sausages with pepper poured thick.

"Not here, no, but we can go elsewhere."

"That's okay. Food's gotten better in Dublin over the years."

"Yes, though I still can't understand why Irish stew has no carrots." She smiled impishly over her wineglass. "Even the British have carrots in their stew."

"And that's exactly why the Irish don't."

Later, as they were finishing their meals she said, "So what were you doing in Amsterdam this time?"

"As little as possible."

"Your consultancy work slowing down?"

"Come on. I have a place I want to take you to."

Shaw could feel the strain in his voice and sensed that Anna could too.

"Are you all right?" she asked. "You're acting very mysteriously."

Shaw tongued his dry lips and attempted to smile. "I thought that was one of the things you liked about me. Mystery?"

He didn't believe his own words and it was clear she didn't either.

He rose. His legs quivered a bit and he silently cursed himself.

I jumped into a damn canal from four stories up and beat a gang of nuclear terrorist nutcases almost single-handedly.

You'd think I could manage this without acting like a lovesick teenager.

A little later they entered a small pub north of the Liffey, which was the decidedly poorer and less glamorous half of Dublin. Yet Shaw liked it here, as did Anna.

As she'd once said, "How can you possibly not love every molecule of a city that produced Swift, Stoker, G. B. Shaw, Yeats, Wilde, Beckett, and Heaney? And the master, Joyce."

Just to see her reaction he'd answered, "I'm more into Roddy Doyle."

"And I'm more into Maeve Binchy," she'd shot back.

He ordered for them, which was unusual. When it arrived she said, "What is it?"

"Barm brack. It's sort of a fruitcake."

"Fruitcake! Don't they use those for doorstops and to poison people?"

Shaw cut her a slice. "Just try it. You're an adventurous gal."

Anna stabbed the cake with her fork and it clinked against something. Her wide eyes grew even wider as she probed the barm until her fingers closed around it.

Shaw said, "Legend has it that if you find the ring in the barm brack, you're destined to be married."

There was no turning back now, he knew. The

next few moments would decide his entire life, and the sweat burned through his shirt. He drew a deep breath, slipped from his chair, and rested one knee on the old plank floor that was worn smooth from centuries of drunks and at least one man proposing. Taking her shaky hand in his firm one, he slipped the ring on her finger and said, "Anna, will you marry me?"

13

The drum-drum of the rain woke him. As he tried to get back to sleep the vibration next to his head elicited a small groan from him.

Shaw snatched up the device and read the message he'd just been sent.

Frank.

In the bed next to him was Anna. They'd properly consummated their engagement and then drank a bottle of Dom, glasses balanced precariously on flat bellies.

She slept soundly as Shaw rose, walked into the adjoining room, and punched in a number, knowing it would be answered immediately.

"Your gig over in old Dublin?" Frank said cheerfully. Shaw could imagine the man lounging in a chair somewhere, probably several time zones away, wearing the smug, shit-eating grin that masters reserved for conversations with their servants.

"What, your men not checking in with you regularly? Not that you need them to." Shaw stared at his right side when he said this, where the old scar was.

"And by the way, it's 3 a.m. here. The thought ever run through that thick head of yours?"

"We're a 24/7 op, Shaw. You know the rules."

"*Your* rules."

He yanked open the drapes and stared out at a dismal curtain of rain drenching the area.

"We need you, Shaw."

"No you don't. And even people like me need some damn R&R."

"I can tell from your grumpy tone that you're not alone."

Shaw of course knew that Frank knew exactly where he was and who was with him. Yet the other man's tone made him look away from the window and then race back to the bedroom to check on Anna. She was still sleeping peacefully, blissfully unaware that he was currently haggling with a professional psycho.

One of the woman's long, elegantly formed legs lay on top of the sheet. It made Shaw want to wake her up, make love to her again. But then he had Frank on the phone. He returned to the other room and gazed out the window, exploring every crevice of the streets and alleys below for Frank's boys. They were down there. They were always down there.

"Shaw, you still breathing?"

"I told you where I was going. So why keep me under the scope?"

"You did it to yourself. With all this crazy talk about retirement."

"It *wasn't* crazy talk. I'm done, Frank. The last one *was* the last one."

Shaw could envision Frank shaking his head with the dent in the back from where he'd been shot at close range with a nine-millimeter SIG Sauer sporting custom grips. Shaw knew these intimate details because he'd been the one who'd shot Frank.

"We have a lot of work to do. The world is a very dangerous place."

"Yeah, because of people like you."

"It's noble what we do, Shaw. It's a matter of honor."

"Save the babble for the rookies."

Shaw heard the squeak of the chair as Frank sat up straighter. *Okay, here it comes.*

Frank's voice was tight and hard as cement. "And where exactly are you going to retire *to*, you prick? A supermax facility?"

"The deal was for five years, Frank. I've hung on for almost six."

"You nearly killed me."

"You had a gun pointed at me. And you didn't show your badge. I thought you were just one more goon looking to shoot me in the back."

"So if I'd flashed my badge you're telling me you wouldn't have shot me in the frigging head?"

"I *did* take you to the closest hospital. Otherwise you would have bled to death."

"Hospital!" Frank roared. "You left me holding what seemed like half my brain in the parking lot of a human chop shop in the middle of Istanbul."

"You really think it was just half?"

"Look—"

But Shaw cut in. "I shot you in self-defense, but when your guys showed up in Greece a month later they obviously didn't see it that way. So we made a deal and I lived up to it. There's nothing else to talk about." They did have a deal, Shaw knew. In return for not spending the rest of his life at hard labor in some hellhole in Siberia that Frank would've gleefully arranged once he'd recovered from the large-caliber hole in his head, Shaw had spent nearly six years running around the world risking his life so, as Frank quaintly put it, others could live in peace and security. Well, Shaw wanted a little peace and security in *his* life and he wanted it right now. With Anna.

Yet arrangements with men like Frank were sort of like hanging off the Golden Gate Bridge by your pinkies while high winds kicked off the bay. And Shaw couldn't exactly grab a lawyer off the street and sue in open court for his contractual freedom. That was why he'd agreed to spend an extra year getting nearly shot, stabbed, poisoned, and even blown up. When he'd implied that tangling with the Amsterdam Islamic nuke squad was a cakewalk, he'd meant it.

"But for your special 'skills' I wouldn't have offered you anything except a prison cell."

This was news to Shaw. "So *you* were the one? Why?"

"After my brains got put back in my head I realized anybody who could almost take me out was somebody we needed on our side."

"Then you should understand that I've done my duty."

Frank said slowly, "I don't know. I'll have to talk to my people about that. Maybe I could bring myself to cutting you loose, but I don't think they'll be too happy about it."

Shaw had never been able to go over, around, or through Frank. The burly baldy had stood his ground like a stone wall.

I should have shot him between the eyes.

"I don't care if they're happy! Just tell 'em what I said."

"In the meantime I need you in Edinburgh and then Germany, Heidelberg. You don't come through on that you can forget me talking to anybody except your new warden."

Shaw was silent for a few moments, trying to get his anger under control. "This is the last time, Frank. This is it! You can tell your people whatever the hell you want. Understood?"

"Instructions the usual way. Two days. Enjoy Dublin. And your friend."

"You really don't want to go there."

"Just making an observation." The line went dead.

"I hate your guts, Frank," Shaw whispered to the empty air.

14

Shaw slipped into the small bathroom. Most European baths were small; these folks apparently required far less space to relieve and bathe themselves than the rest of the world. He splashed water on his face, looked up and caught his reflection in the mirror.

Rugged is how most would describe his features. Even Anna had called him ruggedly handsome. The bones and skin were in decent shape. The eyes had always been his most distinctive element, though. Not only were they the lightest of blues that eyes could generate without artificial aids, they didn't go with the rest of his coloring. His skin was swarthy, more Italian or Greek than Irish or Scottish, and his hair was dark and wavy, often with a mind of its own. Fetchingly rumpled, Anna had once described it. Yet when Shaw looked at himself all he saw was a haunted man with scars that ran far too deep to endure.

As though she had sensed her presence in his thoughts, Anna appeared behind him, wrapping her long arms around his bare and brawny shoulders.

She was wearing his T-shirt. On Shaw, the breadth

and cut of his delts and chest made the shirt a tight fit. Yet even on the tall Anna, it was more like a dress.

"Trouble sleeping?" she asked.

"Rain. Don't like rain at night."

"I thought I heard you talking to someone."

Shaw stared at her in the mirror's surface as her fingers traced a small scar near his throat. It was a little souvenir from a visit to the Ukraine. He'd told her it was from falling off a bike. Actually it was from a knife thrown by an ex-KGB agent whose only qualification for the job was that he was a homicidal maniac. It'd missed Shaw's jugular by about two centimeters. Still, he'd come pretty damn near bleeding to death in a place that would have made the chop shop in Turkey he'd dumped Frank at look like Johns Hopkins.

He had another scar on his right side that he'd never explained to her for a simple reason: he wanted to forget it was even there, because every time he did think of it, he felt shame. Branded. Like a horse. No, like a slave. In fact, that was the other reason he was in Dublin, to do something about that little present.

She said again, "*Were* you talking to someone?"

Frank, scars, and the KGB butcher passed from his mind. What Shaw was really wondering was whether Anna was now having second thoughts. His proposal had been followed with a tearful "yes" from her that he could barely hear. And then the bride-to-be's enthusiasm and excitement ratcheting up, she'd accepted his marriage proposal in *nine* other languages, her tears leaching onto his skin, finally bringing Shaw the man as close as he'd ever come to crying.

But something in her tone now was signaling a message other than happiness. It really was time, he thought.

He splashed water on his face, licked some off his fingers, and turned to face her.

"I'm not really a business consultant specializing in international mergers and acquisitions," he said.

"I know that."

"What?" he said sharply.

"I know many business consultants. They rarely can beat unconscious two armed men. They rarely have knife scars on their bodies. And they almost always want to show off their wealth. I've never even seen where you live. We always stay at my London flat."

"And you're just telling me this now?"

"It's different now. I just told you I'd marry you."

"And if I'd still said nothing about what I did?"

"I'd have asked. Like I am now."

"But you already said yes."

"And I can also say no."

"I'm no criminal."

"I know that too. I can tell. Otherwise I wouldn't be here. Now tell me the truth."

He leaned back against the sink basin and marshaled his thoughts. "I work with an international law enforcement agency funded by several of the G8 countries. We handle stuff that's either too dicey or too global for one country. Sort of like Interpol on steroids. I'm not in the field anymore. I'm in a desk position now," he lied, carrying it off reasonably well, he thought.

"And what laws do you enforce?" she asked firmly.

"We try to stop bad people from doing bad things. Any way we can," he added.

"And what you do now isn't dangerous, though you get calls in the night?"

"Living is dangerous, Anna. You can turn the corner and get nailed by a bus."

"Shaw, don't condescend."

"It's not dangerous, no." He could feel his skin growing hot. He could lie to a Persian madman with ease. But not to Anna.

"Will you continue to come and go as you have been?"

"Actually, I'm planning on retiring. Start doing something else."

Her face brightened. "This . . . this is a surprise."

I hope I live to carry it out. "Marriage is supposed to mean two people together, not apart."

"You would do this for me?"

"I'd do anything for you."

She stroked his cheek.

"Why?" he asked suddenly.

"Why what?"

"You could have any man you wanted. Why me?"

"Because you are a good man. A humble man. And a brave one. But as capable as you are, you need looking after, Shaw. You need me. And I need you."

He kissed her, ran his fingers along her cheek.

"Do you have to leave now?"

He shook his head. "Two days."

"Where to now?"

"Scotland."

He took Anna in his arms, let her blonde hair touch his face, her scent mingle with his, canal stink and all.

"But first, to bed."

They made love again. After she fell asleep, Shaw put one hand behind his head and the other protectively over Anna's arm.

He listened to the rain and envisioned Frank chuckling at having screwed him again. He touched Anna's face. Yes, it *was* different now.

The Dublin torrent poured on; each drop of water was a jacketed round fired right into his brain. Shaw had asked her to marry him. But after his conversation with Frank, he feared it might turn out to be the biggest mistake of his life.

15

"R.I.C.?" Anna said as she held the paper up to Shaw, who was pouring coffee, still dressed in his boxers. She pushed the room service cart away a bit and unfolded the insert that had slipped out from the *Herald Tribune*.

Shaw looked over her shoulder. The article was long, brimming with factoids, and constituted another compelling broadside fired against the government of the Russian Federation. The title of the article might have been, "The Evil Empire, Act Two."

Shaw read out loud, "The Russian Independent Congress, or R.I.C., and its adjunct division, the Free Russia Group, appeal to free countries everywhere to stand up to President Romuald Gorshkov and an administration of terror and oppression before it is too late."

Anna glanced at another section. "The Gorshkov administration has filled secret prisons with political opponents, murdered rivals, instituted a policy of ethnic cleansing at the highest levels of power, and are secretly manufacturing and stockpiling WMDs in clear contravention of myriad disarmament treaties." She gazed up at Shaw. "First the Konstantin business, then all those allegedly dead Russians, and now this? Have you ever heard of this organization, the R.I.C.?"

He shook his head. "There's a Web site listed at the bottom of the page."

She slid her laptop out, fired it up, and within a minute was hooked to the hotel's wireless network. Her quick fingers skimmed across the keys and a colorful page sprang up on the screen.

"Look at this Web site." She pointed to the screen. "This wasn't online yesterday, I would've heard about it."

Anna snatched up her ringing cell phone, listened, asked questions, and listened some more. She clicked off and glanced over at Shaw. "Well?" he said.

"That was my office. Everyone's buzzing about this new article. Gorshkov and his ministers are said to be furious. They're denying everything and demanding to know who's behind what they call a grand smear campaign."

"Any idea who did do it?"

She shook her head. "As yet unknown. It needn't be a large group behind this. Or even lots of money. Although this newspaper insert wasn't cheap, a few good computer people can swamp the globe with propaganda, we've all seen that."

"And everyone else has sort of jumped on the bandwagon."

She looked back at the computer and scrolled through the site. "It's Russian evil this and Russian evil that. My office has done several white papers on the Russians' slide back to an autocratic system of government. It's of concern professionally *and* personally. Tensions are very high between Moscow and the rest of the world right now. And all of this certainly hasn't helped matters."

"Well, forewarned is forearmed," Shaw said.

She looked at him thoughtfully. "That's the problem. When one is forearmed, one tends to pull the trigger faster than one should."

"Like old times, though," he said. "Cold war redux."

She stared at him strangely. "Perhaps someone wants the old world order back."

The rain had broken. He only had two days left with Anna. Perhaps forever.

He took her in his arms and said, "Screw the Russians."

He held her so tightly she said, "Shaw, I can't breathe."

He let her go, stepped back, staring down.

She cupped his chin with her hand. "We're engaged. You should be happy."

"I am, happier than I've ever been."

"You don't look very happy."

"We have to leave each other."

"But not for long. We'll be together again soon."

He wrapped his arms around her again, though not as tightly.

There is no guarantee. None.

16

Two days later Shaw kissed a tearful Anna good-bye.

"We need to set a wedding date," he told her.

She looked at him strangely. "Yes, of course."

Shaw drove off in a rental car, but didn't head to the airport. He was going to Malahide Castle.

Malahide, in Gaeilge, means "on the brow of the sea." It is situated on the Howth peninsula at the north end of Dublin Bay. Built on a small rise, it has a commanding view of the water, because in those days enemies would often come by boat to pillage and slaughter. Now Shaw passed broad fields on the grounds of the castle where local teams played rugby and cricket, without an ax-wielding pillager in sight.

He paid his euros and was admitted to the oldest inhabited castle in Ireland. It looked like one would expect of a medieval keep: built of sturdy stone block, with wings of imposing circular turrets and ivy grafted onto its hard skin. It had belonged to the Talbot family from 1185 right up to the 1970s.

He waited until the current tour was over and then walked up to the small, thin woman who'd just finished telling a gaggle of tourists all about Malahide Castle, the Talbot family, the Battle of Boyne, the disappearing virgin, and the building's four ghosts, including the puckish "Puck."

"Hello, Leona."

She turned, hesitantly at first, and then swung around to stare straight up at him. Leona Bartaroma was in her sixties, her long hair still dark, her face mostly unlined, her lips full and painted a muted red that coexisted nicely with her natural coloring.

She said nothing, but took his arm and quickly guided him into a small room and shut the door behind them.

"What the hell are you doing here?" she spat out.

"I take it you're not happy to see me."

"If Frank finds out . . ."

"Frank always knows exactly where I am, thanks to you." He pressed his finger against his right side. "That's why I'm here."

She sat down behind a small wooden desk with cherubs carved into its sides. "I do not understand you, Shaw. I never have."

"I want you to take it out."

"I'm retired. I give tours. I don't perform surgery."

He stepped closer to the desk. "You have *one* more operation inside you."

"Impossible." She started sifting papers on her desk.

"Nothing's impossible if you want it badly enough."

"You are a fool."

"I'm retiring soon too, Leona. And I want it out."

"Find someone else, then." She waved a hand carelessly around the room as though another person with surgical skills was lurking somewhere there.

"You, Leona. I know how you put it in me. If it's taken out incorrectly . . ."

Her dark face turned noticeably paler. "I have no idea what you are talking about."

"Dirk Lundrell, Leona, remember him? He tried to have his removed. They still haven't found all the pieces."

"Lundrell came to me too. And I told him the same thing I'm telling you. No!"

"What if Frank approves it?" He cocked his head at her. "What then?"

"You think Frank would okay something like that?" she scoffed. "I have heard he and you still don't get along." She smiled. "And retiring? You don't retire from your line of work, Shaw."

"I'm getting married. Two more jobs, I'm done."

"You, married?" she said incredulously.

"Yeah. What, you don't think people like me get married? I've spent six years of my life nearly getting killed. I'm tired. I'm done."

"I know what you have done these last six years," she said more calmly. "I know well the risks you've taken." She paused to study him. "What is the woman's name?"

"What?"

"Your fiancée? What is her name?"

"Anna."

"I was married once." Leona looked down at her hands. "You love her very much?"

"I wouldn't be marrying her if I didn't."

Leona was silent for a long moment while Shaw simply stared at her.

"If Frank approves it, I will take it out of you."

"And I'll still be alive when you're done?"

"Surgery always involves risk," she began. But then she added, "You will live."

He rose. "That's all I needed to know. I'll be in touch." He turned to leave.

"Where is this Anna from?"

"Germany."

"German women make good wives, or so I've heard."

Shaw closed the door softly behind him. Now all he had to do was convince Frank. *And* survive the next few days.

Three hours later, he was on a high-speed catamaran crossing the Irish Sea to England. Normally he would've just flown to Edinburgh from Dublin, but his instructions had been clear. Take the ferry. And then, at Holyhead, an express train through Wales to London. And from there an overnight sleeper to the Scottish capital. He would arrive in the wee hours, whereas a direct flight from Dublin to Edinburgh would've taken less than an hour.

In the lounge of the catamaran, Shaw sat at the third desk from the right set along one wall. There was a light on the desk. He turned it off, on, and then off again in accordance with the instructions he'd been given.

While he was waiting he opened the book to read Anna's inscription to him. Her message was written in French, but his language skills were sufficient enough to translate. It was short, simple, and hit him like a sledgehammer.

Love without trust is nothing.

As Shaw slowly closed the book he instinctively glanced up.

Tipped off by his signal with the lamp, a man was coming his way. They always were.

17

Shaw arrived in Edinburgh and walked from the train station to the Balmoral Hotel at one end of the North Bridge. Anna's inscription in her book was seared across his brain. *Love without trust is nothing.* Around three in the morning he fell asleep, thoughts of a possible life and family with Anna drifting through his mind.

And maybe that's why it began. Again.

"Mudder? Where's Mudder?"

"Shut the hell up, you dumb shit. You ain't got no mum!"

The little boy, just awoken from a nightmare, cried louder, "Mudder!"

One of the older boys mimicked the child's speech. "'Mudder, where's Mudder?' Mudder's dead. That's why you live in an orphanage, you idiot."

Another older boy chuckled and said, "Mudder's dead. Mudder's dead. Mudder is absolutely, positively dead."

Then they all heard the slow footsteps and the room grew quiet save for the little boy's choking cries.

"Mudder? Where's Mudder?"

The squat old nun came into the room and glided to the bed. She obviously knew the destination well, even in the dark. She took the little boy in her arms, rocked him, patted his head, and kissed his cheek.

"Just a bad dream, that's all. I'm here, child. It's all right. Just a nightmare."

Her presence always calmed the boy, and he finally fell silent. He was big for his age, but the nun, though old, was strong. The years did not seem to have worn her down, though she had much to weary her here.

She laid him back on his small cot, of which there were twenty-six in a room meant to hold half that number. The nun knew the boys could walk on the beds to reach the two bathrooms they all shared, so closely stacked were the cots. Yet they had a bed, a roof over their heads, and some food in their bellies. For such children, that's all that mattered to them now. Or probably ever would.

As the nun trudged back to her room, fifty-two ears listened to her measured footfalls. When the sound of her door closing was heard, an older boy said, "And your father's dead too. Drank himself right into the gutter. Saw him do it."

"Mudder's dead," the other boy started chanting again, but in a quieter voice, for while the nun was a good woman her patience had its limits.

The little boy did not cry out this time. His body did not start shaking, as it sometimes did when they taunted him. An hour later the chanting and verbal barbs stopped. All were asleep.

All except for one.

He climbed down from his bed, dropped to the floor, and slid on his belly like he'd seen soldiers do on the black-and-white TV in the nun's part of the building. She would let him come there sometimes, for a drink of fresh orange juice and a slice of bread slathered in rich butter and thick jelly.

He reached the bed, sat up on his haunches, coiled into a ball, and pounced.

His hands closed around the other boy's throat. One fist connected to the far larger child's face. Blood spurted onto the bedcovers, and he felt it splash on his arm. He smelled sweat. And fear. It would be the first of many times he would experience it in someone else.

He aimed another fist and connected with soft flesh. Then something hard struck him in his right eye. It stung, and his face immediately felt puffy. A bony knee wedged painfully into his belly, forcing the breath from him. Still, he hung on. He hit with his hands, his feet, even his head, driving it deep into the chest cavity of the boy under him. He felt his own blood rush down his face, tasted it when the wet ooze hit his lips. It was salty and thick and made him sick. Yet he didn't let go.

"Mudder!" he heard his voice cry out. His arms and legs worked like pistons; his chest was so heavy from exertion it felt like his lungs had solidified.

"Mudder . . . is," he panted.

Hands tore at him, nails like claws ripped at his back. Someone was screaming into his ear, but it was as though they were on the other side of a waterfall.

He struck, flesh, bone, cartilage. The claws ripped. The blood poured into his mouth. The taste of the ocean.

"Mudder . . . is . . . not."

He drove a knee right into the boy's privates, something that had been done to him here, more than once. The older boy whimpered and instantly fell limp under him.

He found the air to scream, "Mudder . . . is . . . not . . . dead!"

Then the claws gripped hard and he let go and like a bent, rusty nail in an old fencepost he finally came free and fell to the floor, panting, bleeding. But not crying.

He had never cried again. Not once.

18

Shaw sat up in bed. He smelled his adult sweat, tasted it too as it trickled into his mouth. He rose, opened the window of his hotel room, and let the cool Edinburgh air sweep away the terror of a six-year-old boy.

His room at the Balmoral looked out onto Princes Street, a grand thoroughfare of shops, pubs, and restaurants. On a high hill to his right lay the imposing footprint of Edinburgh Castle that would dwarf Malahide if they'd been set side by side. The Palace of Holyroodhouse anchored the other edge of the city and was the official summer residence of the British royal family.

Must be nice, Shaw thought, to have an official residence.

"Mudder," he said in a low voice. He hadn't experienced the pain of that nightmare in nearly a year. He thought it was gone forever. As with many important things in his life, he'd been wrong.

He'd been thrown out of the orphanage the next day despite the old nun's impassioned pleas to allow him to stay. The other boy, a bulky lad of twelve, had been severely injured by the young Shaw. Some had wanted to call in the police. Yet how could one hold a six-year-old criminally liable? Shaw remembered terms like malicious intent, willful assault. He hadn't known what they meant. But he did know that he wanted to kill the other boy. Kill the other boy so he would hurt as much as Shaw did.

In the end it was determined that a child who couldn't even pronounce the word "mother" properly because he'd never really had one could not be charged with a crime.

Sister Mary Agnes Maria, what a truly beautiful name that had been. They all called her Sister MAM, which Shaw had translated to MOM. She was as close to a mother as he would ever get in life. He'd never had another.

He hadn't called himself A Shaw because he was *a* Shaw. It was because of the orphanage. Painted on the wall over the bed of the boy who slept opposite his was the letter "A." It was not just randomly there; not the beginnings of an alphabet train. It had once been part of a word, but the "M," "E," and "N" had been worn away over time, and poor busy Sister Mary Agnes Maria had never had the time or apparently the paint to put the M-E-N back into AMEN.

Shaw wasn't sorry about that. He would look at the letter and imagine the long vertical lines of the "A" softening to form the rounded face of his mother.

The horizontal slash connecting the two long lines would curl into a smile on his mother's face, because she was so happy to see him. She had come back for him. They would leave together. They would leave right now. The "A" was his friend. It held so many good possibilities. And then the sun would rise and vanquish them all. Ever since then Shaw had enjoyed the night far more than the day. He would always be a person of the night now.

The years had passed swiftly with a quick succession of orphanages, none of them with a Sister Mary Agnes Maria. Then came foster homes, and other facilities for children who, while not technically criminal, were so close to the line that no one wanted the problem. That was every day of his life until Shaw the boy became, at age eighteen, Shaw the man.

By then he could clearly say "mother" but had not a single reason to do so.

He shut the window and sat on the bed. The man on the high-speed ferry from Dublin had connected with him. They'd gone to the open boat doors at the stern. With the wind and the engines covering their conversation he'd told Shaw the first phase of what he needed to know. As he was leaving the man had stared back at Shaw, his expression clear. *If you survive this, it'll be a miracle.*

On the express train from Wales to London, Shaw had stared out the window, alternately taking in the sea vistas and the views of the Cambrian Mountains, shutting out the desultory conversations from the passengers around him. There was nothing normal about his world, and he felt it nearly impossible to relate to anything outside his own sphere.

Except for Anna. She was his first and only connection to the rest of humanity.

On the overnight train to Scotland he was visited again, in his sleeper compartment, this time by a woman. She was young, but looked old. She was physically attractive but her spirit seemed to be gone. She was a vessel only. People like Frank had torn her soul right out so they could fill it up with what they wanted. In a monotone she told him the second phase of what he needed to know. Nothing was ever written down, so he memorized every detail. If he made one slip he was dead. It was that simple.

He rose, dressed, and looked once more at the book Anna had inscribed for him.

Love without trust is nothing.

She'd be asleep. He called anyway. Surprisingly, she answered on the second ring.

"I hoped it might be you," she said, her voice wide awake. "How was the trip?"

"I read the inscription."

She said nothing.

He swallowed hard. "I want to trust you. I *do* trust you. I told you what I did. Do you realize how hard that was for me?"

"Yes, but there are obviously things you can't tell me."

"There are," he admitted.

"So after we're married, you will go away without a word and show up without one either?"

"I'm retiring. I told you. And I have a desk job."

"Don't insult my intelligence with tales of luggage falling from aircraft bins. And people behind a desk don't go to castles without bothering to take a tour. Or take the time to travel by ferry from Ireland to Scotland. Was it to meet someone?"

Her words stung him. "You followed me?"

"Of course I did. I'm planning on marrying you. And I hate that I have to even think of following you, much less do it." Her voice shook and he heard a small sob. Shaw wanted to reach across the phone line and hold her, tell her everything would be okay. Yet he had lied to her enough.

He found his own voice. "There's still time to back out, Anna. You said yes, you can also say no. I'll understand."

Her tone became harsh. "I don't like that you would understand. You should *not* understand. The same for me if you walked away. I would *not* understand."

"I love you. I will make this work. I will."

He thought he heard another sob escape her lips and his guilt increased.

She said, "And how you will make this all work, you can't tell me?"

"No," he admitted. "I can't."

"Where do you go after Scotland?"

"Heidelberg."

"My parents live about an hour from there. In a small village called Wisbach, near the town of Karlsruhe. They run a bookshop, the only one in Wisbach. Go to see them. Their names are Wolfgang and Natascha. They are good people. Kind people. I wanted you to meet them before now, but you were always too busy."

He hadn't always been too busy, Shaw knew. He'd been too afraid.

"You want me to see them without you?"

"Yes. Ask my father for my hand in marriage. If he says yes, we will be married. If you still want to."

This request stunned him. "Anna, I—"

She rushed on, "If you think it is worth it, you will go. I will tell them you are coming. If you do not go, then I will have my answer."

The line went dead. Shaw slowly put down the phone and looked at the blotting paper on the desk where he had written the name Anna Fischer over and over, driving the letters hard into the thin surface. He tore the paper up, left the Balmoral, and walked down Princes Street, past all the closed shops. Two hours later he was still wandering through the ancient Scottish capital as the sun started to creep up, illuminating the aged stone bridges and casting shadows behind which Shaw could imagine every single one of his nightmares. And he had more than most.

He would go to see her parents at the bookshop in Wisbach. He would ask for their daughter's hand in marriage.

Yes, he would do all that. If he was still alive.

"Where's Mudder?" he whispered to the semidarkness as he walked back to the Balmoral to prepare for what might be his last few hours on earth.

19

The high-rise along the Dulles High-Tech Corridor was mostly dark. One firm, Pender & Associates, owned the entire building, having paid eight figures in cash to buy an office tower smack in the middle of some of the priciest dirt in the country. And even though it was called Pender & Associates, the firm was run by one man, its founder, Richard "Dick" Pender.

He possessed a face that was as chiseled, a grin that was as toothy, and hair that was as perfectly primped as any gospel-spouting televangelist. He had the silky smooth delivery of a trial lawyer in his polished prime. And he would continue to smile while the knife he held repeatedly connected with your spine.

His motto was simple: *Why waste time trying to discover the truth, when you can so easily create it?*

Pender's line of work was called perception management. PM firms, as they are known, were paid to establish what was true or not, all over the globe. Some traditional lobbying firms considered themselves to be PM firms but they really weren't. There were only a very few pure PM players and Pender & Associates was one of the best in the world.

Dick Pender could bury any secret, despite the attempts of the press to ferret it out. He had also, on occasion, started or enhanced wars based on certain *truths*. And when people started poking around, he had hidden those reasons under such bewildering layers of facts, figures, and falsehoods that no one could ever reach them. Yet mostly he was retained to create the truth.

He was paid enormous amounts of money to do this, both from government and private sources all over the world. For his clients, *creating* the truth was critical because real truth was too unpredictable. Created truth was controllable. And thus the difference between the real and the created was the difference between a bomb and an A-bomb in its effectiveness.

Pender had a special visitor coming tonight. The private elevator took his guest up to the top floor. A door was opened, and Nicolas Creel, wearing a black-hooded coat, was ushered into a room that was dominated by a large one-way glass window allowing the defense contracting magnate to see into the high-tech, digitized war room of Pender & Associates.

Pender sat down next to him. "I trust the flight was good, Mr. Creel."

"I have no idea. I slept the whole way."

"Someone mentioned to me that you'd cracked the top fifteen on the Forbes List."

"That's right," Creel acknowledged in a clearly disinterested tone.

"Eighteen billion dollars?" Pender estimated.

"Actually twenty-one."

"Congratulations."

"For what? When I passed my first billion, what did it really matter? It's not as though another twenty billion has greatly altered my lifestyle. Let's hear the report."

Pender pointed to the one-way glass where dozens of people were working hard. "We've devoted our entire war room to the effort. Thirty people, hundreds of computers, enormous databases, and an Internet pipeline that rivals anything Google has."

"And you're absolutely certain there can be no trace back here?"

"We took the most extraordinary security measures, including stealing the electronic identity of hundreds of Web sites and Internet portals. So if someone tries to trace it back to its origin the electronic tunnel will lead them directly to, say, the official Vatican Web site, or the Red Cross site. We also included our own site in the mix along with several of our competitors."

"So if someone does track it back to you, you can just claim identity theft?"

"Why try to hide the needle in the haystack, when you can just make lots of needles?" Pender replied smugly.

"Your people?"

"Extremely well paid and dedicated to me. They have no idea of your, um, interest in this matter. Not that they would care, actually. We do not employ conscience here. We do not worry about the consequences of our work. That's for the *client* to do."

"Refreshing attitude. And the initial impact has been all that we hoped it would be."

"A bit more sophisticated than stories about brutal foreign invaders tearing desert babies from incubators in order to make certain countries enter a war," Pender said quietly, but with a superior smile. "But then you picked well, Mr. Creel. All we had to do was get the ball rolling and everyone jumped on."

"The Bear is an easy target. Where'd you get the thousands of Russian dead?"

"Basically Photoshop stuff cranked up several levels. But we worked in some real victims that we got from old KGB files we bought years ago. You have five authentic dead bodies everyone assumes the other thirty-two thousand are legit as well."

"Prescient of you."

"That's my business. I can visualize the aneurysm slowly building in President Gorshkov's brain. Let me see, we've had the 'gripper' strategy, then the 'Vesuvius' tactic." He gestured at Creel. "You're arranging for the leak. Correct?"

"Yes. But forward to me anything that comes across your desk that looks promising. I'll follow it up from there."

"Not that your motivation concerns me in the least, but I did read that Ares has missed its quarterly projections four times in a row now."

"Tip of the iceberg. We're positively hemorrhaging money. I was convinced Iraq was the beginning of Armageddon in the Middle East and we ramped up for it. But a few months of shock and awe was followed by a years-long pissing contest using basically popguns. I didn't build a $150 billion company to have my people sling potato salad in Anbar for soldier boys. It was a monumental cock-up and the responsibility rests with me. But I'll get us out of it. That's why I hired you. I have my people to take care of."

"Of course you do," Pender agreed demurely. "And we have celebrity interest too. They'll throw on a 'Remember Konstantin' T-shirt which we'll provide, plug their new movie, raise a fist to 'Free Russia.' And maybe even go to Washington and get star-screwed by assorted politicians."

"Any problem areas?"

"Three." Pender checked his computer screen. "There will be 148 feature stories running on the Red Menace across the globe in the next week or so. All but two follow our take to the letter. One in Spain. One in New York. The fellow in Spain is particularly tenacious, but he's also been working for two years on a scandal involving the royal family. Tomorrow he will receive documents that will rekindle his interest in that story."

"And the fellow in New York?"

"His wife has suspected for some time now that her husband is being unfaithful to her. Tomorrow she will also get a present that will show her instincts were right. That will take her hubby out of the game completely. Divorces can be so messy and time-consuming. I speak from experience, unfortunately."

"You just had these things lying around?"

"I have files on virtually every journalist worth a damn. We collect secrets, craft half-lies, and anonymously release those items when it best serves our clients."

"You said there were *three* problem areas?"

"Senator here in the States who fancies himself an expert on Russian affairs. Word is he plans to call for hearings on the matter using a very skeptical prism."

"What are you going to do about it?"

"Next time he steps into a public men's room we're going to Larry Craig him."

"So Senator Craig *was* set up?"

"Who knows? Who cares? But it'll take *this* senator right off our backs."

"And what do you call that tactic?"

"The 'I'm screwed' maneuver," Pender said smiling.

"An apt name."

"I actually prefer a more subtle approach where the target doesn't even realize what's happened. You recall reporters were embedded with troops in Iraq?"

"So they could see the war firsthand?"

"No, so they could be told the story only from the point of view of the Pentagon. That was my idea, and every general and administration official involved has personally come here and kissed my ass for coming up with it."

"You know your field well, Dick."

"I learned from the best."

"Where was that?"

"I started out in the White House Press Office."

Creel pointed to a large worktable in the war room where two people were laboring over some written materials.

"Explain."

"That's the 'Tablet of Tragedies.' We recently discovered that one of our competitors was hired to put something like this together during Persian Gulf One to help convince the West to defend Kuwait. It worked brilliantly there. So we thought we'd use the same concept here. But instead of printing hundreds of thousands of glossy copies we opted for handmade rudimentary stuff. That'll give it a realistic homegrown feel to balance the high-tech attack so far. We'll only make a dozen but send them out to optimal targets for maximum effect."

"Boots on the ground," Creel muttered thoughtfully.

"That was to be on your end," Pender pointed out. "I can make anyone believe a lie is true. However, there's no substitute for real blood spilled."

"I have the boots quite figured out. In fact you'll see evidence of that very soon."

"What about the other piece of the equation?"

"What about it?" Creel said sharply.

"Only that you said you would advise us of the timing of it."

"Have I advised you yet?"

"No."

"Then it must not be time!"

A moment later Creel was gone. Pender had helped make the man a fortune during the cold war, and when that dried up, they'd engineered numerous smaller global conflicts until the first Iraq War had literally fallen into their laps followed by the lucrative second Iraq War. But as he'd recently told Pender, "The Americans are completely tapped out. And the EU's in a peace mode, pouring their money into education, infrastructure, and health care instead of defense. The idiots never stop to think that it would be damn hard for the kiddies to go to school and Grandma to the doctor if they can't protect their countries from ending up pledging allegiance to Allah. But with all that going against me I'm going to win *this* war."

And Dick Pender would never bet against the man.

20

Sergei Petrov walked down the street, his collar upturned against the chill that had descended on New York in the last two days. He'd just finished a taping for a local television show, recounting the considerable horrors that he'd witnessed under the Putin/ Gorshkov regimes as the number two man in the Federal Security Service before fleeing the country. The westerners ate up what he was selling and paid well for the privilege, Petrov had found, far better than playing lapdog to dictators disguised as presidents. He didn't know where the Red Menace campaign had originated from and didn't really care. Gorshkov was evil. Petrov's homeland was going in the wrong direction. Whether all the horrors that had come to light recently were true or not he also didn't care about. Some of them probably were. That was good enough.

He felt for the gun in the pocket of his coat. Petrov was a careful man. He knew he had become a target. If Gorshkov had a top hit list he would be high on it. He always went out armed, never strayed from public places, and his trained eye was ever watchful. He would never drink or eat whenever anyone else was present. He would not die as Litvinenko had. There would be no polonium-210 cup of tea for him.

He walked to the corner and hailed a cab. One drew to a stop beside the curb; the driver looked out.

"Grand Central Station," Petrov said. The man nodded and he climbed in. As he did, the rear door on the opposite side opened and a man jumped in. At the same instant another bulky gent pushed Petrov from behind and slid in next to him. The doors closed and the cab raced off.

Petrov didn't even have time to look at his kidnappers. They pressed against him, their bulk pinning his hands to his body, his gun remaining in his pocket. The knife slashed once against his throat even as he felt another blade bite deeply into his right side. And then another bite and then another.

He fell forward as his life drained away.

The cab drove out of town and into Westchester. Next to a small, dark park it stopped and the three men climbed out and into a waiting SUV. It drove off, leaving Petrov's still body lying on the floor of the cab.

Written on his forehead with a black Sharpie pen was one word in Russian. Its English translation made perfect sense.

Traitor.

Back in the SUV Caesar took off his hat and mask.

This was Nicolas Creel's opening salvo in the "boots on the ground" department. Caesar had one more task to complete tonight. The SUV rolled on for a long time until they reached their destination. Arrangements had been made and money paid and they drove in without a problem. The SUV made its way to the very back edge of the place where a large crater had been dug in the earth. The men got out, opened the back of the truck, and slid out the body bag.

Caesar unzipped the bag and peered in at the face that looked blankly back at him.

Poor Konstantin, his Latino soap opera career never had the chance to take off. Caesar closed up the bag, hoisted it over his shoulder, carried it to the side of the crater, and tossed it in. A dump truck immediately started up, crept to the edge, and tons of construction debris poured over Konstantin's "grave." After that a bulldozer drove up and proceeded to push a mountain of earth back into the hole. By the next morning there would be no crater left. Caesar gave the man an informal salute.

Good-bye, Konstantin, we'll never forget you.

As Caesar and his men drove off he called a private number and reported the success of his mission.

Thousands of miles away, Nicolas Creel scratched another item off his to-do list. Dick Pender was a smart man who knew just how to play the world for a sucker with his head games. But sometimes one "real" dead body could break a million souls. And no one played *that* game better than Nicolas Creel. And if you could accomplish all that with one dead body, think what you could do with *lots* of them.

21

Katie James extended her stay, unwilling to return to New York and the next big death. She'd taken a First ScotRail train over from Glasgow to Edinburgh, soaking in the alternately stark and then lush Scottish countryside during the fifty-minute ride, near where the Firth of Forth dug a notch out of the country right above the capital city.

She checked into the Balmoral and had a quick bite of lunch in the restaurant before setting off. She bumped into a tall, broad-shouldered man on the way out. He politely apologized for the collision and strode quickly away. Katie rubbed her bruised shoulder and stared after him. It'd been like hitting a damn wall. He was probably a rugby player.

She passed the doorman in his full kilt outfit, right down to the ceremonial dagger in the sock. After a pleasant day touring the city and taking tea near Holyroodhouse Palace, she dodged myriad pubs trying to draw her in like a nail to a magnet and made the pilgrimage up the hill to the crown jewel of the city, Edinburgh Castle.

The dark crag of Castle Rock lurching skyward above the setting-sun end of town was the sole reason Edinburgh existed. The rock-strewn volcano remains sat like an anchor between central Scotland and England, the land many Scots still referred to as the "Auld Enemy." Katie passed the Entrance Gateway, flanked by statues of Robert the Bruce and William Wallace, who'd each built their legends on kicking English ass. She'd missed the firing of the one o'clock gun, a World War II twenty-five-pounder, but she did see the Stone of Destiny. It had been taken by the English in the thirteenth century, who'd kept it until the twentieth. In the intervening seven hundred-odd years it had rested under the Coronation Chair at Westminster Abbey, on which every monarch from Edward II to Elizabeth II had perched their royal bums.

A bit later she walked to the peak of Castle Rock where sat St. Margaret's Chapel, the oldest surviving building in Edinburgh. It was here, inside the chapel, that she saw him again, the big man who'd bumped into her at the hotel. He was kneeling in front of the third pew. As she drew closer, Katie spied another man next to him. He looked like a typical tourist. She would've turned and walked out except for what she suddenly glimpsed. She quickly knelt down in the rear pew, slid out her camera, and used the zoom to confirm her initial observation.

The tattoo on the man's right forearm. She'd seen one just like it years ago while covering yet another war overseas. Her senses heightened now, she could tell they weren't praying or reciting well-worn catechisms. They were whispering to one another.

She could not hear them clearly enough to make out the words, so she left the chapel but remained within a few feet of its front door. Ten minutes later the tattooed man came out. She was debating whether to follow him when he was suddenly lost in a gaggle of passing tourists.

The tall man stepped out a minute later and Katie focused on him instead. If he was staying at the Balmoral, she thought, he might be heading there now. She had no reason really to follow him, or to become involved in any of this. Yet she was a reporter, a reporter at rock bottom desperately looking for any way to crawl her way off the obituary page. She had no idea if this would lead to anything, but it might. And it wasn't like she had anything else to do.

He didn't return to the Balmoral. Instead, he headed north of the city center, two miles to be exact, to Leith, where he plopped his money down to tour the royal yacht *Britannia*, out of commission and anchored there.

Katie slipped off her shoes and rubbed her sore feet. Her quarry had been inconsiderately a very fast walker. She paid her pounds and crossed the gangplank. She tried her best to blend into the crowd, because if the man she was following recognized her from the hotel? The chapel? He looked powerful enough to strangle a bull.

Katie half listened to the guide as he recited yacht facts to the crowd. She did focus when the man pointed out the mahogany windbreak on the balcony deck in front of the bridge. It had been built to prevent sneaky breezes from suddenly lifting royal skirts and revealing royal panties. Katie kept a firm grip on her own skirt even as she watched the tall man wander away. She followed. He looked out over the water. Another person joined him at the rail. Katie moved as close as she dared. She managed to hear three words that summed it all up for her. *Tonight*, and *Gilmerton's Cove*.

She immediately left the yacht and grabbed a cab back to the hotel. She didn't have much time to get ready. And she had a little research to do first. She didn't know what she'd stumbled onto. Yet experience had taught her that some of the biggest stories started from the most unexpected encounters.

22

This crew made the Iranian and his bloodthirsty boys look like a bunch of four-year-old thumb suckers, thought Shaw. He was sitting in a car, a block of granite from Tajikistan on one side of him with a small mountain from that same Asian country on the other. It was a wonder even the large Mercedes's front wheels weren't off the road with the half ton of flesh perched in back. But then again it might have been due to the pair in the front seat, both also Tajiks, who pulled at least seven hundred pounds between them, and very little of it from fat that Shaw could see. Add one more guy and they could have made a decent line for any NFL team.

Shaw had never met a Tajik who didn't seem angry. Perhaps living in a brutishly mountain-bound country that had been used by the Soviets as a toxic waste dump and had an eighty percent poverty rate gave them good reason to be perpetually ticked off.

He said something in Russian and received what could only be described as a growl in response. Tajiks didn't see themselves as Russian; culturally they along with the Persians were part of the Iranian ethnic pool. Shaw had never bothered to learn Tajik. He hoped he didn't live to regret that decision.

He settled back in his seat. The Tajiks were selling drugs, heroin specifically, made from opium produced in neighboring Afghanistan, the country's most lucrative export crop. This was possible because coalition forces had largely abandoned Afghanistan to go make Iraq a beacon of democracy. Drug-dealing empires of the world thanked them every night for their thoughtfulness, because without opium one could not make heroin, one of the most popular street drugs of all time. The sheer misery this one bastardized chemical time bomb had imposed on the world was beyond calculation.

Shaw was here to purchase one metric ton of the misery, one thousand kilos with a street value U.S. of fifteen million dollars or $120,000 a gram. The drugs would be shipped out from Scotland to New York concealed inside thousands of soccer balls. Imports from Scotland, the Tajiks had discovered, received far less scrutiny from undermanned U.S. customs inspectors than, say, a large package from Iran or North Korea with "Death to America" written large on the outside.

Of course, if things went according to plan, the cargo Shaw would be purchasing tonight would be confiscated at New York Harbor. The seizure would be touted in the press as a huge blow to international drug traffickers and a testament to the efficiency of global law enforcement efforts. That's if Shaw succeeded in his mission and managed to walk away with all his organs intact. Although he seriously doubted that Frank would see his survival as a necessary gauge of triumph.

Yet making U.S. customs agents look good was not why Shaw was here. It was to prevent the *proceeds* of the drug deal from flowing to an international crime syndicate that had been partially taken over by Islamic fundamentalists who were all over Tajikistan. Their share of this take tonight could buy a few dirty bombs or ten thousand IEDs, neither of which was a good thing for the civilized world.

They weren't that far from Edinburgh but the land had quickly turned open and isolated. Far to the north was the Firth of Forth. As one of the Tajiks rolled down his window to blow out smoke from his cigarette, Shaw thought he could smell the heavy sea air. Thirty minutes later they turned onto a gravel road and were quickly swallowed by dense trees on either side.

The driver of the truck waiting at the end of the road nodded at his colleague in the sedan as it slowed to a stop next to the truck.

Shaw and the four men climbed out of the car.

"Soccer balls?" Shaw asked, pointing to the cargo in the truck.

The man to his left grunted, which Shaw took as a "yes" in Tajik.

The only reason Shaw was still alive was because these men thought he would be a good future customer on the other side of the pond. South American cartels ruled the U.S. illegal drug market, the world's biggest, but the Tajiks had long had their eye on it. If they had to fly to Colombia and rip the throats out of a few thousand Spanish speakers they would be more than willing.

Shaw slit open one of the soccer balls using a knife handed to him by one of the Tajiks. Inside were plastic baggies filled with a white powder. He didn't slice open a baggie and taste the stuff like they did on TV since he didn't want the crap in his system. The only thing worse than heroin on that score was meth. It seemed if you even sniffed the stuff from a hundred yards you were a candidate for detox.

"And what, I only have your word that it's heroin and all the other balls are filled with it right up to a thousand kilos?"

The four men stared back at him; none seemed inclined to answer. The passenger side of the truck opened and a small, slender man sprang down, landing lightly on the soft ground. He had thinning blond hair, wore an expensive suit and a perpetual smile showing a new set of implants.

"We've been doing this a long time," he said, any

119

accent he might have had barely discernible. He extended his hand to Shaw.

"All new clients have the same question. But they are never disappointed." He pointed to the split soccer ball. "That is the best heroin in the world. Guaranteed seventy percent pure even with all the shit you'll put in it before it hits the streets in the U.S. Most heroin, you need ten kilos to get a little over two salable kilos. That's a forty percent purity rate. That's for shit. That costs you money, my friend. With our product you'll make double that."

Shaw imagined himself standing in a product demo line listening to the pitch.

The man continued, "And I threw in ten kilos at no extra charge. That's a million-two U.S. on the street. It's for new customers only, to show our good faith. One time only," he added firmly, but still smiling. "We sell it to you for five million euros and you get twelve to fifteen U.S. for it in New York, L.A., and Miami. Not a bad markup. And we can do this every other week. Easy money."

"It's a big risk pushing drugs in America," Shaw pointed out.

The man chuckled. "That's not what I heard. Candy from babies because all Americans are addicted. Fat, greedy, and sex maniacs. And now that you've seen our product, I'd like to see your money."

"How do I get the balls to the port?" Shaw asked, buying time. *If Frank screwed me? The Tajiks will feed me to the squirrels one finger, toe, and critical organ at a time.*

"We put it right on the ship for you. Nobody the wiser. Now, your money?" The man looked in the Mercedes. "I see no briefcase. Five million euros take up a lot of space even in large notes." He looked at Shaw inquiringly. "We don't accept checks or credit cards," he added with a flicker of a smile, and then his mouth tightened. "Where the hell is the cash?"

"My people are bringing it," Shaw said casually.

"Your people? What people?" The small man looked around at the emptiness that surrounded them.

"You have your people, I have my people."

"We were not told about this."

"Come on. You think I'm getting into a car alone with four T-Rexes I don't know from Adam with millions of euros burning a hole in my pocket? If I were that stupid, I wouldn't have lasted one week in this business."

The little man motioned to his men and four MP5 submachine guns emerged from the trunk of the Mercedes. A metallic sound Shaw heard from the truck indicated that the driver was also armed.

Where the hell are you, Frank?

23

Katie James adjusted her small binoculars at the same time she placed a hand on her chest to try and stop her heart from beating quite so violently. She'd followed the Mercedes from the Balmoral. Having heard the destination earlier on the *Britannia*, she'd even been able to pass the car a couple of times to avoid suspicion before falling back. When they'd turned onto the gravel road she'd driven on, then doubled back, counting on the fact that they would not have gone far. She'd parked her car behind a bend in the road, set out on foot, topped a knoll, slunk through some trees, and settled herself down behind a berm to watch.

She was close enough to catch snatches of what the men were saying. The tall man from the Balmoral was a drug buyer, that much was clear. This surprised her because of the man she had seen with him at the chapel. The fellow had sported a tattoo Katie had only known Delta Special Forces to have carved on their skin. Yet even such men can go bad, she thought. The other men were selling. The drugs were in the soccer balls and they had been discussing money when the machine guns came out.

Katie had contemplated using her cell phone to call the police, but now she'd decided to change her tactics. With the sudden appearance of the guns she was instead going to run. She'd started to back away when a sound froze her.

To her extreme far right it was like a wave of black moving through the forest. She dropped to the dirt and tried to burrow in. When the guns started firing she tried to dig in even deeper. Yet something, perhaps her journalistic instincts, made her look through her binoculars in time to see two of the dealers riddled with machine-gun fire, their bodies literally opening up with holes awash in blood. They dropped to the ground dead without having uttered a sound.

As she continued to watch, the tall man managed to wrestle the submachine gun from one of the giants and then, with a nimbleness that belied his size, he landed a kick to the gut and then the head of the larger man, felling him. He turned and held the gun up, as though in surrender, but as machine-gun fire hit all around him he seemed to think better of this.

The other drug dealers had taken up cover behind the truck. They were shooting at whatever was coming their way, while the wave that had passed Katie was laying down walls of intense fire. And the tall man was caught right in the middle.

"He's dead," Katie whispered fearfully to herself.

Shaw dodged behind the Mercedes as another blast of fire missed him by centimeters. The Tajiks were shooting at him from his rear flank and his own men were doing the same from the front. What, had Frank failed to mention to the strike team that they were supposed to leave at least one man standing? *Him.*

He got off a burst of submachine fire at the Tajiks and then slid into the front seat of the Benz. He cranked the engine and slammed it in gear. Another bullet blast from the rear took out his back window.

He crushed the accelerator and the S600 leaped forward, gravel firing off the tires and spraying the truck. Holding the MP5 out the window, he emptied his clip at the truck, catching one of the Tajiks flush in the face and ending his career in international drug dealing.

Shots pinged all over the car like hail, and water and oil started spraying from under the hood. He slid the car into reverse, burned down the gravel strip backwards, and spun the wheel, whipping the Benz into a J-turn. He came out of the one-eighty, slammed down the gas, and hurtled forward, hitting a hundred on the straightaway and getting almost clear of the trees when the engine started vomiting black smoke and the car died. His gaze swept over the car's interior, before coming to rest on the SIG nine-millimeter partially stuck under the passenger floor mat. He grabbed it, kicked the door open, and ran.

And he wasn't the only one.

He changed course, rounding the bend, his long legs eating up chunks of ground, and caught up to her right as she was climbing in the car, a black Mini Cooper.

"Let me go!" Katie screamed as he grabbed her arm.

"Give me the keys!" he yelled back.

He ripped them from her fingers and opened the car door, sliding his big body into the small space.

"Get in!" he cried out, because she was just standing there.

"No!"

"If they find you here, they'll kill you."

"You mean *you'll* kill me." She eyed his gun.

"If I were going to do that, you'd already be dead. I wouldn't be offering you a ride."

"A ride to a *hostage*, you mean."

"These guys don't give a shit about hostages. Now get in."

In the near distance they could both hear something coming their way.

"Your last chance!" he said in a voice that clearly meant it.

The truck exploded out from the treeline fifty feet from their location. It was the cargo truck and it was being driven by one of the big Tajiks. The small man with the wicked grin who didn't accept credit cards or checks was sitting next to him. His gaze suddenly found them and his smile widened as he rolled down the window and took careful aim.

"Look out!" Shaw exclaimed.

His eyes had seen what Katie's hadn't. He grabbed her arm, yanked her through the open window and into the car, and hit the gas all in seemingly the same motion. Seconds later the ground that Katie had been standing on was obliterated by an RPG.

Shaw pushed Katie to the floorboard and gunned the engine. He shifted gears and wound the engine way past the manufacturer's maximum RPM range. And it still might not be enough.

Machine-gun fire came at their rear like a swarm of bees with fifty-caliber stingers. He pushed Katie down to the floor again as she tried to sit up. "Keep down!"

Shaw checked the mirror. He thought about veering off the road and taking his chances racing through the green fields. The only problem was the shoulders of the road were simply deep ruts the Cooper would never make it over. And even if it did, the land was so rough here that only a four-wheel drive could manage it.

The Cooper *was* far more agile than the truck, but on straightaways Shaw couldn't get out of the range of another RPG strike. Any second now he expected

one right up his ass. He thought he could see the big
teeth of the little Tajik as he smiled, no doubt thinking
he was in the driver's seat. And he was, actually, but
that was about to change.

"Hold on!" Shaw yelled to Katie. He whipped the
wheel around, did another one-eighty, and mashed
the gas to the floor. Now they were rocketing right at
the truck.

Katie sat up in time to see this. "What the hell are
you doing?" she screamed.

The game of chicken was five seconds from its
conclusion as the big truck and little car bore down
on each other. Katie closed her eyes and gripped the
dash.

As the headlights drew closer, the Tajiks glanced at
each other, apparently unable to believe what was
happening. If they collided with the car it might
disable the truck. And with the men in the woods
coming for them they needed their wheels.

And that was exactly why Shaw had pointed his
ride at them.

The big Tajik cut the wheel to the left. It would
be his last evasive driving maneuver.

Shaw's pistol fired and three bullet holes appeared
in the windshield on the driver's side of the truck.
The little man's smile disappeared along with his
wheelman's life. Shaw cut the car hard to the right
and whipped around the truck, the Cooper's wheels
digging an inch-wide gouge in the top layer of the

dirt shoulder before regaining firm traction and racing on.

The driverless truck kept going for another five hundred feet, slipped off the road, hit the rough shoulder, kicked up a wedge of dirt and grass, and slid over on its side.

Only then did Katie James open her eyes.

24

When they were ten miles away from where their deaths should have occurred, Shaw slowed the Mini, rolled his window down, and took a long breath. Even for him that had been close.

For the first time Katie noticed the red patch near his shoulder. "You've been shot!"

He glanced at the wound with little interest, his mind racing through what had just happened. "Just a nick, bullet didn't go in."

"Look if you let me go I promise I won't say anything."

"You watch too many movies."

"You mean you're really just going to let me go?"

"Well, I sure as hell don't want to hang around with you."

"Who were the men all dressed in black doing the shooting?"

"I gave you a lift, I'm not delivering testimony."

She looked at him curiously. "You're not a drug dealer, are you?"

"Met many, have you?"

"Yes, as a matter of fact, I have."

"What were you doing back there anyway?" His features turned grim as he suddenly recognized her. "I bumped into you at the Balmoral. And you were at the yacht. You've been following me!" He grabbed her by the shoulder. "Why? Who put you up to it?"

She gripped his hand. "You're hurting me. Please."

With one final squeeze he finally let go. "What were you doing back there?"

"It was an accident."

"Lying makes me very unhappy."

"Okay, okay, you were acting suspiciously and I followed you."

"Why? Are you a cop?"

"No. I'm a . . . I'm a reporter."

"A reporter? Investigating drug dealers in Scotland?"

"No, I . . ."

"Tell me the truth or I might change my mind about letting you go."

"I was in Scotland doing a special obit piece on the death of Andrew MacDougal," she said in a rush.

"Which paper?"

"The *New York Tribune*."

He paused and then said, "You're Katie James?"

"How did you know that?"

"I read the obit piece on MacDougal. It had your byline on it. But MacDougal died in Glasgow. What are you doing in Edinburgh?"

"On vacation. Reporters do get those from time to time."

"Snooping around in stuff that doesn't concern you part of your vacation plans?"

"I wish it wasn't."

"Guess you screwed up somehow to get stuck on the obit page before you turned seventy."

"Go to hell."

"I've actually been to hell. It's just as bad as people think it is."

He said this so matter-of-factly that even the seasoned journalist could only stare at him before stammering, "What do you mean by that?"

"If you have to ask, then you wouldn't understand the answer."

Actually, Katie thought she knew exactly what he meant, yet she chose to say nothing. They drove on in silence. Thirty minutes later the Cooper pulled up next to the Balmoral.

Shaw turned to Katie. "Okay, now get out of town as fast as you can."

"How about you? They were *shooting* at you."

"I can take care of myself."

She reached over and grabbed his hand as he started to climb out. "What's your name?"

"I've followed your work over the years, so I know you're not that dumb."

"Can you at least tell me what happened back there?"

He hesitated.

"I'm not going to write the story, if that's what you think. I don't know enough to write it anyway."

"If you do write the story, you'll ruin a lot of hard work and help the bad guys."

"I've never been into helping the bad guys."

He paused, studying her closely. "It was a drug transaction. We're trying to keep cash out of the hands of terrorists. There, now you know all."

"Good guys don't open fire like that."

"I know," Shaw admitted. "I don't know why they started shooting."

His candor seemed to melt away most of Katie's doubts. She added in a cautious tone, "But then why were your own people shooting at you?"

"That's exactly what I'm going to find out." He leveled his gaze directly at her. "And get out of Edinburgh. You survived tonight. It'd be a shame to waste it."

In a few seconds he'd disappeared.

Katie sat back into the leather of the Mini. She'd seen much death in her career, heartbreaking stuff that you never really got over. But there had been something about tonight . . . And she had never met anyone quite like this guy.

Had everything he'd told her been a complete lie? As a veteran journalist she often found that to be the case. But he *had* let her go. And he had saved her life. She realized a little guiltily that she hadn't even thanked him for that. If not for him she would've been bits of flesh scattered across Scotland.

Katie snagged her bag from the backseat and drew out a notepad and a pen. Before she'd switched to journalism, she'd been an art major. She flipped open the pad and quickly sketched a drawing of Shaw. She also jotted down notes.

She talked to herself as she wrote. "Dark hair, about six foot five, two-forty. Shoulders the size of Nebraska. Amazing blue eyes." She put down her pen. *Amazing blue eyes? Where did that come from?*

It didn't matter. The odds of her ever seeing him again . . .

She climbed over into the driver's side, drove down an alley, left the car, and ducked back in the Balmoral through the delivery entrance.

25

Shaw didn't bother to get his clothes from the hotel. He'd placed any personal items he had with him in a storage locker at the train station. He called Frank as soon as he was safely away from the hotel. The man waited until the fourth ring to answer.

"What the hell game are you playing?" Shaw barked into the phone.

"You should be celebrating another successful mission. We got the drugs, the bad guys didn't get any cash, and we got one guy left standing who's talking like a mynah bird as we speak. I've personally already popped the champagne."

"Your guys opened fire unprovoked."

"Wow! Really?"

"Yeah, really. What happened to you have the right to remain silent *and* keep the blood in your veins?"

"So we took out some of the Tajiks, so what? You know how much those suckers can eat? And my budget is strained as it is."

"And your guys were shooting at me."

"Then maybe you should pay attention."

"Pay attention to what?"

"We don't like retirees, Shaw. You go when we say you can, if ever."

"My deal—"

"Your deal is shit. Your deal has always been shit, but you never wanted to face up to it. Well, tonight was your wake-up call, my friend. Your only one. Next time maybe they don't miss. And consider yourself lucky. Oh, by the way, your orders for Heidelberg are waiting at the airport. Chartered jet, wheels up in two hours. Man will meet you at the front entrance of the airport. Meanwhile, enjoy the rest of your evening in lovely Scotland."

Frank clicked off and Shaw simply stood there on Princes Street in the middle of the ancient city of Edinburgh with thousands of people all around him.

He had never felt more alone.

Katie took an empty notebook from her bag, inserted something in it, and walked into the lobby of the Balmoral. The receptionist on duty was a tall, thin young man. Katie strode up to him and held up the notebook.

"A man dropped this in the lobby. There's no name in it, but he may be staying at the hotel. He got in a cab before I could stop him." She described Shaw in detail.

"Yes, he is staying here, miss," said the young Scotsman. "A Mr. Shaw. I'll put it in his box here."

She watched as he placed the notebook in the slot for room 505. When he turned back around she'd skittered away.

God bless the Scots, she thought. If she'd tried that stunt in New York they would've thrown the book in her face, wrestled her to the floor, and then called the cops.

She waited for two hours in the lobby, her gaze flitting to the front desk from time to time as she sipped a Coke and chewed her nails till they bled. She stirred when the young Scot turned his position over to a middle-aged woman whom Katie had never seen before. As soon as the man was out of sight Katie approached the front desk.

"I'm staying in room 505 with my fiancé," she began. "I gave him my key when he misplaced his, but he was supposed to put it in a notebook he left for me so I could get back in the room."

The woman glanced at the wall of slots behind her. She reached into 505's box and pulled out the notebook.

"This notebook?" she said.

Katie nodded and took it from her. She looked through the notebook and was careful to let the object she'd placed in there earlier fall out on the front desk. The woman picked it up for her. It was Katie's American driver's license. The woman looked at the photo and then at Katie, who said, "I've been looking all over for that. He must have found it in the room and put it in the notebook for me."

"And where is your fiancé?" the woman asked pleasantly enough, but with the tone of someone who had a job to do and intended to do it.

"Glasgow." She flipped through the pages. "He'll be back tomorrow, but he didn't leave the key. How can I get in the room?"

"Have you tried calling him?"

"Yes, he doesn't answer. Service can be a bit spotty."

"Don't I know it," the woman agreed heartily.

She glanced at the driver's license again.

"Well, we can't have our guests sleeping on the sidewalk, now can we?" She pulled a spare key from the slot and passed it and the license to Katie.

Katie glanced at the woman's nametag. "Sara, I can't thank you enough. I still can't believe he forgot to leave the damn key."

"I've been married to my Dennis for twenty-six years and the poor bloke can't remember birthdays, anniversaries, or, on occasion, all the names of our five children. So if it's just keys your man forgets to leave I'd go ahead with the marriage and count your blessings, ma'am."

Katie headed to the elevator.

A minute later she was opening the door to 505. She had watched Shaw walk away from the Balmoral so she was reasonably sure he wasn't in the building. But she still told herself she had just ten minutes to search the place.

Nine minutes later she'd gone over every square inch of the room and the few belongings he'd left behind and come up with a total zero. Well, not exactly. In the pocket of a jacket she'd found a sales receipt for a book purchase in Dublin. But that wasn't terribly helpful.

She walked along the perimeter of the room and stopped by the desk, her gaze running over the items there, all hotel-issued. That's when she saw it. She sat and pulled the blotter toward her, took a pencil off the holder, and carefully brushed the pencil point across it. A name slowly emerged from the white paper where Shaw had carved it with such pressure that it had been imprinted on the page underneath the one he'd written on, an amateurish mistake. Katie had no way of knowing he'd committed this blunder while distressed about Anna.

"Anna Fischer," Katie said. The name was not uncommon, but for some reason Katie thought she recognized it.

And then something clicked in her memory. She looked at the sales receipt she'd found in his jacket pocket.

"*A Historical Examination of Police States*," she read. Again, something was percolating in her mind.

She left the room and called the phone number of

the bookshop on the receipt. She didn't expect anyone to answer at this hour, but a woman's voice came
on. Katie asked if they carried that book. They did,
she was told, but they only had one copy left. "And
the author's name?" she said. "I can't remember."

"Anna Fischer," answered the woman.

26

Anna Fischer walked slowly along the streets of Westminster in London. Many tourists tended to congregate in this area of the city, craning to catch a glimpse of the Queen or other royal at Buckingham Palace or visiting the graves of long-dead monarchs at the famous abbey. The West End theater district was also here, as well as Lord Nelson looking pensive in Trafalgar Square on the giant granite shaft even as the birds crapped all over him.

She entered St. James's Park, passing foreign nannies and British moms pushing prams and enjoying an evening jaunt under clear skies. Weather such as this was not particularly plentiful on the little isle in the middle of big water, so Londoners leapt to take advantage of the sun when they had the chance.

Anna kept trudging along, passing the King Charles Steps, and then stopped and stared over at Duck Island in the middle of St. James's Park Lake. Here she chose to sit down, her skirt gathered around her long legs.

Had she been too hard on Shaw? Part of her said yes but the other part held forth with a resounding

No! Marriage, at least for Anna, was a commitment for life. Yes, she should have pressed this point before, but now that Shaw had officially proposed, the matter had taken on a greater urgency. He had to see that, and if he didn't, well, perhaps it would be best if they didn't stay together.

She'd had other suitors over the years, educated, articulate men who held important positions in the world or had obtained considerable wealth. None of them, she had to admit, not a single one, had stirred in her the tender, far-reaching emotions that Shaw did. Yet would he even go to Wisbach to see her parents?

She rose and sat on a park bench. Next to her was a discarded newspaper. She picked it up. The *Guardian* was having a good run with the evil Russia story. The headline indeed said it all: "Return of the Red Menace?"

And something called the "Tablet of Tragedies" had just been received by select major news outlets and world leaders. The rudimentary packaging and grainy photos of allegedly murdered Russians, their tragic stories written in simple language, carried a potency a million-copy glossy release could never have inspired. Anna's brow wrinkled as she skipped across the story's contents. It regurgitated much that was already known and then built on that. It was like the game of whispering a story in one ear in a group of people and seeing how much the tale had changed when it came out of the last person's mouth. And yet the murder of Sergei Petrov, the Russian word for traitor inked on his forehead, had been pretty much conclusive proof of Gorshkov's guilt, at least in the minds of the Western press.

The Russian president had put his military force on full alert as mass demonstrations were breaking out across the country. It seemed like the place was imploding. Anna had even heard scuttlebutt from her old colleagues at the UN that if the Red Menace was not explained soon in a way favorable to Gorshkov, Russia's seat on the Security Council might be in jeopardy. Whatever had happened to Konstantin and his family, the man was certainly getting his revenge now.

Yet had anyone bothered to verify any of it? Unlike some other people who might have these same questions, Anna had the means to try and get answers. Perhaps to take her mind off her personal troubles, she decided to do something about it right now.

She walked to her office, a 175-year-old row house nestled in a quiet dead-end street near Buckingham Gate. The buildings on either side of hers were empty, but scheduled to be renovated in about six months. She would cherish her peace and solitude for now until it was destroyed by jackhammers and the sounds of sawing. The smell of fresh paint was in the air. Her building had just gotten a face-lift, including a fresh coat on all the windows and doors.

She unlocked the thick front door on which a gold-plated plaque announced the firm's name: The Phoenix Group Limited. When she'd first started working here, Anna had been told that the firm was bankrolled by a very reclusive and wealthy gentleman who'd been born in the United States, Arizona specifically. So private was he that no one who worked at The Phoenix Group even knew their benefactor's name. Nor did he ever visit them. Yet they did receive communiqués from him from time to time and encouraging words about their important work. And representatives of the man had visited from America to meet with them and answer questions. The owner had been described to her as an intellectual interested in the vast questions that continued to befuddle mankind. And he paid people like Anna to figure them out. Whoever he was, he gave Anna and the others free rein to follow their passions. There were few jobs anymore that had such latitude. It was the most stimulating work Anna had ever done. Now if she could only get her personal life in such shape.

She locked the door behind her and headed up the stairs. Her cluttered office was at the end of the hall on the top floor. She passed other rooms, all empty save one near hers where a coworker, Avery Chisholm, a crusty old academic, toiled away on a project, his circle of white hair barely topping the piles of books in front of him. He lifted a hand in response to her greeting and she hurried on.

Anna settled behind her large desk crammed with books and stacks of papers. Her job was to try and make sense of the world, one complex factor at a time. She and her colleagues wrote paper after paper, published book after book, gave talk after talk in which they laid out precise, detailed analyses that should have proved a treasure trove for government and business leadership from the United States to Japan. Yet she was painfully aware that hardly anyone in power bothered to read them.

She went online and entered some chat rooms. Whenever she raised any questions about the culpability of the Russians, or the "real" origins of the Red Menace, she was attacked by all sides with people questioning her religious faith and her patriotism, though they didn't know if she even had a religion or what country she was from. She was also labeled a Gorshkov ass-kisser, a traitor to humanity, and a royal bitch.

She retreated from that world and expanded her search until she focused on one obscure blogger in a far-off galaxy of the cyberworld. He was raising some of the same questions and doubts that Anna had. She sent him a detailed e-mail and hoped she would get an answer back soon.

She would, but not in any way she could have possibly imagined.

27

Anna Fischer was a remarkably intelligent woman with multiple degrees from world-class universities. Yet she had just committed a critical mistake. In her defense, the woman would have had no way of knowing it was a mistake. Which are often precisely the sort of errors that come back to haunt you.

The blogger she had e-mailed with her own misgivings was not who he seemed to be. It wasn't even a person. It was essentially digital smoke and mirrors.

Dick Pender and his people had been monitoring the goings-on within several thousand chat rooms spread across the world. The rapid-fire repartee bounding kilobyte by kilobyte across his massive computer screens rivaled anything the agony columns of late-nineteenth-century British newspapers had ever inspired. The Red Menace was of course the topic on everyone's mind, and Pender smiled as he totted up those convinced the Russians were behind it as opposed to those who weren't sure. The tally ran nearly ninety-eight percent in his favor.

He noted with glee that as soon as anyone said

something against the "truth" he had established they were electronically "piled on" by armies of chatters. Across thousands of discussion sites, Pender posted prewritten responses spouting fact after fact, which actually had no basis in fact, and grinned as he was hailed as a hero and a speaker of supreme wisdom by the chat hordes.

God, Pender thought, it was so easy to support a popular—if completely wrong—position. It required not a scintilla of courage.

A minute later his smile grew even wider. He had just checked what he termed his online bear traps. One of them was the blogger Anna had sent her query to. Pender's people had set it up, along with several others, to gauge the interest of anyone who might believe the whole Red Menace campaign was a sham. It was critical to know if there was a reverse wave of doubt about the horrors perpetrated by the Russians.

If Pender detected any such movements he had numerous strategies he could employ to dispel this belief. One of his favorites was crafting an outrageous event that drew everyone's attention from a problem area. He'd been retained on short notice to do this for administrations in Washington, London, Paris, Beijing, and Tokyo over the years. Such things were usually needed around elections, scandals, wars, and budget fights.

Not many people had sent e-mails to the planted

Web sites. The vast majority of the world seemingly had accepted on faith that everything being said about the Russians was true. Most people were perfectly fine with being sheep their whole lives, and this suited Pender's business well. There were, of course, some who wanted to know everything about the R.I.C. and were digging deeply to get there. Thus, Pender was feeding them bits and pieces to appease their hunger. It wasn't that hard to stay ahead of them, actually. The media had many stories and fronts to cover, whereas Pender had only one agenda to worry about: Nicolas Creel's. This technique he referred to as "timing the tap," turning on and off the info tap at the most optimal times. He had the media right where he wanted them—in a purely reactive state.

The limited number of people who had made inquiries on the planted sites had already been checked out by Pender's folks and deemed to be unimportant. Unlike the basic chat rooms, one had to really search to find these online bear traps. That hinted of a more determined effort than most casual chatters would ever muster. Pender had no idea who Anna Fischer was, but the name on her Web address intrigued him.

"The Phoenix Group," he said to himself as he sat at his desk in the war room. He'd already electronically run to ground the geographic origin of the message. The Phoenix Group was located in London. He had a file on his desk that he'd quickly assembled.

The Phoenix Group was a think tank located in Westminster near Buckingham Palace; its precise ownership was unknown.

Pender had a lot of things on his mind. The *Wall Street Journal* was running an article soon that would cast a bit of doubt on the tens of thousands of Russian dead. Pender knew the journalist who'd done the piece. He was a good reporter but a bit lazy and had a reputation for not following up on a story if things got tough or his angle became publicly unpopular. Pender instructed his staff to issue four stories on the Web that would strongly imply that while some of the thousands of dead Russians' past might be incorrect, that was due to faulty government records and should in no way dilute the significance of such an indisputable holocaust against the Russian people. To do so was to besmirch the memories of murdered people. Pender would also arrange for several "experts" to go on national shows and remake this point in the strongest possible terms.

Pender was certain that the *Journal* reporter, not wanting to be branded a cynical, dictator-loving pig, would never go near the story again. He'd also gotten wind of the BBC doing a piece but the producer was unsure what angle to take. Pender had an anonymous note and three "published" articles penned by his ghostwriters sent to the harried producer, giving the woman an inspired take on how to do her show that dovetailed nicely with Pender's and

Creel's goals. He looked forward to watching the program.

Yet Pender instinctively knew that this "Phoenix Group" might be precisely what Creel had instructed him to keep a lookout for. Thus he electronically forwarded all this information to his client.

Then he went back to doing what he did best: selling the truth to a gullible world.

There was no more exhilarating game ever invented.

28

Nicolas Creel sat in the lavish home movie theater in his estate on the French Riviera, watching the end of *Saving Private Ryan*. He loved this film, not because of the first-rate acting and directing or the moral message inherent in this classic war story. No, he loved seeing the world at war because it made dying so noble.

Creel had made his fortune building and selling machines that could kill thousands, even millions of people, and yet he was a peaceful man. He'd never struck anyone in anger; never even fired a weapon of any kind. He detested violence. He made the most money while the world was at peace—a very specific type of peace. It was really only a *sense* of peace laced with fear that at any moment war could break out. For Creel a peace based on lurking terror was the best kind of all.

Creel loved *Saving Private Ryan* for another reason. World War II was the classic conflict of good versus evil, a noble war that had enabled a deserving generation of Americans to fulfill their destiny and become the "greatest" generation. Whether the world was aware of it or not, such a conflict was occurring now. And Creel was positioning unsuspecting global players to rise to the occasion, to crush the evil and make the world safer than it had been in decades. The short term would be a bit bumpy of course, but there were always casualities. In the long run it would all be worth it.

He rose, went to his bedroom, and gave Miss Hottie a peck on the cheek as she lay passed out on the bed after performing her usual service for him.

Even as he gazed down at her, he knew it was coming to an end. Hottie liked her newfound wealth, social status, and also her drink a little too much. She routinely screamed at the servants, put on airs she had no business going near, and managed to terrorize Creel's grown children from his previous marriages whenever they stopped by to visit. This wasn't necessarily a bad thing, because Creel wasn't overly enamored with any of his children. Still, the rages could be awkward.

Indeed, his dear wife could be the poster child for insecurity. She had barely a high school education tucked inside a supermodel shell. Yet when he'd seen her flounce down that runway in New York he knew he just had to have her, because everybody else so desperately wanted the lady. Creel always wanted to be first.

As was his custom at night, he went to his office to work. The space was probably not as large as one would expect a man of his net worth to have, but it was efficient. He sat down at his desk, flicked on his computer, and saw the e-mail and attached files from Pender.

He read through them thoroughly, coming away considerably interested.

The Phoenix Group? It didn't ring any bells.

He made a call with one request. "Find out *exactly* who's behind The Phoenix Group, a think tank based in London, and do it as fast as possible."

Every instinct Creel had was telling him this might turn out to be one more missing piece he needed to complete his grand puzzle. It would perhaps take a bit of luck, but even billionaire merchants of death were entitled to good fortune sometimes.

Several hours later his wish came true. His people were very good. They'd ripped through several façades set up to hide the true ownership of The Phoenix Group. And when people went to all that trouble to deceive, it was usually for a good reason. Now Creel could hardly believe his luck.

The Phoenix Group ownership had no ties to Arizona. The phoenix was mostly thought to be of Egyptian origin. But it also hailed from another part of the world. In that ancient land it symbolized power sent from the heavens. It also stood for loyalty and honesty. It could not have been more perfect.

Into the phone he said, "Keep The Phoenix Group building under twenty-four-hour surveillance. And I want complete files on everyone who works there. And the plans for every nook and cranny of that building. No detail is too small."

Creel then called Caesar. It was very nearly time for his boots on the ground to go to work.

29

Shaw was standing inside Heidelberg Castle in front of the largest wooden barrel in the world ever to hold wine. He'd flown into Frankfurt from Edinburgh the night before and driven to Heidelberg that morning. His assignment this time was relatively easy, passing some papers to another man to be carried up the line.

After the task was completed he was supposed to drive to see Anna's parents at their bookshop in the little town of Wisbach. Should he still go? Frank had made it clear that Shaw's enslavement was not going to end anytime soon. In fact, it might only terminate when his life did. So what was the reason to go to Wisbach? He could not marry Anna and continue to work for Frank. He never should have asked her to marry him. Now that he had, he should just get the hell out of her life so someone else could give her what he couldn't.

That would be the noble, unselfish thing to do, and yet Shaw felt neither noble nor unselfish. He did not want to lose Anna. He could not lose Anna. He would drive to Wisbach and perhaps on the way he would miraculously think of some way out of this nightmare.

The papers were passed a half hour later with nary a glitch to a young man who looked like an American college student right down to the Red Sox ball cap, grungy jeans, and Nike tennis shoes. Shaw continued his role as tourist by taking pictures of the castle and its grounds and learning about the history of one of Germany's most famous castles and its seven-meter-thick walls. When it was safe to leave, he nearly sprinted back down the hill to his rental car and drove off for Wisbach.

He passed through the edge of Karlsruhe on his way to Wisbach. As Anna had said, the bookshop was easy to locate, being on the main road of the quaint village.

Natascha Fischer met him at the door. There was much of her daughter's height and good looks in the mother. However, where Anna was talkative and outgoing, her mother was reserved and did not meet his eye as he introduced himself.

The bookshop was small but the shelves had good bones of aged pine and dark walnut. There was a rolling ladder perched against one wall of old volumes, and against another was a large desk littered with papers. Here sat a man even larger than Shaw. Wolfgang Fischer rose and extended his hand. Anna had told them he was coming. Natascha put a "Closed" sign on the door and locked it. She then followed her husband and Shaw through a door into the adjoining flat where the Fischers lived.

Like the bookshop it was neat and nicely decorated with many photos of Anna from infant to grown woman. While Natascha put on a pot of coffee, Wolfgang pulled out a small bottle of cognac from a cupboard.

"An event like this calls for something stronger than coffee, eh?" Wolfgang said in English, but with a heavy German accent that Shaw had a little difficulty following. Wolfgang poured out the drinks, sat down, and stared expectantly up at Shaw, who leaned nervously against a rough-hewn wooden mantel.

"Anna has told us much about you," Wolfgang began in a helpful tone.

Natascha came back in with the coffee and some cakes on a tray. She looked disapprovingly at the glass of cognac in her husband's hand.

"It is not yet four o'clock," she said in a scolding tone.

Her husband grinned. "Shaw here was just about to say something."

Natascha sat and poured out the coffee, but she shot anxious glances at their visitor.

Shaw felt the perspiration staining his armpits. He almost never broke a sweat from nerves, even when people were shooting at him. He felt like a schoolboy on his first date. His mouth was dry; his legs seemed unable to support his weight.

"I came here to ask you something," he finally said, sitting down opposite them.

I might as well just say it. He looked directly at Dad. "Would you have a problem with me marrying your daughter?"

Wolfgang glanced at his wife, his lips curling into a smile. Natascha dabbed her eyes with a tea napkin.

Wolfgang lurched up, pulled Shaw to his feet, and gave him a bear hug that made Shaw's ribs ache. Laughing, he boomed, "Does that answer your question?"

Natascha nimbly got to her feet, took Shaw's hand in a firm grip, gave him a kiss on the cheek, and said in a quiet voice, "You have made Anna so happy. Never has she talked of anyone as she does you. Never. Has she, Wolfie?"

He shook his head. "And she makes you happy, yes, I am sure?"

"Happier than I've ever been."

"When will the wedding be?" asked Natascha. "It will be here, of course, where her family is?"

Wolfgang looked at her crossly. "Well, what of Shaw's family? Maybe they do not like to come to a small village like this." He slapped Shaw on the arm, unfortunately on the spot where he'd been winged by the bullet in Scotland. It was all Shaw could do not to cry out in pain.

"Here will be fine," he said. "I, uh, I have no family." The Fischers looked at him curiously. "I was an orphan."

Natascha's bottom lip trembled. "Anna did not tell us this. I am sorry."

Wolfgang said, "But now you have family. Lots of family. In Wisbach alone there are ten Fischers. If you include Karlsruhe and Stuttgart, it is many more. In Germany, thousands, is that not right, Tasha?"

"But not all will be coming to the wedding," Natascha said hastily.

"Grandchildren," Wolfgang said, staring at Shaw, a broad smile on his face. "Finally, I will have grand-children. You and Anna will have a big family of course."

"Wolfgang," Natascha said sternly, "that is none of our business. And Anna is not that young anymore. She has a career, a very important career. And it is in the hands of God. We wanted many children but only had Anna."

"Well, not a huge family then," Wolfgang amended. "No more than four or five."

"We'll do the best we can," Shaw replied uneasily.

"Anna said you were a consultant," Wolfgang continued. "What is it that you consult in?"

Shaw wondered if the daughter had suggested this line of questioning to force him to tell her parents what he'd already confided in her.

"International relations," he answered.

"Is there much work in this international relations?" Wolfgang asked.

"More than you can possibly imagine." Then he added, "Well, actually it's a bit more than that." As they looked on expectantly, he leaned against the wall. The stout wood seemed to stiffen his resolve. "I work with an agency that helps make the world safer."

They exchanged glances. Wolfgang said, "You are like a policeman? A policeman of the world?"

"Something like that. But I'm planning on retiring when Anna and I get married."

Gratefully, they only asked a few more questions about his job, perhaps sensing it might entail classified information.

If they only knew.

Shaw stayed with the Fischers for over an hour. As soon as he'd passed out of sight a man walked up to their front door and knocked. When Natascha opened the door, the man said, "Mrs. Fischer, I need to talk to you about the man you just met with."

He swept past her without waiting for an invitation. As Wolfgang joined her the fellow said, "I think both of you should sit down."

30

Russia again did something utterly foreseeable, much to Nicolas Creel's delight. Isolated and pushed to the edge, it flexed its muscles by dropping from a Tu-160 aircraft the granddaddy of all non-nuclear bombs. Its thermobaric explosive yield was equal to 120,000 pounds of TNT, or over five times that of a similar bomb the United States had previously dropped, leaving a crater with a radius of fifteen hundred feet and painting the sky with a terrifying but fortunately nonradioactive mushroom cloud. The detonation was termed part of a routine readiness drill by President Gorshkov, who immediately thereafter put the Russian military on the highest alert. He also declared in the strongest possible terms that when Russia found out who was behind this smear campaign, it would be considered an act of war.

"I pity the country or organization behind it, whoever they are and however powerful they might be," Gorshkov added ominously, verbally lifting a middle finger to the United States, which had strenuously denied any connection to the anti-Russia campaign. However, in diplomatic circles this was considered almost an admission of guilt, for who else had enough money or motive to do such a thing other than the Americans? they reasoned.

Nicolas Creel laughed as he read this latest report. He was in the conference room of his Boeing jet thirty-nine thousand feet over the Atlantic. Caesar sat across from him. Creel spun the paper around so Caesar could see the headline about Russia dropping the bomb and Gorshkov's threats.

Creel scoffed. "An act of war? To fight a war you need an army, and the Russians don't have one. They're sitting on a mountain of oil revenue but by presidential decree, the idiocy of which strains credulity, they can't spend more than three and a half percent of their GNP on the military. That comes out to twenty-two billion U.S. a year, and only eight billion of that is earmarked for arms purchases. You can't build major weapons systems for that kind of chump change. Look at the Americans. Including supplemental budgets they spend over seven hundred billion a year on defense, over twenty percent of the federal budget. The Yanks outspend every other country in the world *combined* on weapons. And that's the way it should be. Superpower status doesn't come cheap, but it sure as hell is worth it. Because when you want to kick ass, you can kick ass, my friend."

Creel pointed to a statistical graph on the paper detailing Russian troop strength.

"The Russians may have five army divisions combat ready, *five*, if they're lucky. They used to build a third of the world's naval ships. Now they can't even construct an aircraft carrier because the idiots don't have a single shipyard dock in the country large enough to do the work. Some planning that was, comrade. And since their own government won't use their money to buy anything, the Russian arms manufacturers have to export their junk out to India and China and any other suckers looking to buy cheap and not sweat the specs too hard. The Yanks, Brits, Germans, and French wouldn't think of putting a single penny down for the Russians' crap. And the reformed communists haven't added any new aircraft to their frontline defenses in fifteen years. They've got over three thousand planes but they're nowhere near the standard of the West and half their military bases don't even have fuel for them. Their latest-generation combat fighter never even got funded. They've still got nukes, but they can't use them. If they fire one off, the Yanks will send ten back in retaliation.

"Their vaunted navy consists of twenty creaky ships, including one decades-old carrier, but not counting the subs that tend to find their way to the bottom of the ocean with regularity and stay there. The Americans have *three hundred* ships including ten nuke-powered *Nimitz*-class carriers. And that doesn't even take into account the dozen or so *Ohio*-class ballistic subs. Each one of those suckers can take out an entire country. I should know because one of my subsidiaries built them. Hell, the Yanks could wipe out the Red Menace in a week without breaking a sweat." Creel chuckled again. "But still I'm a happy man."

Caesar finished reading the article. "Why? The Russians obviously won't be buying what you're selling."

Creel took a moment to light up a cigar. "Last year, President Gorshkov, in a rare moment of sanity, implemented a new eight-year state armaments program worth nearly five trillion rubles, that's $186 billion U.S. That's over and above the current defense budget."

"Okay, I see your interest."

"That's what I thought when I had my people over there get the plan pushed through. But sorry, that doesn't get me excited. It was only a start."

"Excuse me saying so, but I just don't get you, Mr. Creel."

The billionaire smiled. "Join the rest of civilization. So let me explain. The bulk of those dollars are going to Russian outfits. But if the Russians would match the U.S. in defense spending as a ratio of GNP, that would mean an extra seventy billion per *year* on top of what they're spending now *plus* the new armaments program. There is no way the homegrown war machine over there can do that amount of work. And the buildup they need would take about ten years. That means they have to look to the West, to me actually, to get it done. In inflation-adjusted dollars that's nearly a trillion dollars U.S. Let's say Ares gets seventy percent of that work. That's seven hundred billion dollars U.S. Now, *that* gets my blood pressure going."

"But why would they do that – match the U.S.?"

"They would if they feel they have to."

"Konstantin? This publicity campaign you've put together? Think that'll force them to become like the old Soviet Union and fill your coffers?"

"Not that simple. The Red Menace campaign has isolated them from the rest of the world, sure. And right now you could claim that Gorshkov eats babies for breakfast and half the world would believe it. But for my plan to work I've got to raise the stakes. The Russians are not fools. If they're going to pay for the best, they need a damn good reason."

"So how do you raise the stakes?"

"That's where you come in. I need a dozen men all Russian, or at least Russian-looking."

"No problem. Unemployment's high over there, so I've got Russians coming out of my ass. They'll kill with guns, knives, or their bare hands, it doesn't matter to them."

"I didn't think it would. I also need some of them to be computer whizzes."

"Again, not a problem. Russia leads the planet in world-class hackers."

Creel leaned forward and drew out a file. "Good, now here's the boots on the ground."

31

Anna Fischer was just about to open the door of her flat in London when the man walked up behind her. Sensing someone's presence, and always on guard after her mugging in Berlin, she whirled around, her fingers clasping the pepper spray that was attached to her key ring.

The man already had his badge out.

"Ms. Fischer? I'm Frank Wells. I'd like to talk with you about Shaw."

She stared at his badge and then up at him.

"I do not recognize that agency," she said.

"Most people wouldn't. Can we go inside?"

"I don't have strange men to my flat. You *say* you know Shaw. You could be lying."

"Should've known. A lady with all your degrees isn't stupid."

"All my degrees? How do you know that?"

"I have a two-inch file on Anastasia Brigitte Sabena Fischer. Your parents, Wolfgang and Natascha, live in Wisbach, Germany, where they run a bookshop. You're an only child. A champion swimmer. Advanced degrees from, among others, Cambridge. A stint at the UN and now employed at The Phoenix Group here in London." He eyed the ring on her finger. "And currently engaged to Shaw." He looked away from her astonished face and glanced at the front door. "Now can we go up to your flat? It's important."

They sat in her small front room overlooking the street. Frank looked around her apartment.

"Nice place."

"Why have you come here?"

"Like I said, to talk to you about Shaw. Just like my men have done with your parents."

"My parents! No, you're wrong. They would've called . . ."

"We told them not to, so I'd have a chance to see you first." He eyed her keenly. "He proposed to you in Dublin, didn't he?"

"I can't see why that's any business of yours."

Frank ignored this. "And he told you he was retiring from his job."

Anna found herself nodding in spite of herself.

"Let me tell you the truth. Would you like that?"

Tears gathered in Anna's eyes. She whisked them away with her hand and composed herself.

"If you have something to tell me, say it. But I will determine for myself if it's true."

Frank chuckled, then nodded. "Fair enough." He leaned forward and cocked his head so she could see the sunken hole in his scalp. "See that little divot? That was courtesy of a round Shaw fired into my brain when I was trying to arrest him."

Anna eyed him coldly. "Arrest him? For what?"

"That's classified. But it wasn't for not paying a parking ticket, I *can* tell you that. After I recovered and we caught up to him again, he started working for us."

"*Working* for you? After he almost killed you? You said you wanted to arrest him. If he's a criminal and you say he shot you, why isn't he in jail?"

Frank held up a cigar. "Mind if I smoke?"

"Yes."

He put the cigar away. "My world doesn't strictly involve good and bad, right and wrong. Shaw would be in prison right now, but for one thing."

"What's that?" she said fiercely.

"Your *fiancé* possesses some pretty incredible skills. No one I've ever worked with in the field can touch him. He can walk into a room full of terrorists loaded for bear, con the turbans off them, take 'em down, and walk out alive. Pretty much one-of-a-kind stuff. And for that we make exceptions." He tapped the dent in his head. "Even if the exception almost killed me."

"So he works for you. He told me he worked for a law enforcement agency."

"He did, huh? And that he runs around the world

never knowing if he's going to come out alive?" He studied her closely.

Anna nervously twisted her fingers. "He said . . . he said he worked behind a desk now."

"A desk?" Frank grinned. "And he said he was retiring too." He leaned so close she could smell his tobacco breath. "Let me tell you something. People like Shaw don't retire. He goes until he either dies or we don't need him anymore. He tries to leave before that, his ass goes right to the scummiest prison I can find." He leaned back.

"Why did you come here to tell me this?"

"Because I thought you needed to know the whole truth."

"The man you have described to me is not the man I know. He saved my life in Germany. He is the most kind, most wonderful man I have ever met."

"He kills people, Ms. Fischer. They're bad people, for sure, but he still kills them. I do too. Or did. See, *I* actually have the desk job. Your fiancé is a brave man, I'll give him that. Nerves like I've never seen before. But I've also seen him gut a man, here to here." He drew his finger from his navel to his neck. "Guy deserved it, but Shaw doesn't bake cookies. When the man's on the hunt he's an alpha with a capital freaking A! You know what I mean?"

He stopped and studied her again, a smile edging across his face. "You know, I have to tell you, I'm impressed. I figured you'd have started crying five minutes ago."

"Have you ever loved anyone, Mr. Wells?" Anna said suddenly.

Frank's eyes narrowed and his jocular manner faded. "What?"

"You seem to think all of this is funny somehow. Do you so enjoy the pain of others? Is that what your agency looks for in its employees? No soul? No compassion?"

"Look, I came here to tell you the truth."

Anna went to the door and opened it.

Frank stood stock-still for a moment and then shrugged. "Okay, you can't say I didn't warn you."

As he passed her Anna said, "Why do you hate him so much?"

"He shot me in the head, lady!"

"I don't think that's the real reason."

"What are you doing, playing shrink?"

"You've never had anyone in your life, have you? That you really cared about? Or that cared about you."

"This isn't about *me*!"

"I guess you're the only one who can really answer that truthfully. Good night, Mr. Wells."

As she closed the door behind him, Anna clutched at her face, stifling a sob.

Her phone rang. She almost didn't answer it.

The voice said, "Anna Fischer, please."

"Speaking," Anna said a little hesitantly. "Who is this?"

"Do you know someone named Shaw?"

Anna stiffened. "Why do you ask?"

"He's a big man, dark hair, blue eyes?"

A lump formed in Anna's throat. *Please, God, don't let it be . . . This is all too much.* "Yes, I know him," she managed to say.

"Then I think we need to meet."

"Is he all right?" Anna gasped.

"He was when I left him. But that's not to say he'll stay all right."

"What do you mean? Who are you?"

"My name is Katie James. And I believe Shaw is in serious trouble."

32

The two women sat opposite each other at a café on Victoria Street. It was a cold, dank afternoon of intermittent rain; the kind of day that Londoners knew all too well.

Katie James swirled her spoon in her coffee while Anna Fischer stared out the window where a flock of umbrellas paraded past. A single tear slid down her face. Katie pretended not to notice.

"You told me what happened in Edinburgh with Shaw, but you never really explained how you found me," Anna said.

"Several years ago you delivered a paper at The Hague about the balance of preserving civil liberties with the fight against terrorism. I covered it for my newspaper. I was doing a stint in the Middle East at the time and the subject matter was certainly relevant to that part of the world. Then I found a sales receipt that Shaw had. He'd purchased a copy of your book. I recalled that you discussed it at your lecture. It was a brilliant discussion."

"Yes, well, too bad no one was listening."

"I'm sure many people were, Ms. Fischer."

Anna looked up from the remains of a barely eaten lunch. "Please, it's Anna. We should be on first-name basis considering what you've just told me about the man I'm engaged to," she added in a resigned tone.

"And you had no idea?"

"Of course I had *some* idea. And I had my suspicions."

"But you never pushed him on it?"

"I did. After he asked me to marry him," she added, her voice choking. When she started to snuffle, several other patrons looked around to stare at her.

"Would you like to go to someplace more private?" Katie suggested in a low voice.

Anna wiped her eyes and rose. "My office. It's close by."

A few minutes later the women sat in Anna's book-lined office at The Phoenix Group. A secretary brought them in hot tea and then retreated. Katie gazed around the room with interest.

"So what is it that you do here?" she asked, obviously trying to break the ice a bit.

"Here, we think," Anna replied. "We think about vitally important global issues that most people have neither the time, expertise, nor desire to dwell on. Then we write our white papers, publish our books in hundred-copy runs, and make our speeches to half-filled rooms and the rest of the world goes merrily along ignoring us completely."

"Is it really that bad?"

"Yes." Anna took a sip of tea. "You said Shaw had been wounded?" Her face twitched even as she tried to appear casual.

"He didn't seem to even care. Bullet didn't go in, he said, or something close to that. But they were shooting at him. His own people, the good guys."

"Or so he told you they were the good guys," Anna said sharply.

Katie was taken aback for a moment. "Well, I guess I only had his word for it. It wasn't like I had the opportunity to ask everyone for official IDs."

Anna rose and paced the room, making precise ninety-degree turns as she did so. "It could very well be that Shaw is *not* who I thought he was."

"He saved my life, Anna. And he let me go."

As though she'd just used up all her energy, Anna slumped down in her chair, put a hand to her face, and quietly sobbed.

Katie rose and put a comforting hand on her shoulder. "Is there something else?"

Anna took a deep breath and wiped her face with a tissue. "Shaw went to see my parents, in Germany. He did so at my request. To ask for my hand in marriage from my father." She glanced up at Katie. "I know, it's silly. But I just wanted . . ."

"To see if he'd do it?" Anna nodded. "And what happened?"

"My father happily gave his consent."

"So what's the problem?"

"After Shaw left another man came. He told them things about Shaw. Very disturbing things. Then the night you called me, a man came to see *me*. He was with an international agency I've never heard of. He said Shaw worked for them."

"So he is a good guy!" Katie exclaimed.

But Anna shook her head. "He said that Shaw was *forced* to work for them."

"Forced to? How?"

"To avoid going to prison for serious crimes. This man told me Shaw shot him in the head. Almost killed him."

"If he did that why wouldn't they just put him in prison? Why cut him a deal like that?"

"I asked that same question. And this man—he said his name was Frank Wells—he said that Shaw was very good at doing what they needed done. He was brave with strong nerves. That he could walk into dangerous situations and come out alive like no one else."

"From what I saw I can believe that. So he *is* working for the good guys."

"Wells said that Shaw kills people."

"When they're trying to kill him."

"Why are you defending him so?" Anna asked in a sudden fierce tone. "You do not know him. You met him, by your own admission, one time."

"That's true, but it was a helluva one time. You

learn a lot about someone in a situation like that. There's no opportunity to put on a false front. He saved my life and he let me go, Anna. So, I feel like I owe him. But it doesn't matter what I think. What counts is what you believe."

"I *thought* I knew Shaw." She paused. "My father has revoked his consent."

"You're a big girl, you don't need your father's permission to marry."

"Would you marry a man under such conditions?"

"I'd talk to him about it *before* I made any decisions."

"I'm . . . I'm afraid," she admitted.

"Anna, if he were going to hurt you, he would've done it by now."

"I'm not afraid of him hurting me physically. But what if he did commit these crimes the man spoke of? What if he tells me so? I cannot live with that. I don't want to know."

"But then he doesn't get to tell you his side of things. That's not fair to him."

"And he told me he had a desk job. According to you that's not true. So he lied to me. And he said he was retiring. According to this Frank Wells that is not an option. If he quits he goes to prison."

"Anna, I don't have all the answers, but I do have a suggestion. Talk with Shaw. He needs you right now. His own people tried to kill him. Maybe he's trying his best to get out and they gave him a pretty deadly warning. But you have to talk to him."

Anna composed herself. "I want to thank you for coming here and telling me all this."

"You're welcome," Katie said a bit resentfully. "But you're not going to talk to him, are you?"

"Please, that is not your concern."

The door opened and a man came in. "Anna, Bill wants to speak to you for a moment."

She turned to Katie. "I'll be back."

"There's not much else left to say, is there?"

Anna hurried out while Katie slipped on her rain-coat. Her gaze caught on some papers on Anna's desk. Ever the curious soul, she drew closer.

"The Red Menace," she read from the top of a printout. Anna's desk was littered with research related to the world's number one story along with her handwritten notes. She ran her gaze over the desk, taking in as much as she could. Names, dates, places, Web sites. She had a wonderful short-term memory. When she got outside she would write these things down. She didn't know why. Well, she did—it was just who she was.

Then her eye caught on something else. She picked up the photo from the desk. Shaw and Anna looked very deeply in love as they stood there, arms around each other. In the background the Arc de Triomphe watched over them.

"Well, if you can't fall in love in Paris, you're not meant to be together," she said quietly to herself.

She glanced up as Anna hurried back into the room.

"So you're 'analyzing' the Red Menace?" Katie said, pointing to her desk.

"Just curious, like everyone else."

The next moment Anna saw what Katie was holding. "Please put that down."

As Katie passed Anna she pressed the picture into her hands and said, "Don't expect that kind of love to come around again. Most people don't even get it once in their lives. And I speak from experience." She handed Anna a business card with an address written on the back. "Here's where I'm staying in London, if you want to talk some more."

Katie left Anna clutching the photo as she headed down the stairs.

33

Shaw was waiting in the British Airways lounge at Frankfurt Airport. He, along with the other passengers, was watching the news on several TVs sprinkled around the room. On one screen indignant senators from the United States were on the floor of that august chamber taking turns lobbing potshots at the Russians and their downward spiral into an autocratic state that rivaled the ruthless machine Papa Joe Stalin had cobbled together.

On another screen the BBC was showing the British Parliament giving the same treatment to the former Soviet Union. On yet another screen the German chancellor was putting her two cents in. While she was asking for calm and urging others not to rush to judgment, the chancellor still made it quite clear that the Russians should be deeply ashamed of themselves. This was the same tack the French president was taking, although he was erring more on the side of caution than his fellow leaders.

Shaw was not focused on the great international political question of the day. He'd made up his mind.

He was flying to London and would tell Anna the truth about what he did for a living. If she still wanted to marry him, which he doubted she would, then he would figure out some way to do it. He was actually surprised that he hadn't heard from her after his meeting with her parents. He'd called and left her a message telling her he was coming to London. She hadn't called him back, which was also unusual. He was thinking about this when the men approached him. They didn't have to flash their creds; he recognized them.

Frank's goons.

A few minutes later, deep in the bowels of the airport Shaw entered a small room where Frank sat at one end of a table and a man Shaw didn't recognize at the other. There were four other men here, all fit and, Shaw assumed, amply armed.

"I did Heidelberg."

Frank nodded. "I know. Nice easy job, just like Scotland. How was the side trip to Wisbach by the way? Work out okay for you?"

This didn't surprise Shaw. He knew that Frank tracked his every movement. "As a matter of fact it did."

Frank glanced at the men standing against the wall and nodded. They each crept forward a bit, putting a wall of flesh and guns between Frank and Shaw.

"The Fischers are nice people, aren't they?" Frank said. "My guy really enjoyed his chat with them. And

I really enjoyed getting to know Anna when I visited her in London. Though I was really surprised at how clueless she was about you. But now, just so you know, she's all filled in."

About a minute of absolute silence followed as Shaw stared at Frank and Frank smiled at Shaw.

Shaw instantly sized up the situation. They would kill him long before he could reach Frank. But if the last six years had taught him anything, it was patience.

He turned to the short, thick-necked, curly-headed man about Shaw's age seated at the table. "Who's this, Frank? Your boss or another flunky?"

If Frank was disappointed that Shaw had not tried to attack him he didn't show it. Hs just continued to smile and motioned with his hand at the other man.

The man said, "I'm actually neither. The name's Edward Royce, MI5." He handed Shaw his card.

"And what's so important that you had to pull me away from a comfortable chair and a bottle of Guinness, Mr. MI5?"

Royce glanced at Frank, his eyebrows slightly upraised. "Sorry to inconvenience you."

"No you're not and hurry up. I have a plane to catch." Shaw stared directly at Frank as he said this.

That comment got another eyebrow hike from Royce. "Well, frankly, if it were up to me, Mr. Shaw, I wouldn't even be here. MI5 is working with Interpol in investigating this Red Menace phenomenon. I think we're perfectly capable of handling the situation, but it's not my call. And my superiors have asked Mr. Wells's people for assistance. And he, in turn, recommended that I meet with you."

"What do you want me to do about it?" Shaw said bluntly.

"I've been told that you have very good contacts in Moscow, speak fluent Russian, and can handle yourself in dangerous situations. That makes you pretty unique."

"The time I spent in Russia was against my will. So you might want to find another *unique* person to carry your bags."

"Don't you want to find out who's behind the Red Menace?"

"Why?" Shaw asked pointedly. "Is what they're saying about Russia not true?"

"Who the bloody hell knows?" Royce exclaimed. "Well, some of it undoubtedly is. But the truth is quite beside the point. In fact, it's really the last thing we need. As you probably know, MI5 protects the UK against terrorists, spies, extremists, and the like. Well, the Red Menace business has opened quite the Pandora's box. The world is in a delicate state right now. Many countries are powder kegs ready to blow."

"Really? I must've missed the warning signs," Shaw said.

This response drew a snort of laughter from Frank.

Royce hurried on. "Anyway, this campaign is driving the Russians in a direction neither we nor the rest of the EU want them to go. A brooding, hunted Russian Bear is dangerous to everyone, Mr. Shaw. We have to defuse the situation. To do that we have to find out who's really behind this whole campaign."

"Why not team up with the Americans? They can pull the bear's claws if it comes to that."

"The Americans are, as usual, going their own way on this matter. But Wells here has agreed to allow you to work with us. He said you even knew Sergei Petrov, who was just murdered."

Shaw shot a glance at Frank, who stared back at him imperturbably.

"That was very generous of Frank to offer my services. But I respectfully decline."

Royce said angrily, "Fine. No bloody skin off my nose."

Frank stood. "Look, Shaw, you get this done, then maybe we talk about those other things."

"Is that right?" It was all Shaw could do not to leap over the table and rip out the man's throat.

Frank hitched up his pants. "That's right. I'm giving it to you straight, Shaw. I always do."

"I'll have to get back to you."

"What? Why?" Frank exclaimed.

"I've got something more important to do right now."

Royce said, "More important than the whole bloody world going to hell?"

"Yep."

"What could that possibly be?" Royce demanded.

"I need to go see a lady," Shaw answered, staring at Frank before walking out of the room.

Royce glanced at Frank. "Not exactly what I was hoping for, Wells," he barked.

Frank was solemn-looking, staring after Shaw. "Surprised me too, but for a different reason."

"Why? What the hell were you expecting?"

"For him to try and kill me."

"Good God. And the man *works* for you! You're both bloody insane."

"The man doesn't really *work* for anybody, Royce."

"But I thought you said . . ."

"Yeah, well, Shaw's a special case."

"Do you have anyone else that can do what he can?"

"Not even close."

34

Anna nearly screamed as she awoke to see the man hovering over her while she lay in bed in her London flat. She sat up, clutched the sheet around her.

"What are you doing here?" she demanded.

Shaw sat on the edge of the bed. "I think you know," he said quietly.

"How did you get in?"

He held up a key. "You gave it to me, remember?"

"I remember," she said groggily.

"I went to see your parents, but I'm sure you know that."

"And do you know about the man who visited them later? And the man who came to see me?"

"What did he tell you?"

"Would you like to guess? It's actually not too difficult. What I need to know is, was it the truth?"

"Anna, I'm sorry. I never meant for this to happen."

"You should know that lies always hurt people."

"I know you're upset. That you probably hate me

right now. And you have every right to. But I came here to tell you the truth."

"And I'm simply supposed to believe that it *is* the truth this time?"

Shaw glanced around the bedroom. Many happy hours had been spent in here. He knew every inch of Anna's flat better than any place he'd ever called home. "All I can do is try."

"Let me get dressed. You can wait in the other room."

"It's not like I haven't seen you naked a thousand times."

"You won't see me naked tonight. Go!"

He left and she joined him a few minutes later, a long dressing gown wrapped around her. She remained barefoot. They sat at the small table overlooking the street at which she and Frank had sat.

"So explain," she said tersely.

"Frank Wells is my superior at the organization I told you about."

"Yes. Where you work at a *desk* job? How is that going, by the way? Any interesting work come across your nice, safe desk job?"

Shaw stared down at the floor. "The work I do is highly dangerous. There's hardly ever a time when I go into a mission where I'm sure I'll come out alive. That's the truth."

Anna let out a noticeable moan but then caught

herself. "And you do this out of the goodness of your heart?"

"Seven years ago I shot Frank Wells in the head in Istanbul. He pulled a gun on me. I thought he was going to kill me. When I realized who he was I took him to a hospital. Otherwise he'd be dead. He probably forgot to mention that part."

"He said he was trying to arrest you for some criminal activity."

"That's his story, but it doesn't make it true."

Anna sat back and pulled the robe closer around her. "So what is your version? What were you doing when you shot him?"

"I can't tell you. Only that I'm not what Frank thought I was. But I couldn't really prove it."

She stared at him incredulously. "So I'm just supposed to take your word for it? You don't have a good track record for veracity."

Shaw mulled this over for a few moments. "Okay, but this can go no further, Anna. Seriously. No further." She quickly nodded, her face strained. "I was in Istanbul that day to find out who was trying to frame me for working with a very violent drug cartel operating out of Tajikistan. I was a freelancer back then. I worked for the Americans, the French, the Israelis, among others, and none of it criminal."

"Who would try to frame you?" Anna said, but her tone was more conciliatory now.

"There were lots of potential suspects. The work I did had put a dent in a lot of the bad guys' activities. And I guess Frank's organization got involved, became convinced I had gone bad, and were going to take me in. I thought Frank was one of the guys who'd framed me. I believed they'd laid a trap in Turkey and he was there to finish the job. So I shot him before he shot me."

"Why would you later agree to work for Frank if you weren't in the wrong?"

"Let's put it this way. If it had gone to court I would have probably never seen the light of day. I had no proof, and the frame job was pretty convincing. Working for Frank isn't exactly easy, but it seemed better than the alternative. And I think Frank and his people suspected I'd been set up, but instead of investigating further to establish my innocence they used it as an excuse to make me work for them, fine people that they are."

"So why did your own people shoot at you in Scotland?"

"Who told you that?" he said sharply.

"Perhaps it was Frank."

"Don't lie to me, Anna."

"That is a fine one, coming from you."

"I've never really lied to you. I just didn't tell you everything."

"A distinction that is beyond absurd," she retorted.

Shaw looked angry for a moment and then his face

cleared. "You're right, it is. Anyway, they'd agreed that I'd work for them for five years, and if I survived, I was a free man. As of right now I've stayed on for nearly six just to make sure."

"Why would you work for these horrible people for an extra year? It makes no sense."

"I did it because I wanted to be sure they'd let me go. I *had* to be sure because, well, because of a very important reason. I'd worked for them for nearly three years when I made that decision."

"And when exactly did you decide to work for them for an extra year?"

"Three years ago. At 12 a.m. In Berlin."

Their eyes met and held as Anna's breath caught in her throat. That had been the exact moment when he'd saved her from the muggers. They knew this because a street clock had chimed the hour.

"But he told me that you're not free. That you still work for him. That people don't retire from that job. Ever."

"I just found that out myself."

He sounded so utterly crushed that she gripped his hand with hers.

"Can't you just stop, just walk away?" The tears had started to gather in Anna's eyes.

"I could, but I'd be dead or more likely in prison in less than twenty-four hours if I did."

"But these people are the law! How can they possibly do that?"

"They are the law, a law unto themselves. They kill when the ends justify it. It's a dangerous world and the rules of the game have changed."

"That's very comforting."

"Do you want to be safe?"

"At any price? No!"

"That makes you a minority."

"So where exactly does that leave us?"

"I asked you to marry me. You accepted. You asked me to get your father's permission. I did. But I wasn't truthful with you. And I can't stop doing work for Frank. And I can't expect you to marry me under these conditions. It's not fair. And it's not right. And I love you too much to do that to you. And now I'm going to do the hardest thing I've ever had to."

"What is that?" she said in a hollow whisper.

"Walk out of your life."

Shaw started to rise. "Wait!" she exclaimed. He sat back down.

Anna dabbed at her eyes with the sleeve of her robe. "Do you still want to marry me?"

"Anna, that's not the issue anymore. When I go away you'll never know if I'll come home alive."

"What do you think the spouses of soldiers and police officers do every day?"

"Anna, that's easy to say but . . ."

She sat on his lap and placed his large, muscular hand over her engagement ring.

"You only have to ask yourself one question, Shaw.

the whole truth

Just one. Do you still love me? If the answer is no, your problem goes away."

He placed his head gently against hers. "Then I have a big problem."

35

Nicolas Creel had never been an overly religious man, yet this amount of good fortune must surely have at its epicenter a divine light. His life of balancing good works with the sale of deadly weapons was clearly paying off, judging by the latest golden opportunity to present itself.

He'd reviewed the surveillance tapes of The Phoenix Group's building and watched in astonishment as a woman identified as Anna Fischer and none other than the legendary journalist Katie James walked into the place practically arm in arm!

He now had the remaining piece to his game plan. Creel had dossiers on a dozen promising candidates, yet Katie James had never even occurred to him because she'd dropped off the radar screen. He'd had an entire file assembled on her within an hour of seeing the woman on the video. And the man liked what he had seen.

Her fall from the top had been swift. Allegations of alcoholism, stories botched or never written. Relegated to the obit page and she was several years shy of forty. Her two Pulitzers had not saved her from that fate. She looked hungry on the film.

Well, Creel would play her dreammaker. He would give her the one story that would catapult her right back to the top.

He called Caesar and told him to be ready to go in two days. Putting down the phone, he sat back in his chair as the door to his study opened and Little Miss Hottie sauntered in holding a bottle of champagne and wearing only what she'd been born with.

"I love your office," she said. "It just feels like you. I come in here sometimes and just soak it in." She sat down in his lap and drank straight from the bottle.

"This is a nice surprise," Creel said as he ran his hand along her naked thigh. "It wasn't on the schedule, sweetie."

"A thank you for that kickass ring you got me, baby," she slurred. She was drunk, and, from the shrunken appearance of her pupils, also high. Yet Creel had found his wife was at her lovemaking best while stoned out of her mind.

"It's amazing, really, what twenty carats will get one these days," sighed Creel, as Hottie slid up on his desk.

The buzzing sound woke Shaw. He instinctively sat up and scanned the room, until he realized where he was. Next to him Anna was still sleeping. He rubbed his face and glanced at his phone. It was Frank. He snatched it up and went into the next room, looked out the window onto a moonless London night. The rain had passed but a chill mist still floated down the street obscuring everything it touched.

"What do you want?" Shaw said.

"Spending the night? The lady must really love you."

"You go near her again, Frank, I'll kill you."

"Don't make promises you can't keep, my friend."

"What the hell do you want?" Shaw snapped.

"Well, since you didn't seem all that interested in the assignment from MI5 it's my job to put your ass back to work. And I hope you've got the notion of freedom right out of your head. Or else the little woman can come and visit you in the biggest shithole prison I can find."

His reconciliation with Anna was so powerfully euphoric that Shaw found himself immune even to Frank's taunts. "Where?" he asked curtly.

"Paris. You'll take the Eurostar over this afternoon. Initial instructions at St. Pancras. The rest in Paris."

"Piece of advice, Frank, always watch your back."

The line, however, was already dead.

Shaw smiled and clicked off. He had Anna. That's all that mattered. The enormous weight lifted off him almost made Shaw feel he could fly.

He ate breakfast with his fiancée, kissed her good-bye, and was about to leave the apartment while she showered when he remembered he'd left his jacket in her cluttered office off the dining room. When he retrieved it, he happened to see the card on her desk and picked it up.

"Katie James, *New York Tribune*," he said slowly, his anger rising.

He flipped the card over and saw the London address penciled in there. *That's* how Anna had known about Scotland. He checked his watch. He had time. He slipped the card into his pocket.

36

Shaw could sense the eye burning into him from the peephole. He would have laid down a bet that she wasn't going to let him in. He would have lost.

Katie got right down to business. "Look, I can tell you're upset but did you see Anna?" Her voice was anxious, her features worried.

She sat down on the small sofa and curled her legs under her. She had on a hotel bathrobe and slippers covered her feet. Her hair was wet and straight. Shaw could still sense the steam coming from the bathroom. Her shampoo's aroma drifted into his nostrils. Yet he barely noticed. He was so angry he could barely keep from shaking.

"Can I ask *you* a question?" he said.

"Go ahead."

He exploded. "What the hell do you think you're doing getting involved in my life?"

"I was just trying to help."

"I don't need your help, lady."

She sat back and crossed her arms. "Really? So you're totally oblivious to the fact that you have this amazing woman head over heels in love with you but trying to figure out whether you're her knight in shining armor or a psychopath?" Her tone was far more aggressive now.

"You have no business, no right butting into this."

"I told Anna to talk to you before she made up her mind. I told her I thought you were a good guy. Well, are you or aren't you?"

"Right now I'm having a hard time making up my mind."

"Why?"

"Because part of me wants to strangle you."

"Okay. I can understand that. Would you like some coffee instead?"

For the first time he noticed the room service table with her breakfast on it.

"No."

"Well, I'm sure you won't mind if I help myself."

She poured out a cup of coffee and took a bite of bagel. "Well?"

"Well what?" he shot back.

"Did you talk to Anna?"

"Yes."

"And?"

"And it's none of your damn business."

"So that's the only reason you came here? To read me the riot act?"

He moved so fast her eyes could barely follow. The

room service table smashed against the wall with a loud crash.

Unperturbed, Katie finished her coffee and put her cup down. "Are you finished with the histrionics?"

"Stay out of my life."

He turned to leave.

"I actually have one question for you. And it doesn't involve Anna," she quickly added.

He stopped at the door and glowered at her.

"What did you mean when you said you'd been to hell and it was just as bad as everyone thought it was?"

"Like I told you before, you wouldn't understand the answer."

In response, Katie slid her robe partially down, exposing a blistery red gash on her upper right arm.

"Try me."

Shaw eyed the old wound on her shoulder. "Gunshot?"

"I figured you were the sort of man who could tell. Fired by one ticked-off Syrian. Good thing he was such a lousy shot. He said later he was aiming at my head."

She picked up an unbroken coffee cup and the carafe that miraculously hadn't burst open and poured him a cup of coffee. As she handed it to him she said, "Whenever Clint Eastwood got shot in the arm in a movie they'd just pour some whiskey on it, wrap a little sling around it, and he'd get on his trusty horse and ride off. They never bothered to dwell on what happens when the bullet enters your arm and keeps going, shattering an artery here, ripping up muscle and tendon there, or nicking my left ventricle on its pinball ride through Katie's organs. I was in rehab for three months after they finally weaned me off the ventilator. They had to cut a nice little hole in my back to get the slug out. It was flat as a pancake."

Shaw sat down. The sight of the wound seemed to have wilted his anger. "Soft head. Designed to tumble through your body, trashing everything in its path. And it tends to stay in you, which means a surgeon has to cut you open in another place, while you're just about dead, to get the sucker out."

She eyed him from over the rim of her cup. "How many gunshot wounds do you have? You can show me, I won't tell."

"A good plastic surgeon could take care of that scar."

"I know. They wanted to when I got back to the States."

"So why didn't they?"

"I didn't want them to."

"Why not?"

"Because I wanted to keep the scar. That explanation cover it for you?"

Her face softened and she said in a calmer tone, "Look, you have every right to be pissed off at me. If you were messing in my life—not that I have one right now, but if you were—I wouldn't be happy about it. For what it's worth, I was just trying to help. You picked a great lady and it's easy to see how much she loves you."

Shaw drank his coffee but said nothing.

Katie continued. "And no more meddling from me. I swear. I hope things work out for you both."

He finished his coffee and rose, looking very uncomfortable. "Anna and I are fine. I told her . . . I told her things I should have told her a long time ago." He took a few steps toward the door before glancing back. "I'm glad to see you got out of Edinburgh okay."

"It's coming in awfully late, but I want to thank you for saving my life back there. I mean really thank you."

"How'd you find out about Anna?"

"Hey I *am* an award-winning investigative reporter. Your hotel room. You left her name engraved on the blotter. And I found a book receipt in your jacket pocket. I'd actually heard an Anna Fischer speak a few years ago and was very impressed. Figured it was worth a couple of phone calls to see if it was the same one. From what I'd seen of you it would take an exceptional woman to keep your interest."

Shaw looked a little surprised by this praise, but didn't say anything.

He happened to look at her desk parked next to the hotel room door. Piles of papers, news clippings, and writings were scattered over it. On the laptop screen was a headline detailing the recent events with Russia.

"Your next Pulitzer?" he asked.

"A girl has to keep trying. And do it far better than the boys just to stay equal."

"You sound like Anna."

Shaw hesitated and then slowly pulled something from his pocket and passed it to her. It was a card with no name on it, just a phone number.

"I don't give that out to many people."

"I'm sure you don't."

"But if you went to see Anna there's a chance the man I work for might come creeping around. If he does."

"You'll be the first one I call."

"Take care of yourself. I doubt we'll be seeing each other again."

"I thought that the last time and look where we are. Having a nice cup of coffee together."

A second later he was gone.

37

After Shaw left for Paris the Russians publicly announced that if they were so terrible the world would not, of course, condescend to use all their filthy oil, so they cut their exports in half. As the number two exporter of crude behind only Saudi Arabia, and the possessor of the globe's largest proven natural gas reserves, this was not an empty gesture. Russia exported more oil than the next three countries—Norway, Iran, and the United Arab Emirates—combined. Global production had barely kept pace with demand when all export cylinders were firing. With the Russian black gold not totally available there was no way to make up the shortfall.

The world markets were hardly pleased. The price of crude hit $130 a barrel within hours of the announcement and stock markets around the globe suffered enormous, unprecedented losses even with automatic trading stops in place. Gas at the pump and airline ticket prices soared. And since many things people used every day were made with petroleum products, the cost of everything from toys to trucks shot up too.

OPEC, so long in the driver's seat on the world's economic stage, scrambled to try and at least make up some of the difference but they couldn't come close. And rather than making the Arab world more untold riches with the price of oil so high, it was actually costing them billions because, unlike Russia, desert countries imported just about everything they needed. So while crude had skyrocketed forty percent, the cost of derivative products had doubled. Because of the price increase and Russia's stockpile of cash and foreign investments and its proportionately low level of imports and per capita consumption, it was believed that Moscow could keep this position up for quite some time.

If that wasn't enough for the world to absorb in a week's time, the Russians had more up their sleeve. Their minister for foreign affairs announced that a Taliban-occupied sector of Afghanistan had been caught red-handed using Uzbekistan and Kazakhstan to smuggle drugs into Russia, which promoted criminal activity and corrupted innocent Russian youth. Everyone knew that this was true, of course, but the Russians had never done much about it before. The Russians would not follow diplomatic channels in dealing with this serious problem, the minister stated. Afghanistan had allowed this activity for years and Moscow was tired of it.

And when the Russians made up their minds, they acted.

One day later five large cruise missiles fired from a Russian submarine hit a Taliban training compound that the Russian minister later said was instrumental in this drug trafficking. In seconds one thousand Taliban fighters were obliterated and their caches of weapons and equipment destroyed. The Russians warned every Arab country in the Middle East that if there was any retaliation by them against Russian interests they could expect the same treatment multiplied a hundredfold.

The Afghan president released an official statement denouncing this "unwarranted intrusion into a sovereign nation's borders." But in diplomatic circles this was seen as only perfunctory considering that the Taliban was doing its best to overthrow the Afghan government and had attempted to assassinate the current president twice. The Afghan leader therefore was probably doing cartwheels down his presidential corridor at the same time he was telling off Moscow.

Tehran fired off an angry response saying they were appalled by what they termed the Russians' barbaric behavior, and then hastily turned to the UN for help.

The United States also immediately filed a protest against Russia with the United Nations and began withdrawing its troops from Iraq and Afghanistan. The Pentagon announced that this was not connected to the attacks on the Taliban, but merely in keeping with previously stated administration policy. Insiders knew, along with probably most Americans, that this consolidation of troop strength had everything to do with the looming Russian threat. The Middle East was no longer that important. Generals from every NATO nation pulled out their old attack-and-defend plans against Soviet aggression.

One major newspaper succinctly if melodramatically stated it in a four-inch headline: "THE COLD WAR IS BACK."

Privately, military and administration officials in the United States were rejoicing that with one stroke the Russians had wiped out a large measure of the Taliban's terrorist capability. One four-star general complaining to his aide said, "If only *we* could do that shit and get away with it."

When the first major American pullouts from Iraq began, Shiite and Sunni tribal and militia elements commenced probing attacks on each other in preparation for what many believed would be the long-feared all-out civil war. That story was relegated to the interior pages of most major newspapers, and was not the top story on any mainstream television news program. Iraq, as a newsworthy subject, was now very much second-tier. Islamic-based terrorism was listed in recent polls as the eleventh most important subject for citizens across the globe, falling right after too much sex and violence on TV.

Russia was the number one target of concern, and the reason was abundantly clear. Terrorists had little bombs; Russia possessed tons of real nukes and had apparently lost its collective mind.

The search for the forces behind Konstantin and all the rest took on a much greater urgency now. The world probably figured if they could at least get the Russians one target to crush, they might leave the rest of them alone.

Yet what if the force behind the Red Menace *was* the United States, many wondered with dread. The Russians had said it would be considered an act of war. Was this really the beginning of the end? Could the Americans have made such a colossal miscalculation? People across every nation on earth braced for the next crisis to happen.

They would not have long to wait.

38

The final elements of the mission in France had taken an inordinately long time to complete. Typically Shaw would get to town a day or two before the big event, receive his briefing, and hit his marks. Whether he lived or died was really the only unanswered question. This time had been different.

Frank had even flown in with a team to go over everything in meticulous detail. At the final prep meeting before D-day, he'd hammered the essentials home to Shaw again and again while they sat in a little cottage twenty miles outside of Paris.

He warned, "These guys are good, Shaw, really good. They don't trust anybody, and anybody they don't trust, they kill."

"Thanks for the pep talk, Frank, I really appreciate it." Shaw sat across from him, rubbing his hands slowly together and not meeting his colleague's eye.

Frank observed this and suddenly slammed his fist down on the table. "Are you freaking nervous!"

Shaw looked up at him. "What the hell do you think?"

"I think I need the old Shaw, the man who never sweats. If these guys even smell your stink, they'll put a slug right here faster than you can say, 'Oh, shit!'" He pointed to the center of his forehead. "And then chop your body up while they chitchat about the weather and women."

"I'll be fine, Frank."

"It's the lady, right? You're getting married now and you finally got something to lose." Frank sat back and shook his head, a patronizing look spreading across his face. "Well, keep this in mind, lover boy, you screw up tomorrow, there's no wedding, just four funerals. One for each part after the scumballs quarter you up."

"How long have I been doing this? And I've walked away from every one."

"There's a first and *last* time for everybody. Just don't make it happen on this one, I'm not done with you yet."

Shaw reached over and gripped the man's arm. "Tell me why you really went to see Anna."

"I told you. I was being fair. And *you* should've been the one to tell her, not me. She had a right to know what she was getting into."

"She's not a little girl, Frank."

"Did you tell her you weren't retiring? That any second your ass could be grass?"

"What the hell do you care?"

Frank looked uncomfortable and shrugged. "She

seems like a nice lady. You ever stop to think about what you getting killed might do to her? Or if one of the wackos we deal with on a daily basis gets wind of her?"

"I would never let anything happen to Anna."

"But you're not in control of that, are you? You're not an accountant, Shaw. And in our line of work, you make a mistake, you get dead real fast. And maybe she does too." He paused. "So with all that you don't think she had a right to know?"

Shaw didn't say anything, because more than a little bit of him was arriving at the conclusion that Frank, the hated Frank, might be right.

Frank rose, grabbed his overcoat, and headed to the door. "Good luck, Shaw. And if I don't see you again, well, I'll have to find somebody else, won't I?"

"You'll never find anybody as good as me."

Frank considered this as he slipped on a battered hat. "You're probably right about that. But I'll settle for *almost* as good. And if they do end up killing you, right before the bullet hits you in the brain, just ask yourself one question: was the lady really worth it?"

Frank slammed the door behind him, leaving Shaw alone with only his thoughts.

"Yes," Shaw said to the empty room. "She is."

39

Shaw was on the move. The warehouse was in an area of Paris where people who liked to avoid violence never ventured. This small patch of French earth wasn't controlled by the police; it belonged to others who called it home. And they did not encourage visitors.

Four skinheads came out of the darkness toward Shaw, who stood at one end of the warehouse, a few dim bulbs overhead the only illumination. The young men encircled him; they didn't even bother to hide their weapons. They probably ate breakfast, lunch, and dinner holding them closer than any woman they'd ever bedded.

Three of them wore tank tops though it was chilly outside. They were all white, though it was actually hard to tell because their torsos were so blackened with tattoos. The skin engravings were all different, except for one that appeared on the right triceps of each man: a swastika. One of them, who looked about twenty, had an entire dragon wrapped around his upper body, in black, green, and salmon colors, the fangs spreading across the bottom part of his face. He was carrying a pump-action twelve-gauge in one hand with "I don't give a shit about nuthin'" attitude awash in his brown eyes that stared at Shaw with a convincing mix of hatred and contempt. He loaded up and sent a wad of spit an inch from Shaw's foot.

Your mother must be so proud.

Shaw turned to another man who was walking up to him. He wore a jacket, pressed jeans, and tasseled loafers instead of black cammie pants, muscle shirt, and head-busting combat boots. But his attitude mirrored his men's. He moved with a conceited swagger that just made you want to reach for a gun or ball up your fist and squash him for the good of humanity.

He couldn't have been more than thirty but his scarred face and expressive features intimated a far greater experience level than three decades normally provided.

He shook Shaw's hand and motioned him over to a small table set up in one corner. Only when he took a seat did Shaw follow. The skins now encircled the table. They were pack animals, Shaw observed, always waiting for the order to kill.

"*Je suis* Adolph, monsieur. And you go by?"

"Nothing," Shaw said. "I have all you need."

"The price was never mentioned," Adolph said. "Unusual, yes?"

Shaw leaned slightly forward. "There are some things more important than money."

"Most things are more important than money, but you need money to accomplish all of them." The man smiled and lit up a cigarette. "If only Sartre were still alive, he could give us the precise philosophical analysis, or perhaps he would simply answer, '*C'est la vie.*'"

"You want to kill President Benisti," Shaw began. "That will throw France into near anarchy."

Adolph shook his head. "You overestimate the French love of politics. You say I want to kill Benisti? That is your opinion only. But even if I did, it's only one dead president. They will simply elect another idiot."

"This is the land of political revolution," Shaw retorted.

"*Au contraire.* This *was* the land of political revolution," Adolph answered. "We have been truly Americanized. All my fellow citizens care about now is whether they have the latest iPhone. But we are the real revolutionaries, *mon ami.*"

"And what is your revolution about?"

"What do you think?" he suddenly snarled, grabbing one of his men's arms and pushing the swastika right in Shaw's face. "Unlike Hitler's phonies who only wore this on their uniform, we have *stained* it into our skin. It's our permanent identity. And I have taken the master's name as my own."

"So Jews are the root of all evil?

"Jews, Muslims, Christians, they share equal culpability. Benisti's mother was a Jew, though he tries to hide that fact. You said you have the information and credentials to get us into the hotel where he will be?"

"I do. Not all here. But I brought a sampling to show you I'm serious." He slowly reached in his pocket and pulled out an official-looking press badge and a ticket to the president's upcoming speech at a Paris hotel.

Adolph looked at them, impressed. "*C'est bon. Bien fait!*"

"I have five more of these," Shaw added. "Plus you will be included on the official VIP list."

"Weapons?" Adolph asked.

"The French aren't as paranoid as the Americans. VIPs don't get run through the detectors." He looked at the snarling skins. "But you have to look and act like VIPs."

Adolph laughed. "These are my personal body-guards. We grew up together on the streets of Paris. Each one of them would gladly give up his life so that I would live. I am the chosen one. They all understand that."

Shaw looked at the dragon skinhead. *Yep, he looks stupid enough to die for this megalomaniac asshole.*

"So you've got others to do the deed. And look the part?"

Adolph nodded. "When can we have the rest of the documentation?"

"As soon as my price is met."

"Ah, now we get to that." Adolph sat back, crossed his legs, and blew a circle of smoke toward the warehouse ceiling thirty meters above them. "I will tell you up front, monsieur, we don't have much money."

"I thought I made it clear that I'm not interested in money."

"Everyone says they're not interested in money until they ask for it. We are not drug dealers or desert terrorists grown fat on oil. I do not have billions of euros in a Swiss account. I am a poor man with rich ideas."

"My father died in a French prison last year."

Adolph sat up straighter and looked at Shaw with some interest now. "Which prison?"

"Santé."

The man nodded and crushed his cigarette with the heel of his shoe against the cold concrete floor. "That is one of the worst. And French prisons are for shit anyway. Several of our men reside in Santé now, their crime only that of cleansing the streets of filth. And for that, they are locked up like animals? The world is insane."

Behind Shaw the dragon skinhead let out a grunt.

Shaw turned to look at him and watched as another gob of spit hit near his shoe.

Adolph said, "Victor's brother was also one of them. He committed suicide at Santé last year. You were very close to your brother, weren't you, Victor?"

Victor let out another grunt and racked his shotgun.

"I'm sure they were very tight," said Shaw dryly.

"So your father died in prison. For what crime?"

"My father was an American who immigrated here to start a business, a business that became competitive with several others run by friends of Benisti, too competitive, in fact. So when Benisti was a prosecutor for the government he framed my father for a number of crimes he never committed, just to ruin him. It was all lies and Benisti knew it. My father spent twenty years in that hellhole and on the eve of his release he died of a heart attack. A broken heart. Benisti as good as put the knife through his chest."

"And if we check your story out, we will find it is true?"

"I speak the truth," Shaw said emphatically, his gaze leveled on the other man. "Otherwise I would not have walked in here."

"So you want revenge. That is all?"

"Isn't it enough? I give you the information, you kill Benisti." He paused. "And someone else," he added slowly.

"Who?" Adolph said sharply.

"Benisti's father. He cost me my father, I will now take his."

Adolph sat back and considered this. "I understand that he is also guarded."

"I have it all planned out. I have spent years planning it out." He looked around at the skins.

"These men can do it. It only requires a little courage and a steady hand."

"And how did you come by this intelligence? That interests me greatly."

"Why?"

"Because it has been rumored that Benisti is not above setting traps, that is why."

Adolph motioned to his men. They seized Shaw, pulled off his jacket, and stood him up. Victor pulled out a knife and slit open Shaw's shirt, checking for a wire. They pulled his pants off doing the same. After a search that would have made a proctologist blush with its intimacy, Shaw was allowed to put his clothes back on.

"I'm surprised you waited until now to search me," Shaw said as he buttoned his shirt.

"What would it matter if you were a *poseur* and wearing a wire? You would be dead anyway. And I would be long gone before the idiots showed up here."

"They could have surrounded this warehouse," Shaw pointed out.

Adolph smiled patronizingly. "No, no, monsieur, they could not come within ten blocks of here without my knowing. The gendarmes, they control the parts of Paris where the tourists go, but not here I think, monsieur, not here."

Shaw sat back down. "I am close to Benisti. He trusts me."

"Why, after what he did to your papa?"

"He doesn't know the man was my father," Shaw said simply. "I left France, changed my name, assumed a new identity, and then returned. I do his dirty work behind the scenes. Oh, he trusts me, like a son. I think about the irony every day."

"Your hatred is inspiring."

"Do we have a deal?"

"*Vive la révolution, monsieur.*"

40

Anna Fischer was in her office at The Phoenix Group building where she continued to pore over the documents that littered her desk. She actually now had more questions than answers about the Red Menace. And every day, sometimes every hour, a new revelation would burst to the surface like the aftershocks of a tsunami, and the earth would shake.

What bothered Anna the most was that there was no face, no name behind the R.I.C. Press releases were done over the Internet exclusively. No one had come forward and said *I* am the R.I.C. And with the murder of Petrov, and the attack on Afghanistan, Anna could perhaps understand why. Gorshkov had stated very clearly that whoever was behind this was going to be punished, and there were few nations on earth as good at punishment as the Russians.

Had this somehow backfired on the people who had perpetrated it? Were they running scared, unsure of what now to do? Anna couldn't answer any of those queries. All she knew was that the effort had been extraordinarily well planned. Yet was it for benign or evil motives? She could understand the benign argument; Russia after all did not have an exemplary track record on human rights and there were many people and organizations out there that would love to put them in their place. The evil side Anna had a more difficult time conceptualizing. What purpose would be gained by turning Russia into an even more isolated and paranoid country? It would be akin to giving North Korea free nukes and telling them to fire away.

She rubbed her temples. She couldn't spend all her time on this. Yet she was certain lots of other people across the world were doing the same thing right now. Someone had to find the truth at some point.

She checked her watch. It was nearly three o'clock. There was a firm-wide meeting today and all the staff was required to attend. She wasn't looking forward to sitting through what usually turned out to be a boring discussion. But at least she had a half hour to work on something of importance. And then this evening she had something still more critical to do.

She was going shopping for her wedding dress. Her in a wedding dress? Anna smiled at the thought and her skin actually tingled. The only thing better would be seeing Shaw in a tux. She had no doubt he would carry it off wonderfully.

With the world in crisis, it seemed ludicrous to be thinking about dresses and weddings. On the other hand, if the world were going to blow up sooner rather than later, she had no desire to wait to legalize her relationship with the man she loved.

A few minutes later she was so intent on her work that she never heard what was going on downstairs.

At precisely the same instant the front and rear doors of the building burst open and twelve men wearing long coats swarmed in. From under their coats they drew silenced weapons, took aim, and started firing.

When they charged in the receptionist in the front foyer had just lifted up the phone to make a call, but the line was dead. A moment later she was too as a bullet hit her in the forehead. She slipped off her seat and fell limp beside her desk, the blood from her head wound staining her dress front. A middle-aged analyst had unfortunately chosen this moment to come into the foyer. A second later he lay dead next to the receptionist. Some of the armed men headed to the basement. Others went room to room on the first floor, kicking open doors and killing anyone inside. Still others raced to the upper floors. There were twenty-eight people in the place today. Not a single one of the twenty-eight would be going home tonight.

When the screams reached Anna's ear, she thought someone had injured themself. She jumped up and rushed to the doorway. When she heard a muffled sound, she didn't immediately realize what it was. When she heard it again, the truth hit her.

That was a gunshot! Then she heard several more.

She slammed her door closed and locked it, raced

back to her desk, and tried the phone. The line was dead. She grabbed her purse off the shelf and slid out her cell phone. The sounds of footsteps were growing closer. She heard more bangs, more screams, and more thuds as bodies presumably hit the floor. She tried to remain calm but her hands were shaking so badly she could barely hold the damn phone.

She punched in the emergency number for the police and then watched in disbelief as the phone tried to connect, but no ringing came. She had made many calls on her cell from the building. What was going on? She looked at the tiny screen. She had *no* bars of reception. She tried again and again with no luck. She finally threw her phone down and ran to the window. She was three stories up, but she had no choice. She heard the sounds of feet pounding up the stairs. Her office was the last one on the hall. Still, she probably had barely a minute if that.

She struggled with all her might to raise the window. The exterior had recently been painted and Anna suddenly realized that the idiots had painted the window shut. She dug her fingernails into the wood frame, applied every ounce of strength she had. It would not budge. The sounds were coming down the hall. She heard a door kicked open, and next came a scream. Then a sound like a book being dropped as another body hit the floor.

In the midst of her terror, this actually gave her an idea. She grabbed a book off her desk and used it to smash the window glass open, and then to clean out all the shards. She leaned out the window and screamed.

"Help us! Help us! Call the police."

Unfortunately it was a quiet street with unoccupied buildings on either side of her and no one was down there to hear. She saw a large van parked at the curb. She called again, but apparently no one was in the vehicle. She was going to throw something at it when she noticed what appeared to be a small satellite dish attached to the van's roof. It was pointed right at the building.

Her panicked mind still working at incredible speed, the truth came to her. That's why she had no reception bars on her phone. Whatever was coming from the van was blocking them. She glanced up and down the dead-end street and noted the temporary barriers that had been set up at one end, preventing traffic from coming through.

She slipped off her pumps, climbed onto the windowsill, and looked down. There was an awning over the first-floor window. *If I can hit that and then roll to the street.*

She had no idea whether there was anyone left in the van. She only knew that if she stayed here she was dead. She steeled herself to jump. Tears were sliding down her face as she heard another door crash open next to her office. A scream, a thump, and then a thud. That was poor Avery. Gone.

God, if only Shaw were here.

She said a prayer, took aim, and tensed her legs for the leap. As soon as she was safely out, she would run like she had never run before, to get help. Although she doubted there was anyone left alive to save. Except her.

The two bullets fired right through the door hit Anna directly in the back and exited out her chest into the fresh air of a London afternoon. She squatted there frozen on the windowsill, seemingly unaware that she had just been shot as blood gushed all over the floor and window. And all over her. As her eyesight began to fade, the blue sky turned brown, the small patch of green grass across the street eroded to yellow. She could no longer hear the birds in the sky or the cars passing along on the next block over. She gripped the wood of the window with all her strength, but within a few seconds, as her blood left her far too fast, she had no strength left.

When Anna Fischer fell, it wasn't forward and out the window, but backwards, and into the room. She lay there spread-eagled staring at the ceiling of her office.

The door was kicked open and two men came in to stand over her. One of them slid off his mask and looked down at her, shaking his head.

"Damn lucky shot," he said. "I was just trying to blow the door."

The other man took off his mask and gazed down

at her. "How the hell?" Caesar began. "Two chest shots dead-on and she's still breathing?"

The other man said, "Give it a minute; she's about to kick."

"I don't have a minute. Look at the window. She was trying to get away."

The other man followed his gaze to the shattered glass.

Caesar took careful aim even as Anna's chest started heaving erratically with the last throes of life.

The shot hit her directly in the forehead.

As she let out what was to be her last breath, it sounded very much like a name. "Shaw."

Caesar used his boot to push roughly against the woman's shoulder, but it was crystal clear she would never bear witness against them as to what had happened here today.

The second man spoke into a walkie-talkie. He listened for a moment and then nodded.

"All dead," he told Caesar.

"All dead," Caesar repeated back. "Hack Squad?"

"Almost done."

"Tell them they've got two minutes. Send somebody down to the street to see if anyone saw the chick at the window. If they did, they know what to do. The plane's waiting. If they ain't on it, they ain't on it. Let's hit it."

He and the other man opened their backpacks and took out notebooks, reams of paper, charts, graphs, and other documents and then proceeded to press Anna's fingertips to many of the documents.

As the men started to spread the material over Anna's desk, Caesar said, "Damn." He was looking at the papers that were already on Anna's desk.

"What?" asked his companion.

Caesar pointed at one of the papers Anna had printed out showing her interest in the Red Menace.

He said, "Lady was obviously already curious. But it'll tie in okay."

He took out a camera and started snapping pictures of the office's interior.

They received an all-clear that no one had seen Anna at the window, though some of her blood had made its way to the small garden standing to the left side of the building entrance. The orange daylilies had grown a shade darker on impact.

Soon, a third man joined them. He sat down at Anna's computer and slid a CD into the intake slot. The man typed so fast his gloved fingers were a blur and the keyboard was rattling like a train car over bad tracks.

Sixty seconds later he took out the CD. "Download's finished." He got up and raced out.

Thirty seconds later there wasn't a living person left inside The Phoenix Group building.

41

As President Benisti was leaving the Ritz in Paris after giving a speech, six men were arrested for attempting to assassinate the French leader. The news reports touted it as miraculous police work, for the would-be assassins, who'd gained access to the event with cleverly forged documents, were apprehended before they could get close to Benisti. In a related story, an attempt was made to attack Benisti's elderly father but the criminals were caught before they could enter the senior Benisti's apartment. Two of them had been shot dead by authorities.

The men appeared to be members of a well-known neo-Nazi group operating on the outskirts of Paris. Further arrests were expected. Authorities said this had likely dealt a fatal blow to the ultraviolent organization.

Shaw listened to this report on the TV as he packed his bag in his hotel room. His phone vibrated and he picked it up.

"Congratulations," Frank said. "Your stink stayed away."

"You always had a way with words."

"Ready for some more work?"

"No, I'm headed out."

"Let me guess, London?"

"I just can't keep any secrets from you, can I?"

"Two days. Then I need you back."

"Three. And consider yourself lucky."

He clicked off, picked up his suitcase, and walked to the door. It opened before he touched the handle.

The pistol was leveled right at Shaw's chest as he backed up, still clutching his case.

Victor fired off a ball of spit at Shaw, drilling him right in the face.

Another man carrying a small rucksack slipped in behind Victor and shut and bolted the door.

In Shaw's pocket his phone started vibrating. It was probably Frank warning him, but far too late.

Adolph grinned. "No, no, *mon ami*, you must not leave Paris yet. The show, it is not over yet."

Shaw took another step back until he butted up against the wall. His gaze flitted from the gun to Adolph as the spit from Victor's launch trickled down his face.

Adolph drew a hacksaw and a small ax from his rucksack as Victor spun a suppressor onto the end of the pistol.

Shaw said, "You must be the only two left."

"I can always get more men," Adolph said. "For every one I lose, I can get five to replace them."

"The French really need to do something about their unemployment."

Adolph lifted the ax up. "Are you a Jew?"

Shaw eyed the tool. "Why, would you cut me up kosher?"

"I want to know why you set me up. I want to know this before you die. It will be good to cleanse your soul. Confess to me. Confess to Papa Adolph."

"I tell you what. I'll give you one chance to get out of here. Only one. Then all bets are off."

Adolph looked at Victor and laughed. "We have weapons and you have nothing. So that must mean you are full of bullshit." He brandished the saw and smiled maliciously. "If you are full of shit, I will certainly find out."

Shaw pressed a button near the lock on his suitcase. A second later an earsplitting siren erupted all around them.

Startled, Adolph and Victor glanced toward the window, no doubt thinking the police were coming.

In the next instant Shaw was charging directly at the pair, his suitcase held out in front of him. Victor took aim and fired at the suitcase, thinking it would easily rip through the cloth and hit Shaw in the head. He thought wrong.

The bullets did hit the suitcase but bounced off the super-strong composite lining and embedded in the ceiling. The impact of the shots staggered Shaw but he managed to keep his forward momentum. When he hit Victor the collision was so violent it ripped the gun from the man's hand and also tore off the skinhead's trigger finger.

Victor screamed in pain as he clutched the bloody stump. He stopped screaming when Shaw's suitcase smashing against his head sent him flying over a small couch.

Before Shaw could turn to face Adolph the man slashed his left arm deeply with the hacksaw. As he staggered back Adolph raised the ax but Shaw managed to kick his legs out from under him. Adolph went down hard, the ax slipping from his hand. He slid across the floor toward it, grabbed the weapon, and hurled it at Shaw. Fortunately the handle rather than the blade slammed into Shaw's thigh, but it still hurt like hell.

He didn't feel his phone vibrating once more in his pocket because Adolph was coming at him with the hacksaw and Victor, half his face a busted-up, bloody mess, had risen shakily to his feet looking for his gun.

Shaw launched himself at Adolph and drove his shoulder right into the man's gut, propelling them both onto the bed and over it, where they landed hard on the floor, Shaw on top. Adolph grabbed Shaw's face, gouging at his eyes. Partially blinded, winded badly, and his wounded arm and leg throbbing, Shaw still managed to lever his arm against Adolph's windpipe. But when he tried to press down to finish him, his normal strength simply wasn't there.

He glanced at his arm. The blood was pouring out thick and fast.

Shit! The blade must have hit an artery. He felt his fingers growing numb.

He pushed away from Adolph and managed to stand up on legs that unfortunately were starting to fail. As he turned looking for some way out, he froze.

Victor was pointing his gun right at Shaw's head, his middle finger on the trigger.

The skinhead's malevolent grin was apparently going to be Shaw's last conscious memory. *What a shitty way to go.*

The door crashed open and Frank and six of his men burst in. Frank immediately sized up the situation and fired two shots. Both hit Victor in the head and he dropped to the floor.

With a scream Adolph jumped on Shaw, his hands around his throat.

"Damn it, get him," yelled Frank, and four of his men raced to Adolph and tore him off the badly wounded man.

"Get that piece of crap out of here," ordered Frank, and Adolph was hustled from the room.

When Frank turned back to Shaw the big man's face was chalk white and a moment later he slumped to the floor.

"Shaw!" Frank raced across the room and knelt next to him.

"Get the EMTs up here now!" Frank roared.

Frank cradled Shaw's head with his hand. "Shaw? Can you hear me? Shaw!"

Shaw's head rolled back and forth in Frank's grasp. Frank glanced down at the deep tear in Shaw's arm, ripped off his necktie, and fashioned a tourniquet above the wound.

"Hang on, Shaw, hang on, the EMTs are coming right now. Right now!"

He screamed at his men, "How the hell did these bastards find him? He was supposed to have cover!"

"Frank?" the faint voice said.

Frank looked down at Shaw, who was now staring up at him.

"Shaw, it's gonna be okay. I hear the EMTs on the stairs."

"Call Anna," Shaw said, his breathing growing very shallow. "Call Anna for me."

The EMTs burst into the room and surrounded Shaw and Frank. As Frank tried to pull away from Shaw, the injured man clutched at him with the little strength he had left.

"Call Anna. Please."

"Right, I will. I'll do it right now," Frank said quickly.

Shaw drifted into unconsciousness and his arm fell to his side motionless.

A few minutes later they were hustling him out on a stretcher.

Victor the dragon-tattooed skinhead made his final exit in a body bag.

Frank watched from the window as the ambulance raced off. The room would be sterilized, the local police dealt with, and this would never appear on the French news. Frank mentally went through the steps of getting this done.

"Who's Anna?" one of Frank's men asked as he walked up to his boss.

Frank pulled his BlackBerry out of his pocket and read the e-mail on the screen for the fourth time. "Urgent Alert: Attack on The Phoenix Group in London. No survivors." That's why he'd been trying to call Shaw at the hotel. When he didn't get an answer he was on his way over to tell him in person when he'd gotten the distress signal from Shaw. He let out a deep breath as he surveyed the wreckage of the room. "Just a woman he was really close to."

42

Katie James was sitting in her small apartment on the Upper West Side in New York staring at a bottle of gin she had placed carefully on her kitchen counter. An empty glass sat next to it. She put five ice cubes in the glass and then added two fingers of tonic. She sat back and examined what she had done so far. She swirled the tonic around with a spoon, the ice clinking enticingly against the sides of the glass. She eyed the bottle of gin. One drink, that was all. And didn't she deserve it?

She had nearly been killed, for starters. And then she'd flown home to New York to find she'd been canned from her job on the death page due to budget concerns. They'd replaced her with a freelancer who was pushing eighty.

They'd also given her a hearty "Good luck, Katie!" as they had her escorted from the building by security. She wanted to run back in, take the Pulitzers she'd won, and cram them down their fat throats.

Instead, she'd come home and was staring at the gin. She would stop at one. She knew she could. She could just feel that she had the strength to stop at one. She unscrewed the top, smelled the delectable gin. She dropped a wedge of lime in the glass, swirled it around as she worked herself up for the final step, the adding of the Bombay Sapphire. It would be a toast to her new career—in what she didn't yet know.

But that wasn't the whole story. The thing was, when she was sober she saw Behnam in her dreams. The little Afghan boy who had died so that she could win her second Pulitzer always came to her when she slept. He seemed very much alive, his curly hair being lifted by a stifling desert wind. The smile on his face would melt the hardest heart, light the darkest night. But the dream always ended with him lying dead in her arms. Always dead was Behnam.

It was only when she was drunk that she didn't see him. It was only when she was wasted that he stayed away. And that meant she had seen him pretty much every night over the last six months. He had died hundreds of times after being resurrected in her dreams three or four times a night. She was tired of the spectacle. She wanted a drink. No, she wanted to be drunk. She didn't want to see Behnam alive and then dead.

As she sat back on her bare haunches, a ratty old sweatshirt her only clothing, she stared out the window. There was a rally going on in Central Park today. It was a protest against the Russian government. Tens of thousands of people were marching and waving "Remember Konstantin" flags. Katie couldn't know the flags had been secretly delivered to the rally organizers by a firm working for a shell corporation with an untraceable connection to Pender & Associates. Twenty million of the flags had been manufactured and distributed throughout the world for rallies just like this one.

Katie had decided not to attend the protest. She had other things on her mind.

She glanced away from the window and happened to stare through the blue glass of the gin bottle to the TV beyond.

Breaking news. Right. There was always breaking news. The next big story. In the recent past she'd already be on a plane, hurtling five hundred miles an hour right to the epicenter of the storm. And loving it. Loving every second of it until it was over and the next big story came along. And then the one after that in a psychotically charged, adrenaline-burning race that had no finish line.

London again. Well, London had its share of breaking news, though nothing bad had happened while Katie had been there. Just her luck. She took a deep breath and idly looked at the building with police tape all around it. It looked familiar. She sat up straighter and forgot about the gin.

What was the woman saying? Westminster? What group? Katie jumped to her feet, jogged into the living room, and turned up the sound.

The newsperson was standing in the rain while police and people in white uniforms raced here and there. A curious, neck-craning crowd was being held back by portable barriers. TV film crews were arrayed up and down the street, their satellite masts flinging the story electronically around the world one frantic byte and pixel at a time.

"The Phoenix Group would be the last place most people would expect something like this to happen," the reporter was saying. "Situated on a quiet London street, it has been described as a think tank conducting research on global policies covering myriad social and scientific subjects. Virtually all the people who worked here were scholars and scientists, many of them former academics that one would hardly expect to be the target of a brutal murder rampage. An official list of the dead has not been released pending notification of family. While details remain sketchy it appears that the massacre—"

Massacre? Did the woman say massacre? Katie slumped down on the carpet, her heart thudding against her chest. Her limbs felt dead.

The reporter continued, "As of right now, the authorities are only saying that there are nearly thirty victims inside the building. There has been no indication of any survivors."

No indication of any survivors? Katie glanced at her watch and did a quick time zone calculation as her reporter mentality kicked in despite her rising panic. It was evening in London now. A few hours for the bodies to be discovered, the police called, and the news people and crowds to get there. It might have happened around three or four that afternoon. Then the panic resumed.

No survivors.

She bolted up, raced to her phone, grabbed the business card Anna had given her, and made the call. It went immediately to voice mail. Katie choked back a sob as Anna's precise voice came on the line asking her to please leave a message. Katie hung up without saying anything.

Her next thought hit her like a lightning bolt. "Shaw!" she exclaimed.

She called the number he had given her. It rang four times and she thought it too was about to go to voice mail when someone answered.

"*Allo?*" a woman's voice said in French.

Confused for a moment Katie said, "Um . . . can I speak to Shaw?"

The woman at the other end spoke to her again in French.

Katie thought quickly, trying to conjure up her college French and the little she had learned while overseas. She asked the woman if she spoke English and she said a bit. Katie asked her where Shaw was.

The woman did not know that name.

"You've got his phone."

Now the woman sounded confused but asked her if she was family.

That didn't sound too good, thought Katie. For a surreal moment she wondered if Shaw had been with Anna at The Phoenix Group and been killed too. Yet why would a Frenchwoman have his phone if the massacre had taken place in London? "Yes," she told the woman. "I'm family. His sister. Who are you?"

The woman said that she was a nurse and her name was Marguerite.

"A nurse? I don't understand."

"This man, this Shaw is in hospital," Marguerite said.

"What's wrong with him?"

"He has been injured. He is in surgery."

"Where?"

"In Paris."

"Which hospital?"

The woman told her.

"Will he be okay?"

Marguerite said she didn't know the answer to that.

Katie ran to pack. Using her millions of frequent flyer miles, she booked a seat on an Air France flight leaving JFK that night.

She tried to sleep on the flight over, but couldn't. As other passengers dozed all around her, Katie's eyes were glued to the news channel on her personal monitor. There was a bit more information about the Phoenix Group massacre, as the media had initially termed it, but nothing really enlightening. Katie had tried to call Anna before boarding the plane, but it still went to voice mail.

As the jet zoomed across the ocean, Katie asked herself why she was doing this. She barely knew Anna or Shaw. And as Shaw had made quite clear, and quite correctly too, she had no right butting into their lives.

So why are you doing this, Katie? Why?

Perhaps the answer was as simple as she had nothing else in her life. And while she didn't know Anna and Shaw very well, the very dramatic way in which she had met them both made the pair seem far more than mere acquaintances. She cared about them. She wanted them to be happy. And now? And now she felt as though a very close friend had died.

She landed at seven in the morning local time, passed through customs, and grabbed a taxi to the hospital, which was near the center of Paris.

She paid off the cabbie and ran through the front doors. Using her broken French she quickly found someone who spoke English and asked for the location of Shaw's room. There was no one here under that name, she was told.

Damn it! She mentally kicked herself for not asking the nurse on the phone the name Shaw had been admitted under.

"He was badly injured. He was in surgery yesterday. He's a big man, six-five or so, dark hair, really blue eyes."

The woman looked at her blankly. "It is a large hospital, madame."

"I spoke to a nurse here about him. Her name was Marguerite."

"Ah, Marguerite, *bon*, that is helpful," said the woman. She made a call, spoke for a minute, and then nodded at Katie. "Monsieur Ramsey is in room 805."

As Katie ran to the elevator bank, her small carry-on rolling behind her, the woman started speaking into the phone again, her worried gaze on Katie's back.

43

An hour after Anna Fischer was killed, Nicolas Creel's BlackBerry buzzed. He rolled over in bed, picked it up, hit a key, and five words appeared on the screen: "All's well that ends well." It was from Caesar. Who would have thought such a man would have been a fan of the Bard? Creel checked his watch. Afternoon in London, right on schedule. He rolled over and went back to sleep.

Later that evening, Creel smoothed down his tuxedo jacket, adjusted his French cuffs, and rose from his seat to thunderous applause. As he strode to the lectern, he shook the hand of the governor who'd just introduced him to an elite crowd that had paid five thousand dollars a pop for the privilege of seeing Nicolas Creel named man of the year for his philanthropy, the latest of which had been a donation of eighty million dollars for a state-of-the-art cancer wing for children at a major hospital. The wing was not named after Creel, though. He had enough buildings named after him. He'd christened it in his late mother's honor.

The governor of California had been effusive in his introductory remarks, calling the billionaire arms manufacturer a man for the ages with unsurpassed vision and unbridled compassion for others. Had Creel's mother been alive, she no doubt would have shed many tears over that description. Creel's eyes never even grew moist. It was just not his way. As with everything else in his life, every action had multiple motivations. Tonight's event was no exception. Indeed it was money well spent. He had no problem helping kids who were sick. He'd nearly lost his oldest son to leukemia, which had spurred his interest in cancer research and treatments. He might be more greedy and ambitious than most, but he was far more successful than most too.

He actually had a generous heart. And better still, he had plenty of money. Over the decades Creel had given away billions to charity, far more than most of his fellow super-rich. And spreading the wealth made you feel good, made others feel good, and did some good all at the same time. It was also a fine way to honor his mother, to give her the immortality she deserved. But doing good works gave you friends in high places when you needed them. He had a feeling the governor of California and the state in general would be his friend for life. It was a win-win, a classic no-brainer. At eighty million bucks it was actually cheap.

He drew his speech from his pocket and looked

out over the adoring crowd, suddenly wondering if there was a brand-new Miss Hottie out there. There was a good reason he'd left his wife at home. It was definitely time for a change there. She was bored with him and the only asset she possessed of interest to him had long since lost its appeal. He figured he'd opt more for brains this time so long as the lady had an exceptional exterior. He was a man who loved beautiful things around him.

He started off his remarks with a reference to what the media were now callously terming the London Massacre. He then asked for a few moments of silence in respect for those killed. He thought it a nice touch. He bowed his head and even thought of the dead and their families. With this his eyes did grow moist. It really was horrible. He was sorry he'd had to do it. If there had been any other way. What a tragedy. The world had grown so damn complicated and with it good and bad lines blurred to near extinction.

He looked back up and saw a sea of glistening eyes staring back at him. It was a magical moment, it really was. In those few precious moments, he and the audience had bonded. They were in this together. The world had grown a bit closer with this calamity, just as it did when other disasters had occurred. From adversity, from catastrophe come astonishing things. It was no coincidence that the greatest American presidents had all served during wartime. Armed conflict did that to you. Or rather *for* you. You either soared or crashed. There was no in-between, there was nowhere to hide. It was the most perfect scorecard in all of history. It was only with loss, Creel believed, that people fully realized the potential of life.

As he finished his remarks about ten minutes later and returned to his seat, humbly playing down the lengthy standing ovation he received, he reflected for a moment on Caesar's message.

It really had been a remarkable evening, even for him!

Caesar and Pender no doubt thought that this was all about money, about bringing Ares back from the corporate dead. That certainly was one of the reasons, but only one and not the major motivation at that. Only he, Nicolas Creel, realized why he was doing this. And if people had known his reasons, he was certain many would applaud them. Sometimes the ends really did justify the means. In that old cliché, so abused and discredited over the years, existed a gem of wisdom that Creel believed others were finally starting to comprehend.

The ends did justify the means, but only if the ends were truly critical enough. Yet few were. In every endeavor humanity undertook there was an evaluation done. Whether it was to give expensive medical treatment to a ninety-year-old who had little time left anyway, or to stop oil fields from being exploited so that a certain owl could survive, or to spend trillions of dollars and sacrifice hundreds of thousands of lives to establish a beachhead of democracy in Muslim lands in the hope that freedom would spread. Those decisions were made every day. And no matter which way they were decided someone was hurt, often many died, many more lives were destroyed, but the decision had to be made. And that was exactly what Creel had done. Indeed, he had executed it with far more planning and thought than most governments exercised when contemplating something as monumental. Above all, Creel had an exit strategy, whether his plan worked or not.

In the reception that followed the awards ceremony, he did meet several women who might make the cut as future companions, not wives: he'd made up his mind on that. They were always at these types of events, even the ones with brains and degrees from fancy schools. He was just too damn rich and socially well connected to ignore.

Later, as the tall, elegant woman he'd selected to take out for a drink stepped into his limo, Creel had a sense that nothing would ever go wrong in his life again. It was a vitally empowering and—even for men like him—rare moment.

He intended to savor it for as long as he could. For Creel well knew that tomorrow all of that could change.

A smart man understood that victory was not

inevitable. An even smarter man knew that defeat was never really total if you figured out how to handle the aftermath with skill and just the right spin.

And the smartest men of all, even when they lost, they actually won.

Nicolas Creel had always considered himself to be just such a man.

44

When Katie stepped off the elevator and onto the eighth floor a large hand immediately pressed against her shoulder. Her immediate reaction was to rip it off, but when she looked up into the eyes of the broad-shouldered man with the serious expression she thought better of it.

"Come with me," he said in a clipped British accent.

"Why?"

The man's grip tightened on her shoulder. At the same time another man in a suit joined them, even larger and more powerful-looking than the first. He flashed a badge so fast that Katie couldn't see what it said.

"We have some questions for you," the second man said.

"Good, because I've got some questions for you."

The pair bracketed her as they strode down the hall. A door opened and Katie was ushered into a small room and told to sit. She remained standing, arms crossed and a defiant look on her face. One of the men sighed.

"We'll be back in a minute."

Sixty seconds later they returned with another man, older, bald, and wearing a rumpled suit that needed a good cleaning.

He sat down and motioned Katie to do the same. "You want something to drink?"

"No," she said as she sat down across from him. "What I want is to see Shaw."

Frank sat back and studied her. "You mind my asking how you know him?"

"Yes, I do mind."

He nodded at one of his men, who ripped Katie's purse out of her hand. She clutched at it, but the other man held her back. Her wallet and passport were plucked out and given to Frank.

He perused them for a minute. "Katie James, name rings a bell. Reporter, right? You doing some kind of story on Shaw?"

"No, he's a friend."

"That's funny, because I happen to know all of Shaw's friends and you're not one of them."

"I'm a *recent* friend. And can I see your badge or credentials? I want to get my facts right for the exposé I'll do on you if you don't let me the *hell* out of here!"

"How recent?" asked Frank calmly.

She hesitated. "Edinburgh."

"He never mentioned it." Frank studied her passport more closely. "So you flew all the way over from New York to see your *recent* friend? Why?"

"Who the hell are you?"

"Why are you here?" Frank said again.

"Is he alive or dead!"

"Alive, barely. Now answer my question."

"I called him yesterday. A woman answered. She said he was in the hospital, that he was in surgery. So I came."

"I see. And why did you call him?"

"Do *I* get another question answered?"

"Why did you call him?"

Katie glanced nervously around the room. The two other men stared impassively back at her. "Because I heard about The Phoenix Group."

Frank did not look pleased by this at all. "What about them?"

"Oh come on!" Katie exploded. "I doubt you missed the *massacre* in London."

"What's the connection to Shaw?"

"Anna Fischer. And I can see by your expression that you know all about that, so don't try and bullshit. It doesn't sit well."

"How do you know Ms. Fischer?"

"Is she dead?"

"How do you know her, Ms. James?"

Katie debated whether to tell the whole truth or not. She decided on a complete fabrication that would

249

sound plausible. "I was doing a story on The Phoenix Group. I met Anna that way. And through her I met Shaw. We became friends."

"You said you met Shaw in Edinburgh. How did you know he'd be there?"

"Anna told me."

"No she didn't. I can read bullshit as well as you can. Now, you have two options. Either tell me the whole truth, or you can go cool your heels in a French jail as a remand prisoner. And French courts are notoriously slow. You might be in there for a few years before somebody remembers to bring you to trial. And the French aren't known for the cleanliness of their incarceration system."

"I know. I did a story on the French garbage cans they call prisons five years ago and won a major journalism award for the effort. By the way, what offense am I being charged with? Because even the French require that before throwing somebody's butt in jail."

"How about being stupid and uncooperative?"

"How about taking me to the American embassy? I have the address memorized."

"We seem to have reached an impasse." He tapped his fingers on the table. "Will you tell me the truth if I let you see Shaw?"

Now Katie sat back, not looking as defiant or as confident. This time she opted for the truth. "Okay, I was in Edinburgh on holiday. I saw Shaw and another man at the chapel at the castle. Something made me suspicious." She went on to explain what had happened near Gilmerton's Cove, Shaw saving her life, and her following up the clue Shaw had left at his hotel. And then her meeting Anna that way.

"I'm surprised he didn't tell me any of this."

"He barely survived that night. And he didn't know about my tracking Anna down until very recently. And he wasn't happy about it. In fact he got quite angry."

"I'm sure he did."

"Now you know all." Katie hesitated hoping against hope. "Was Anna killed?"

"Yes. Along with everyone else in the place."

Katie looked down at her hands. "Why? They were just a think tank. Anna said no one even paid attention to their work."

"Apparently someone did."

"Does Shaw know, about Anna?" She glanced up at him.

"No," Frank said quietly, not meeting her eye.

"Is he going to be okay?"

"He lost a lot of blood, but the docs say he came through the surgery fine and that he's out of danger. He's a tough guy."

Katie let out a long breath. "Thank God."

"But when he finds out about Anna . . . ?"

"Someone has to tell him."

"I'm not sure it should be anytime soon," Frank said candidly.

"But if he finds out on the TV, newspaper, telephone?"

Frank shook his head. "We've got that covered."

"Won't he wonder why she's not here with him at the hospital?"

"I'll tell him I made her stay away."

"But he'll want to talk to her, at least by phone." She paused. "I never got your name."

He hesitated. "Frank."

"First or last name?"

"Just Frank."

"Okay, Just Frank, they're engaged to be married. He's not going to buy for one second that he can't talk to her or see her."

"I didn't say it was a perfect plan, okay!" Frank suddenly exploded. "He asked me to call her when he thought he was dying. And I told him I would even though I already knew she was dead." He jumped up and started pacing around the small room, hands shoved deep in his pockets, his gaze on his shoes.

"Can I see him? You said if I told you the truth I could see him."

Frank stopped pacing. Without looking at Katie he gave a curt nod to his men.

As they were escorting her out Frank called after her, "Tell him."

She turned back. "What?"

"You were right. Tell him about Anna."

Katie looked stunned. "Me? I . . . I can't. I . . ."

"You said he saved your life. That you're his friend. So start acting like it."

A terrified Katie started to say something else, but Frank slammed the door in her face. A moment later she was walking toward Shaw's room.

And it felt like she was traveling the last, lonely mile to her own execution.

45

With the aid of a red-eye flight on board his private jumbo jet Nicolas Creel had exchanged Los Angeles for Italy and was playing captain today aboard his massive ship, *Shiloh*. The giga-yacht was far longer than a football field with a beam of over seventy feet and boasted nine floors of opulence. Creel's master suite alone measured five thousand square feet, or far larger than the average *house*. It could carry up to thirty guests in extreme luxury since it also housed an indoor pool, cinema, disco, gym, wine cellar, basketball court, every water toy imaginable, two helipads, several hot tubs, and its very own private submarine with a capacity of forty passengers. The sub exited the ship via the bottom of the hull, so Creel could come and go in privacy. The *Shiloh* also carried a crew of several dozen superbly trained professionals whose only goal was to serve with pleasure.

The *Shiloh* was also a very safe ship with state-of-the-art security, motion sensors, and even a special missile-detection system. And while he was parked here in Italian waters, the Italian government, ever mindful of Creel's prestige and his humanitarian and political connections in their country, provided a couple of police boats to stand guard.

Despite its gigantic size, it being far larger than many naval vessels, the *Shiloh* could still manage a top speed of twenty-five knots, allowing it to easily outrun any storm.

All in all, Creel had considered it a bargain at a mere $300 million. Of all his residences around the world, he loved the *Shiloh* the best. As a youngster he'd had a secret passion for the sea and a desire, never fulfilled, to join the merchant marine and see the world as a sailor.

In keeping with his nautical surroundings, today he had on a dark blue double-breasted jacket, cream-colored slacks, and a white seaman's cap. He watched as the chopper headed toward the ship, covering the still waters below at just over a hundred knots. The aircraft slowed, hovered, hit its pad mark, and the blades wound down. Dick Pender stepped off, shrouded in a wide-brimmed hat, large sunglasses, and a long leather coat. He carried a slim briefcase that flapped against his leg from the prop wash.

Creel met him on the aft deck and escorted him down wide polished teak stairs to a large walnut burl-paneled room amidships. Outside the large porthole windows the coastline of Italy was visible across the dark brooding plain of the Mediterranean.

"Is the missus with you?" Pender asked as he

removed his hat and coat and threw them over a chair.

"No. The crew enjoys her *nude* sunbathing habit a little too much. She's in Switzerland at some spa rejuvenating herself. From what exactly I was never clear about."

Pender glanced at the flat-screen TV on the wall where scenes of the London Massacre were being replayed.

"Quite a mess over there," Pender said. "You've been a busy man."

Creel had enough information to bury Pender many times over and the man knew it. So he never worried about Pender turning on him. And no one knew Pender was here. He came in secret and he would leave in secret. It was just the way Creel worked. When you basically had your own airline, there was nothing easier to accomplish.

"Let's get down to it."

Pender spread out the contents of his briefcase. "I'm assuming the appropriate materials were left behind at The Phoenix Group?"

"Correct."

"Any indication whether the police have gone over them?"

"It's early yet, but they're easy to find. Only a matter of time."

"You have someone on the inside?"

Creel simply nodded at this question.

"You know when you called and told me what you'd discovered about The Phoenix Group it seemed too perfect."

"I thought the same thing," Creel admitted. "But it all checked out, or else I wouldn't have done it. So tell me the steps you have planned to get our next 'truth' out to the public."

Pender picked up a piece of paper. "For maximum exploitation and dissemination we recommend going to the Web first and letting the mainstream outlets reverse engineer the story. The major networks don't like to acknowledge the fact but they troll the blog world constantly looking for cutting-edge stories and trends. It'll make it appear to be more grassroots and homegrown that way. Lends credibility and throws off suspicion."

Creel nodded in agreement. "So we get the payoff of Phoenix's true ownership that way, which will segue nicely into the inevitable leak that will come out of what's discovered in London."

"That's how I see it playing out. We have the revelation of ownership and then the really earth-shattering news of the activity having been conducted there coming out. It'll be disputed, of course," he added.

"Of course it will, and that will only lend credibility to it being true. If you dispute, you lose."

"Your boots on the ground worked to perfection."

"Well, they're not done yet," Creel responded cryptically.

"When will the leak come?"

"She is primed and ready. I'll pull the trigger on that when I deem the time right."

"And she can be trusted?"

"It's not a question of trust."

"And after she's performed the leak?"

"Then I will decide what to do, Dick."

"In my experience," Pender began, before Creel cut him off by lighting a cigar and turning away from him and picking up a decanter.

"A glass of port? I always find port particularly supportive of grand scheme-making."

"I'm sure your port is better than anyone else's," Pender said, smiling.

A ship's horn sounded.

Pender glanced out the starboard porthole in time to see a twenty-six-foot launch pulling up with about a dozen excited children dressed in shabby clothing on board.

He looked at Creel with an amused expression. "You running tours on the *Shiloh*, Mr. Creel? Earning some extra income from the dirty-faced Mediterranean rabble?"

Creel didn't return the smile. He rose from the chair and pressed down his sailor's jacket and reset the cap on his head. This was why he'd worn the uniform today, for the children.

"They're Italian kids from a local orphanage. They

never get to do anything. So when we're at anchor here I always have them come out. For a good meal, new clothes, toys, and some fun. They're just children; they should have some fun, Dick."

"Very generous of you."

"It's why I didn't have my wife come. It's impossible for the woman to keep her clothes on while on this boat, even with little kids running around. I mean, adults are one thing, and if the crew wants to ogle her, but children? It's really quite an appalling facet of her personality. Had I known before the wedding? Well, there you are."

"A small dent in your aura of omniscience," Pender said, not bothering to hide his smile.

"Dick, I've found that you occasionally take liberties with me that you have no right to take."

Pender looked startled. "I'm sorry, Mr. Creel. I had no intention—"

Creel set a glass of port in front of him. "By the way, it is the best."

A pale-faced Pender nervously lifted his glass with Creel.

Creel said, "To a better world."

"To a better world," Pender mumbled nervously.

"Don't look so glum, Dick, I wasn't being *entirely* serious."

This comment didn't seem to make Pender feel any better at all.

"I'll be back in a few minutes after I get the kids settled down to eat. Then after that I'm going to take them on a submarine ride."

"You have a submarine!"

"I have everything, Dick. I thought you knew that."

"Yes, but Italian orphans on a submarine?"

"And when one has everything, one needs to share," Creel added firmly.

As Creel headed abovedeck to see his youthful guests, Pender set back to work. However, part of his mind was contemplating the oddness of mankind in general and the peculiarity of one enormously rich man in particular. He also made a mental note to never, ever treat himself as an equal to the billionaire. That, he knew, could be deadly. It was perfectly true that there were only a very few people who could do what Dick Pender could do.

But it was also true that there was only *one* Nicolas Creel.

46

Shaw slowly opened his eyes. His first image was the far wall where a small cabinet sat. When he moved his gaze to the right, his line of sight took in the pair of long shapely legs standing next to the door.

He smiled, even though the painkillers were beginning to wear off and it felt like his left arm had been amputated.

"Anna?" he said, trying to lift up his good arm to reach out to her.

The legs moved forward, coming more sharply into focus.

"It's Katie, Katie James. Do you remember me?" she said awkwardly, her voice actually cracking.

God, he mistook me for Anna!

Katie stopped next to the bed. Shaw very slowly moved his head up so he could see her standing there.

He said in a drug-induced, halting voice, "What are you doing here?"

Katie was momentarily frozen. She hadn't thought of that one. What was she doing here, other than because of Anna? Her mind suddenly snapped into action.

"I called your cell phone and a nurse answered. She said you'd been hurt, so I came to, um, check up on you. See that you were okay."

"You came to Paris?"

"Well, I was just over in London," she lied. "It was a quick trip."

Katie pulled up a chair, placed her purse on the nightstand, and sat down next to him. She slipped her hands through the side rails of the bed and took his large hand in hers, squeezing it. She saw the huge bandage covering his left arm, and the stain of blood streaking its outer edge, and also the bruises and cuts on his face and neck.

"Boy, you look like a train wreck, but they say you're going to be fine."

"Where's Anna?" he said groggily.

She started to speak, but couldn't say it. She couldn't. The news might kill him. "I'm not really sure. Has she been contacted?"

Shaw nodded absently. "I told Frank. He took care of it," he said vaguely.

He suddenly winced and clutched at his wounded arm, his left side obviously seizing up in pain.

Katie looked frantically around, saw the call button and hit it. A voice came on, Katie spoke to the nurse, and a minute later she arrived. More medication was sent through his IV drip and Shaw slowly drifted off.

Katie held on to his hand, kicked her shoes off, and leaned against the rail, watching the rise and fall of the man's chest.

She sat there, unaware of the time passing. Exhausted by her travels and lack of sleep, her eyes finally closed. More time skipped by as she and Shaw slept heavily. Katie finally opened her eyes and found Shaw's gaze locked on her. She slowly let go of his hand and sat back.

"How are you feeling?" she asked.

"Why did you come here?" His tone was harsh and cut right into her. The meds-induced fog was clearly gone now.

"I told you. I heard you were hurt. And I mean, you know, you saved my life. One good deed deserves another," she added lamely, instantly wishing she hadn't said the stupid words. He seemed to stare right through her skin, peering directly into her soul of souls, a place not even she had ventured that often. It was completely unnerving.

"Are you hungry or thirsty?" she asked quickly, hoping to find shelter from his withering gaze in mundane matters.

"Where's Frank? You had to get past Frank to get in here."

"He's around somewhere."

Shaw tried to rise from the bed, but Katie gently forced him back down.

"You've got tubes coming out all over the place," she warned him. "Just lie still or you'll really do some damage."

"I want to see Frank," he said firmly. "I want to know where Anna is!"

"I'll go and see if I can find him."

"You *do* that!"

She found her mouth running dry as he stared at her accusingly, as though she'd committed some crime. And in truth Katie felt as though she had. She had lied to him and knew he could sense it.

She nearly ran from the room.

"So you didn't tell him?" Frank said with the same accusatory tone Shaw had just used. They were back in the small room.

"He's hurt and vulnerable and depressed enough," Katie snapped. "It's not right to tell him now."

Frank didn't look convinced, but he also didn't argue the point.

"He wants to see you," Katie said.

"I'm sure he does, but I can't tell him what he wants to hear."

"So what do we do?"

"We could keep him drugged up until he's healed a little more."

"How did he get hurt?"

Frank looked at her incredulously. "What, you want me to give you a debriefing?"

"If he keeps working for you he's going to end up dead, you know that, don't you?"

"It's a risky profession. We try to be as careful as we can."

"Does that include having your own men shoot at him? Because that seems a bit much even for your 'profession.'"

Frank spun around to stare at her. He was about to say something when the sounds of a commotion reached their ears. Katie and Frank raced out and headed toward Shaw's room. Screams pierced the air, there was a crash like a table had been overturned. A door slammed open. Multiple pairs of feet were racing over the tile floor.

Another cry seemed to rise above all the others.

"That's Shaw!" Frank exclaimed. "What the hell's going on?"

Katie suddenly glanced down at her hands. "Oh my God!"

"What?" Frank said quickly.

"My purse. I left my purse in his room. My cell phone was in it. It has Internet capability." Katie's face turned deathly white.

"Son of a bitch!" Frank screamed as he rushed down the hall.

They turned the corner and stopped.

Shaw was standing at the other end of the corridor, his hospital gown nearly torn off, blood running down his arm and tubes hanging off his body. Katie saw her phone clutched in his bloodied hand.

Katie's gaze spun to Shaw's face and she found she couldn't look away. His features held anguish and heartbreak like she had never witnessed before.

"Shaw!" she cried out and ran to him.

He had dropped to his knees by the time she reached him. She threw her arms around him, tears spilling down her face.

"Anna!" he screamed. "Anna!" He did not even seem to be aware that Katie was there.

"I'm sorry, I'm so sorry," she said into his ear. "Oh, God, I'm so sorry."

Hands pulled her away. People were shouting in French at her, but she wouldn't let go. She couldn't let go of him.

Then a voice barked at her in English. "He's bleeding to death! Let him go! Or you'll kill him, lady!"

Katie immediately released her grip, backed off, but continued to stare at Shaw as the hospital personnel put him on a gurney and whisked him away.

Frank glared at Katie, reached down, picked up her phone where Shaw had dropped it, and tossed it back to her.

"Thanks for all your help, James!" he said bitterly. "Next time, why don't you just bring a gun and pop a round right in his brain? It's quicker that way." He stalked off.

Katie stared after him for a few moments then fearfully glanced down at the phone's screen. Emblazoned across it was the headline "London Massacre." She threw the Nokia down the hall and sank to the floor with fresh tears pouring down her face.

47

Shaw slowly put on his loose-fitting shirt, careful to work around the thick bandage on his left arm. The wound was so deep and wide that the surgeon had had to staple the folds of skin back together. A plastic surgeon had also been called in and had done the best she could at the time. There would be scars, the doctor told Shaw, who really could have cared less.

"We can do another surgery later, after the staples come out, fix it up better," she'd told him.

"No," Shaw answered without hesitation. He could still fire a gun, that's all he cared about right now.

Fortunately, the hacksaw blade had managed to miss his tendons and there had been no nerve injury either. Yet as the doctor had told him, "If that blade had struck a centimeter to the right or left, we might not be having this conversation."

It would be a while before Shaw was at full strength, but the doctors assured him he would make a complete recovery.

"I want to go to London, today," Shaw announced

to Frank as he finished packing his bag in the hospital room.

Frank sat moodily in a chair. "Let me guess why."

"How fast can I get there?"

"Chunnel train's quicker than planes these days. You can be in London in the same time it takes you to get through De Gaulle."

"Private wings?"

"Sorry, I don't have any available right now."

"Then book me on the train. Make it for early this afternoon."

"Are you sure you want to do this?"

"Book me on the train, Frank."

"Okay, then what?"

"Where's Katie James?"

Frank looked surprised. "Why?"

"I want to thank her."

"Are you out of your frigging mind? After what she did?"

"What she did was fly halfway around the world to see if I was okay. Where is she?"

"Hell if I know. I'm not the lady's keeper. I've got my hands full with your ass."

"Tell me where she is," Shaw persisted.

"What happened to me giving the orders and you following them?" Frank said spitefully.

"It stopped when Anna died because I don't give a shit anymore. Where's Katie?"

"I told you, I—"

Shaw interrupted. "You don't let anybody just walk away. Now *where* is she?" he barked.

Frank glanced out the window. "Staying at some friend's apartment off Rue de Rivoli near the Hotel de Ville while the guy's out of the country."

"I'll need the address. Can you get me a car?"

"Can you drive with that busted wing?"

"So long as it's not a clutch."

Frank helped Shaw slip on his jacket. Shaw picked up his bag using his good arm.

Frank said, "Look, I'm sorry about Anna, Shaw. Really sorry. And believe it or not, I was going to let you go when you got married. And you can take as much time off as you need now."

Shaw's features clouded. "Why the hell are you telling me this now? And just for the record, why are you cutting me any slack at all?"

Frank stepped over to the window. He turned back. "Just looking for skinheads," he said, smiling.

"Why, Frank? You hate me. I hate you. Not a great working relationship, but at least the ground rules are understood."

Frank plopped back down in the chair, his gaze on the wall. "How do you think I came to work for this fine organization?"

"Tell me."

He looked at Shaw. "I had the same choice you did. And my ass is still here."

Shaw gaped at him. "You got railroaded too! And, what, you paid it forward to me?"

"Yeah! So what? And *just* for the record, I still hate you."

"Thanks, Frank. And here I was thinking my life couldn't get any better."

Frank looked down at his beefy hands. "She must've really loved you. I never had anybody like that."

"Well, now I don't either." Shaw paused at the door. "Is Anna's body still at the morgue in London?"

Frank nodded slowly. "They haven't released any of them yet. Ongoing investigation," he added unnecessarily.

"She'd have wanted to be buried back in Germany. I'm sure her parents are making arrangements." A part of Shaw's mind couldn't even contemplate, much less understand, that he was talking so calmly, so rationally about Anna's upcoming funeral. He suddenly felt as though if he didn't get out into the open air, his skin would catch on fire.

Frank followed him out. "Are you going to see James now?"

"Yes."

"Want me to tag along?"

"No." Shaw suddenly stopped and held his injured arm, evidently in pain.

Frank put a supporting arm on his shoulder. "Sorry

271

about the screwup with the Nazi freaks," he said in what seemed a sincere manner. "Right-hand, left-hand crap. It won't happen again."

"Yeah."

Frank made a call as they were heading out of the hospital to the car waiting for Shaw on the street. He wrote something down on a piece of paper and handed it to him. "James's address."

"Thanks."

Shaw slid into the driver's seat and then popped his head back out the window. "Call me with the train info."

Frank nodded glumly. "You're just going to see Anna's body, right? You're not going anywhere near where it happened. Right?"

"I'll see you later."

"Damn it, Shaw, you are not to go anywhere near The Phoenix Group. Do you hear me?"

"I'll make a deal with you, Frank. A deal so good you can't refuse. Wanta hear it?"

Frank looked at him suspiciously. "I don't know, do I?"

"You let me poke around The Phoenix Group."

"Shaw," Frank began, but Shaw kept talking over him.

"You let me do that, I'll work with this MI5 guy Royce on the Russian piece."

"I don't think that's—"

Shaw interrupted. "And I'll sweeten the pot. You

sign off on it, and I'll keep working for you until I drop."

Frank was silent for a long moment, then slowly said, "But what about retiring?"

Shaw gave him a look that somehow contained both helplessness and menace. "Retiring to what, Frank? Is it a deal?"

Frank hesitated. "Yeah, sure."

Frank started to say something else but with a squeal of tires, Shaw was gone.

Frank turned and walked down the street to find a bar and a drink.

48

A wisp of rising sunlight managed to slip by the window blinds, creep across the floor, and end up briefly settling on the bare calf that poked out from under the sheet. Later it traveled ruler-straight across the bed and slid to the floor where it glanced off the empty blue gin bottle lying there, causing beads of swirling, reflected light to kaleidoscope off the ceiling.

The demons had finally caught up to Katie James. The last few days were lost to her in a drunken binge of such mammoth proportions that the only thing she remembered later was the feeling of deep shame. *And* the worst hangover she'd ever had.

In the throes of some nightmare she kicked off the sheet and lay there in a long-sleeved T-shirt and baggy gym shorts, perspiration rising through her pores and moistening her clothes. Her breathing became normal and she finally grew still, the slight lift of her chest and her pink flesh the only real evidence that she was still alive.

She never heard the front bell, the accompanying

knock, the pounding on the door, or the call of her name. She never heard the front door open, or the footsteps traversing the small living room, or the bedroom door swinging wide. She never felt the other person's presence in the room, never felt anything when the intruder lifted the sheet off the floor and covered her with it.

The slight creak of the bedsprings as the visitor sat down didn't arouse her either. The quiet call of her name? Oblivious. The gentle shake of her shoulder? No response.

However, the glass of water thrown in her face? Now *that* got the lady's attention.

She sat up sputtering, rubbing at her eyes and nose.

"What the—" she began angrily until her eyes focused on Shaw sitting there holding the empty glass and staring at her.

She let out one more gag as the rest of the water that had made its way into her windpipe went down hard. "How did you get in?"

"I rang the bell, pounded on the door, called out your name. I did the same thing when I got in. You never let out a peep. I didn't think anyone was here until, well, I actually saw you lying in this bed."

She rubbed at her throbbing temples. "I . . . I'm a heavy sleeper."

Shaw picked up an empty bottle of gin. "You're a heavy something." He hooked a second empty bottle and then a third and then a fourth.

"You mix gin, bourbon, and scotch?"

"When in Scotland, you know."

"We're in *France*," he said, frowning.

She ran a hand through her tangles of blonde hair and yawned. "Oh, right, Paris," she said absently. Then something seemed to strike right through the clouds of alcoholic stupor. "Oh my God, *right*." She hastily sat up straighter.

"Shaw, I am so sorry. For everything. For the stupid cell phone, for lying to you." She paused. "And about Anna."

Shaw took his time lining up the empty bottles on a bureau set against one wall. "I actually wanted to thank you for coming to see how I was."

Katie seemed surprised by this. "You didn't have to do that. Especially after yesterday at the hospital. It was yesterday, right?"

"Actually, it was five days ago."

She looked stunned. "Five days! You're joking?"

He glanced over at the line of bottles. "Does your head *feel* like I'm joking?"

She stared at him, then at the bottles, and sat back on the bed. "I hadn't touched a drop in over six months, can you believe that?"

He glanced at the line of bottles. "No, I can't."

She let out a deep groan. "Well, it's true. I . . . I can't believe I did this. I can't believe I fell off the wagon."

Shaw looked at the line of bottles again. "It wasn't

a wagon, it was a *cliff*. I'll wait in the next room. Get showered and dressed. Then I'll buy you some breakfast." He headed to the door.

"Wait a minute, what are you doing out of the hospital?"

"I'm done with hospitals."

"You really think so?" she said doubtfully, eyeing the bulge under his left jacket sleeve.

"I'm heading to London later today on the Chunnel. But first I wanted to talk to you about Anna."

"What do you want to know?"

"Why someone would have wanted to kill her."

Katie stared at him blankly. "But I don't know anything about that."

"You might think you don't. But you also might have seen or heard something when you visited her that could help me."

"Shaw, do you really think you're well enough to take this on?"

He turned and fixed his eyes on her, eyes that were so blue and potent that Katie found herself holding her breath, digging her fingernails nervously into her palms like a schoolkid in serious trouble.

He said quietly, "My life is over, Katie. But whoever did this to Anna is going to die. And soon."

Every hair on the back of Katie's neck stood straight up and her skin actually goose-pimpled for the first time in years. Her head was pounding and her stomach gave a sudden disquieting lurch.

"Now get dressed. Please."

As soon as he left the room she sprinted to the bathroom and threw up five days' worth of liquid hell.

49

They ate outside at a small brasserie that had partial views of the Seine across Quai de Gesvres. If Katie craned her neck just a bit she could glimpse the spires of Notre Dame Cathedral in the middle of the famous river. The Louvre was less than half a mile to their west, the Bastille a little farther than that to the east.

The coffee was strong, the bread hot, the simple egg dish as delicious as only the French seem to be able to accomplish.

"You met her in London," Shaw said. "At her office? Her flat?"

"We first met at a café, then we moved on to her office."

"Anything strike you as out of the ordinary when you got there?"

Katie shrugged as she delicately took a forkful of eggs while her stomach continued to do little flip-flops. "It seemed ordinary and extraordinary at the same time. A beautiful old row house on a quiet street in the heart of London filled with a bunch of scholars who write things no one reads, or at least that last part was Anna's description." She glanced over at him. "Have you ever been there?"

Shaw nodded. "And just for the hell of it about a year ago I checked the real estate records to see how valuable that building was. Care to guess?" Katie shook her head and bit into a piece of toast as she stared at him curiously. "Sixteen million pounds."

The toast nearly fell out of Katie's mouth. "That's over thirty million dollars."

"That's right. And that was just the *purchase price* ten years ago. It's obviously worth a lot more now."

"How long had Anna worked there?"

"Five years. She was a senior analyst, one of the best they had."

"I'm sure. She told me basically what they do there. But who owns the Phoenix Group?"

"She said once. Some rich American recluse living in Arizona, hence the name. Although she also told me she thought it came from the mythical bird, the phoenix."

"The one that never dies," Katie said, and then her face reddened when she found Shaw staring at her.

"Didn't turn out to be a very apt name, did it?" he noted.

Katie said quickly, "But there must be more to The Phoenix Group than people knew. So we really need to nail down who or what it is."

"No, *I* need to do that."

"I thought we were working this together."

"You thought wrong."

"I want to find out what happened to Anna too."

Shaw just shook his head. "What else can you tell me?"

"Why should I tell you anything now?"

"Because I asked you politely."

His eyes locked on her again and Katie felt herself quivering under their burn.

"Well, when I was about to leave I noticed she had all this research on her desk."

"She always did. That was her job."

"No, I mean it was about one thing, the so-called Red Menace."

Shaw sat forward. "Did you ask her about it? Was she working on it for The Phoenix Group?"

She shook her head. "Anna said she was just curious. That it was just something she was working on in I suppose her spare time."

"When we were in Dublin she was very interested about this R.I.C. organization. She went online trying to dig up some stuff but didn't find much."

"Well, it seemed like she was still very curious." She looked thoughtful for a moment. "You don't think her employer had anything to do with any of that? I mean trying to find out who was behind the Red Menace? And maybe they did and that would explain the shooting?"

Shaw slipped a business card out of his pocket and looked at it. Edward Royce, MI5. The man Frank had wanted him to team with on the Red Menace investigation. He was based in London. Shaw didn't believe for an instant that The Phoenix Group had been investigating the Red Menace and that was the reason for the slaughter. Yet Royce probably had the connections to get Shaw at least into the building if Shaw agreed to help him on the Red Menace situation.

"Anna would've told me if she were working on it for them."

Katie licked her lips and said nervously, "Take this in the spirit in which it's offered."

Shaw looked up from the card. "What?"

"Could Anna have been keeping things from you, I mean about what she really did?" She added quickly as his features turned grim, "Look, you weren't exactly truthful with her. It's just a thought."

"It *is* a thought. I'll keep it in mind. Thanks."

"So when do you leave?"

"Soon."

Shaw's BlackBerry vibrated. He had some difficulty getting it out of his coat pocket so Katie helped him pull it out. "Do you want me to bring up your messages?" She asked this as she watched him struggling with the device basically one-handed.

"I can manage," he said, perhaps suspecting that this was a ploy on Katie's part to read his mail. He glanced at the screen. He had a first-class ticket on the Eurostar out of Gare du Nord station to St. Pancras in

London. He'd be staying at the recently reopened Savoy. At least Frank didn't do things on the cheap. It was partial compensation for a job that involved the potential of violent death on a minute-by-minute basis.

"Will you at least call and let me know what you find out?"

He stood after dropping some euros on the table to pay for the meal. "Sorry, I can't do that."

"Why?"

"Because I don't want to. That explanation cover it for you?"

It took Katie a moment to realize he was merely throwing her own words back at her, when he'd quizzed her about not getting plastic surgery done on the scar on her arm.

"No, but I guess I don't have a choice."

"Thanks for your help. Now go back home and get on with your life."

"Oh, yeah, great," she exclaimed in mock delight. "I hear the *New York Times* needs a new managing editor. Or maybe I can take over Christiane Amanpour's slot on CNN. I've always wanted to cross over to TV. I'll make millions. I have no idea why I didn't do it years ago."

"Take care of yourself, Katie. And lay off the drink."

He left her sitting there at the table, her head pounding. Five minutes passed and she hadn't moved, just sat staring at nothing, because that's apparently all she had left, nothing. Her ringing phone jolted her. It was a stateside number she didn't recognize.

"Hello?"

"Katie James?"

"Yes."

"I'm Kevin Gallagher, features editor at *Scribe*. We're a fairly new daily based in the U.S."

"I've read some of your stuff. You've got some good reporters."

"Quite a compliment coming from a two-time Pulitzer Prize winner. Look, I'm sure you're busy, but I got your number from a buddy at the *Trib*. I understand you're no longer there."

"That's right," Katie said, then quickly added, "Irreconcilable differences. Why are you calling?"

"Hey, it doesn't take a rocket scientist to figure out that a reporter at your level doesn't become available all that often. I'd like to hire you to cover the story for the paper."

"*The* story?"

Gallagher chuckled. "At least the only story anyone cares about right now."

"The Red Menace?"

"Nope," he said. "We've already got a team on that. I meant the London Massacre."

Katie's heartbeat quickened.

"Katie, you still there?"

"Yeah, yeah. How would we work it?"

"We can't pay what you're used to at the *Trib*. But we'll pay you per story at the going rate for somebody like you plus reasonable expenses. You break anything big I can go back for more. You have free rein on how to get the story. How's that sound?"

"Sounds like exactly what I've been looking for. I happen to be in Europe right now as a matter of fact."

"I call that a kickass coincidence."

I wouldn't.

"I can e-mail you the contract and other essentials."

They spoke for a couple more minutes and then Katie clicked off. She couldn't believe this incredible turn of events. She checked her watch. She'd just have time to catch the one o'clock Eurostar to London.

50

The yellow-and-blue Eurostar train left right on time, and once past the suburbs of Paris quickly accelerated to over two hundred kilometers an hour. The rails were designed for high-speed trains and the ride was smooth, with just enough gentle swaying to induce a nice nap if one were so inclined.

Shaw was in first class where he enjoyed a wide comfy chair and a three-course meal complete with wine, professionally presented by a smartly uniformed steward who spoke both English and French. Shaw, however, didn't eat or drink anything. He just stared moodily out the window.

He rarely thought about the past. But as the train sailed along, he did so if for no other reason than he no longer had a future to ponder. Life had come full circle for him. Abandoned in an orphanage by a woman who was his natural mother but someone he could no longer remember, and then thrown onto the garbage heap of a string of fake families who'd done him no good and much harm, he had constructed his adult life around being a loner. Before he had involuntarily joined Frank's group he had spent his years going from country to country doing the paid bidding of others. He neither cared about the personal risk nor the moral implications of his actions. He had hurt people and been hurt by them. Some of what he'd done had made the world safer; some of it resulted in added danger for the six billion other people who shared the planet. Yet all of what he had done had been authorized by governments, or organizations acting on behalf of such governments. And that had been the sum total of his existence.

Until Anna had come into his life.

Before he met her he believed his life would end when one of Frank's missions went seriously awry. And he was perfectly fine with that. You live, you die. Before Anna, Shaw had no reason to draw his life out other than from innate self-preservation. Yet when one is only living half a life even that instinct becomes worn down, dulled over the years. With Anna, he suddenly had a real reason to survive. He prepared harder and harder for each job, because he wanted to come back. To her.

And then he had planned his escape from Frank. And his future life with Anna. And it seemed that he was so close. Even with Frank being Frank, it was still possible, so long as he could stay alive.

And that was the heartless irony that tore at him now.

It had never occurred to him, never even entered

his personal equation, that Anna would be the one to die a violent death instead of him. *Never.*

He stared out the window at the rolling landscape of breathtaking beauty. It meant nothing to him and never would. The only thing of beauty he had ever cared about was currently inside a refrigerator in a London morgue. Her beauty now only existed in Shaw's mind, in his memories. That should have been a comfort to him, but wasn't. Eyes open or closed, all he saw was the one person he'd ever allowed himself to love. That image would be with him forever, his penance for thinking he could ever possibly deserve to be normal. Or happy.

He only had one goal now. To kill. After that, he would end his life as he had started it. Alone.

Katie was in another train car one down from Shaw, though she didn't know it. As the picturesque French countryside raced past, she was focused, despite her new assignment, on the grieving Shaw, and what would happen when he got to London. He would, of course, go to The Phoenix Group building and, with his connections, probably get in somehow. He would also visit Anna's flat. He would have to go there, she told herself. There would be no way he could avoid it.

So deep in thought was Katie that she didn't even notice the train passing through Calais and then entering the tunnel, heading downward and eventually making its way underneath the bedrock of the English Channel. With billions of tons of water overhead, she looked out onto the well-lighted tunnel, unconcerned with leaks or walls of water smashing the train flat.

Twenty-five minutes later the train emerged into bright sunshine. They were in England. The whole trip would take about 140 very pleasant minutes and Katie had electricity for her laptop computer and the convenience of her cell phone, though she had no one to call. Indeed, after the episode at the hospital, she had no desire ever to use her cell phone again.

She thought too about Shaw's words: *My life is over. But whoever did this to Anna is going to die.* She had no doubt that he meant it. She had no doubt at all he would try to kill the person or persons with his bare hands, injured or not.

But after that? What would he do? Or what if he died in the attempt? Someone who could orchestrate the slaughter of nearly thirty people was not someone who could be easily killed.

And she had stories to write now. What would Shaw think if he found out she was reporting on the London murders, earning a living from Anna's death? But that was what she did. She was a journalist. Still, though, he would be angry. Very angry.

As she was thinking about this, she noticed the small bottle of red wine on her tray that had been served with lunch. She'd kept it when the steward had cleared the tray. Katie kept staring at it as the train rolled on. Twenty minutes later when the Eurostar reached the outer fringes of London and the old dwellings with their unique chimneystacks, she was still gazing at the wine. She unscrewed the top, took a whiff and a quick gulp, and felt immediate gratification followed by crushing, searing guilt. Yet she took another swig. And the guilt grew a thousandfold. She screwed the cap back on, dropped the bottle on her pulldown tray, and muttered, "Shit."

The fellow next to her heard this, glanced at her and then at the wine. "Bad year?" he asked with a smile.

She gave him a burning stare. "Bad life!"

He quickly went back to his newspaper.

Katie knew she could not do her job this way. She could not help herself as a drunkard. She could not wallow in self-pity, no matter how enticing that might seem right now. When a steward walked by she stopped him and asked him to take the bottle away.

A few minutes later they pulled into St. Pancras Station. Katie detrained and quickly made her way to the cab stand.

Like Shaw she would be staying in the Strand in the West End of the city, but not at digs as nice as the Savoy. London was not cheap at any time, but one could find bargains, and Katie had traveled enough to where she knew them all. If her stay in London was going to be a long one, she hoped, much as she had done in Paris, to crash at the flat of another news correspondent friend of hers who was away more than she was home.

She checked into her cut-rate hotel, dropped her bag in her room and took a cab to The Phoenix Group building. At some point she would probably run into Shaw. If she did, she felt fairly confident of her action plan.

I'll run like hell.

51

On the drive over to Anna's former office, Shaw pulled out the business card he'd been given and called MI5 agent Edward Royce. The man answered on the second ring and Shaw explained that he was in London and had reconsidered helping Royce on the Red Menace investigation.

When Royce asked about his change of heart, Shaw said, "Long story not worth going into, but I've got a favor to ask. I've already cleared it with Frank."

"He called me."

"Really, and said what?"

"To help you any way I could. He told me of your . . . personal connection to the murders in London."

"Can you get me access to the building?"

"Well, we might be able to kill two birds with one stone, actually. How does that plan work for you?"

"What are you talking about?" Shaw said curiously.

"You'll see when you get here."

"Here? Where?"

"At The Phoenix Group building."

Shaw's mouth sagged. "What are you doing there?"

"I'll see you when you get here," Royce said tersely.

Shaw put his phone away and leaned back, rubbing his injured arm.

What the hell is going on?

After he'd gotten to Katie's cell phone and found out about Anna's death, the next two days in the hospital had been worse than any mission he'd ever done, worse than any nightmare his subconscious had ever conjured. He did remember being sedated again and again after busting up his hospital room and actually throwing someone against a wall. This outlet for his grief, his fury, hadn't helped. It just kept building until his mind and body had been unable to endure any more. And he had just collapsed. He actually thought he'd died. And a real big chunk of him wished he had.

For twenty-four hours he didn't move or speak. He just stared at the white wall of the hospital, much as he had done as a little boy at the orphanage, trying to fashion a different reality from the abject collapse of his life. Yet when he'd finally risen from his bed, Anna was still dead. She would always be dead.

The only thing keeping him going now was the thought of finding and killing whoever had done it. It was the one goal that could possibly keep him from simply disintegrating. He hadn't lapsed into melodrama when he'd told Katie that his life was over. It *was* over.

All he had to do now was finish it right, by avenging Anna.

He grabbed a cab and headed to the place where her life had ended. What he really wanted to do was run the other way.

52

Royce met Shaw at the front door where police lines were still strung across. Inside the building the activity was intense, with police and forensic teams examining every square inch of the place. As Shaw stepped carefully around their work he saw the pools of dried blood and white tape outlines that distinctly marked where a body had dropped.

Royce eyed his injured arm. "What the bloody hell happened to you?"

"My dog bit me. What did you mean about killing two birds with one stone? And why are you here in the middle of a homicide investigation?"

"I'd like you to see this first."

He led Shaw into a room on the first floor that had been set up as a crime scene investigation office. On one table was a computer terminal. Royce sat down in front of it and started hitting keys.

"We got a video feed from a surveillance camera on the street that was put there to record license plates for the congestion charge. Here's what it captured on the day the killings happened."

Shaw looked over Royce's shoulder as the screen sprang to life. The positioning of the camera up on a pole afforded a complete exterior view of the building. A van with a satellite dish sprouting from the top pulled up in front of the building and two men got out.

Royce explained, "The uniform of the London road crews."

The men pulled a number of traffic cones from the van and used them to cordon off one end of the street and the sidewalks in both directions. The instant this was done Shaw noted the satellite dish started moving.

"They're jamming cell phone reception," he deduced.

Royce nodded. "After having earlier cut the hard-line phone wires to the building."

Shaw stiffened as the next frame on the screen showed a half dozen men erupt from the van and race into the building. It happened so fast it was almost impossible to clearly see their movements. Even someone looking out a window or passing down the street might not have thought anything was out of the ordinary.

"Slow it down," Shaw instructed.

A minute later, the scene was replayed again at half speed and the picture was zoomed in. The men were all tall and fit-looking. Lifelike masks covered their faces, and any weapons they might have been carrying were concealed under the long coats each wore. Shaw scrutinized each figure, looking for anything of distinction, any exposed skin that might have a memorable marking on it, but he came away disappointed.

Royce, who'd been watching him, nodded in sympathy. "I know, we've been over it a dozen times and nothing hit us either. They were obviously pros. They knew the camera was there and acted accordingly."

"I take it the camera feed isn't reviewed in real time?"

"Unfortunately not, otherwise it would have elicited an energetic response from the Metropolitan Police, I can assure you. They also must have been aware of that."

"I probably shouldn't even bother asking this."

"License plate and vehicle are dead ends. Van was stolen from a junkyard in Surrey about a week ago, the plates off a wreck at a repair garage here in London. The back door to this building was kicked in, so evidently an assault team came through there as well."

"I think you hit it on the head, an *assault* team. Front, back, hit each floor grid by grid. They probably had a list of everyone who worked here and the physical layout of the place." Shaw said this more to himself than to Royce. "Okay, run the rest of the feed."

Shaw stiffened once more when the shattered window glass poured down on the street. He saw a head emerge and the person started screaming. He couldn't hear her, because there was no audio. But he didn't need to hear.

"That's Anna!"

"I thought it might be," Royce said.

Shaw stared hard at him. "How much did Frank tell you about her and me?"

"Not all that much, but enough. And I've been in Ms. Fischer's office. I saw the photos of you and her. I'm sorry. Had you been together long?"

"Not long enough."

"Again, I'm sorry. I can only imagine what you're feeling."

"Don't even try to imagine it," Shaw said back.

Royce cleared his throat and turned to the screen. "The windows were accidentally painted shut and she had to break the glass."

"Accidentally? You're sure?"

"We checked out the painting company. They're legit, been doing buildings around here for decades. All hands accounted for and all. It's not such an unusual thing apparently, shoddy work I mean. I had my flat done three years ago and I still can't open the damn windows."

Shaw wasn't listening. He was watching the image of Anna as she called out the window, obviously for help, help that would never arrive. Then a moment later he saw her climb up onto the windowsill.

"Was she going to jump?" he said sharply.

"To that awning below, we're guessing."

"But she never made it," Shaw said dully. "Why?"

"I have to warn you that the next few frames are . . . Well, they're not easy to watch." Royce turned to look at him. "Are you sure you want to keep going?"

"I need to see it."

The next scenes were played out quickly. Anna was on the sill of the window, in her stocking feet, grasping both sides of the window with her hands.

Mentally, Shaw was telling her to jump, jump, before it was too late, even though he knew it already was. It was an agonizing moment for him; he couldn't even imagine how terrifying it had been for her. The next frame, however, sent his agony to an entirely new level.

He saw the first bullet pass through her chest and a wash of blood and tissue was propelled from her body. A split second later another chunk of Anna was blown out into the fresh London air. As she toppled back inside her office, Shaw finally looked away.

"We can finish this later," Royce suggested.

"Keep rolling, I'm okay."

Several minutes later the men emerged from the front door. Seconds after that the van was gone.

"And no one heard or saw anything?" Shaw asked. "Even a woman screaming out the window? Shots fired, her blood hitting the street?"

"The buildings on either side of this one are scheduled to be renovated so they were empty. The buildings opposite *are* occupied but the tenants were notified that the city was doing some hazardous gas work in the area that day and they were to leave their premises before noon or risk a hefty fine."

"And no one bothered to call and check whether that was true?"

"There was a phone number on the notice. Several tenants did call and received confirmation that it was true."

"Only the number was phony."

"Correct. And the cones blocked off the normal automobile flow and foot traffic. And it's a dead-end street. There're never many vehicles down here anyway."

"Leaving The Phoenix Group all alone. It was well planned out," Shaw grudgingly admitted. "I'd like to see Anna's office now."

"Well, first I'd like to introduce you to an owner of The Phoenix Group."

"They're here?" Shaw said sharply.

"One of them flew in as soon as he was notified."

"Where from?"

"What do you know about the phoenix symbol?"

"Bird that never dies. Rises from the ashes. Egyptian origin."

"Your description is accurate, as far as it goes. The phoenix is actually a symbol that has various origins. Egyptian as you said. It's also Arabian, Japanese, and at least one other."

"Which is?" Shaw said impatiently.

A small man appeared in the doorway. He was dressed in a black suit and his expression matched the color of his clothing. Royce rose to greet him.

"Shaw, let me introduce you to Mr. Feng Hai. Of China."

53

While Shaw was inside the building Katie had been busy outside. She'd actually gotten there before him and had hidden around a corner when she saw him arrive by cab. She'd flashed her no-longer-valid press badge at the officer on duty outside the entrance and fired off a series of questions to which the man in blue offered not a single answer.

"Move along," he said, his beefy face showing considerable irritation.

"Not into a free and independent press, Constable?" she asked.

"What I'm *into* is you blokes letting us do our bloody jobs without you poking your noses into places it don't belong."

"Your name will never appear. You'll be an unnamed source."

"You're bloody right my name won't appear. Now move along!"

Katie walked slowly down the street a bit, staring up at the windows of the building as she did so. Shaw was in there getting the whole story while she was out here with zip.

If I could just . . . Back on top. Another Pulitzer.

She was so intent on her thoughts that she nearly jumped when something touched her arm. She whirled around and saw him, his soft felt cap in hand, his wide, nervous eyes squarely on her.

"Can I help you?" she asked suspiciously.

"You are a journalist, yes?" His voice was squeaky and not exactly brimming with confidence. She easily guessed that English was not his first language. He was short and painfully thin. His teeth were crooked and yellowed. His clothes barely rose to the level of threadbare.

"Who wants to know?" She peered over his shoulder as though expecting to see someone else there.

He looked back at The Phoenix Group building. "I have come here every day to see it. This place, I mean." He gave an involuntary shudder.

"It *is* disturbing," she said, still wary of the man.

He seemed to sense her discomfort. "My name is Aron Lesnik. I am from Krakow. That is in Poland," he added.

"I know where Krakow is," Katie said. "I've been there. What do you want with me?"

"I saw you talking to that police officer. I heard you say you are journalist. Is that true? Are you journalist?"

"Yes. So?"

Lesnik glanced once more at the building. When he turned back to her, his eyes were filled with tears. "I am so sorry for those people. They were good people and now they are dead." He wiped his eyes with the back of his sleeve and looked at her pitifully.

"It was a real tragedy. Now if you'll excuse me." Katie wondered why she always seemed to attract the nutcases. The man's next words made her forget that thought.

"I was in there. On that day." He said this in a hoarse voice.

"What?" Katie couldn't have heard the man right. "In where?"

Lesnik pointed to The Phoenix Group building. "In there," he repeated, an agonizing pitch to his voice now.

"Where the murders happened?"

Lesnik nodded, his head bobbing up and down like a child making a confession.

"What were you doing in the building?"

"I was looking for work. A job. My English is not that good, but I am good with computers. I go there because I hear they need people who are good with computers. I have appointment. It is on that day. That . . . bad day."

"Let me get this straight," Katie said, trying but failing to hide her excitement. "You were in that building for an interview when the people were killed? *While* they were being killed?"

Lesnik nodded. "Yes." His eyes filled with tears again.

"Then how come you're not dead?" she said suspiciously.

"I hear the guns. I know about sounds of guns. I was young boy in Krakow when the Soviets would come with guns. So I hide."

A bit of Katie's suspicion drained away. She'd had to hide from men with guns when she'd been reporting overseas. "Where did you hide? I want precise details."

"On the second floor there is machine in a little room they use to make copies of papers. It has doors in back. A little space to hold things. It was empty. I am not big. I crawl inside. I stay there until the shootings stop. Then I come out. I think they shoot me too when they find me. But they do not find me. I am lucky."

Katie was nearly vibrating off the pavement. "Look, it's probably not a great idea to talk about this here. Why don't we go somewhere else?"

Lesnik immediately backed away. "No, I say enough. I come here every day. I come, because I can't stay away. Those people, all dead. All dead except me. I should be dead too."

"Don't say that. It obviously wasn't your time to

go. Like you said, you were lucky. And besides it'll be good to get it off your chest," she urged.

"No. No! I only come up to you because I hear you are journalist. In Poland we have journalists who are heroes, heroes in Poland. They stand up to Soviets. My father, he is one of them. They kill him, but he is still hero," he added proudly.

"I'm sure he is. But you can't just not tell anyone. You have to go to the police."

Lesnik took another step back. "No, no police. I do not like police."

Katie looked at him warily. "Are you in some sort of trouble?"

Lesnik didn't answer her. He simply glanced away. "No police. I must go now."

She clutched his arm. "Wait a minute." Katie thought quickly. "Look, if I promise not to reveal my source, can you at least tell me what you saw? I promise, I swear on a stack of Bibles I won't ever tell who told me. After all, you came up to me. You must want me to help somehow."

Lesnik looked unsure. "I don't know why I come up to you." He paused. "You . . . you can do that? Not tell?"

"Absolutely." She looked over his anguished face, his small, childlike frame, and his shabby clothes. She could easily envision him hiding terrified inside a copier as gunfire erupted all around him. "How about I buy you something to eat and we can talk? Just talk.

If you're still uncomfortable, you can walk away." She put out her hand. "Deal?"

He didn't take her hand.

"I'm sure your father would want to see the truth come out. And to see murderers punished."

He slowly slipped his fingers around hers. "Okay. I go with you."

As they walked along Katie said the one question she'd been dying to ask.

"Did you see who did it?" She held her breath waiting for the answer.

He nodded. "And I hear them too. I hear them good. I know the language they speak very good."

"Language? So they were foreigners?"

Lesnik stopped walking and stared at her. "They were Russians."

"You're sure? Absolutely certain?"

For the first time his face took on a confident expression. "I am Pole. From Krakow. I know Russian when I hear it."

54

"We named the company after the Chinese phoenix, the *Feng Huang*," Feng Hai said as they sat in an office off the main foyer. "In Chinese mythology the phoenix stands for virtue, power, and prosperity. It was also said that the bird represented power sent down to the empress from above. You might know that *Feng* means male phoenix."

"And Feng is also your surname," commented Shaw. Unlike the West the Chinese put their family name ahead of their given one. So Hai was the man's first name.

Feng nodded. "That also gave me the idea, that is correct."

"And the connection The Phoenix Group has to China?" Royce asked.

"It is simply a Chinese company doing business in London, like many others."

"Your employees seemed to think a wealthy American from Arizona owned it," Shaw noted.

Feng shrugged. "Rumors, obviously."

Shaw said, "I think it was more than that. I think it was a deliberate cover."

Royce sat forward while Feng glared at Shaw. "So it was basically a think tank that studied global issues funded by you and your partners? That was the business model?"

Feng nodded.

"And you set it up for what reason?" Royce asked.

"To find answers to complicated questions," Feng said. "The Chinese too have an interest in such problems and solutions. We are not all heartless polluters and people who put lead in children's toys, gentlemen," he said, attempting a weak smile.

"Did The Phoenix Group make any money for you?" Shaw asked.

"We did not do it for money."

Shaw looked around at the elaborately decorated interior of the office. "This building must be worth, what, thirty million pounds?"

"It has been a good investment. But as I said, money is not our chief concern. We, my partners and I, we are good businessmen. We make lots of money in other things. The Phoenix Group was our way of doing some good. Giving back, I think you say."

"And you have no idea why anyone would have wanted to attack this place and kill everyone?" Royce asked, the skepticism in his voice unmistakable.

"None at all. I was most distressed when I heard. Most distressed. I . . . I could not believe that such a thing could happen. The people here were scholars, intellectuals. They work on issues of water usage rights, globalization of world economies, atmospheric warming due to carbon-based fuel use, energy consumption, matters of international financial assistance to third world countries, political dynamics. Benign intellectual subjects, gentlemen."

"Anna Fischer wrote a book on police states," Shaw pointed out. "That hardly qualifies as a benign intellectual matter."

"Ms. Fischer was most excellent at her job."

"You knew her?"

"I knew *of* her."

"Had anyone here met you before?" Shaw asked quickly.

"We, my partners and I, prefer to keep a low profile. But we received regular reports."

I'm sure you did, Shaw said to himself.

"Have you found any evidence that will lead to the people who did this?" Feng asked anxiously.

Royce shook his head. "No fingerprints, no shell casings, no trace at all, I'm afraid." He did not mention the video feed.

"That is most discouraging."

"But we did find one thing of interest, Mr. Feng," Royce said. "Would you care to see? It's a real eye-opener."

55

Aron Lesnik wolfed down his sandwich and drank his coffee in large slurps. Part of Katie was disgusted by his eating habits, and part of her was sympathetic. He must be terrified, she thought. Terrified, probably broke, and obviously hungry.

Lesnik wiped his mouth and let out a small sigh. He caught her staring at him and his features turned embarrassed. "Thank you for food."

"You're welcome. Do you mind if I use this?" She pulled out a mini-recorder.

"No. I tell you, but I don't want people to hear me." He looked around nervously. "I am scared."

She put the recorder away. "Okay, I'll just write it down."

He relaxed and sat back.

"Now tell me everything you saw and heard," she said.

Lesnik's story only took a very few minutes. He'd been interviewing with an older man named Bill Harris on the second floor.

"Why weren't you killed then?" Katie asked sharply.

"I go to the bathroom down the hall from his office," Lesnik explained. When he was coming back he heard shots and screams. He ducked into an empty room, saw the copier machine, and climbed in. He heard more screams and shots. He listened to people walking nearby. He thought they would find him. He told Katie he was convinced he was going to die. He had to interrupt the story several times to drink some water and calm down. Katie's pen flew across the page as she recorded everything he said.

"Then what happened?"

"I think, I hope, they all gone now, the men with guns I mean. But I hear something."

"What did you hear?"

"I hear two men talking. They come into room where I am hiding! They speak in Russian. I know Russian. I can speak it, yes."

"What did they say?"

"They say they have list of names and every name is dead."

"So they knew who worked in the building?"

"I think they do, yes."

"What else?"

"They talk about someone else coming in building. But they don't have his name. And they don't think he is dead."

Katie immediately got it. "They were talking about *you*!"

Lesnik nodded. "I think this too. I think they search

building again and this time they find me. I am trapped. I know I am going to die now." The tears slid down his face.

She poured him some more coffee. "So why didn't they find you?"

"One man say to other that they must leave now. A window has been broke in office. A woman has screamed out window. They must go in case police show up."

"So then they left?"

"Yes, but as they go they keep talking. One man, he say Gorshkov will be pleased when he hears from them that mission went good."

Katie nearly dug a hole in the paper with her pen. "Gorshkov? Russian president Gorshkov?"

Lesnik nodded. "I hear his name and it frighten me much. Everybody know that like Putin, Gorshkov is ex-KGB. He spits at democracy. Everyone in Poland know this."

"Why would Gorshkov target a think tank in London?" Katie said in a confused tone.

"I do not know."

"How did you get away?"

"I wait for men to leave. I hear door close and wait some more, to be sure. Then I go out back door. That is way I come in."

"Why not the front?"

"The man I talk to, Mr. Harris, he say come in that way. He say it is easier for me when I tell him where

I coming from." His face clouded over. "And I no go out front door because . . . because there is two bodies there. One old man, one young woman, shot in face." He pointed at his right eye. "Shot there. I can no go by them. I go out back door. And then I run. I run all the way to where I staying."

"And you haven't told anyone else about this?"

Lesnik shook his head. "If I tell, then people come kill me. I just go there for job. I no want to die."

"Okay, okay," Katie said, laying a calming hand on his slender shoulder. "This was a big first step."

"You write story now? You no use my name?" he added anxiously.

"I promised that I wouldn't. But where can I reach you if I have any more questions?"

"I stay at hostel by river." He wrote down the address for Katie on a piece of napkin. "It is all I have money for."

Katie again ran her gaze over his old, patched clothing and emaciated body. She reached in her pocket and handed him some pounds. "It's not much, but I'll try to get you some more."

"*Dziekuje*. That is 'thank you' in Polish."

"You're welcome."

Lesnik rose from the table.

"Do you have a phone where I can reach you at?"

He smiled wearily. "I have no phone. I be at hostel. *Powodzenia!*"

"That's 'good luck' in Polish, right?"

His face brightened for a moment. "How did you know?"

"Just a guess."

As he walked off Katie slumped back against her chair. "Now what the hell do I do?" Part of her couldn't believe that any of this was true. A Polish guy speaking passable English walks up to her on the street. Her! And starts to tell her the story that everyone in the world is dying to hear. A story she had just been assigned to work on. No one was that lucky, certainly not her.

And yet, taking the facts as she knew them into account? His story was plausible. He had details of the inside of the building, details Katie would have to verify. He seemed legitimately scared, and if he was telling the truth he should be scared. And why would he lie to her? Because he was a nut looking for fifteen minutes of fame? But this guy didn't want his name used. He didn't want fame. What if he was telling the truth?

Katie jumped up and dashed back to The Phoenix Group building. There was one man who could help her verify the man's story. And that was Shaw. She did not relish this encounter, but all her journalistic instincts were on fire, propelling her forward to that most elusive of quarries: the truth.

56

The items were neatly laid out on the table. Next to them was a computer terminal. Royce had just been showing some things on the screen to Shaw and Feng. Feng sat in a chair with a stunned look on his face while Shaw slowly perused some of the written materials.

"So you're saying you weren't aware of any of this?" Royce said, the disbelief in his voice ricocheting around the room like a stray slug.

Feng wagged his head. "That is correct," he said firmly. "I knew nothing."

"Mr. Feng, let me make this clear to you. There are paper records all over this building which show quite clearly that The Phoenix Group was part of the propaganda campaign against Russia. And they have the fingerprints of your employees all over them. The computer hard drives here also have thousands of files on them chronicling everything from the creation of the so-called 'Tablet of Tragedies' to the details of this Konstantin fellow to composite ads that were circulated in connection with said propaganda campaign.

There are over thirty thousand names of Russians on your hard drives, the same names and backgrounds that were slung across the Internet along with claims that they were all victims of the Russian Red Menace."

"I have no idea how any of that got here," stammered Feng. "None!"

"Do you not oversee the work that is done here, sir?"

Feng said indignantly, "We let our people explore what they wish to explore. Our involvement is minimal. I have never even been to this building before."

"Well, it appears that your employees' *exploration* got a bit out of hand. Do you understand the magnitude of the situation we have here?"

Feng looked at Royce questioningly. "I do not understand what you mean."

"Do you have any ties to the Chinese government?"

"I fail to see what that has to do—"

Shaw interrupted. "Gorshkov has sworn that whoever was behind the smear campaign would be viewed as having committed an act of war against his country. If you have any ties to the Chinese government, then you might just have started a war between the People's Republic of China and the Russian Federation."

Feng sprang to his feet. "That is preposterous!"

Royce exclaimed, "It will hardly seem preposterous to the rest of the world, sir."

Shaw added in a quieter tone, "*Do* you have any ties to the Chinese government? Better it come out now rather than later."

Feng suddenly looked uncertain and sat back down. "It could be construed, that is to say, some people might . . ."

Shaw leaned down into Feng's troubled face. "I'm sure you understand that telling us the truth is really your only option."

Feng licked his lips and fiddled with a ring on his finger. "Part of our funding comes from the government." He started speaking rapid-fire. "My partners and I have done much work with the Communist Party with respect to economic development both in China and in other countries. We started The Phoenix Group with the sole purpose of trying to better understand global issues that will help China adapt more readily to an expanded role in world affairs. There is no question that our economy will at some point become the world's largest. With that comes a responsibility, a responsibility that we take very seriously. And thus we sought to educate ourselves as to critical issues around the world. Creating a think tank and staffing it with some of the best minds seemed a reasonable pursuit."

Shaw snapped, "And yet you deliberately hid your ties to the Chinese government behind this Arizona millionaire façade?"

"We are misunderstood in many parts of the world."

He shot a glance at the MI5 agent. "Including in your country, Mr. Royce. We did not want any lingering doubts or misconceptions to taint the important work The Phoenix Group was undertaking."

"Did any of the people who worked here have any idea of these ties?" Royce asked.

Shaw already knew the answer to that question. Anna would've told him.

"No," Feng said. "We did not think it important or relevant to their work. What did it matter who they were working for if the goals were good ones?"

"Are you a member of the Communist Party?" Royce asked.

"I fail to see—"

"Please answer the question."

"You have to understand—"

"Are you!" Royce bellowed.

"Yes. I am, like many of my fellow citizens," Feng said defensively.

The MI5 agent threw up his hands. "This is a complete and total *cock-up*."

A pale Feng said, "No, gentlemen, this is ludicrous. The Phoenix Group was not involved in any of this Red Menace business. It is absurd to even suggest it."

"Since you said you've never even been here before, you're hardly in a position to know that, are you?" Royce shot back.

"But why would they do such a thing?" Feng said in a near wail.

"How many other partners do you have?"

"Four."

"I think somebody should ask them," Royce said. He looked at Shaw. "For now, this stays among us. If any of this comes out, I can hardly imagine greater consequences for your country, Mr. Feng."

"You cannot believe that Russia would attack us."

"Gorshkov has staked his reputation on the fact that he will do just that. Go ask Afghanistan if you don't believe me."

"Who else knows?" Shaw asked Royce.

"A very few of the crime scene team. We hardly expected anything like this when the investigation started. Once they knew what they were facing, they cut off access to everyone else and called me in."

"I'm surprised you allowed me in here," Shaw said bluntly.

"Wells told me that you are the absolute best he has. So I thought I could rely upon your discretion and I desperately need your help."

"You're welcome to both."

Royce turned back to Feng. "I'd like your passport."

Feng's features darkened. "You cannot possibly mean that."

"Give it to me." Royce held out his hand.

"I have committed no crime."

"That remains to be seen, doesn't it?"

"You will create an international incident?"

"What's one more?" Royce retorted.

"I want to go to the Chinese embassy. Immediately."

"Passport first and then I'll see if I can get you a lift over," Royce said pleasantly enough, even tacking a smile onto the end of his offer.

Feng very slowly handed over his passport. "This is outrageous."

"Absolutely," Royce agreed. "Everything we've discovered here so far *is* outrageous."

As Feng and Royce headed out, Shaw said, "I'm going up to Anna's office."

"Shaw, we only removed the body. The rest of the place is untouched. It's not very . . ."

"I know it's not."

57

Shaw took the steps two at a time and followed the carpeted floor down to the end of the hall. The door on the left stood open. He closed his eyes and willed himself to focus on the task at hand—finding anything that could help lead him to Anna's killers.

He walked into the room and suddenly grew very cold. His gaze wandered over the room, the books, the old desk, and the chair he had sat in when visiting her here. His eyes took in the small patch of oriental carpet in the middle of the room, her plants, and the sweater that still hung on the back of her chair. He touched the sweater, and his wall of professionalism started to crumble when he breathed in Anna's scent that somehow still lingered on the fabric, despite the still-present stench of discharged weapons and the antiseptic vapor trail of the forensic team.

His professional demeanor started to crumble a bit more when his gaze went to the bookshelf right behind her desk where there were several photos of him and Anna. Their broad smiles seemed to pile up on him, like grain into a silo, threatening to bury him with their collective tonnage.

When he glanced down at the floor and saw her blood where it had leached into the wood, he had to sit down. In those dark stains he saw his past, present, and even his bleak, lonely future in one crushing vision. When you gave your heart to someone, you were never free ever again. And you had better be prepared for something like this. Only you never really could be.

The shattered window had been taped over, but he rose and studied it anyway, telling himself that if he broke down now, it would not help avenge Anna. He saw the scratches her desperate fingers had made in the window frame. She must have been seconds from jumping. He glanced back at the door and the twin bullet holes there. His practiced eye did the rough trajectory. It would have indeed hit her chest-high as the video had shown. Yet with the door closed the shooter could not have known Anna was trying to jump out the window.

A lucky shot, he concluded painfully.

She had fallen back inside the room. He knelt down and looked at the bloodstains and taped outline. Outside he could hear the normal sounds of a large city. In here there was only the silence of death. And yet sometimes the dead speak loudest of all.

Talk to me, Anna. Tell me what happened.

He looked closer and thought he saw the faint trace

of a footprint in the blood. It wasn't large enough to help with the investigation, which was probably why Royce hadn't mentioned it. He moved to Anna's desk and sat down in her chair. Her computer had been removed for examination by Royce's people, but her desktop was still covered with things she'd been working on. The only difference was that each item had been sealed for evidence.

Shaw picked up one bundle. Through the plastic he saw Anna's precise handwriting in the margins of the typed pages. He had joked with her more than once that she was an inveterate scribbler and annotator; that she never saw a piece of writing she couldn't comment on. He put it down and picked up another bagged stack.

The documents in here purportedly showed that Anna had been engaged in putting together elements of the Red Menace propaganda. Even though her fingerprints were supposedly all over the documents, Shaw knew the idea that Anna had helped propagate the Red Menace campaign was ridiculous. And if he had any doubts as to Anna's involvement they were dispelled by these pages not having a single mark from her pen on them. Anyone who knew the woman well would have spotted that glaring omission. Yet Shaw was aware that that would hardly be conclusive proof for the rest of the world.

They must have pressed everyone's fingers against the papers after they were dead. And they'd shot Anna in the head, even though the chest wounds would've been fatal. And I will take great pleasure in killing every single one of the heartless bastards.

He also suspected that every computer in the place had had incriminating files downloaded onto it. Careful scrutiny might show that they had been put there on the day of the killing, but if someone really knew what he was doing they might never be able to prove that.

He wasn't going to tell Royce his doubts about the evidence because he wasn't sure how all this was going to turn out. While he made a show of working with Royce, he knew that his and the MI5 agent's interests were going to diverge at some point. Royce wanted merely to arrest whoever had done this. Shaw simply wanted to kill them.

Feng had admitted that the Chinese government had ties to The Phoenix Group. So was someone trying to make it seem as though the Chinese were behind the Red Menace? But who would do that and why? Russia against China? What maniac would want that global scenario to play out?

And Anna had been caught right in the middle. But why had they chosen the Phoenix Group out of all the places they could have targeted? Was it just a coincidence that it had ties to the Chinese government? *No, it can't be.*

The killers had obviously found out the connection, which must have taken some legwork. Yet there must be tens of thousands of entities with ties to China spread all over the world. Why here? Why Anna?

He went to the shelf and picked up one photo. It'd been taken the night he'd proposed. Anna had gotten a waiter to snap the picture of them together, with particular emphasis on the new engagement ring on her finger. Her smile, so full of the bright future ahead, made him forget about the pain in his arm, because the agony in his heart hurt so much.

He suddenly realized he couldn't stay here for another second. He pounded down the steps and threw open the front door. He felt like he couldn't breathe, his lungs hard as stone. The image of Anna falling dead back into that room, the imagined vision of her killer standing over her and Shaw far away and helpless seared his brain.

He rushed past the officer on duty and catapulted out onto the street, where a split second later he knocked a person flat to the pavement.

He reached down to help, an apology ready on his lips, an apology he would never deliver. He merely gaped.

Katie slowly got to her feet. "We need to talk. Right now."

58

Nicolas Creel had had a busy day even for him. He'd ridden on his private jet from Italy to New York and then on to Houston where he'd picked up his executive sales team. They spent the considerable flight time going over last-minute details for their upcoming high-level sales presentation in Beijing.

Creel was now in his stateroom staring at a picture of a man he'd just been sent, along with accompanying details. His name was Shaw and he was working on The Phoenix Group massacre. He was attached to a highly secretive international law enforcement agency; though, Creel had been informed, the agency often went outside the law to achieve results. Shaw was one of their best operatives and he apparently had a personal motivation to solve the crime. That was troubling. What was even more irritating was the e-mail he'd just received from Caesar. He had men watching The Phoenix Group building of course. And they reported seeing Shaw and Katie James going off together. He'd instructed Caesar to have them followed. He didn't want this man Shaw to interfere with James's unwitting role in his plan.

He returned to the jet's conference room where his executives were putting the finishing touches on a sales pitch that they hoped would lead to the largest defense contract China had ever awarded to an outside firm. Actually, this was only the opening salvo, Creel alone knew. When the events in London were more fully explained to the world, the Chinese would understand quite clearly the precarious position in which they stood. The Asian Dragon would become a bull's-eye for the Russian Bear. And the communists would triple their weapons order if for no other reason than to ward off the madman Gorshkov. With any luck, they'd be in bed with Ares Corp. for the next two decades at minimum.

That would have been plenty for most business-men. But not Nicolas Creel. The Beijing piece was only half the equation.

After China, Creel would continue flying west and visit Moscow. He fully expected much resistance from the former Soviets, who as yet did not see a great need for the latest and greatest in military hardware. They, like the rest of the world, had ceded the field to the Yanks, who simply outspent everyone. Yet Creel was one of the few, perhaps the only visionary who saw that that need not be the case forever. World powers came and world powers went. The Americans had been on top for a very long time, at least by recent historical standards. They were due to be overtaken. Whether by the Russians or the Chinese, or both, Creel didn't really care. He just wanted to be the one to arm the next superpower.

He would not dwell on, or even mention to Gorshkov's and China's defense ministers, the issue of Russia versus China and the heightening tensions between the two nations. Instead, he would take a more positive tack. *This is your time*, he would tell both countries. *This is your century. You must seize it or someone else will.* He would let their respective imaginations fill in the identity of that someone.

His underlings could sweat the actual numbers and details. He was along for the ride to deliver the closer, to put into clear perspective what was at stake for both countries. And trillions of dollars were at stake for Ares, because once Russia and China undertook a substantial rearmament, so would everybody else with dollars to spend and egos to defend. That would include the Yanks, who would most certainly see their world leadership rank being usurped. What was a few trillion more in debt anyway? It wasn't like the Americans could possibly pay back what they owed already.

Creel swiftly ran through the numbers in his head. National debt at about ten trillion dollars, not counting the Social Security accounting charade. Just interest on what amounted to America's credit card debt was over $300 billion a year, along with $700 billion in defense spending, which totaled a full trillion annually, or about one-third of the total budget. Social Security, Medicare, and Medicaid costs were well over $1 trillion, collectively. Welfare and unemployment expenditures were about $400 billion. That left a paltry few hundred billion dollars for everything else. In the grand scheme that was chump change. And every day the Yanks went hat in hand to the likes of China and Japan and Saudi Arabia essentially begging for money to finance their consumption. Creel had long ago figured out the ending to that song. He had to because it was in his business interests to know. Despite the Americans' well-deserved reputation for ingenuity and resilience, the veteran businessman knew that the dollars never lied.

Unless the country does a complete turnaround, in thirty years or less the Yanks will be finished. That's why I'm buying euros, yen, yuans and rupees and looking to expand my clientele well beyond the land of the free, home of the brave. No one with that much debt is free and the home is mortgaged to the hilt. Still, they can enjoy it while it lasts, credit card their way for another couple decades anyway. Future generations will have to pay the piper and all hell will break loose when that bill comes due.

Clearly, several other major defense contractors would get a piece of the global pie, but Creel's firm was perfectly positioned to get the bulk of it. It would be the crowning jewel of his lifetime. His company would be saved, his legacy ensured. And, most importantly, the world's natural equilibrium reinstated.

It was everything he could have hoped for. And they were almost there.

Yet he kept going back to the photo Caesar had sent him. His gaze burned into the tall man's eyes. Creel didn't like those eyes. He had made several fortunes by reading correctly the expressions, the poker faces of his opposition. And he didn't like this man's at all. In fact the eyes he was looking at in the photo seemed very familiar to him. As he glanced into a mirror hanging on the wall opposite he suddenly realized who it was.

They remind me of me.

Creel sat back and listened to his sales team drone on as they covered 550 miles an hour on the way to sell peace and security at the end of a tank muzzle to another satisfied customer.

And yet his mind kept going back to those eyes. And that man. Only one man for sure. Yet sometimes it only took one to bring it all down.

Creel would never let that happen. He was not afraid of much, but one thing that terrified him was uncertainty. That's why he'd hired Pender, who made the world believe what Creel wanted it to believe. It was often a war of attrition. You made up the truth and then buried the real thing under so much garbage that people grew weary of trying to dig through it and instead just accepted what you offered. It was the easy way out and humans were programmed to always go that way. After all, there were bills to pay, shopping to do, kids to raise, and sports to watch, so who had time for anything else? Yes, you cover every base, but sometimes something or someone slips in and undoes it all.

But not this time.

No, not this time.

59

"Take me to see this guy," Shaw said to Katie as they sat in his room at the Savoy. She had just finished telling him about her meeting with the Pole.

"I can't do that," Katie replied. "I promised."

"I don't care what you promised. He's a material witness in a murder investigation."

Katie looked out the window where Big Ben, the Houses of Parliament, and the pie-shaped London Eye stared back at her with the narrow Thames in the foreground. "You don't think I know that?"

"Okay, tell me his name then."

"Yeah, right. How about I show you his picture and give you his mailing address while I'm at it?"

"This isn't a joke! People have died."

She whirled around. "Don't throw that crap in my face. I do the journalism thing for a living, okay? Ever heard the phrase 'source protection'? Journalists invoke it every day. Some even go to prison in defense of it, which I happened to have done in the past. So save the guilt act for somebody else."

Shaw looked down and Katie realized she had gone

too far. She sat across from him and said quietly, "Look, there's no one in the whole world who wants to find Anna's killer more than you do. And I want that too. But I've got a job to do. I've been assigned to write about this story, and I have to go about it as a professional."

"You tell me what the guy told you, and you expect me to stop there? Why tell me at all if you won't take me to see him?"

Katie sat back, kneading her fists into her thighs. "I wish I had a stellar answer for that, but I don't. I just wanted you to know. I guess I just wanted you to say he's telling the truth."

"Do you believe him?"

"The details I told you, the copier, the bodies near the front door, the guy named Bill Harris? Can you verify that since you were in there?"

"The copier on the second floor and the bodies near the front door, yes, that's all accurate. I'll check to see if the storage in the copier was big enough to hold him. I didn't get a complete roster of the dead, so I can't vouch for this Harris guy, but it'll be easy enough to check that. You said he entered and left through the back?" Katie nodded. "Then that's why we didn't see him on the video footage. It only recorded the street entrance."

"So he seems legit," she said hopefully.

"He would also know all of those things if he were in on the murders."

"I thought of that, but he didn't seem the type. He's basically a skinny little Polish kid scared out of his mind."

"Who just happened to walk up to you on the street in front of the murder scene? Bit of a coincidence, don't you think?"

"It would be, but he heard me talking to a cop. Pegged me as a journalist. And it's not so unusual for a survivor to come back to where it happened. Guilt and all."

"You sound like you're trying very hard to convince yourself."

"Trust me, I'm going to check this guy every way there is."

"So what do you want from me?" Shaw asked.

Katie let out a breath. "You've pretty much confirmed for me that he was in there. I think, well, I keep working on the story."

Shaw rose and stared down at her. "What the hell are you talking about? What story?"

She looked back at him with equal incredulity. "An eyewitness to the London Massacre? Don't you think that's newsworthy?"

"Katie, he said the killers were speaking Russian."

"Yeah, so?"

Shaw looked very troubled as she eyed him suspiciously.

"Is there something you haven't told me?" she said.

"I'll only tell you if you promise not to write the story."

"I can't do that, Shaw. I can't. I won't! This is news."

"Even if it might start a world war?"

"What world war!" she exclaimed.

"If I tell you, you can never repeat it, to anyone, anywhere, including in print. Those are my terms. Take 'em or leave 'em."

Katie hesitated for an instant and then nodded. "Deal."

"They found evidence inside the building that purportedly shows The Phoenix Group was behind the Red Menace campaign."

Katie sprang out of her chair. "What? You're sure?"

"Sure the evidence was there? Yes. What it really means, I don't know yet."

"And my eyewitness also overheard the killers saying they were there on orders from Gorshkov."

"Damn it, why didn't you tell me that?"

"Look who's talking about holding things back? Like you, I tend to keep things close to the vest. But if The Phoenix Group was involved in putting together the Red Menace campaign, that would explain why the Russians on orders from Gorshkov attacked the place."

"But it's *not* true. The Red Menace stuff was planted."

"How can you be certain about that? I *did* see those

materials in Anna's office. Maybe she wasn't research-
ing it. Maybe she was doing it."

"And just left the stuff lying around for you to see
while the whole world is trying to find out who's
behind it?" he said incredulously.

Now Katie looked unsure of herself. "I guess that
doesn't make sense, but where does the world war
thing come in? I must have missed that."

"Gorshkov has pledged that whoever was behind
the smear would open itself up to attack."

"The Phoenix Group was attacked, not a country."

Shaw took a deep breath and said, "The Phoenix
Group is run by the Chinese, or at least has deep ties
to them."

Katie exclaimed, "The Chinese? You're sure?"

"Yes. I met with one of the owners. He confirmed
it."

"But do you seriously believe Russia will attack
China?"

"Who knows? But the last thing we need to find
out is that the answer to that question is *yes*."

"But if the Russian government sent their killers in
as retribution against The Phoenix Group, *and* they
know about the Chinese connection, then that seems
to be an act of war right there. I'm actually surprised
Gorshkov hasn't gotten on the world pipeline and
told everyone he did it."

"He can't. Most of the people killed were British citizens. Blowing up a bunch of Taliban in the

mountains of Afghanistan is one thing. But you don't waltz into London and wipe out nearly thirty of their people and then start bragging about it. I don't care if you are Russia. The Brits have nukes too. And their closest ally is America. And not even Gorshkov wants to take on that eight-hundred-pound gorilla. And we don't know for certain that the Russians *are* aware of the Chinese connection."

"But nothing you've told me is a reason not to write the story. An eyewitness says some Russians in Gorshkov's pay did it. I'll say nothing about the Red Menace stuff or the Chinese connection because I told you I wouldn't. But the fact that the Russians hit that building came from my source and is a story the world needs to know."

"Come on, who can't read between those lines! And if the Chinese think that the Russians took out one of their offices? *They* might retaliate against Moscow."

"But even you said the Red Menace stuff was bull crap. It was planted. The Chinese weren't behind it."

Shaw shook his hands in exasperation. "Exactly, Katie. Don't you get it? The Russians wouldn't have planted that stuff, especially if they knew of the Chinese connection. What would have been the point? They wouldn't go out of their way to pick a fight with China by framing them. The two countries are too evenly matched militarily. If they were going to pull a stunt like that they would've chosen a country a lot easier to blow out of the water. Hell, start with the A's and nail Albania. That war would be over in twenty-four hours. But China? They have three soldiers for every Russian grunt. And they have nukes too."

Katie looked confused. "So what exactly are you saying?"

"That the Russians *didn't* do it. And The Phoenix Group *isn't* behind the Red Menace and neither are the Chinese."

"Okay, then *who is* behind it all?" she said doubtfully.

"There's a third party involved. A third party that is playing a game I don't completely understand, but that I know is somehow designed to pit Russia and China against each other."

"So you're saying my source is lying about the Russian involvement?"

"If he said he overheard people speaking in Russian who said they worked for Gorshkov, then, yeah, I think he might be lying, because I don't believe the killers were working for Russia. Or else, and it's a real stretch, they somehow knew he was in the building and let him live so he could tell what he'd heard, or what they *wanted* him to hear."

She snapped her fingers. "He did say he overheard the Russians, or according to you, the fake Russians talking about someone else being in the building. If they were watching the back of the office they would've seen him go in. But they didn't do another search because a window was broken and a woman was screaming out of the office and they were afraid the police would show up."

Shaw's expression grew clouded. Katie said, "Did that happen?"

He nodded slowly. "The woman was Anna. She broke her office window, tried to get out that way, but was killed before she could."

"How do you know that?"

"The street camera recorded it."

"My God, you saw it happen?" She put a hand over his. "Shaw, I don't know what to say."

"Say you won't write the story."

"I can't do that. The world deserves to hear it."

"Really? Even if it's all lies? Or maybe Katie James believes she deserves to get back on top, any way she can? Even if it means the end of the world as we know it?"

Katie's face flushed and she drew away from him. "That is not why I'm doing this!"

"Then tell me why you are doing it."

"I'm a journalist. I have a story. A story of the decade! I can't just sit on it because you have a bunch of pet theories, or because you say the world *might* end."

"And what if I'm right? Are you prepared to deal with it?"

"Yes," she said, but her voice shook slightly.

the whole truth

"Then we have nothing else to talk about." He rose and held the door open.

"Shaw, please don't do this."

"We have nothing else to talk about," he said more firmly.

She slowly walked past him and he slammed the door shut behind her.

60

Nicolas Creel's trips to China and Russia had been successful. No firm deals had been announced, but he had laid the groundwork for that to almost certainly happen and soon. When the "real" truth of The Phoenix Group came out—and Creel expected Katie James to publish it anytime now—the dynamic between China and Russia would quickly change from regional competitors to that of absolute enemies. And the trillions of dollars would begin flowing his way.

Yet with that triumph just behind him, he still had a problem.

He once more sat on the top deck of the magnificent *Shiloh*, one of the world's greatest super-yachts, while his ditzy wife lay sprawled naked on a plush chaise longue on the foredeck. Creel had finally gotten fed up and demanded that she put *something* on. She flatly refused, claiming that even a string bikini would unbalance her tan.

She'd told him in a pouty voice, "My body is perfect. No tan lines. No lines, Nicky! You can't make me."

How could one respond to such stark logic, to such earnest narcissistic proclamations? Creel had almost laughed, as he would've when a child had done something silly. No, this marriage was clearly not going to last. His ship phone rang. It was the captain. Mrs. Creel had finally fallen asleep.

"Then put a damn blanket over her, neck to toes," Creel instructed and hung up.

The woman he'd met in L.A. when he'd been given the philanthropic award was an art curator at the Met in New York. With multiple degrees from Yale, she was stunningly intelligent, world-traveled, attractive, nicely built, and he seriously doubted she would have been the least concerned about tan lines across her ass. He'd had a wonderfully fascinating evening with the woman that had involved no physical contact at all. He'd have his attorneys draw up the divorce papers when he returned home.

But that looming domestic change was not the problem Creel was troubled by.

He stared down at the photo of the man with Katie James. James had left Shaw's hotel in tears, Creel had been told. Was the man going to screw this up? He wanted revenge. He was highly skilled. Yes, a potential problem. Shaw's days were probably numbered. But then what was one more?

Creel gazed out onto the calmness of the Mediterranean where a hot sun slowly burned its way downward to the lazy shimmer of sea. Despite selling the best military hardware on earth, he was a peaceful man. He had never struck anyone in anger. He had, it was true, ordered the deaths of people, but it was never done with malice.

Yet from the first club wielded in anger to an A-bomb that wiped out six figures' worth of people in a few ticks of the clock, physical conflict was an essential part of humanity. Creel knew this, just as he knew that war had many positive attributes. Most significantly, it made people forget the frivolous and bond together for the greater good.

He certainly felt guilt for what he'd done. In fact he'd already pledged ten million dollars to a fund set up for the families of the victims of the London Massacre. It was the least he could do, he believed. And while across the Atlantic in England people were trying to make sense of what seemed senseless, he had gotten down on his knees in his $175 million aircraft, and asked his god, who surely couldn't be that much farther above him, to forgive him. And when Creel rose off that wool-carpeted floor and got back into his luxurious bed and turned off his ten-thousand-dollar designer lamp, he was reasonably certain his god had accommodated him.

While Pender was busy manufacturing something and selling it to everyone as the truth, Creel clearly knew what "real" truth was.

The world is a much safer place when the powerful actually use their power and much less safe when they don't.

The United States could wipe out the problem in the Middle East in days. Certainly there would be innocents who would die. But what was the difference between millions killed in ten minutes or ten years? They'd still be dead and you would have avoided a decade of misery and uncertainty. And Creel would gladly provide every weapon needed to extinguish the savages. It really was all about us versus them. And only the strong survived.

"And the weak perish," he said to the setting sun as it colored the water and the Italian coast a noble burgundy. The weak always did die. It was the natural order.

If Creel had his way the big boys would be back in control. Mutually assured destruction, or MAD, was a term from the cold war and the subject of much fear, all of it misplaced. MAD was actually the greatest stabilizing force in history, though so many people, ignorant of how the world really functioned, would be appalled by such a statement. MAD provided certainty, predictability, and perhaps annihilation of certain elements of humanity for the greater good.

He walked to the upper deck railing and looked down at his sleeping wife. She was an idiot, like most people. They were blind to everything but themselves. No vision. Simple, weak, lazy. He gazed once more at the photo of Shaw. He didn't look simple, weak, or lazy. Because he wasn't.

It would be a pity to have to kill him. Yet Creel would, if necessary.

He lifted the ship's phone. The *Shiloh*'s captain, a man with thirty years' experience on the open seas serving a variety of rich masters, answered in a brisk positive tone.

Creel said, "Arrange to bring *all* the children out tomorrow. Take in the sixty-footer to get them. And bring the mother superior. I want to give her a check."

"Very good, Mr. Creel. Will you want to launch the submarine again? The kiddies certainly enjoyed it last time."

"Good idea. Have it ready. And have the chopper prepped to take Mrs. Creel to the small jet. She'll be going to the South of France in the morning. And have her maid lay out some suitable clothing. The *more* the better."

"Right you are, sir."

Creel hung up. The good captain might not have been so pleasant had he known what Creel had done. The captain was British, London born and raised.

But the children would come tomorrow. Creel's life had become a series of balances. One bad deed weighed against one good one. Yes, he very much looked forward to the children coming tomorrow.

And to building them a brand spanking new place to be orphans in.

61

The steel bed rolled out with a clanking sound that Shaw felt down to his toes. The place smelled of chemicals and urine and other things he didn't want to think about.

Frank stood next to him.

"Look, Shaw, you don't have to do this. In fact I'm thinking you shouldn't be doing this. Why remember her like this? In this place?" He waved his hand around the antiseptic space.

"You're right," Shaw said. "But I still have to do it."

Frank sighed and nodded at the attendant.

For an instant, as the man's fingers clutched the sheet, Shaw wanted to run, run to daylight before it was too late. Instead, he simply stood there as the sheet was lifted up and Shaw stared down at Anna. Or what was left of her.

He tried to avoid staring at the wound in the middle of her forehead, or the V-shaped suture tracks where the medical examiner had cut her open looking for helpful clues as to what had killed her, or at the twin bullet holes that had erupted through her chest. Yet he found that was all he could look at, the absolute destruction of the most beautiful woman he'd ever seen. He didn't even have the gentle embrace of her green eyes, since they were closed forever.

He nodded at the attendant again and turned away. The bed rolled back and the door clanged shut and with Frank's help Shaw left the death room on shaky legs.

"Let's go get drunk," Frank said.

Shaw shook his head. "I have to go to Anna's apartment."

"What, are you some sort of masochist? First you see her on the slab and now you want to go rip your heart out some more. What's the point, Shaw? She's not coming back."

"I'm not asking you to go. But I have to."

Frank hailed a cab. "Right, but I'm still going."

They climbed in the taxi and Shaw gave the driver the address. Then he hung his head out the window trying to fight the waves of nausea that were pounding him.

He shouldn't have gone to the morgue. Not to see her like that. *Not Anna.*

Shouldn't have, but had to.

He opened the door to her apartment a few minutes later, entered, and sat down on the floor while Frank stood nearby, his gaze on him. As Shaw looked around at the familiar sights, he slowly calmed. This was the living, breathing Anna here, not the butchered object he'd just left lying on unforgiving stainless steel. Here, Anna was not dead, not murdered.

He rose, lifted a photo off the mantel; it was of him and Anna in Switzerland last year. She was a fine skier, he was less than that. But the fun they'd had. Another photo of them in Australia. A third shot of them atop an elephant she'd nicknamed Balzac for its love of coffee that it would slurp right from the cup with its trunk.

Everywhere were her belongings, her loves, her passions.

Her.

He sat down again. In a few seconds he endured a million obvious thoughts that run through a bereaved person's mind at a time like this. The bite of Adolph's saw blade didn't even come close to the pain he was feeling now. One bloody wound versus your entire mind, body, and soul being slowly crushed. They had no painkillers that could fight that.

Frank must've noticed the change in his expression. "Come on, Shaw, let's go get that drink now."

Shaw finally realized he couldn't stay here either. In some ways the living Anna was more catastrophic to him than the dead one on the metal slab. It brought back so clearly what he'd lost, what they'd both lost together.

He struggled to his feet, but before Frank could reach it the knob turned and the door opened.

The next moment Shaw and Frank were standing eye to eye with Anna's parents.

Wolfgang's face flushed. He reached out to grab Shaw, but Shaw stepped back, out of the man's range.

"No, Wolfgang, no!" screamed his wife.

"This monster, this monster." Wolfgang was so incensed he was sputtering, choking on the few words, his eyes all the time shooting dangerous volleys at Shaw, who hung back, unsure of what to do.

"Now just hold on," Frank said. "He's hurting too."

"What are you doing here?" demanded Natascha, clutching at her husband's arm, trying to hold him back.

"Do not talk to him, to that filth," yelled Wolfgang. "He killed our daughter. He killed Anna."

Now Shaw took a step forward, his eyes flashing like blue acid. "What the hell are you talking about? I had nothing to do with Anna's death."

"Shaw, let me handle this," Frank said.

Wolfgang pointed a fat finger directly in Shaw's face. "Anna would not be dead but for you. You killed her."

Frank yelled, "Wait a minute. That's bullshit!"

Shaw started to move past him, but Wolfgang suddenly charged forward, grabbed him around the throat, and his heavy bulk caused both men to fall back hard against the wall. Natascha screamed and tried to pull her husband off. "No! No! Wolfgang. No!"

Frank tried to tug Wolfgang off Shaw but the man was too heavy.

Wolfgang's thick shoulder collided with Shaw's wounded arm and he grunted in pain. He managed to lever the big German away from him by pushing a knee against his gut. When Wolfgang charged him again, Shaw sidestepped the far slower man, who was breathing so hard and whose face was so red, Shaw thought he might be having a heart attack. Wolfgang struck the wall. Before he could turn around again and attack, Shaw used his hand to pinch a nerve right next to the man's thick neck. Wolfgang slumped to the floor crying out in pain.

The next instant Natascha's heavy purse struck Shaw in the face, cutting his cheek. He felt the blood ooze down. Frank ripped the purse from the woman's hand and threw it across the room. Natascha knelt next to her husband, her arms protectively around him.

His chest heaving, blood running in his mouth, Shaw stared down at them. "Is he all right?"

"You go. You go now!" Natascha screamed at him. "You leave us alone. You have done enough. Enough!"

"I had nothing—" Shaw stopped. *What the hell is the use?*

Frank was pulling him to the door. "Let's get out of here before somebody really gets hurt."

Shaw wiped the blood off, turned and left, shutting the door behind him.

As they walked down the stairs Frank said, "They were not told you were some kind of monster, Shaw. We just—"

Shaw suddenly stopped, sat down on the steps, and let out a sob so loud that it seemed to clang off the walls like the boom of artillery. The remaining blood on his face was washed away by the tears that were coming in droves. For ten minutes he wept uncontrollably, his body thrashing from side to side.

Frank just stood there looking down, his hands clenched in fists, his own eyes moist.

And then Shaw stopped crying as abruptly as he'd started. He stood up, wiped his face dry.

"Shaw?" Frank said, eyeing him warily. "You okay?"

"I'm perfect," he answered in a mechanical tone. Then he rushed down the steps, leaving Frank to gape after him.

When Shaw hit the street he started jogging. Jogging with a purpose. He was done with mourning. What was the point of trying to cope by letting the normal grieving process take place? He would never get over Anna's death. So now he had to get back to something that really mattered: revenge. He would not lose sight of that again. And he would never stop until he'd gotten it.

And he knew just where to start.

Katie James.

This time he wouldn't take no for an answer.

62

"I checked on your story about Krakow and about your father," Katie said. She and Aron Lesnik were sitting in his tiny room at the hostel near the Thames in a far less fashionable part of London than The Phoenix Group digs. She'd brought him food and coffee, which he was devouring as she spoke.

"You check?" he said between mouthfuls of ham sandwich and crisps.

"Of course I checked. Journalists just assume everyone is lying to them."

"I not lie to you!" Lesnik exclaimed and then took a gulp of coffee.

She looked at her notes. "Your father was Elisaz Lesnik, editor of a daily newspaper in Krakow. He was killed in 1989."

"The Soviets murdered him. Poland was fighting for freedom then. We had Lech Walesa, the liberator, fighting for us. But my father he writes the truth and the Soviets they do not like that. They come one night when I am little boy and then he is dead."

"That was never proven," she pointed out.

"I do not need proof! I know!" Lesnik pounded his fist against the wall.

"So you have quite the grudge against the Russians?"

He gaped at her. "You do not believe me? You think I make this up because I hate Russians? I see people dead. I see blood everywhere. You ask me questions, I tell you truth." He stared at her defiantly and took a vicious bite of his sandwich.

"So why are you afraid to go to the police?"

"I go to police and they think I have something to do with it. To them, Pole is like Russian. And then they tell people and killers come after me. I see what they do to my father. I no want to die like that."

"You say you're good with computers; mind if I ask you a few questions?"

"Ask."

She fired off some highly technical questions that she didn't understand at all, but that a techno-friend had given her along with the answers. Lesnik responded to each of them correctly.

"Do you have computer you want me to fix, if you still not convinced?" he said crossly.

"Can't blame a girl for checking," she said sweetly. "Now about this Harris fellow? Tell me about him." She'd gotten a description of Harris and wanted to see if it jibed with what Lesnik said.

"He is okay guy. Old. White hair, smells like cigar. We talk about job. He likes me, I think. He say it is good place to work, this Phoenix place. I drink some water and then I go to bathroom down the hall. Coming back is when I hear shots downstairs. I hide. Like I say already to you."

Katie was writing all of this down. "Okay, now talk to me about—"

She didn't finish because the door had been kicked open and he was standing there.

"Shaw! How did you know . . . ?" She glared at him. "You followed me!"

He didn't bother to respond. Shaw only had eyes for Lesnik, who'd shrunk back in the corner, his half-eaten ham sandwich forgotten, his coffee spilled on the floor.

He marched toward the small man, who pressed back until the wall stopped him from going anywhere else. Lesnik cried out, "Don't let him hurt me. Don't let him. Please!"

"Shaw, you're scaring him."

Shaw took a fistful of Lesnik's shirt in his good hand. "He should be scared."

"You say no one else know!" screamed Lesnik as he looked pitifully at Katie.

"Shaw, let him go."

"You're going to tell me everything you saw and heard that day. And you better not leave one damn apostrophe out! I just heard the part about you going to the john and hiding, now pick it up from there."

Lesnik looked ready to faint, his knees buckled. "Shaw!"

Katie grabbed at his good shoulder to try and pull him off, which was akin to a gnat harassing an elephant.

"Don't get in the way, Katie," Shaw said menacingly as he glanced at her.

Lesnik, however, used this moment of distraction to pluck up his courage and nail Shaw with his fist directly on the man's bandaged arm.

"Damn it!" Shaw doubled over in pain.

The Pole leapt past him, pushed Katie down, and sprinted through the door. Shaw recovered and, holding his arm, ran after him, Katie right on his heels. They clattered down the steps, Shaw moving as fast as he could with his bad wing, but the much smaller Lesnik was seemingly jet-propelled. He hit the door to the street and was through it while Shaw and Katie were still a flight above.

Shaw smashed the door open and skidded to a stop to survey the street. Katie bumped into him. She grabbed his jacket.

"Have you lost your damn mind!" she screamed.

He suddenly saw Lesnik across the street, on the Thames side. He bolted across the road, car horns blaring, taxis swerving to avoid him as Katie followed in his wake yelling at him to stop before he killed himself.

Shaw shouted at Lesnik, who was running down the sidewalk. The Pole turned around for an instant, his face full of fear.

The shot struck him right between the eyes. He stood there for a moment, seemingly unaware his life had just ended. Then he pitched backward and over the railing. A few seconds later his body hit the flat surface of the river. A few moments after that Lesnik disappeared under the dull-colored Thames, the water briefly turning a murky crimson.

At the sound of the shot, Shaw had immediately hunched down. As Katie started to run past him yelling for Lesnik, he reached out his good arm and snagged her leg, wrenched her down, and then pulled her over behind a parked car for cover.

"Stay down!" he urged. "That was a long-range rifle round." He edged his head above the car's fender and took a look around, checking for an optics signature from the sniper gun but seeing none.

He looked back at Katie and his expression softened. She was shaking.

"It's okay now." He put an arm around her.

"No, it is *not* okay," she snapped, ripping his arm off her. "You had to come here. You had to butt in. And now an innocent man is dead! Because of you!"

"Neither one of us knows how innocent he really is," Shaw said calmly. "But right now we need to get out of here. The police—"

"You can run. I *want* to talk to the police. It'll be good background for the story."

"You're still going to write it?" he said incredulously.

"You bet I am. And you want to know something funny? Until you bulled your way into this whole thing I'd decided to table it, at least for a while. But now?" She looked in the direction of where Lesnik lay dead. "Now, I changed my mind."

"Katie, listen to me—"

She cut him off again. "No, you listen to me, Shaw. I know the woman you loved got killed. I know you're hurting. I know your life is even *shittier* than mine right now, but you crossed the line back there. No, you *obliterated* it. And I will never trust you again."

The sound of a siren reached them. Shaw glanced away and then looked back at her.

"You better get going. The police won't be your best friend right now."

"Katie, I don't think you know what you're getting into."

"What I'm getting into, you sorry-ass son of a bitch, is the truth. Now get the hell out of here."

Shaw's eyes flashed at her for an instant, but they seemed to have lost their effect on the woman.

"Now!" she screamed at him.

As he rose to go, she said, "Don't worry, I won't mention you in the story. Consider it a *parting* gift."

63

Katie called Kevin Gallagher and filled him in on what had happened. When he finally stopped hyperventilating, he only had one question: "When can you deliver the story?"

"It's already written. I can e-mail it to you right now. You can fact-check the crap out of it and then run it."

"Your contact is dead?"

"Yes. The police are investigating."

"Did they talk to you?"

"I only gave them the barest essentials and didn't reveal anything he'd told me. This is front page, right, Kevin?"

"Front page! Front page! Four-inch headline, Katie. Just like we do when war's declared. Send the story right now and I'll call you after I read it."

She put down the phone, hesitated for a moment, hit the send key, and the e-mail sailed to the man. *Just like when war's declared.* She thought about Shaw's words. What if a world war happened? She felt a tingle shoot down her spine.

Gallagher called back twenty minutes later; she could sense his drool from across the ocean.

"We'll run this in the morning edition," he promised. "We still have time." He added worriedly, "No chance we'll get scooped?"

"Lesnik won't be talking to anybody else, if that's what you mean. But look, Kevin, I can't absolutely prove that my contact was actually in the building that day. It's all circumstantial. I have no corroborating source. That's not how I usually do things."

"There's no way in hell he'd have those details if he hadn't been in there, Katie. The London police haven't released any of that information, and believe me we've tried to get it. And the fact that someone killed him? I think that's proof enough. I've led off stories with less, just like every other newspaper. I mean look at the Duke lacrosse team and Richard Jewell fiascos."

"Operative word being *fiasco*, Kevin." Katie suddenly wasn't that certain anymore.

"Don't worry. Here's to your third Pulitzer, Katie. Go have a drink on me."

Katie flinched. "I actually have a little problem in that regard. I thought you would've heard."

"I did, but so what? Get wasted. A story like this deserves it."

Whether it was this callous remark or something embedded deeply in Katie's soul, there was a definite pop in her brain.

"Wait a minute, Kevin!"

"What?"

"You can't print the story, not yet."

"Are you kidding?"

"You wait until I call back and give you the go-ahead. I have to check out something first."

"Katie! My instincts are telling me—"

"Shut up and listen," she screamed into the phone. "You don't *have* instincts. It was my ass running all over the world getting shot at while people like you sat behind your nice safe desk, okay? You don't give a shit about anything other than selling newspapers. You will hold that story until I tell you otherwise. And if you screw me, I will personally come to your house and rip your face off. And now I'm going to hang up and go have that drink you so graciously suggested, you bastard!"

She threw down the phone in disgust, took a deep breath, and tried to stop shaking. A few minutes later she was in the hotel bar steeling herself with a whiskey soda for what she was about to do. And then she had a second one. A third would have followed, but she somehow wrenched herself off the barstool after watching a guy next to her pass out in his own drool.

She walked outside, passing the Charles Dickens House. It was one of the many residences that the author had occupied in London but the only one now used as a museum. She wondered if even Dickens's prodigious imagination could have contemplated the absolute nightmare she found herself in. Probably she would have had to look to Kafka to do it justice.

She reached a small park, sat down on a bench, took out her cell phone, and called him.

He answered on the second ring. "Yeah?"

"Can we talk?"

"I thought you made your position perfectly clear already."

"I want to see you."

"Why?"

"Please, Shaw. It's important."

The café was near King's Cross Station. She sat outside and waited for him, watching the "bendy-buses," as Londoners had dubbed them. They had taken the place of the double-deckers and were basic-ally two buses joined together by a flex joint. They were not liked very much by Londoners because they often clogged the city's narrow intersections when making a turn.

That's my life, thought Katie. *I've got a dozen bendy-buses blocking every possible direction I could take.*

She saw him before he saw her. Even with the wounded arm, he moved effortlessly, seeming to glide above the pavement like a heron over water, just waiting to strike. She rose and motioned to him.

She ordered some food; he only had coffee and a biscuit.

"Did you talk to the police?" he asked.

"Briefly. I only told them what I saw. I didn't

mention that I was there interviewing him. Not a can of worms I wanted to open. As far as they knew I was just a passerby."

"They'll know you lied to them when the story comes out. Which is when, by the way? I'm sure you've already written it."

"I have. That's why I wanted to talk to you."

He sat back and looked expectant. "So talk."

"I don't want to start a World War III."

Shaw took a sip of his coffee while Katie picked at her salad. Neither said anything for about a minute.

"What do you want to hear from me?" he said. "That you shouldn't publish the story? I already told you that."

"Do you really think the truth coming out will do more harm than good?"

"Yeah, I do. But let's take a step back. We don't know if what your story says *is* true."

She bristled a bit. "How do you know? You haven't read my story."

"You didn't let me," he shot back. Then his tone softened. "Look, Katie, I'm sorry about what happened with Lesnik. I have no idea if he's involved with the bad guys or not."

"Someone gunning him down on the street probably shows he *wasn't* involved with them. He knew the truth and so they tracked him down and killed him."

"That theory has a few holes in it. How did they

track him down? Why kill him? Because he might talk about the Russians? But it looked like they wanted him to."

"We seem to be having the same discussion as last time."

"Yeah, we do." He sat back and looked everywhere except at her.

"Why did you come bursting into that hostel?"

"Let's just say I was having a bad day."

She gazed at him curiously.

He caught her look. "I went to see Anna's body at the morgue."

"Why would you do that?" she said incredulously.

"I don't know. I felt like I had to. Then I went to her apartment and it didn't get any better there."

"All the memories."

"And running into her parents, and having her father attack me."

"Good God!"

"But that wasn't the worst of it. The worst part was him blaming me for what happened to Anna."

Katie sat back, looking stunned. "Why would he do that?"

"If you see it from his perspective, it sort of makes sense. He finds out I run around the world and duke it out with men who have guns. And on top of that he's told I'm basically a criminal. Then Anna gets shot. My fault."

Another few seconds of silence passed. "Look, I'm

going to hold off on the story. For now. Until I know more."

"I think that's a very wise move, Katie." He paused. "And I appreciate it."

"What are you going to do now?"

"My plan hasn't changed. I'm going to find Anna's killer."

64

Nicolas Creel was growing impatient. He would have thought that the *Scribe* would have published the story by now. Lesnik was dead; he had told James all. She had the story of the century. The very thing she needed to take her back to the top. So what was the problem?

He had his people place certain tactful phone calls to various sources, including the *Scribe*. Creel was actually a passive investor in the newspaper and he'd been the one who'd discreetly behind the scenes orchestrated the assignment for her. There seemed to be some tension there, he had learned. She had submitted the story. But they were holding on to it for some reason. Well, he would put a stop to that.

He phoned Pender and explained the situation to his "truth manager," as Creel liked to refer to him.

"I don't want to be seen trying to influence the paper, so shake this story loose from them, Dick, any way you can."

"Never fear, Mr. Creel. I have the perfect way to get it done."

Pender hung up the phone. There was one surefire way to make a newspaper sitting on a story publish it. And that was make them think they were about to be scooped. In the age of the Internet, it was the easiest thing in the world to do.

By that evening, Pender had planted in several different but highly visible places on the Internet entries implying that a drastic turn of events regarding the London Massacre was about to be revealed.

"Startling new revelations," one fake blog entry proclaimed. "Insider's account to be revealed."

Another said that "global consequences are resting on the murders in England and what really happened there and why," and that it was connected to another recent murder in London. And that the story would be revealed in full any minute and the truth would be astonishing.

Pender had had these statements placed on sites that he knew most newspapers, including the *Scribe*, trolled hour by hour for material.

He sat back and waited for them to pull the trigger.

It didn't take long.

Kevin Gallagher was made aware of the claims on the Web barely an hour after they'd been posted. Like other papers he had staffers posted there to snatch up items of interest. Well, what his people were dropping on his desk were not only matters of interest, they were slowly eating away at Gallagher's stomach lining. When the higher-ups at the paper discovered that they were about to be beaten to the punch on the biggest story any of them could remember, Gallagher was told in crystal-clear terms that if the *Scribe* was scooped on this story, it would be the last thing that he ever did as an employee of the paper. And if Katie James wouldn't agree to release the story, Gallagher had better damn well find a way to do it.

With thoughts of his career and a Pulitzer for the paper going down the tubes, Gallagher did what he felt he had to. And then he called Katie.

"We have to run the story, Katie," he said. "We're about to get scooped."

"That's impossible. No one else knows."

"I'm looking at four different Web sources that say otherwise."

"Kevin, we're not publishing."

"Why not?"

"Because it's not right." *And I gave Shaw my word.*

"I'm sorry, Katie."

"What do you mean you're sorry?" she said sharply, her heart starting to pound.

"I didn't call asking for your permission."

"Kevin!"

"It'll be in the morning edition."

"I am going to kill you!" she screamed into the phone.

"They were going to fire me. I'll take death over

that. Sorry again, Katie, but I'm sure it'll turn out all right."

He clicked off and Katie sat there staring at the wall of her London flat. God, did she need a drink.

Then she stopped thinking about booze. *Shaw!*

She called him, part of her hoping he wouldn't answer, but he did.

"I have some bad news," she began lamely.

When she'd finished, he said nothing. She said, "Shaw? Are you there?"

Then the line went dead. She did not take this as a good sign.

The next day the world learned that, according to an inside source, the killers behind the London Massacre were Russians sent there allegedly by Russian president Gorshkov. Their motive was as yet unknown. To say that this hit the earth like a molten-lava tsunami would have been the grossest of understatements.

Dozens of lawsuits were immediately filed by the victims' families against the Russian government in British courts, even though those tribunals had no jurisdiction. A small bomb exploded outside the Russian embassy in London. Security was beefed up as protestors marched in front of the building, while the grim-faced ambassador was holed up inside burning up the phone lines to Gorshkov. On the streets of

London thousands of marchers carried flags reading "Gorshkov is a murderer." They'd been discreetly supplied by people working with Pender.

The families of the victims appeared on the BBC, all major U.S. networks, and also in several other countries. All denounced Russia's atrocity, and their tearful faces and crushed hearts made a stunned world reach a level of apoplectic fury that had been seen very few times in history.

Stoking the inferno even more was the revelation that the inside source, Aron Lesnik, had been shot down in broad London daylight. In fact, he'd died right in front of Katie James, who'd just zoomed back to the top of the journalism world after her exclusive bombshell.

The Russians again issued stern denials of it all. And these statements made not a dent in the opinion of the world. Gorshkov was said to be so crazed that he was walking around the Kremlin carrying a gun and threatening to blow his and anybody else's brains out at any moment.

Everyone wanted to find Katie James. As did the London police once they realized they'd been snookered by the intrepid journalist. Only she'd disappeared. There were rumors flying around that Gorshkov had ordered her killed.

Was she already dead? A few billion people wondered.

As soon as Shaw had hung up on her Katie had

packed her bag and fled. She'd found a room at a decrepit boardinghouse that accepted cash and asked no personal questions at all. She settled in—no, burrowed in was a more appropriate term. She vowed that if she survived all this, her first order of business would be to fly to the States and take a baseball bat to Kevin Gallagher's knees.

65

A shell corporation owned by Nicolas Creel held title to a thousand-acre estate in Albemarle County, Virginia, within a short drive of Thomas Jefferson's beloved University of Virginia. It was a working farm with stables of horses bred to run and then stud out. It had some cattle, some crops, and a mansion so large that it could fit several Monticellos inside of it comfortably. Creel had flown in today and his chopper had delivered Dick Pender here to discuss and implement the next step in the plan.

The men sat at a small conference table in a room that was totally sound- and bugproof. Pender asked, "Did your wife come back with you from overseas?"

"No. That relationship is now over."

Miss Hottie was still in the South of France and would be receiving the divorce papers just about now, Creel silently calculated. And the odds were better than even that she would be completely naked when that event occurred. He wondered briefly how she would be able to manage on the $5 million a year "stipend" the prenup provided for the next decade.

Well, at least her predilection to nakedness should save the lady some money on clothes. And then Miss Hottie disappeared from his mind completely.

"I see."

Pender noticed the architectural sketches on the table. "Building another grand palace somewhere?"

"No, an orphanage in Italy."

"Your range of interests never ceases to amaze me, Mr. Creel."

"Glad to hear it," the billionaire said coldly.

"James's one story has already surpassed everything we did," Pender added. "I have never seen media activity like this before. Never."

"Wait until we finish the story for her."

"Let me see, that includes Chinese ownership of The Phoenix Group," Pender said, glancing at his papers. "And files showing that Phoenix was behind the Red Menace campaign were found in the building, but the police have covered it up to prevent an international crisis." The man recited these items as though he were reading off a grocery list. He looked up and smiled. "That, may I say, is a true showstopper. You've never risen to greater heights, and I don't bestow that compliment lightly considering what you've accomplished in the past."

"The situation would require no less, Dick," Creel said sharply. "How soon can you let it fly?"

"Give the word and it's all over the Internet. Five

minutes after that, every major news outlet will have it in their greedy little claws."

"You sure they won't sit on it? Try to verify things?"

Pender laughed. "Verify? In this day and age? Who cares about verifying anything? It's all about speed. Who gets there first defines the truth. You know that as well as any man living."

"Then do it. Now."

Pender typed on his BlackBerry one word. *Launch.* He said the word out loud as he typed it. "I thought the term appropriate for someone in the defense industry," he said.

"Inspired," Creel said dully.

The two men worked for several more hours and then Pender packed his bag.

"What's next?" he asked the billionaire.

"Another boots on the ground," Creel answered. "Have a nice ride back to D.C. Oh, and Dick, when we sign the official deals with China and Russia I believe a substantial bonus will be in order for you."

Pender couldn't hide his pleasure. "Just doing my job."

"Oh, does that mean you *don't* want the bonus?"

Both men laughed, Pender a little nervously.

"Thank you, Mr. Creel."

After Pender left, another door to the conference room opened. Caesar sat down across from his master.

"Of course you still know where James is," Creel said. It wasn't a question.

The other man nodded. "Hiding out in London, but we kept her on a tight leash after we took care of Lesnik."

"Aron Lesnik. I never trust people who do things for altruistic reasons. You never know when they might want to do the right thing again and end up screwing you."

"He was pissed about his old man getting killed by the Soviets, that was for sure. So do you want us to kill this guy Shaw?"

"No. At least not yet. If I were a betting man, and occasionally I am, I would say the time will come when the answer to that question will be yes."

"How about James?"

"She's performed her part and I see no reason to keep her around for a return engagement. She did reveal the Russian piece in her story so the solution is fairly obvious." He eyed Caesar suggestively.

"Not polonium-210," Caesar protested. "That shit is dangerous to handle and it'll take me a while to get some."

"It would be stupid to make it that obvious." Creel sat forward and peered directly into Caesar's eyes. "But once upon a time there was a Bulgarian dissident named Georgi Markov, who ironically enough was killed in London with an *umbrella*. I trust you're familiar with the tale?"

Caesar grinned wickedly. "I am."

"Then do it."

Creel waved his hand and Caesar vanished as quickly as he'd appeared.

66

Shaw watched silently as Royce's men continued to scour the interior of the massacre site for clues that just wouldn't come. The MI5 agent had gone outside to meet with someone, leaving Shaw to wonder if things could get any worse. Royce had been furious about the story Katie James had written but he could hardly blame Shaw for that, because he'd told the man nothing about his involvement with James and the late Aron Lesnik.

Lesnik had been pulled from the Thames with the slug that ended his life still parked in the back of his brain. He wouldn't be giving any answer sessions.

Frank walked down the hallway and joined him. "You never told me where you took off to after we left Anna's apartment."

"That's right, I never did."

"Have anything to do with Katie James or her *exclusive*?"

"I don't hang out with the woman, Frank."

"Right. So how the hell did she get that story with the Polish guy? And who killed him?"

"No clue," Shaw said dully as Frank scowled at him.

A forensic tech Shaw had never seen before passed by him at the same time that he heard the front door downstairs slam shut. The tech said, "You mind? I need to use the facilities."

Shaw looked over his shoulder and realized he was standing in front of the bathroom door. He moved aside and the man went to open the door, or at least tried to.

Feet were stomping up the stairs. Shaw could hear Royce yelling. The agent was clearly upset about something, and from what Shaw could make out, that something was him.

The tech jiggled the handle of the bathroom door as a uniformed sergeant who'd been on duty here from the first day passed by.

The sergeant said, "You must be new here. You'll have to use the loo in the basement, lad, that one's busted."

Shaw could hear Royce clearly now.

"Shaw? Damn it, Shaw!"

The MI5 agent appeared at the top of the stairs, breathless and red-faced. He charged right at Shaw waving a piece of paper.

"What the hell do you know about this?" he demanded.

Shaw read the paper. It was a printout from an online news service. The story was short but to the point. The Chinese government owned or had ties to The Phoenix Group. And it was also revealed that evidence found inside the building allegedly proved that The Phoenix Group was behind the Red Menace campaign, which implied, of course, that the Chinese had been behind it. That, according to the news service's unnamed source, was why Gorshkov's men had attacked the place. It was a simple connect-the-dots explanation that would play very well all over the world.

"This is all over the Net," Royce yelled, pointing a finger at Shaw. "And now all over the bloody world."

Frank had read the story over Shaw's shoulder. "So why is that *his* problem?"

"I'm not the source," Shaw said calmly. "I haven't told anyone about anything that's gone on in here."

Royce's features clearly showed he didn't believe that answer. "Not even your friend, James? Another scoop for her maybe?"

"I don't know what you're talking about!" Shaw said heatedly.

"Are you denying that you know the lady?"

Shaw hesitated.

"I already know the answer to that question, so don't lie to me, damn it."

"How did you know?" Shaw said impassively, even as he glanced curiously at the uniformed police sergeant.

"I'm a bloody intelligence agent, that's what I do."

"I haven't seen her lately. And I have no idea where she—" Shaw froze as the tech walked past him and down the stairs.

Frank faced off with Royce. "If you've got a problem with leaks, Royce, why don't you discuss it with your people?" he said. "Because there is no way in hell that Shaw is the source for that story."

"I can't believe any of my lads would have anything to do with it," Royce said indignantly.

While Frank and Royce were arguing Shaw grabbed the sleeve of the sergeant who'd issued the warning about the bathroom.

In a low voice he asked, "How long has that toilet been broken?"

The sergeant gave a weary smile. "Ever since we got here, sir. Right inconvenient. Locked up it was. Pipe broke, or so's I could see when I finally got the door open. It's an old building after all. And not like those poor folks ever had a chance to get it fixed. So I locked it back up. Now the gents got to go to the basement to take a pee 'cause the only other loo is for the ladies on the first floor. Though some of the lads have been using that one too. Guess it don't matter now, does it?"

"Exactly where is the first floor ladies' room located?"

"End of the hall, furthest from the stairs, near the rear of the building."

Shaw walked down the hall and saw the nameplate set into the wood of the door: William Harris. He looked at the room where the copier was. It was equidistant between Harris's office and the locked bathroom.

Royce came thundering down the hall with Frank scurrying after him. "Shaw?" Royce said. "I want the bloody truth!"

Shaw looked down the stairs, the mental images racing across his brain. Even if Lesnik had misspoken and had used the basement bathroom or even the ladies' room on the first floor instead of the locked-up one on the second it couldn't have happened the way he said it had. Katie said he'd told her that he'd heard shots when *leaving* the bathroom. The assault team was already on the first floor covering both ends by then. Coming back from the basement and especially the first floor he'd have run right into them. He'd be dead. He'd never hid in the copier. He had probably never been in the building.

And it all came down to where you took a leak. Or didn't *take a leak.*

He sprinted down the steps, leaving Royce to scream after him, but he never heard the curses raining down on him. He called the number Katie had left him.

"Come on, answer, answer the damn phone." It rang three, four, five times. Shaw was sure it was going to go to voice mail. *Sonofabitch!*

"Hello?"

A rush of relief hit him when he heard her real voice. "Lesnik was lying," he said.

"What?"

"On the day of the killings the toilet on the second floor was busted and the door was locked shut. He'd have to have used the one in the basement or the first floor near the rear entrance. He would've run right into the killers. He'd be dead. He was lying about the whole thing. You were set up, Katie."

There was only silence on the other end. He wondered if she'd hung up on him.

"You're sure?" she said shakily.

"They briefed him well otherwise. But for the slip about the john, which they obviously forgot to check and assumed it was working, and a bit of luck, I'd never have known."

"My story. It was a lie?" she gasped in disbelief.

"Where are you?"

"I can't believe this. I can't. I told that idiot Gallagher I didn't have corroboration."

"Katie, where are you?"

"Why?"

"Because now that you've written the story you're dispensable."

"I'm safe."

"No, you're not safe! They probably know exactly where you are. Now tell me."

She gave him the address.

"Do not open the door to anybody. And be ready to run."

He sprinted into the middle of the street, stopping a taxi dead, ripped open the door, hauled the surprised passenger out, jumped in, and told the stunned driver exactly where to go. The diminutive cabbie took one look at Shaw's massive size and glowering expression and the taxi roared off.

67

Only twenty minutes had passed since Shaw's call when the buzzer on the entrance to Katie's building went off. She ran to the door of her flat and spoke into the call box.

"Shaw?"

"Yep."

She hit the button to release the door and then froze. *Had* that been Shaw's voice? In her excitement she'd just assumed . . .

From down below she heard measured footfalls coming up. That didn't sound like . . .

She bolted the door, grabbed her hastily packed bag, and looked frantically around for another way out. There was only one. The window overlooking the back alley.

She threw it open and peered out. It was a two-story drop. In the movies there would've been a convenient fire escape or mounds of soft garbage down below, but in real life there never were. And she had no time to knot sheets into a rope. What there was on the alley level was a guy, a big guy wearing jeans and a rugby sweater and reading a newspaper in the fading light while sitting in a beat-up lawn chair.

"A hundred quid if you catch me," she called out.

"Pardon me?" he said, gazing up at her quizzically.

She climbed onto the windowsill, her bag slung over her back. "I'm going to jump and you're going to catch me. Understood?"

The man dropped his newspaper and stood up looking around, perhaps to see if this was some sort of prank.

"You say you're going to jump?"

"Do not drop me!"

"Oh, dear Lord," was all he could manage.

There was someone right outside of Katie's door now. She heard something pushing against the wood. For an excruciatingly long moment all she saw was Anna Fischer, positioned just as Katie was, and the bullets ripping through her body. If only she'd jumped an instant sooner.

"Here I come," she called down to the man, who was hopping around, his thick arms flying in all directions, trying to best gauge her trajectory. "Do not miss!" she added firmly.

She leapt and a couple seconds later she and the man tumbled down in a tangle of arms and legs. Katie got to her feet, all body parts seemingly intact, and except for a bruised arm and cut shin she was fine.

She shoved five twenty-pound notes into his hand, gave him a kiss, and ran for it.

She turned the corner and headed away from her building. She didn't look back and didn't see the man change direction and head her way. She didn't see the door of her apartment building fly open either as another man hit the street and hustled after her. But she could feel their presence and picked up her pace. Should she start screaming? There were plenty of people around. But what if they had guns? They'd shot poor Lesnik with a million people around. She desperately looked for a cop yet saw none.

She never saw the third man, because he was ahead of her but coming her way. He was the safety valve in case the first team missed, and it looked like he would get his chance. He slid the syringe from the sleeve of his coat, uncapped it, and held it ready as he picked up his pace.

68

The taxi turned onto the road and Shaw scanned the street. His gaze caught and held on Katie. Her look of terror was clear. She was running. He caught sight of one of the men behind her. But there would be more than one.

And then it happened. Shaw saw a glint of sunlight reflect off the object in the man's hand. He jumped from the rolling cab and sprinted forward.

Katie and the man were inches away from each other. He drew back the syringe and then swung it forward, aiming for her belly.

Katie gasped as the fellow in front of her was knocked aside by a far larger man. She felt something slide across her arm. She looked down and saw the needle as it missed going into her by a bare inch. Then she watched as Shaw grabbed the man's hand, bent it forward, and buried the needle to the hilt in the man's chest, the plunger pushed all the way down. The man looked in horror at the thing sticking out of him, pushed Shaw away, got to his feet, and ran down the street. His lips were already starting to grow numb as the drug began its lethal journey through him. Caesar had not opted for ricin, the poison fired into Bulgarian Georgi Markov's leg using a spring-loaded umbrella. What had entered the man's body was a massive dose of tetrodotoxin, a substance over a thousand times more lethal than cyanide and for which there was no antidote.

He would be dead in twenty minutes.

Shaw grabbed Katie by the arm and they sprinted to Euston Station, jumped on the Tube, rode it to King's Cross, ran back to daylight, and grabbed a cab. Shaw told the man to simply drive and then looked over at Katie.

She hadn't said one word to him, not while running and not in the Tube. A terrible thought seemed to grip him. "The syringe, it didn't . . . ?"

She put a shaky hand on his arm. "No, it didn't. Thanks to you. How did you know?"

"More luck than anything else." He sat back against the seat.

"That was the third party back there, wasn't it?"

He nodded. "That was the third party."

She glanced out the window as the cab struggled along in London traffic. The afternoon was quickly turning to dusk. "Where are we going?"

He didn't say anything.

"Shaw?"

"I heard you. I just don't have an answer."

"I'm sorry I didn't listen to you about Lesnik."

"So am I," he said bluntly.

"I shouldn't have written the story."

"No, you shouldn't."

"We're screwed, aren't we?"

"Looks that way. And I told you not to leave where you were staying."

"They were in the building. I had to run."

"How'd you get out?"

"I—" Katie stopped. She did not want to tell him that she'd jumped from a window and managed to survive. Unlike Anna. "Through the back. Do you have some sort of plan?"

"I have a *goal*. To stay alive. The plan is still coming."

"It's clear now that Lesnik was working for this third party. They killed him and tried to kill me. For all I know they somehow got the *Scribe* to hire me and then dropped Lesnik in my lap. I knew it was too good to be true. Damn it!" Katie slapped the seat.

"Did Lesnik say anything that might give us a lead on who hired him?"

She shook her head. "Nothing. I checked out his background. That was legit. He seemed like a sincere guy. His father *was* killed by the Soviets. He probably held a grudge and these people exploited it."

"But that gets us no closer to the truth."

the whole truth

"We need to go underground to have any chance of finding out what's really going on." She looked at him. "Know anyone who can help with that?"

Shaw already had his phone out. "I might."

69

This should have been one of the happiest days of Nicolas Creel's career. After years of work, and one enormous and recently manufactured international crisis, both the governments of Russia and China were about to sign contracts with Ares Corp. and its subsidiaries to the tune of half a trillion dollars with plenty more to come down the road. It was a testament to the centralization of defense contractors in the modern age that countries on either side of a dispute would buy their weaponry to destroy each other from essentially the same outfit. Yet Ares did not pick favorites. It was an equal-opportunity provider of weapons of mass destruction and always would be.

The final catalyst for the successful deal had occurred when President Gorshkov had sent a strongly worded demand for a public apology to Beijing. And the man also wanted money, in the billions, for the damage done to Russia's international reputation. Beijing, not surprisingly, had not agreed with that position. They sent an equally forcefully worded reply to Moscow stating that the Chinese weren't involved in the Red Menace machine, and thus owed the Russians nothing. Predictably, international relations between the two behemoths went downhill from there at a remarkably brisk clip.

Other countries had stepped in to try and broker a peaceful resolution to this mess. The United States naturally took the lead role, but since the Chinese government was basically financing America's consumption by buying its debt, Washington had little recourse when Beijing told it to back off. The Russians accused the Americans of being in China's pocket for this same reason. Consequently, the U.S. ambassador to Russia was told to stand down or pack his bags when he implored the Russians to do nothing drastic.

France next tried to step in, but Gorshkov would not even return the French president's phone call. The Germans remained silent. Berlin obviously didn't want to get dragged back behind either a new Iron Curtain or a Titanium Coffin. Britain was in an extremely delicate situation. If Russia *had* been behind the massacre and China *had* been operating the Red Menace campaign from London, the poor Brits didn't exactly know what their role or response should be. And when initial diplomatic channels had been opened with China over the matter, the communists had been as stern in their denials of culpability as they had been with Russia, and ended by telling Downing Street to keep clear of the dispute.

The entire world was now arming for a third world war. The new amount of business would be the biggest in the history of the world, the vice chairman of Ares Corporation e-mailed to Creel, his glee evident in every word of his message. "What a stroke of luck, this Red Menace thing," he'd added.

Creel read the message once and then deleted it. *What a stroke of luck indeed.* He made a mental note to find a new vice chairman to replace that idiot.

The cold war was back and better than ever. With a series of deft moves and remarkable planning he'd reshaped the planet's power structure to where it should be. The pissants in the Middle East had immediately tried to suck the world back in, doing a version of "Hey, what about me, I'm still bad news," by cratering another mosque in Baghdad, bombing a market in Anbar, and killing all of eighty civilians and two U.S. grunts. The world's collective response had been swift and unmistakable: "Don't bother us, we've got *real* problems. *Millions* could die!"

Ironically, Creel had made the world far more civilized by getting back to a "real" war mode. That was his plan, after all.

Not a shot fired.

And the money poured.

And the savages without a conscience put in their place.

It is the hat trick. Thank you very much.

It had never been about the money, really. It had been about the world. Nicolas Creel had just saved it.

Yet still, there was something wrong.

He was currently standing on picturesque Italian soil, the beauty of the Mediterranean coast spread out before him. The mother superior was next to him, resplendent in her lovely white robes. She was beaming, as she looked over preliminary plans for the building of a new orphanage to replace the one that had been constructed right after World War II when there had been a large number of orphans.

Speaking in Italian the mother superior said, "It is beautiful. And you are a beautiful man to have done it, Nicolas."

"Please, Mother Superior. It was the least I could do. And I can assure you I will benefit spiritually to the same degree that the children will by having a new home." He said all this in fluent Italian.

Creel was proficient in many languages; he'd learned them solely to gain an edge in business. Some of his biggest deals had come about simply because he could say "Please" and "Thank you" in his customers' own tongues.

Yes, this should have been a time of great triumph for Creel as he strolled around the site where the new orphanage would be. But it wasn't. And for one reason only.

Caesar had arrived from London and ridden a launch out to the *Shiloh*. Katie James had slipped through their fingers. One of Caesar's men had been stuck with the damn needle instead. And Shaw, the man with the eyes like Creel's, had been right in the middle of it. He and James were now out there together. Doing what, only they knew.

According to Creel's sources Shaw had run out of The Phoenix Group building like he was on fire twenty minutes before he arrived at James's flat. And worst of all, Creel didn't know why.

For the first time in a long time, the fourteenth richest man in the world felt a twinge of real fear. Nicolas Creel was not a man who bet the farm or thought himself infallible. He was brilliant enough to know that he didn't actually know everything. He was a man who could adapt a plan on the fly, apply new intelligence to maximum effect, and realized that a plan set in stone was always doomed to failure.

And as he thought about this, the mother superior hugged him, her angelic tears staining his blazer. "God will bless you for this," she whispered in his ear.

And above all, Creel was a man who hedged his bets any way he could.

"Mother Superior, can I ask a favor please?"

"Ask and it shall be done, my son," she said.

"Will you pray for me?"

70

Shaw and Katie had hidden out in a small row house outside London near Richmond that Shaw had previously arranged as a safe house. The next night they had received a visitor, an Italian with a Dutch accent. He was the same man who ran Shaw's favorite restaurant in Amsterdam. He said a polite hello to Katie and then nodded at Shaw, who was scrutinizing him closely.

"How did you get here?" Shaw asked.

"Train," replied the fellow. "A bit more congenial security-wise."

Shaw nodded in understanding while Katie watched curiously.

"You have it?"

The man took out a small package from his pocket and handed it to Shaw.

Shaw tried to give the fellow a roll of euros but he pushed it away.

"At least for your expenses," Shaw said.

"Come see me in Amsterdam, after this is all over. Spend your money there with good food and bad wine."

The men shook hands and then the Dutch-speaking Italian was gone.

Shaw put the package in his coat pocket and looked at Katie, who was staring at him expectantly.

"Care to share?" she asked.

"No."

Shaw next called Frank and filled him in. At the end of his lengthy explanation, Frank's comment was brief but to the point.

"Ho–lee shit!"

"I was expecting something a little more helpful."

"What do you want me to do? You've got no real proof and you still don't know who the third party is."

"Then get me to Dublin and I'll take it from there."

"Why Dublin?"

"I've got people to see."

"Like who? Leona Bartaroma at Malahide Castle? I know you went to see her."

"FYI, I've got Katie James with me."

"Lucky, lucky you."

"So can you get me to Dublin?"

"Look, I had a hard enough time convincing the folks upstairs that your freelancing with MI5 was a good use of your time. If they find out you've split, all bets are off."

"Just get me to Dublin."

"I can, but you've got to swear you won't see Leona about *that*."

"I do."

The next day Shaw and Katie were driven from London to Wales in an old bus. After that they ducked into the damp hold of a ratty tugboat that was now crossing the Irish pond in pitching seas. Katie spent an hour throwing up into a bucket as they bounced to Ireland. Shaw kept handing her soaked towels to wipe her face.

Katie finally sat up, nothing left to heave out of her gut.

"Your sea legs are impressive," she said. "I'm more of a landlubber."

"The high-speed ferry wasn't an option since everyone in the world is looking for you."

"Everybody wants to be famous until they are and finds out it sucks."

"We'll be there shortly."

"Good to know," Katie said, one hand over her still-writhing stomach. "So we get there, and then what?"

"And then we meet someone who can help us go deep underground. Disguises, new IDs."

"And then what?"

"And then we figure out the next step."

Later, Shaw walked over and looked out a port-hole. The tug had slowed, the rocking had ceased. They were past the breakwater and into the harbor.

"Let's go."

Katie rose gingerly, testing her legs. She slid her

bag over her shoulder. "Shaw, we're going to die, aren't we?"

"Probably. Why?"

"Just wanted confirmation."

71

They took a cab from the harbor, driving through small villages on their way west to Dublin proper. A chilly rain was falling and even the pubs they passed were mostly empty. As Katie gazed into the window of one bar and saw a cheery fire and a man pulling down a pint, she didn't have the least desire to join him. Her alcoholism was apparently cured. All it had taken was the end of the world.

Before they'd left England Katie had phoned Kevin Gallagher and explained that her source had probably lied to her.

"Do you have absolute proof that he did?" Gallagher demanded.

"No, not absolute."

"Do you have absolute proof that the facts of your story are untrue?"

"No, I don't."

"Then we're standing by it."

"Even if I'm not?"

"This is the biggest story of my life, Katie, so I'm going to pretend this conversation never happened and I suggest you do the same." Then Gallagher had promptly hung up on her.

"Son of a bitch!" screamed Katie. "I hate editors."

The cab dropped them off and they walked in the rain. Katie looked around.

"Isn't that the university?"

Shaw nodded. "Come on." They headed down a side street.

He knocked on a door where a sign hung.

"Maggie's Bookshop?" Katie said.

The door opened and a tall, stout woman ushered them in.

She closed the door and Katie surveyed the books on all four walls. They were running for their lives and Shaw had forced her to vomit her way across the Irish Sea so he could take her to a bookstore in dreary Dublin?

The woman didn't tell Katie her name, and Katie didn't volunteer hers. She assumed the woman was Maggie.

"I'm so sorry about Anna," the lady said to Shaw.

She led them upstairs where a room had been set up as a hair and makeup area.

"Sit here, please." The lady motioned to a swivel chair in front of a long mirror. Katie sat and the woman picked up a pair of shears and lifted a handful of her hair.

Katie jumped out of the chair. "What do you think you're doing?"

"You didn't tell her?"

"Tell me what?" Katie said, staring at Shaw.

"Haircut," Shaw said. He nodded at the woman. "Do it short and change the color. And then you can scalp me."

An hour later, Katie James was a brunette with spiky hair, her eyes were brown instead of blue, her skin coloring was darker, her eyes rounder, her lips narrower. She wore bulky clothes that added about twenty pounds.

Shaw could not make himself shorter, but twenty minutes later his hair was mostly gone and the woman had done a number on his face, including a mustache and goatee, a bulked-up nose, and contact lenses that turned his startling blue eyes a muted brown. Katie couldn't even swear it was him.

She led them to another room set up as a photo studio.

Katie said to Shaw, "She sure has a lot of sidelines for a bookshop owner."

The pictures were taken and two hours later Shaw and Katie had brand-new passports, driver's licenses, and other official papers showing them to be a married couple from a London suburb.

Shaw thanked the woman and paid her.

"I wish you luck," she said.

"Oh, we're going to need a lot more than luck, honey. Why don't you go ahead and pray for a miracle?" Katie shot back as she slammed the door behind her.

As they walked down the alley she said, "Where to now?"

"Grab some sleep and then I have a doctor's appointment in the morning."

"A doctor's appointment?" she said skeptically.

"Let's get something straight. I'm not going to tell you everything."

"Fine. Just so long as you know that cuts *both* ways."

"The ground rules are set then." He picked up his pace and she had to hurry along to keep up.

72

They'd checked into the hotel as a married couple and thus had only gotten one room. Shaw had told Katie that he didn't want her to be left alone at any time. "They almost got you once, they'll definitely try again."

They ordered some food, although Katie's still touchy stomach could only manage some tea and bread. Then they sat at a little table facing each other to discuss matters.

"What I still don't understand," Shaw said, "is why they targeted The Phoenix Group in the first place."

"It was Chinese-owned," Katie answered as she cradled her tea cup and watched the drenching rain out the window.

"There're lots of Chinese-owned places in London. And why pick London?"

"But a Chinese-owned think tank?"

"Okay, so why a think tank?"

"According to you they *planted* those docs about the Red Menace. A bunch of super-smart people working at a secret think tank being behind the global smear campaign seems plausible. It probably wouldn't have seemed nearly as credible if they'd hit a local fast-food place, slaughtered a bunch of teenagers, and planted the incriminating docs there."

"So they *happened* to stumble across The Phoenix Group, just happened to learn its Chinese connection, and sent in a strike team?"

Katie said, "There has to be a catalyst. Maybe someone they met with. Some project they were working on. They obviously had the place under surveillance. When I was there, I saw lots of people coming and going so we might have to check . . ."

She stopped talking as the horrible, absolutely awful possibility swept over her. She glanced at Shaw. By his look she could tell he'd reached the same conclusion.

"They would've seen *you* there," Shaw said, a discernible edge to his voice.

"Yes, they would have," Katie answered in a hushed tone. "And since they were already using me they might've focused on The Phoenix Group because of my connection to Anna. And then discovered the Chinese element."

"But that's only one possible reason," he said, though the disbelief in his own words was evident.

"Yes," Katie said weakly. "I suppose that's true."

She put down her cup and glanced at the bed. "Um, I'm really tired, Shaw. You can have the bed. I'll take the floor."

"No, I'll sleep on the floor."

"Shaw!"

"Just take the bed, Katie. It's been a long day and we're both exhausted."

Katie changed in the bathroom, came out, and crawled under the covers. Shaw was already on the floor, a blanket over him. Katie turned out the light.

A few minutes later, as the rain continued to pour down, she said quietly, her voice quivering, "I'm sorry, Shaw."

She didn't get an answer.

73

As the dawn began to break outside, Shaw sat up, leaned against the bed, and looked at a wide-eyed Katie. It was obvious from her puffy red eyes that she hadn't slept at all.

"I have something to tell you," she said, drawing the sheet around her.

"Katie, you don't have to—"

She put a hand on his shoulder. "Please, let me just get it out before it burns a hole in my gut."

He waited, watching her.

"I *was* doing this for the story. Even when I flew over to see you in the hospital, part of me was thinking about getting my career back on track. And then I got this new assignment and came to London. I could just feel I was on my way back." She looked down, balling the bedcovers in her hands, cheeks quivering. "I don't even think I'm human, not anymore. I used to be, I'm just not sure when I stopped. It's been a while, I know that . . . I'm sorry."

"Katie, you're a reporter. It's in your blood."

"That doesn't make it right. And I'm a shit, don't ever forget that."

"Okay, you're a shit. But if we're going to work together, we have to trust each other."

"I trust *you*. I think the problem is you don't trust me. And I can't blame you."

"I haven't had a lot of practice, trusting people." He paused. "But I'm going to have to work on it. Besides, I need your help. Sometimes you see things I don't. I haven't found many people who can do that." He managed to smile weakly at her.

She smiled back, the small thaw in their relationship immediately rekindling her spirits. "I'm going to grab a shower. Get up on the bed while I'm in there. You must be stiff as a board."

Shaw pulled himself off the floor and slowly eased down on the bed. He listened to the shower come on. The bed was warm from Katie lying there, and then his eyes closed. The next thing he knew he smelled coffee, bacon, and eggs.

He sat up and looked around. Katie was dressed and sitting in front of a room service table. She poured out a cup of coffee and handed it to him.

"What time is it?" he said.

"Eight-thirty."

He sipped his coffee.

"Hungry?"

He nodded, rose, and sat across from her. "You

should've gotten me up when you got out of the shower," he said grumpily.

"It was a lot more convenient this way," she said. "With you sound asleep I could get dressed in here and not in the tiny bathroom. You know, this marriage arrangement is going to turn out to be awkward," she said, eyeing him over the rim of her cup.

He stretched out his bad arm gingerly.

"Is that why we're going to the doctor's?"

"Yes, but just not for the reason you're probably thinking."

"What a surprise."

They grabbed a taxi to Leona Bartaroma's cottage, a simple stone structure set off a gravel road. It was about two miles from Malahide Castle where Leona was a tour guide. When they got out and looked around Katie said, "Strange place for a doctor's office."

"She's retired."

"Oh, that makes perfect sense."

Leona invited them in, said hello to Katie, and sat them down in her roomy kitchen overlooking the back garden. She said nothing about Shaw's altered appearance but eyed Katie. "May I speak freely in front of her?"

"I wouldn't have brought her otherwise."

"Frank already called."

"Of course."

"He said you promised not to visit me."

"No, I promised not to visit you about *this*." He tapped his right side.

"His men are all around here," she added.

"I know that."

"How?"

"I smelled them."

"So you know I can't do what you want me to do."

"How do you know what I want you to do? I haven't told you yet."

She looked curious while Katie's gaze darted back and forth between the two.

"Tell me, then."

He rolled his sleeve up, exposing the metal staples in his wound.

"My God, how did that happen?"

"I guess Frank forgot to tell you about that."

She looked at the wound more closely. "It looks like it's healing nicely. The surgeon did a good job."

"I'm grateful for your expert opinion. But that's not why I'm here."

"Why, then?"

He took a small metal cylinder from his pocket. "I want you to put this in there," he said, pointing to the rip in his arm.

"You're not serious."

"Shaw!" Katie exclaimed.

"Dead serious."

"What is it?" Leona said slowly.

411

"You don't need to know that," Shaw said. "It's stainless steel, if that helps."

"It doesn't. There's the risk of infection," Leona began.

"Put it in a sterilized bandage. But there's where I need it. Can you do it?"

"Of course I can do it. The question is, why in the world should I?"

"Because I'm asking you. Politely."

"How far in?" she said nervously.

"Not too far. Because I may need to get it out in a hurry."

"This is ridiculous," Katie snapped.

"Not too far in, Leona," Shaw said again. "And you owe me."

"I don't see it that way."

"But I do." He pulled out his shirttail and lifted up the front, exposing the sutured tracks of the scar on his right side. "I do."

Katie looked at the mark and then over at Leona and frowned. "Did you do that to him?"

Leona wet her lips. "I don't have a surgery here, Shaw. No instruments."

"Dublin's a big town. I'm sure you can find what you need."

"It'll take a bit of time."

"This afternoon," he shot back, a tinge of menace in his voice.

"I can't. I have to go to Malahide."

"This afternoon."

"All right. I'll call you."

Shaw rose to leave and Katie quickly stood too.

"I don't have the means to put you completely under," Leona said. "Just a local. There'll be pain."

He tucked his shirt back in. "There's always pain, Leona."

Outside, Katie said, "Okay, who the hell was that, Dr. Frankenstein's wife? And what is going on?"

"It's better that you don't know, Katie. Trust me."

"Trust you? What about trusting *me* like we talked about?"

"I said I was going to *work* on it. I didn't say I was there yet."

74

The rain had passed and it was a lovely day in Dublin. Skittish birds flitted from tree to tree; colorful flowers in neat beds waved in the slight breeze; people walked and chatted, drank coffee at street cafés; cars drifted down wide streets.

Inside the small, antiseptic room Shaw gritted his teeth and crushed the arm of the chair he was in. Leona, gloved, masked, and dressed in surgical scrubs, had pulled out several of the metal staples holding his ripped skin together while Katie gripped his other arm with her gloved hands.

"That was the easy part," Leona said pleasantly as she dropped the last of the three staples she'd removed into a pan. There were four left in his arm.

"Glad to hear it," muttered Shaw.

"Still want to go through with it? It's going to set back the healing process."

"Just *do* it, Leona."

She used a slender instrument that looked like a miniature crowbar to pry open the wound and blood started to trickle out. Droplets of sweat popped up on

Shaw's brow. Katie tightened her grip on his arm. Leona had given him local anesthesia all around the wound but warned him again there would be pain. And the lady hadn't been mistaken.

She'd wrapped the small metal device in a layer of sterilized mesh surgical wrap. "You can't keep this in there long," she said. "I've sterilized it, but there will eventually be infection. It's unavoidable."

"Funny, you didn't say that the last time."

"The last time was different."

"Not for me it wasn't." He touched his side. "You never said me having *this* thing in me long-term was a problem."

"Apples and oranges," she snapped. "That device is like a pacemaker, designed for long-term use inside the body. But not this thing. So, as a doctor, I am giving you that warning. There will be infection here."

"Duly noted." Shaw grunted. "Now stick it in."

She carefully wedged the device into the wound, her nimble, gloved fingers finding a small cavity where it would fit.

The pain made Shaw's entire body shake.

"Take my hand, Shaw, squeeze it," Katie offered.

"No," he grunted.

"Why?"

"Because I'll break every damn bone in it."

A second later, the armrest came away in his hand, the screws sheared off.

Leona withdrew her fingers from the wound and looked with satisfaction at her work.

"I can put new staples back in, or even cauterize it."

"Uh-uh."

"Why not?"

"Because I won't be able to get to the damn thing when I need it, Leona. Which is the whole point," Shaw snapped. "Old-fashioned thread will be just fine."

She shrugged, cleaned the wound as best she could, stitched him up, wrapped gauze around it, and sat back.

"All done."

Katie let go of Shaw and also let out a relieved breath. Shaw slowly sat up, carefully moving his arm.

"Thanks," he said gruffly.

"For you, Shaw, anything," she said sarcastically. "As you said, I so clearly *owe* you."

"Yeah, well now we're even."

"At *least* even," she corrected. "The needle in fact might have swung to my side."

"I don't think so. Calling it even was a gift on my part." He put his shirt on. While he was buttoning it up she glanced at the scar on his right side. "How is it working, by the way?"

"Ask Frank, I'm sure he'd love to tell you all about it." He reached over and pocketed the tiny instrument she'd used to put the metal device in his arm. "For old time's sake," he said, when she looked ready to protest.

As they were leaving Leona stopped him at the door. "Is that thing in your arm what I think it is?"

"You never know, Leona, you just never know."

75

"Shaw, are you going to tell me what's going on? What is that thing in your arm? How do you know that Leona person? Where'd you get that scar on your side?" Katie fired off these questions as they ate dinner at the Shelbourne Hotel across the street from St. Stephen's Green in central Dublin. It was late enough at night that they had a quiet table in the back and could discuss things. Though Shaw didn't appear to be in a *discussing* mood because she'd been asking these same questions for hours and hadn't gotten a single answer in return.

He stoically finished chewing his food. He hated Dublin now. He'd asked Anna to marry him here, at a little place north of the Liffey. On his knee with the damn ring. She'd said yes in nine languages. And now she was dead. There would be no marriage, no four or five kids, no growing old together. Nothing. Everywhere he looked he saw some place, some nook, cranny, smell, sound, even a funny thing the sky did, the drop of the rain, the honk of an Irish car horn that reminded him of her. He could barely breathe here.

He could barely function. Hated it. And that wasn't all.

Anna was on her way back to Germany for burial with parents who blamed him. Blamed *him* for the death of a woman he would have gladly sacrificed his own life to protect. Anna on a cold metal bed in London with a hole in her head. Anna being shipped to cold, lonely ground in Wisbach, for all of eternity, instead of being held in his warm arms. Safe, together.

Katie interrupted these thoughts. "We need to find out who was really behind the Red Menace."

"The whole world has been looking, and nobody seems to have found it yet."

"I'm not sure the whole world *really* has been trying to find out the source. They've just accepted that it was true, sort of a rush to judgment. Or if they did look it wasn't very hard. And then events kept happening and kept people jumping. After a while, the story didn't become *who* was behind it, but what the hell are we going to do about the evil Russians. I think the whole world was basically snookered."

Shaw looked at her with new respect. "That's sort of what Anna was thinking."

"I'll take that as a big compliment."

"Any ideas?" he asked.

Katie pulled her chair closer and lowered her voice. "I've actually been giving that some thought." She dug in her purse and pulled out a battered notepad.

"When I was in Anna's office that day she had to step out to see someone and I sort of looked around."

"You mean you were snooping," Shaw said a little angrily, instinctively defending Anna's right to privacy.

"Do you want to hear what I found or not?"

"I'm sorry, go ahead."

"I looked through some of the Red Menace stuff on her desk and some notes she'd jotted down. One was a list of Web sites or e-mail addresses. Maybe she'd contacted them. Anyway, one stuck with me and I wrote it down."

"Why'd it stick with you?"

"It was called Barney's Rubble-Land. You know, *The Flintstones*? It was one of my favorite cartoons growing up. Anyway, it was a blogger page. I didn't check it out then, but while you were showering back at the hotel after Dr. Doom worked on you, I accessed the site from my laptop."

"What'd you find?"

"This blogger, apparently his name is Barney, had some questions about the Red Menace too. From his postings he didn't think it was legit."

"How does that help us?"

"Well, quite frankly, I didn't think the blogger site was legit."

"What do you mean?"

"I think Barney is a sham. I have lots of friends who're bloggers. You get obsessed with them, write stuff all the time. There's really nothing regimented about them. Free association, spur-of-the-moment stuff. And you usually have a place for people to discuss things. I mean, that's one of the main reasons to have a blog in the first place. Right?"

"Right."

"Well, this blog didn't have that. I checked the dates of the postings. They come out every other day at the same time. That doesn't sound like Barney's Rubble-Land to me. It sounds like it was on some sort of preset spit-out-a-blog mode, bi-daily pattern."

"Why would someone set up a system like that?" Shaw wondered out loud.

"They might if instead of a real blog, it was a way to test the waters."

"Test the waters?"

"Yeah, people in the entertainment and ad fields do it all the time. I actually did a story on it years ago. You put out a product and you want to gauge people's reaction to it. You can have focus groups, opportunities to phone in opinions, Web site discussions. But some companies go a step further. They use blank drops, like a façade to get people to *really* let them know how they feel without feeling pressure. It can be a fake Web site, 800 number phone bank, or a questionnaire put out under a sham company's name."

Shaw looked very interested now. "So you're saying this Barney Rubble might have been a façade to test how people were reacting to the Red Menace campaign?"

"And since Barney's blog was highly critical and suspicious of the campaign . . ."

"They might have put that carrot out there to see if anyone else felt the same way. But you said there was no forum on the site to leave your opinion."

"But if you e-mailed the site, which Anna did—"

Shaw finished for her. "Then they get your e-mail address. And Anna's e-mail was AFischer@The PhoenixGroup.com." He looked sharply at Katie. "That may be how they found out about The Phoenix Group. Not through you."

"That's probably something we'll never know for sure."

A minute of silence passed while they fiddled with the remains of their meals.

"Katie, I . . ."

"Don't even go there, Shaw. This thing is complicated and we've both made mistakes. And we'll both probably make some more along the way."

"Let's just hope one of them doesn't end up getting us killed."

"Can we track this Web site somehow? I'm not that great with technical things." Shaw nodded, made a call to Frank. He put his phone away and finished his wine. "We'll see what he comes up with."

"So are we staying in Dublin?" she asked.

He shook his head. "We're flying out tomorrow."

"Where?"

"Germany. A little town called Wisbach."

76

There is never a good day to bury someone. Even when the sun is shining and the air is warm, there is nothing whatsoever positive about laying a cold body in the cold earth, particularly someone with three bullet holes that cut her life short by at least four decades. And in Wisbach there was no sun, no warmth. The rain was coming down in sheets *and* buckets as Shaw and Katie sat in the car at the graveyard that was set next to a small church.

They'd flown into Frankfurt that morning and driven over. Going through airport security in Dublin the alarms had sounded when Shaw had stepped through the metal detector. The wand the security guard ran over him homed in on his left arm.

"Roll up your sleeve, sir," the guard had ordered, an edge to his voice.

When his gaze hit the row of metal staples revealed under the bandage, he flinched.

"Damn, does that hurt?"

"Only when I roll up my sleeve," Shaw answered.

At the gravesite the rain had turned the mound of fresh earth next to the six-foot-deep hole into a mud pile. Anna's coffin and the people here paying their respects were under a large tent set up next to the gravesite to keep them reasonably dry.

Shaw had decided not to join the mourners. He'd spotted Wolfgang Fischer's lumbering figure, Natascha next to him. Neither looked very tall today. They seemed bent, destroyed. So Shaw just sat in the car. And watched them lower the coffin into the grave. Wolfgang nearly collapsed with grief. It took several men to get him back to the car.

Next to him Katie felt tears slide down her cheeks as she watched. *Thank God*, she thought, *that I don't have to write death lines about this*. She looked at Shaw. His gaze was impassive, his eyes dry.

"It's so sad," she said.

Shaw didn't answer. He just kept watching.

Half an hour later the last person had left and the gravediggers moved in, tempest and all, to plant Anna in the earth of Wisbach for good.

Shaw got out of the car. "You remember what to do?"

She nodded. "Just be careful."

"You too."

He shut the door, glanced around, and headed to the hole in the earth, trying not to think about the much bigger one in his heart.

He pulled some euros from his pocket and asked the diggers, in German, to give him some time alone here. No doubt happy to be relieved of their wet duty, they took the money and fled.

Shaw stood next to the grave and looked down at the coffin. He did not want to visualize Anna inside that box. She didn't belong there. He spoke in quiet tones to her, saying things he should have said while the woman was alive. He had many regrets in his life. The most devastating by far was not being with Anna when she needed him most.

"I'm sorry, Anna. I'm sorry. You deserved a lot better than me."

He grabbed a shovel and spent the next half hour filling in her grave. He felt it was his task to perform, no one else's. He was soaked through to the skin by the time he was done, but didn't seem to notice.

He looked at the headstone. It gave Anna's full name, Anastasia Brigitte Sabena Fischer. Her dates of birth and death. And the phrase at the bottom in German, "May our beautiful daughter rest in peace."

"Rest in peace," Shaw said. "Rest in peace for both of us, Anna. Because I don't see peace ever coming my way again."

He knelt down in the mud, his head bowed.

As he did so the two men stepped clear of the trees, guns in hand.

The car horn instantly split the silence of the cemetery and then Katie slid down in her seat.

Startled, the two men ran straight at Shaw.

A split second later the rear glass of the car Katie was in was shattered by a gun blast.

77

In a blur of motion, Shaw erupted forward like a blitzing linebacker, knocking both men to the ground. In another instant his pistol was stuffed nearly down one man's throat as his partner lay unconscious next to him.

A moment later the men in black swooped in.

Katie sat back up in the car, flicking glass off her. She looked anxiously over at Shaw. When he rose from the ground clutching one of the gunmen, she breathed a sigh of relief and climbed out of the car.

Twenty feet behind the car Frank stood over the dead man who'd tried to kill Katie. She joined him.

Frank said, "Sorry we cut it so close. Bastard got the shot off before we could nail him."

Later, they sat in an empty barn outside of Wisbach. The two would-be killers were manacled together back to back in the middle of the straw floor.

Frank, Katie, and Shaw stood together in an informal powwow.

"Thanks for agreeing to back us up on this," Shaw told Frank.

"Hey, other than keeping the world safe and secure, I've got lots of time on my hands."

They'd already run the pairs' prints through the usual databases and gotten zip for their troubles. Their interrogation so far had resulted in a cascade of foul language from the man who'd ended up chewing on Shaw's gun barrel. By contrast, his partner, a beefy man with a stoic expression, hadn't said a word. He looked like he might not even speak English. They'd tried several other languages out on him but his silence remained golden. They had no IDs. Two pistols and a gutting knife were the only things of interest found on their persons. The dead man had been similarly sterilized.

"Not even a cell phone," Frank said.

"Means they were going to rendezvous with someone after they killed me and Shaw," Katie said. "Probably close by."

Frank turned to Shaw. "What now?"

"Keep pounding away at these two until they pop. We'll be in touch."

Frank put a hand on Shaw's shoulder. "Look, Shaw, watch your back. My gut's telling me something is off here."

"Off how?" Katie asked.

"Off as in it seems like they're always a step ahead of us."

As they drove down the road Shaw said gloomily, "I was pretty sure they'd be watching Anna's funeral in case we showed. That's why I called in Frank for an assist. But it didn't score us anything."

"They might talk at some point."

"I doubt they know much beyond being paid to kill me and you. These people have been really good about covering their tracks."

"They'll make a mistake. They always do," she said confidently.

"Oh, you think so?"

"I *know* so."

He stopped the car. "Why are you so sure all of a sudden?"

Katie could barely contain her excitement. "Because I just thought of a brilliant way to flush them out."

78

By now the entire world was convinced that China was behind the Red Menace for reasons as yet unknown, and that Russia had wiped out The Phoenix Group in retaliation. And no matter how many denials issued from Beijing and Moscow, this belief remained largely unshaken.

Elaborate theories were cropping up everywhere, in both digital and real ink, as to why China would have done such a thing. They ranged from wanting to turn the world against the only country in Asia that was a true rival both economically and militarily to China's ascension to the top spot in the global pecking order, to fears in Beijing that Russia's slide back to autocracy posed a real threat to the region's stability. How making Russia even angrier and more dangerous than it supposedly was would alleviate that threat was still a puzzle. Yet when people wanted to believe something badly enough facts and logic never proved to be difficult obstacles.

Whatever the reason, it was true that both nations were now mobilizing. The two countries shared an enormous border to the east of Mongolia, along with a much smaller wedge of land between Kazakhstan and Mongolia. Russian army units along with armor and air support were being marshaled at both of these sites. It was also rumored that Gorshkov was contemplating going straight through Mongolia in a planned invasion of China, which would have made it a much shorter route to Beijing, despite some political and topographical problems. The Chinese, knowing this full well, had set up thick walls of men and machines at each of these points. Yet war did not seem imminent. Indeed, it was clear that both countries well knew that such a contest would result in them both losing, so closely matched were they. But it was also believed, though no public statement had been made, that both China and Russia had signed long-term deals with unnamed defense contractors to rearm so that if they indeed did go to war years from now, they could each wipe out the other in grandly impressive style.

In response to these developments, many Western countries, the United States included, were doing the same thing, namely rearming. The Pentagon, always unafraid it make its intentions public, announced that the Ares Corporation, taking the lead position with several other major defense contractors in tow, had been awarded a series of no-bid contracts that had long been percolating to rebuild its tank and artillery divisions, upgrade its electronic intelligence-gathering infrastructure, reconfigure its missile defense systems, retool several aircraft carriers, ballistic missile subs, and destroyers, bring online several thousand heavily armored personnel carriers and other troop vehicles, and upgrade the nearly brand-new, and apparently already obsolete, Raptor combat aircraft. It was only American-based Ares, the Pentagon stated, the original manufacturer of much of this weaponry, with its myriad areas of expertise and global management capability, that could carry out this enormous task to the exacting standards demanded by the U.S. military complex.

A Pentagon source said, "This will ensure that the U.S. military retains its position as the number one fighting force in the world for decades to come."

The Congress had quickly passed a spending bill to pay for all this, which the president had just as quickly signed.

In several newspapers, a source who asked not to be identified because he was not authorized to say what he was about to, reported that the Ares Corp. contracts were for eight years and added up to nearly a trillion dollars of taxpayer money. This would ratchet the U.S. military budget up to over $800 billion a year, dwarfing even annual Social Security payouts and making it by far the biggest expenditure of the budget. But, fortunately, it would not *technically* increase the enormous budget deficit and national debt, because some clever bureaucrats backed by equally slick members of Congress were able to get the additional defense funding pushed through on a supplemental spending bill that technically was not included in the official budget. And in Washington, D.C., technical was all that mattered.

"So the next generation can worry about reality," remarked one political insider who requested anonymity, citing a desire to remain a political insider.

After signing the defense spending bill in a grand White House ceremony the embattled president, his reelection chances still hurting from him being painted as soft on Russia, called a press conference where he said, in the most unmistakable terms, "Now anyone seeking to harm the interests of the United States of America will find us superbly prepared to do whatever is necessary to defend ourselves to the fullest. And may God continue to bless the United States of America." He immediately shot up eleven percentage points in the next poll. There was nothing like saber-rattling to win the voters over.

Ares Corp. released a new ad campaign that had been carefully crafted and polished for months. It didn't tout the new contract or the dollars involved. That was deemed too crass by the top New York ad agency that created the message. The narrator merely said, "The United States of America and the Ares Corporation. Together, we are unbeatable." It was quite a statement and its underlying message crystal clear: Ares had just put itself on equal footing with the world's only remaining superpower. This simple narrative was followed by classically styled black-and-white video shots of aircraft flying, tanks rolling, ships sailing, and a platoon of soldiers marching. This was all set to the tune of a very popular song.

It was said that the people in the focus groups previously set up to gauge the emotional impact of the commercial were left weeping in their seats. It was whispered in certain ad circles that it was the best fifty million dollars Nicolas Creel had ever spent.

Everything was all going exactly as planned by Creel and Pender.

All except for one little unexpected bump in the road that would turn out to make things even better.

At midnight, Mongolian time, a Russian field general received a set of garbled orders that he took to authorize a probing attack into China. Being an enthusiastic commander who had never seen combat before and who possessed a personal hatred of all things Chinese, he immediately launched said probing attack without bothering to request clarification from up the chain of command. His artillery roared, hitting previously designated targets, while overhead MiGs rocketed into Chinese airspace with authority. And the MiGs promptly ran into Chinese combat aircraft that, ironically enough, had been legally reverse engineered by the Chinese from the MiG family of aircraft under license from Russia. So in essence the pilots on both sides were flying in the same planes. In keeping with this equality, the ensuing dogfights culminated in a draw, with each side losing two aircraft apiece.

The Chinese, a bit ticked off to say the least by this Russian punch in the face, immediately launched a counterattack. For the next six hours the two armies fired off everything they had at each other.

When it was over, in addition to the lost aircraft the "probe" resulted in a rural Chinese town being pulverized and two thousand citizens killed. Ten tanks, twenty armored personnel carriers or APCs, forty artillery pieces, and nine hundred Chinese uniformed grunts were also wiped out as a million rounds of various Russian ammo rained down on them even though far more missed their mark than hit it.

On the Russian side, six hundred civilians unfortunately caught right between the two armies perished, most of them still in their beds when the ordnance struck their homes. Along with this collateral carnage, eight tanks were blown up, six choppers shot down, twelve APCs flattened, 412 soldiers lay dead, and an entire artillery battery vaporized by a direct rocket attack that ignited an adjacent fuel dump. As an interesting side note, this conflagration also claimed the life of the Russian field commander who'd started the whole thing in the first place based on orders that, on further review, had instructed him merely to launch such an attack only on the occasion of him being attacked first.

It really was in the details, it seemed.

The breathless and shell-shocked armies retreated back to their respective home turfs to regroup and contemplate what the hell had just happened.

If this *was* to be the beginning of World War III, it was truly an inauspicious start.

79

Nicolas Creel, along with the mother superior, ceremoniously lifted the first spade of dirt for the new orphanage to the cheers of the Italian press and public. That done, and the heads of tiny, grateful orphans patted, special treats given out to them, a brief statement read to the press, and the hands of the mayor and other dignitaries shaken, Creel retreated to the *Shiloh* to relish how well things were going.

The Russians had attacked China and the Chinese had counterattacked. As Creel searched the Web for stories on the latest incident, he saw with glee that there were already thousands of them, with more pouring in every minute. This would only cement his contracts with the two countries and encourage other nations on the fence about rearming to jump down on the side of muscling up. He would be only too glad to accommodate them.

While it was true that the Americans, Brits, and French were leading diplomatic efforts to forge a cease-fire and reconciliation between the two Asian lands, Creel knew it was too little too late. A summit-level conference had been set for this week in London. Yet the two warring nations had not even agreed to attend. And even if they did, which was unlikely after this latest incident, it wouldn't matter.

The phone call he received wiped the smile off his face. It was Caesar. The hit at the cemetery in Wisbach had not gone according to plan. In fact, it had gone as not according to plan as it was possible to be.

"One man dead, two others arrested," Creel said, repeating back Caesar's report. "I'm assuming the men you hired know nothing useful?"

"Nothing," Caesar said firmly. "I know this is a setback, but we'll get them, Mr. Creel, I guarantee it. We're close. Really close."

"That's what I thought a while back, Caesar. And look at us now."

He clicked off, took a deep breath, looked out the porthole in the direction of where the new orphanage would spring up, and phoned Pender. "Pour it on, Dick," he ordered. "I want to see the media stream full of vitriolic ammo to support the war."

"Without actually having a war," Pender said warily.

"A cold war," Creel said impatiently. "I make the most money when shots aren't fired."

"But shots *have* been fired."

"A stupid meaningless probe that, according to my

sources, scared the hell out of both sides. Now we can settle down for a nice long rearmament phase."

"But what if they actually go to war?"

"Dick, just do your job and let me worry about the consequences, remember? And if they do go to war, well, it won't be the end of the world. They'll have to have weapons to fight with and what they use up they have to replace. And if they beat the crap out of each other, who cares?"

"But what about the nukes? They have nukes."

"Mutually assured destruction. Neither Moscow nor Beijing wants to disappear. That's why I could never do this with the Muslims. They don't seem to care if they get annihilated so long as everyone else does too. You see, even in war you need a civilized attitude to make it really work. Now pour it on!"

Creel clicked off and Pender immediately instructed his team to pull out all the stops. The mission had been a challenge for Pender, but then Creel always was a challenge. Pender opened up his official playbook and turned his horses loose. He would show Creel very clearly what pouring it on meant. There wouldn't be a news outlet in the world that didn't get his attention. The globe would ring with more lies than ever before in history. It would be the master PM's finest hour.

Now that they were nearing a successful end,

Pender contemplated how large the bonus to his firm—to him actually—would be. Creel did not deal in small numbers. Fifty million? A hundred million? Pender had always wanted two possessions more than anything else: his own yacht and his own aircraft. Not in the same class as Creel's, of course. That would always be beyond his purse strings. Yet a Gulfstream V jet and a trim 120-foot Italian-built double-decker vessel would be perfect. These days those two items were what one really needed to say they had actually made it to the big time. And Pender wanted to say that with gusto.

He daydreamed about this possibility for a few more minutes until his dreams collapsed into a nightmare.

On his computer screen popped up a message from Pender's aide. It read, "Barney Rubble Blog update." An e-mail had come in on the blogger site that according to the aide, Pender needed to see right away.

Pender opened it and began to read even as he multitasked on some other agenda items. As soon as he read the first sentence, he stopped multitasking.

"I know who you are and what you did. I want a face-to-face or I'll retract the story and write the real truth. K.J. P.S. Nice try with Lesnik. And next time you set up a fake blogger site, use someone who knows what they're actually doing."

Instantly gone were all thoughts of a jet and a

yacht. His playbook didn't have a counterattack to this.

The master perception manager had just realized his greatest fear.

The *truth* was literally staring him in the face.

80

Shaw sat watching the computer screen over Katie's shoulder. She'd sent the e-mail ten minutes ago. They'd hoped for an answer before now.

"Should I send it again?" Katie asked him.

"No." Though he looked a bit nervous too.

Fortunately, they didn't have to wait much longer. The message was short. "What do you want?"

Katie and Shaw exchanged glances. "Answer it," Shaw said.

A face-to-face, Katie typed.

"Impossible," the answer said.

Then I'll just write my new story.

"No one will believe you," came the reply.

I can be very persuasive. And I have some facts that will back me up and blow your plan out of the water.

"What facts?"

I'll tell you in person.

"I'm not doing that. This could be a setup."

Shaw and Katie glanced at each other. Of course it *was* a setup.

A phone call, then.

The answer didn't come immediately. "What do you want to talk about?"

Money, Katie typed, adding no fewer than three exclamation points. *Money for my silence.*

"We can do that over e-mail."

I want to hear you sweat. Katie smiled at this intentionally mixed metaphor.

A long minute went by as they anxiously stared at the screen. "When?"

Katie clapped her hands together. *Tonight. Midnight U.S. East Coast time.* She typed in a cell phone number that was untraceable. Shaw had given it to her.

"He'll suspect that we'll try to trace the call when he's on the phone," she said.

"He'll use a sterilized cell phone, believing that even if we trace the signal and burn a target between the cell towers, it's still a big place."

"Well, isn't it?" Katie said.

"The world isn't nearly as large as people think it is. In fact, it's pretty small. If we can track his signal, that'll give us about a city-block footprint to target. Once we get that, Frank can send in people fast. With his connections, he has assets pretty much everywhere that he can call on."

"That's still a big space to search, Shaw."

"It is, but it's better than nothing. And we might just get lucky."

★

Pender sat back in his office after having finished his digital conversation with Katie James. That's who it had to be of course, the damn reporter.

The initials at the end of the e-mail, K and J. The threat to retract her story.

He should have immediately phoned Nicolas Creel, but he couldn't. He'd obviously blundered on setting up the sham blogger site, because the damn woman had seen right through it. He could not let Creel know about that. He had never personally seen what Creel had done to underlings who'd failed him, but he'd heard enough rumors. He would handle this himself. It was only a phone call and he would take all necessary precautions against it being traced. There was no way they would be able to find him.

If it was merely money she wanted, that was doable. James would no doubt be reasonable in her request. If it took millions, he'd just take it out of his bonus. It wasn't like he needed both the yacht *and* the private plane. But what if she kept coming back for more money?

Pender took a deep breath as his nerves began to bunch up and down his spine. This had never happened to him before. He was only used to being behind the scenes, never in the trenches. But he would get through this. He was the master of this game. In the end he would win.

And best of all, Nicolas Creel would never have to know.

He prayed to God that the man would never find out.

81

Next to the table where Katie would be sitting when she made the call, Shaw had set up a large clock with an LED readout down to the seconds. He held a video camera pointed at Katie and the clock; he also had on a headset.

"Just keep him on as long as you can. Once they track the tower locations they can zero in on a more exact location and send in a team."

Right at midnight the phone rang. Shaw started videotaping the clock as Katie answered.

"Right on time," she said into the phone.

"How much do you know?" the voice said tersely.

"More than you want me to."

"How much do you want?"

Shaw motioned to Katie. "Keep him talking," he mouthed as he listened to the man on the other end of the headset phone.

"Don't you want to know how I figured it out?" she said. "I mean in case next time you want to avoid something like this happening again."

"Okay, how?" Pender asked.

Katie took her time explaining about Lesnik, the broken loo, the inconsistencies in his story, and finally the impossibility of him doing what he said he'd done. "You should have just taken him in the place with you," she advised. "Instead of briefing him on it later."

"So why'd you write the story then if you knew it wasn't true?"

"I just found out."

Shaw jerked his head up as Frank's voice came through the headset. He pointed at her. "He's in a moving car. Tell him to pull off the road! Now!"

Katie immediately barked, "Pull your car off the road!"

Pender was so astonished by her observation and demand that he nearly swerved his big Mercedes off the road before regaining control. "How the hell did you know I'm in a car?" he hissed suspiciously.

Thinking fast, Katie said, "You were breaking up. *I'm* not moving, so you must be. And besides, I can hear the traffic noise in the background. Now pull off so I can hear you clearly. We don't want any misunderstandings, do we?"

"Give me a minute." Pender still sounded wary. He pulled off at the next exit and said, "Okay, how much?"

"Twenty million dollars and consider it a gimme."

"That's not a gimme. It's a helluva lot of cash."

"Well, it's a helluva big thing you're involved in.

But if you don't want to pay, fine. I'll retract my story and tell the real one."

"Which is?"

"You can read about it along with everyone else. But the world will know that the Russians did not do the London Massacre and the Chinese are not behind the Red Menace. And this whole war thing goes right down the tubes. That's what this is about, right? War?"

Pender was really sweating now. *Twenty million dollars.*

"It'll take me a little time to raise the cash."

"No it won't, I want it in twenty-four hours. I have, big surprise, an offshore account. You can write down the wiring instructions. I know you'll send it in a way that can't be traced, but that doesn't matter to me. I just want the cash."

"I can't do it that fast. I need more time."

"How much more time?"

"A week."

"Seventy-two hours. And consider yourself lucky. I really want to start my vacation."

"Tired of being a reporter?" Pender sneered.

"I'd much rather be rich."

"Five days," he retorted.

"The negotiations are closed! Three days or your plan goes down the tubes."

"I doubt one story from you will turn such an overwhelming global tide."

"Fine, then don't pay and we'll see what happens. Good-bye."

"Wait, wait!"

"I'm listening."

"All right. Three days. But a piece of advice, Ms. James. If you do something as incredibly stupid as double-crossing us—"

"I know, I know. It won't be pretty. Don't worry. I've already got my Pulitzers. All I want now are the good things in life."

She gave him the bank information and glanced at Shaw. He was making a slashing motion against his neck.

"Nice doing business with you," Katie remarked before clicking off.

She looked at Shaw, who turned off the video camera.

"Well?" she asked.

"Western suburbs of Washington, D.C.; the Dulles Toll Road."

"They know that fast?"

"There're two cell towers right there. It was easy to trace the signal. He would've been far safer sitting in a crowded hotel. Too many signals there to narrow down to one person."

"Okay, but what about just tracing the *number* the man used?"

"We did. He tried to block the number, that's why it didn't pop up on your screen, but we had a wireless intercept on the phone you used. It overrode his block, snagged the number, and sixty seconds later we had our phone number owner."

"Who was it?"

"According to Frank, an eighty-six-year-old priest in Boston who I'm reasonably sure is not running around the world starting wars, and has no idea someone stole his phone number."

"So how does knowing that this guy was driving on that road help us? Could they tell which car?"

He shook his head. "Technology's not there yet. Same as trying to pinpoint a person."

"So *how* do we trace the guy, Shaw?" she said, exasperated.

He patted the video camera. "By using this."

"That? You've been taking a video of me and a clock."

"That's right."

"So now what?"

"Now we fly to D.C."

82

They snagged a ride to America on a private wing that Frank managed to get hold of. The plane had enough range to make it to D.C. without refueling so they settled in for the seven-hour-plus flight from London.

Ed Royce from MI5 was with them. Shaw and Katie strapped into their seats in the back while Frank and Royce went over some details up front.

Katie pulled a blanket snugly around her. She sipped on some club soda and stared over at Shaw as they rode a smooth flight path across the Atlantic.

"This beats the hell out of the trip across the Irish Sea on that roller coaster, doesn't it?" she said.

Shaw nodded, but kept staring at the seat in front of him.

"Do you really think we're going to find out who's behind it?" she asked.

He glanced at her. "If we're lucky, maybe. But finding out and then doing something about it are two different things."

"Evidence that'll stand up in court, you mean?"

Shaw didn't say what he meant. He turned away from her again.

"You okay?" she asked, touching his shoulder. It was his bad arm, so she did it very gently.

"Yeah, I'm good," he said unconvincingly.

"When we get this all figured out and the bad guys are put away, I think I'm going to go see my parents."

"Where are they?"

"In Vermont, at least they were the last time I checked. They like to move around. I think that's where I got the wanderlust."

"What do they do?"

"My father's a professor of English. He teaches creative writing. That's why my middle name is Wharton. Edith is one of his favorite writers. I was actually named after Katherine Chopin, but people have always just called me Katie. My dad grew up in D.C. but went to college at Stanford. That's where he met my mom. He got his Ph.D. and started teaching at Harvard. Mom taught there too until the kids started coming."

"How many?"

"Including me, four. I'm the youngest. I was born in Harvard Square. Literally. After three kids I guess Mom figured she could wait to the very last second before heading to the hospital. She and Dad were running to the car when her water broke. I ended up being born in a spare classroom. How about you?"

"How about me what?"

"I just divulged some details of my earth-shattering past. Now it's your turn."

"No, thanks."

"Oh, come on, Shaw, it's not like I'm going to run out and write a story about it. Just tell me something about your family."

"Okay. I have no memory of my mother other than imagined because she got rid of me when I was about two, at least that's what I was told later. I never knew my father. I lived in an orphanage until I got kicked out at age six. The next dozen years I spent with people I have no reason to remember. I have no brothers or sisters, at least that I'm aware of. So now you know all about me."

He turned back away from her.

Katie just sat there stunned. "I'm sorry."

"No reason to be sorry."

"But that must've really been hard on you."

"Probably the best thing that ever happened to me."

"How can you say that?"

"Because it taught me right from the start to rely only on myself," he said firmly.

Katie drew the blanket tighter around her as Shaw turned his attention to the seat in front of him again.

"So what are you going to do after this is all over?" she asked.

"Depends on which way it turns out to be all over."

"I mean the way where we both walk away from it still breathing."

"Haven't really thought that far ahead," he said.

She glanced up to the front of the plane where Royce and Frank were sitting at a small table going over some documents.

"But not stay with Frank? You need to get out, before it's too late."

"What don't you get? It's *already* too late for me, Katie."

"But Shaw—"

He turned away from her, slid his seat back, closed his eyes, and went to sleep.

Katie kept her gaze on him for a while before turning to look out the window. The sky was black, the wide ocean seven miles below invisible. She'd been on thousands of flights over the years, and, for some reason, had felt cold on every single one of them.

Yet Katie had never experienced the ice in her veins she felt right now.

83

Frank, Royce, Shaw, and Katie sat in a room and looked at the video stream pouring over the large screen. Now Katie understood what Shaw had been talking about.

"There're video cameras mounted on poles all along the highway here," Shaw had explained. "They're as much to address accidents and traffic backups as they are about Big Brother watching, but they're very useful for what we want to do."

On another screen was the video Shaw had taken of Katie talking to Pender with the LED clock readout also clearly visible.

"Okay," Shaw said. "Start the highway video at the same time as the film that I shot of Katie and the clock."

The videos started up and the time ticked away. At midnight there was still traffic on the Dulles Toll Road. D.C. was just that kind of place. But it wasn't bumper to bumper.

"There's the starting position of the cell signal burn," Frank pointed out on the screen.

"Looks like the cars are going about sixty-five," Shaw estimated. "So a minute a mile." He looked at the video of Katie and the LED clock.

He told Royce, "As soon as Frank told me they'd picked up the signal on the highway and that the guy was moving, I had Katie do the 'pull the car off the road' maneuver. That was three minutes and three seconds into the conversation."

Royce nodded. "So about three miles of drive time."

"I thought I could hear the squeal of tires on the cell phone when I told him," Katie said. "And a horn too."

"We're coming up on that time slice now," Shaw noted. He paused. "Five, four, three, two."

He broke off and everyone stared at the video of the highway.

"There!" Royce snapped. He was pointing to the far left lane where a black Mercedes swerved into the middle lane, nearly hitting a pickup truck.

Frank spoke into a headset. "Zoom in on the black Mercedes that almost took out that truck. And then freeze it."

A few moments later the image of the Mercedes grew in size until it nearly took up the entire screen. Unfortunately, the angle wasn't great; the driver, though clearly a man—something they already knew—wasn't completely visible.

"White guy," Shaw observed. "Thin, a little gray

in the hair, but the doorjamb is hiding his face. Looks like he's on the phone."

"So are probably ninety percent of the people on that road," Katie said.

Frank gave instructions to the tech and they tried it from different angles but without much success.

Shaw said, "Keep the film rolling. He pulled off after Katie spoke to him. We might get a good look at him or his license plate."

Unfortunately, that did not turn out to be the case. The Mercedes *had* pulled off, leaving at the next exit, but any more images had been blocked by other traffic. They couldn't see the man or the license plate once he left the highway.

"It's a black Mercedes S500," Frank said. "That narrows it down some. We'll assume it's registered in D.C., Maryland, or Virginia and start looking at motor vehicle records."

Katie said, "This is a very affluent area. I think you're going to find more S500s than you think. And you're just assuming it's from the area. It could be from any state, because we couldn't see the license plate. You might be talking hundreds or thousands of people."

"She's right," Royce said.

"We might have an easier way," Shaw said. "It's a *toll* road."

Frank snapped his fingers. "They'll have a camera there to record people who don't pay. And if they don't, dollars to donuts he's got an electronic toll-paying device. That'll give us a record."

"How can you be so sure he pays his tolls electronically?" Royce asked.

"An S500 costs over a hundred grand. You spend that much on a ride, you're not gonna be digging through your fancy pockets for quarters."

Royce said, "But isn't there a chance that the car swerved to avoid an accident? And isn't connected to this at all?"

"And then shoots off the highway at the same time Katie tells the guy to on the phone? No, it's him," said Shaw. "You heard the tires squeal and a horn blare and the time sequence was dead-on with the film I shot."

"We can check with the toll people and get a record for that booth at"—Frank glanced at the clock—"four minutes past midnight." He looked back at the highway film. "That's the Wiehle Avenue exit off the Toll Road."

"We get this guy and it's all over," Royce said. "We arrest him, extradite him back to London, and bloody well put him and his cohorts away forever."

"Right," Frank agreed.

Katie glanced nervously at Shaw. He was looking away from them, his expression stony.

I don't see it that way, thought Shaw.

84

It had taken the selling of stocks and bonds, the liquidation of retirement funds, the pilfering of corporate accounts, and the rifling of safety deposit boxes, but Pender had raised the twenty million. He rose early on the second day after he had spoken to Katie James. He would now make arrangements for the wire transfer. He was desperately hoping the bonus from Creel would be closer to eight figures to compensate him for this unforeseen out-of-pocket expense. After that, he prayed he could put this whole ugly business behind him.

Divorced with two children in college and another a high school senior at an elite private school in Washington, Pender lived in a mansion in McLean, Virginia, home of many of the Washington area's politically famous, or infamous, depending on one's perspective. He loved his freedom, was immersed in his work, and his only sexual encounters were of the random variety, occasionally involving a young female employee trying to get a leg up in more ways than one. He preferred it that way—no commitments. He had never understood why a man as smart as Nicolas Creel would keep marrying women whose heads contained about as much brain matter as their breasts.

He had the twenty million, it was true, and he would wire it out. But what if James went ahead and wrote the story? Or what if she asked for more money? Or, even worse, what if Creel found out?

It will work. It has to.

He showered, dressed, gulped down a glass of orange juice, grabbed his briefcase, and headed out.

When he reached his garage, Dick Pender's world suddenly turned black.

He awoke several hours later, on a cot in a small room. The only light came from a bright, shadeless lamp on a table. As he sat up and slowly looked around he could sense someone was in here with him, behind the wash of light from the lamp. He put his hand up to shield his eyes from the glare.

"What the hell is going on?" he said as bravely as he could, which wasn't brave at all really as his voice cracked, his lips quivered, and he was nearly hyper-ventilating.

The big, angry-looking man stepped out from behind the light and Pender immediately shrank back against the wall.

A voice came at Pender from somewhere, he wasn't sure.

"We only brought you here to keep you safe."

The door opened, the overhead lights came on,

and Pender found himself blinking rapidly. His face sagged when he saw who'd entered the room.

"You?" Pender said.

"Me," Nicolas Creel answered as Caesar stood silently behind him.

85

While apparently the government could spy on its citizens without benefit of a court-issued search warrant, determining whether a certain car had gone through a certain tollgate at a certain time was far more problematic. Shaw and the others found out that the video camera at the tollbooth Pender had taken was not working. Apparently so many motorists had run the booth without paying, been filmed, gotten a fine in the mail, and refused to pay it that the high-way folks had simply given up. Now the camera was there as a deterrent, they were told. However, everyone knew it wasn't functioning because a local newspaper had done a story on it, and so there went the deterrent.

Frank had next checked with the electronic toll payment company. They had balked at giving out the information to him, despite his credentials. He had summoned assistance from the police in Virginia. Armed with this official backing, another attempt had been made to get the information. Then they were told that there apparently had been a server glitch, electronic bug, or inadvertent file wipeout that happened from time to time. They were working on it and would get back to them.

"Get back to us!" screamed Frank over the phone. "Get back to us? The whole freaking world is about to go up in smoke and you'll get back to us?"

The woman on the other end of the line told Frank that she didn't care for his tone and they were doing the best they could, but that computers were not perfect.

"Well, honey," Frank said, "by the time this is all over and the world has come to an end, who'll give a shit about imperfect computers?"

The woman apparently had not been listening but rather reading from her script. She told Frank to have a nice day and if he had any other questions or concerns they'd be happy to help because customer service was their number one priority.

Frank slammed down the phone and would've ripped the hair off his head if he had any left.

He looked at the others. "Now what? We just wait for the first nuke to launch?"

Royce shrugged. "What's the alternative?"

Shaw rose. "We do a little digging on our own."

Frank said, "What kind of digging?"

"In the dirt," Shaw answered as he closed the door behind him.

Katie looked at the other two men.

"What's with him?" Royce wanted to know.

"He's been through a lot," she said defensively.

"We've *all* been through a lot," snarled Frank.

Katie didn't hear this. She'd already hurried out after Shaw. She caught up with him as he strode down the hall.

"Shaw?"

He stopped, waited for her to catch up.

"What are you going to do?" she asked.

"Just like I said. Dig." He started walking again.

She had to skip along to keep up with his long strides.

"But how, where? It's not like you can just pull this guy out of a hat."

"You never know."

"Do you have to be so damn secretive? Because let me just tell you, it's frustrating as hell." She put a hand on his arm. "And can you please stop for a sec? I haven't run a marathon in a while."

He faced her. "I'm not asking for you to help."

"I know," she said more calmly. "But I *want* to help. I thought we could flush this guy out with my plan."

Shaw's angry features cleared. "Your plan was great, Katie. And we almost got him that way."

"So can I help? I mean, I don't have anything else to do right now. And the whole 'world at stake' thing, you know." She attempted a smile.

"Okay, do you have any ideas?"

"All we have is that video of the car. And I think

it's worth another look. We might have missed something."

Shaw finally shrugged. "I'll scrounge up a copy and we can go through it again."

"A copy? Why not just go back and watch it with Royce and Frank?"

Shaw didn't answer her. He was already walking back down the hall.

86

Creel held up a small recorder. He turned it on and Pender listened to his phone conversation with Katie James all over again.

A gray-faced Pender said weakly, "You knew about it?"

"Of course I *knew* about it, Dick. I know everything. You should have realized that by now."

Pender started to sputter. "I was just trying to take care of it without bothering you, Mr. Creel. I have the money. It's all ready to go."

"I appreciate your effort, I really do. The problem with the blog was unfortunate, however. I would've hoped with the amount of money I was paying you that that would not have happened. But such is life. The unexpected sometimes comes along. I know that as well as any man living."

"But once we pay her—"

Creel stopped him. "Unfortunately it's not that simple. I seriously doubt that someone like Katie James suddenly cares that much about money. I researched the woman thoroughly before deciding to use her in my little plan. Years ago she could've made a fortune becoming a morning TV news personality for any of the major networks, but she refused. She cares more about the story than she does about money. So no, not even twenty million dollars will change that picture."

"Then why did she contact me?"

"To get you to call her. When Ms. James told you to pull off the road, my friend here tells me you almost ran off the highway."

Pender stared at Caesar. "He was following me?"

"Just answer the question, Dick."

"Yes, I did. It was unnerving. It was like she was watching me."

"Someone *was* watching you, Dick. And it wasn't just me."

"What are you talking about? Who was watching me?"

"There are cameras all over the toll road. She made that comment to get you to react. And you did. Now they look at the video, time the conversation, and they see you almost wreck at the precise instant James said what she did. That way they *can* pinpoint the *car*."

Caesar added, "And then she told you to pull off. And you did. Right through the tollgate."

"Oh my God. They could be at my house right now. It's been two days. I . . ."

"Calm down, Dick. If the road cameras had gotten

a clear shot of you, you'd already be under arrest. So it obviously didn't."

"But the toll. I paid electronically. There'll be a record."

"Fortunately, we learned of this development in time. I had some of my best hackers target the firm that operates the electronic toll pay. Quite soon after you went through the gate, they suffered a complete crash of their recordation system."

Pender let out a relieved breath. "As usual, you thought of everything."

"Now I need you to do something for me."

"Anything."

"We'll have to shut the entire project down. Right now. I want you to tell your employees in the war room to go home. We're going to clear it out of everything that shows your connection to the Red Menace."

"My people can do that, Mr. Creel. I can make the call right now."

"In light of recent events, I'd prefer my people to handle the cleanup. I'm sure you understand."

"All right, if you insist."

"And best of all, you won't have to pay the money, Dick."

"I guess that's right. But then she'll write the story, the real story."

"Let her. I believe things have gotten to a point-of-no-return stage. The contracts are signed and China and Russia are still only a few steps from going to war, regardless of this recent diplomatic effort. The only thing James can do is back off her original story. 'I was duped,' she'll claim. But with no corroboration her credibility is zero. She'll simply look incompetent."

"Then we've won."

Creel put an arm around Pender's shoulders. "Yes, Dick, we've won. Now call your employees and let's finish this."

87

They sat in Katie's hotel room going over the video for the hundredth time. A room service table was stacked with plates and cups since they had not bothered to leave the room to eat. The drapes were drawn and the room was dark so they could see every detail on the screen better. They had enlarged all angles of the shots on the laptop and dissected them grid by grid.

And they had come up with absolutely nothing.

Shaw lay on the floor gazing at the ceiling. An exhausted, red-eyed Katie was on the unmade bed moodily doing the same. She slipped off her pumps, padded over to the room service table in her stocking feet, and poured out a cup of coffee.

"You want one?" she asked Shaw.

He shook his head and kept his gaze fixed on the ceiling.

"Frank checked the overseas account he set up for the money drop. No twenty million yet."

"Great," Katie shot back. "I'm clueless and still poor."

She sat down at the desk chair, sipped her coffee, and stared at the screen.

"What's the latest on the diplomatic efforts?" Shaw asked.

Katie hit a few computer keys, accessed the Internet, and read the news. "They're still meeting in London. China and Russia haven't even agreed to send delegations. But they're hopeful of some sort of peaceful resolution."

She clicked off the Net and ran the video of the Mercedes again, this time in slow motion.

Shaw glanced over at her.

She was dressed in a skirt, stockings, and a blouse and her face was wrinkled in concentration.

"Katie, we've done that to death and gotten zip. And the damn toll people still can't tell us anything. And every minute that goes by . . ." He didn't have to finish the statement.

Katie wasn't listening. Her gaze was suddenly riveted on the screen.

"Shaw! Look!"

He hopped up and joined her at the desk. "What?"

"There." She pointed to the bottom of the screen where she'd enlarged the grid section.

"It's the rear fender of the Mercedes. So what?"

"It's a *black* Mercedes."

"Really? Hell, I thought it was white," he said a little heatedly. "Get to the point."

"Hey, keep your pissy attitude under control." She

nicked the screen with her fingernail. "The car is black, but that spot is blue. And gold." She pointed to another smudge of color. "And red."

"I noticed that before. We all did. It's a sticker on the bumper. But that's all you can see. No writing. It could be anything. The techs already enlarged it and came up empty."

"I know that. But wait a minute." Katie was hitting keys, enlarging the section even more. Now was revealed a red top bar, a short line of gold, and a background of deep blue. Katie hit another key, zooming in on the gold and red parts.

"We've seen that, Katie," Shaw said, studying her intense expression. "What's the big deal?"

"When I saw it the first time, I thought I knew that pattern, but nothing came to me so I just thought I was mistaken. But now that I'm looking at it again I know I've seen it before. Somewhere. It's bugging the crap out of me." She looked at Shaw's jacket hanging on the chair. She touched the breast pocket. "Damn, that's it. That's it!"

Her hands flew over the keyboard. She got back online and did a Google search.

When the screen revealed the answer to her query Shaw gaped as he stared at the top of the page.

It was a crest with a red top bar, a blue shield, and a gold X with a red crown in the center. It seemed a fleshed-out match for the bit of sticker visible on the bumper.

Shaw read the name at the top of the screen. "St. Albans School?"

She nodded. "I told you my dad grew up in Washington? Well, he went to St. Albans. It's an exclusive private boys' school in D.C." She held up the sleeve of Shaw's coat. "He still has a jacket with that crest on it. That's where I remember seeing it. And I bet our guy has a son that goes or went there."

A second later Katie was lifted into the air. Shaw's strength was such that he had done it solely with his good arm.

"Great work, Katie," he said into her ear.

He put her down and turned his attention to the screen while she looked slightly flustered.

She said, "So we tell Royce and Frank. They can search St. Albans's database, get a list of names, we match it to vehicle registrations, and we find the black Mercedes and our guy."

"Do you think we can find that out without calling Royce and Frank?" He didn't look at her when he said this.

She answered hesitantly. "I don't know. I mean, you'd probably need a search warrant."

"But you said your father went there. That might make a difference."

"Maybe, but I can't access vehicle registrations. And why don't you want to call them?" She looked uncomfortably at Shaw.

He turned, towering above her. She unconsciously took another step back.

"Why do you think?" he said bluntly.

"I don't know what to think."

"Sure you do. You're a smart woman." He nodded at the screen. "Smart enough to have seen *that* when none of us did."

"I can't help you do what you want to do, Shaw." Her voice was tinged with a quiet desperation.

"Getting squeamish on me all of a sudden? Worrying about the rights of others? Innocent until the trial lawyers cover up the truth so no one can find it and the guilty walk free?"

"I don't give a damn about the people who did this. They can rot in hell."

"So what's the problem then?"

"The problem is *you*. You take the law into your own hands, you go to prison. Or worse. I won't be a part of that. I can't."

He sat in the desk chair and stared down at the carpet.

"Shaw, you can't throw your life away over this."

Shaw didn't appear to be listening. "I thought I knew what real pain was, Katie. What it was to hurt like you've never hurt before. But when Anna died, I discovered exactly what it felt like."

Katie crept forward and put a hand on his shoulder. "You need to let it out, Shaw, before it destroys you."

He stood so quickly that she had to jump back. "I'll call Frank and get him going on this."

"Just like that?" she said, bewildered.

"Just like that. It'll be faster that way," he added ominously.

As he made the call, Katie stared at the crest of St. Albans School and then over at Shaw as he relayed her discovery to Frank.

When he clicked off, Shaw said, "Get your shoes on. We've been stuck in this room long enough. I'll take you to dinner while they bang through the database."

Katie retrieved her shoes, sat on the bed, and slipped on her heels.

He put a hand on her arm and guided her out the door. As they walked down the hall, her heart was thumping in her chest. She didn't believe Shaw. Not at all.

And she was afraid. Not for herself.

She was afraid for him.

88

There were eight families on the St. Albans database that owned black Mercedes S500s, a match with vehicle registration showed. Shaw, Royce, Frank, and Katie sat in a room at the FBI's northern Virginia office studying this list.

"Two in McLean. One in Great Falls. Three in Potomac. The rest in D.C. Four of them have kids currently enrolled in the school," an FBI agent rattled off.

Katie broke off staring at the screen and glanced at Shaw. His focus was totally on the list, she could see. As she watched, she saw him mouthing words to himself.

He's memorizing the names and addresses.

"The smart thing to do," Frank said, "is split up our assets and hit them all at once."

"We can actually narrow the list down even more," the agent said. "The house in Great Falls and the car are registered to a woman; she's eighty-six. The ones in D.C. are men, Stephen Marshall and Sohan Gupta, but they're African American and Indian, respectively. You said your guy was a white guy. We can check out those people later just in case someone had access to their cars, but it makes sense to prioritize."

Frank said, "So that leaves five. Two in McLean, Virginia, and three in Potomac, Maryland."

"We'll have to get search warrants executed," the FBI agent said. "That'll take some time since the circumstances"—he glanced at Frank—"are a little unusual."

"How long?" Royce asked.

The agent checked his watch. "We'll push hard, but tomorrow morning at the earliest."

"Do it."

"Should we post surveillance teams at their houses?" Frank asked.

"Might spook them," Shaw pointed out. "And if we don't have search warrants in place . . ."

"Then they could destroy evidence and there'd be nothing we could do about it," Royce finished for him.

Frank sighed and said to the FBI agent, "Just get 'em as fast as you can."

Katie glanced over at Shaw in time to see a grim smile cross his face. And then it was gone. "I want to go with you when you do the hits," he said.

Frank nodded. "But we let the FBI guys lead the way."

"Absolutely."

Royce nodded in agreement. "I'm clearly out of my jurisdiction here."

The meeting broke up and Shaw walked out. Katie quickly followed him. As he reached his car in the parking lot, she put a hand on the car door.

"Don't do it."

He eased her hand off the door. "Don't do what exactly?"

"You know what."

"I'll give you a ride to your hotel. You obviously need some sleep. You're sounding a little punchy."

She gripped his sleeve. "Shaw, I saw what you were doing back there. You memorized the list. You're not waiting for a search warrant. You're going to go to those places tonight. And——"

"And what? Start killing people? Is that what you think?"

"I'm not sure what to think."

"Good, you can join the club." He pulled his arm free. "You want that ride?"

"No, I don't."

"Suit yourself."

He drove off. Frank and Royce came out of the building and headed toward her. Frank stared after Shaw's car. "Your buddy leave you high and dry?"

"No, I just . . ."

"You want a ride?"

When they got in the car, Frank turned and looked at her.

"Everything okay?"

"Everything's great."

Royce gave her a penetrating stare, glanced at Frank, and shrugged.

When Katie got back to the hotel, she stripped off her clothes, took a hot shower, and nearly scrubbed herself raw. She rested her head against the tile wall of the shower and let the water pour over her.

What do I do now? Tell Frank and Royce? Let them follow Shaw? Stop him from killing somebody? From being killed?

That's what she should do, Katie knew. But it wasn't that simple. What if she was wrong? What if Shaw found out she'd betrayed him? Yet she hadn't promised not to tell. He'd never asked her not to reveal her suspicions.

She got out of the shower, dressed, and put on dark clothing. She couldn't snitch on Shaw. But she also couldn't just stand by and let him destroy what life he had left.

She called his room. When he answered she hung up. He was still there. Two minutes later she was in the lobby sitting in a high-backed chair waiting for him to come down.

An hour later he did. He headed out. And so did Katie.

89

The first two homes Shaw checked out weren't the ones. From a distance Katie watched him enter the places only to come out of each a few minutes later. At the third house, however, a stone mansion in McLean, he didn't come right back out. In fact, he didn't come out at all.

Katie checked her watch. Ten minutes had gone by. This must be the jackpot. She slipped out of her car and crept into the house the same way as Shaw had—through the back door. Her heart was hammering in her ears as she threaded her way down the hall. She almost tripped over something that was in her path. It was all she could do not to scream.

Is it a body?

Is it Shaw's body?

As she groped around with her hand, she felt the overturned chair in front of her. As her eyes became accustomed to the dark, she noticed other things too, things that shouldn't have been where they were, including a smashed photo on the floor. She picked it up, squinted at the picture. It was a man with a young boy.

She put it down and edged along the hall. A box was on the floor. She bent down to see what it was. The box turned out to be empty, but it looked like something had been kept in there. Was this Shaw's doing? Was he looking for something she didn't know about? Was there someone else in here and all this debris evidence of a struggle? She really should just run, but what if Shaw were hurt?

The door was up ahead. She clutched the knob, took a breath, and eased it open. It was a bedroom. A large one. The master suite of this McMansion.

Her breath caught in her throat as she saw the figure in bed. He was propped up on pillows. The weak moonlight that came through the window allowed her to see. The man looked like he was still screaming. But he wouldn't be screaming anymore. Katie had seen corpses before and this was one.

She turned to run.

And smacked right into a human wall.

Shaw clamped a hand over her mouth.

She stared up at him fearfully, every inch of her body sliding into spasms of terror.

He removed his hand and motioned to the body. "He's dead."

Katie slowly nodded, her eyes still wide with a look of terror.

Realization spread across Shaw's features and then was replaced with anger.

"Check the body, it's already cold."

"No, that's okay."

He pushed her toward the bed.

"I believe you," she said, turning back to him.

"No, you obviously don't. So go see for yourself."

She edged forward. Shaw followed her.

"He's in full rigor," he said. "That happens about twelve to twenty-four hours after death. I've only been in here for fifteen minutes."

More curious than scared now, Katie touched the man's arm. It was like a rock. His skin was ice.

"What killed him?"

He pointed to the pillow where she could see dried stains.

"Gunshot wound to the back of the head."

She stepped back from the bed and gazed around the room. Shaw had a flashlight that he used to sweep the area. Furniture was overturned in here too and there were drawers pulled out and contents dumped on the floor.

"A struggle?" she said. "A search?"

Shaw pointed toward the closet. "Look at this."

They stepped inside the room. In the back a portrait was hanging off its hinges. Behind it a chunk of wall had been ripped out, revealing a cavity.

"My guess is there was a safe there. Whoever did this took it with them."

"So it was just a burglary that went wrong? The dead guy is fully dressed. He might have come home, stumbled on them, and they killed him."

He stared at her. "You really believe that?"

"No."

"Good. Because it's all been staged. Just like everything else in this whole damn thing."

"But this is the right house, isn't it?"

He nodded. "I checked the car in the garage first. Sticker's on the back. And there's a slight scratch on the back panel that I noted from the video. It's the right car."

"And the dead guy?"

Shaw picked up a photo that was on a shelf and shone his light on it. It looked like the guy on the video.

"It's the owner of the house. Richard Pender," said Shaw.

"We better get out of here."

"No, I want to finish searching the place first."

"Shaw, what if we get caught?"

"You can leave."

"Damn it, do you always have to make everything so complicated?"

"I didn't ask you to follow me tonight."

"How do you know I was following you?"

"Maybe it's the fact that you're standing in this house with me right now."

"I could've come here on my own. I can memorize addresses too."

"If you had memorized the addresses you'd know this was Pender's house. And last but not least, I saw you about a dozen times tonight in your car following me."

"Wait a minute. If you knew I was following you, why didn't you stop me? Or try to lose me?"

Shaw started to say something but then stopped. He looked away, and said quietly, "I'm no murderer."

"I'm glad you realized that."

A brief moment passed, and then Shaw asked, "Are you going to help me look or not?"

"I'll help. Let's just make it quick."

A half hour later they'd found nothing of any use. Richard Pender owned a firm called Pender & Associates. Shaw had never heard of it. They got the office address from some letterhead they found in a desk drawer.

Katie stared at the paper. "I know this name for some reason." She thought for a moment and then shook her head. "It's not coming."

They left out the back door.

Or tried to.

They never made it.

90

Shaw awoke first, the synapses in his head screaming out intense messages of pain to the rest of his body; yet that busted-up nerve mailbox was pretty full. He tried to sit up and push back the feelings of nausea rolling over him. He assumed he'd be bound. But he wasn't; his hands and feet were free.

He heard a groan and looked behind him over the top of the seat. Katie was lying on the floor there.

"Katie? Are you all right?"

Another groan was followed by a soft moan, and then came a bit of movement as she slowly sat up.

She rubbed her head. "Yeah, but I've got the mother of all knots on the—"

There was a grinding sound, like metal against something equally hard.

"What was that?" she said. "Where are we?"

She looked around. They were in a car. *Her* car. The one she'd followed Shaw in.

"Don't move," Shaw hissed.

"What?"

Another grinding sound came, and Katie had the sickening feeling of the floor slipping beneath her.

"What's going on?"

Shaw inclined his head at the window. Katie stared out and saw nothing but black. No, not entirely black. She saw some trees, large trees and thick bushes.

"Did they leave us in the woods?"

"Yes, but not exactly on level ground."

"What are you talking about?"

"Look out the windshield but do *not* move."

Katie slowly turned her head to stare straight ahead and her breath got lost halfway up her throat. She was looking straight down, or at least it seemed that way. It was like being on a roller coaster about to go over the edge, or a plane in a death spiral and you were the pilot watching the ground coming at you sickeningly fast.

"Where are we?" she whispered.

"In a car on the side of what appears to be a very steep hill with a clear path of two hundred feet in front of us at least until we get to the bottom. Then we hit a wall of trees. And if we manage to plow through those, we go right into the river."

"River?"

"The Potomac." He slowly raised his arm and pointed out the windshield. "That looks to be Georgetown over there, doesn't it?"

She gazed at the pulse of lights from across the water. "Then we're off the George Washington Parkway?"

He nodded.

"Can you open the doors?"

"They're locked, and if I try to open one, we're going for a short ride way too fast."

"How did we get here? The last thing I remember is leaving Pender's house."

"They must've been waiting for us. I'm an idiot! They were waiting for us at the graveyard in Germany. Why not Pender's house? They must have figured out what we'd done on the call, gotten to Pender first, and then waited for us to come poking around."

Katie shuddered. "They made his death look like a burglary and now we're going to end up as a traffic accident."

Shaw grimaced as yet another pain shot through his battered head. "A run off the road and down the hill where we burst into flames when the gas tank ignites as we smash into the trees down there. I'm sure the skid marks off the road were professionally done."

"So why hasn't the car rolled down already?"

"We seem to have gotten stuck on an outcrop of rock."

"Are we really that close to going down or am I becoming almost hysterical for no reason?"

"None of the tires are touching the ground. It's like being on a seesaw and the rock is the fulcrum. We move too much, down we go."

"And if we don't move, at some point, we go down

anyway. Can you call somebody? Frank? Royce? The president?"

Shaw gently felt in his pocket. "They took my phone. How about you?"

"It was in my purse. I left it in the car. Do you see it?"

Shaw eyed the floorboard. "Yeah, but if I try to get it, we're going over."

"Can you slide into the backseat? With your weight back here it might anchor the car."

Shaw tried to ease himself backward, but another long groan and a few more inches of the car sliding stopped him.

"Okay, that's a no-go."

"We can't just sit here waiting to die," Katie exclaimed.

He moved his weight a little to the left. The scraping sound came immediately and they could both feel the car move forward another inch.

"Okay, that tells me something."

"What?"

"Not to move again." Shaw eyed the interior. The keys were still in the car. They would have to be, he thought, to make it look like a real accident when the police found the charred wreckage. He edged his hand forward and carefully turned the keys one click to the right. That didn't turn the engine on, but it did do something else. He slowly reached over and depressed the window button. The

glass slid down even as the car eased forward another inch or so.

"Okay, the window's down, now what? We can't
exactly jump for it."

Shaw reached down, undid his belt, and slid it off.
"Please tell me you're wearing a belt."

"I am."

"Take it off and give it to me. But slowly."

She did so, but it seemed like even moving her
arms made the car wobble on its precarious perch.
She finally got it off and handed it to him.

Using very slow and careful movements Shaw
made a loop with her belt and then slid his belt
through that circle, cinching it tight and leaving a
stretch of leather about four feet long in his hand.

"What's that supposed to be?" she asked.

"A lasso."

"What exactly are you going to lasso?"

"That tree branch outside the car window." He
nodded at the short but thick piece of wood. "If I can
pull myself through the window, with my weight out
of the front seat, the rear should settle back down.
And I can get something to wedge under the front
tires. And then get you out."

"*Should? Should* settle back down? What if it
doesn't? What if you getting out makes the car go
hurtling down to those trees? Are you just going to
wave bye-bye while I plummet to my death?"

Shaw thought for a minute. "Okay. We've got

one shot at this. Just one. If we get out we get out together. If we go down, well . . ."

"Trust me, I get the picture. What's the plan?"

"Basically a thousand-to-one shot."

"Okay, I'm already loving it," she said sarcastically.

"As soon as I get the loop over that branch, you grab on to me like you've never held on to anything in your life. Got it?"

Katie's breaths were coming quickly now as the car started to tilt forward even more. "We're going over, aren't we?"

"Katie, did you hear me?"

"Yes, yes I did. Grab on to you, never let go. Got it."

"But wait until I get the loop over the branch."

"And you're going to do all that in the millisecond you'll have before we fall to our deaths? Pull us to safety using a belt I bought at the Gap for ten bucks?"

"Katie, don't go hysterical on me. I know you've been in plenty of tight places before. This is just one more of them."

She gazed fearfully out the windshield and then looked away. "Okay."

Shaw eased sideways and eyed the branch trying to convince himself that it would not necessarily be a miracle if what he was about to do worked. It would actually constitute more than a miracle, he realized. It would take divine intervention plus luck, plus some unknown element of cosmic wizardry.

"You ready?" he said.

Katie was breathing so hard she sounded like she was about to deadlift a ton of iron as she prepared herself to escape a two-thousand-pound car as it fell away from them at speed. She looked at the window opening. It seemed about three inches in diameter. They were never going to make it. *I can do this*, she said to herself. *I can do this. Oh please God let me do this.*

Shaw tossed the loop. It missed.

Katie cried out, "Maybe I can try it from back here." She hit the window button and the panel of glass slid down.

And then the car suddenly snaked forward.

"Oh shit!" Katie said.

"Hold on!" Shaw called out.

"It's going, Shaw. It's going over. Oh my God!"

The car was indeed going and there was nothing between it, them, and a hundred tons of oak. From where he was sitting Shaw could no longer even reach the branch with his belt rope.

"Shaw!" Katie screamed, gripping the seat with all her strength as the front of the car shot downward and the rear lifted up into the air like the *Titanic* about to take the final plunge.

Shaw swore, flipped backward over the seat, turned in mid-roll, and let the belt lasso fly out Katie's window.

It somehow snagged the branch and Shaw pulled it tight.

the whole truth

Miracles did, it seemed, happen.

The car's momentum had pulled Shaw, who was holding on to the belt with both hands, halfway out of the window.

"Katie, grab hold of my legs. Now!"

He felt her grip his legs. The car was going all the way, no stopping it now.

Shaw slid neatly out of the window but then something felt wrong.

"Katie!"

She wasn't there. He hit dirt hard; a jut of rock nailed him right in the gut. The belt slipped out of his hand and he tumbled down the steep hill. He looked in front of him and watched as the car gained more and more speed. His momentum caused him to flip over and land hard on his back. When he managed to sit back up he saw the car slam into the trees at the bottom. A second later an explosion ripped the air as the gas tank ignited.

Shaw grabbed on to everything he could get hold of, bushes, branches, dirt, and rock to stop his slide. If he went another twenty feet, there was no stopping and he would end up in the inferno down there too. He finally slammed against an old stump.

"Katie!" he yelled. "Katie!"

She didn't answer him.

91

The phone call woke Frank from a sound sleep.

It was the FBI agent they'd been working with.

Frank sat up, already groping around for his clothes that he'd dropped on the end of the bed when he'd turned in. "What's up?"

"One of the people on the St. Albans list, Richard Pender, was just found murdered in his home."

Frank's feet hit the floor. He pinched the phone against his ear with his shoulder while he hopped into his pants. "Sonofabitch!"

"And that's not all."

"Yeah?" Frank said warily.

"A neighbor of Pender's phoned the police; that's how they discovered the body."

"Why'd they phone? Did they see something? Pender's killer?"

"He saw what looked to be two people being carried out of the house and put into a car."

"Two people! Could they ID them?"

"It was dark. He couldn't be sure. But the man was

big. It took three guys to carry him. And the other appeared to be a woman."

"Did they see anything else?"

"He got the license plate of the car they were put in."

"And?" Frank slid into his shirt and tucked it into his pants and then slipped on his socks. "Oh shit, don't tell me."

"We traced the plate. It was James's rental car."

Frank stuck his feet in his shoes and roared, "What the hell were they doing there? We hadn't gotten a search warrant yet."

"Looks like they were doing a little independent snooping."

"Have the police tracked the car down yet?"

"No. They put out an APB, but nothing yet."

"Has anyone tried to call Shaw or Katie?"

"Yes. No answer. We sent people to their rooms. Nothing."

"When did the neighbor phone this in?"

"About two hours ago."

"Christ! They could be already dead. They probably *are* already dead. What's the take on Pender? When did they pop him?"

"Twenty hours ago or more, according to the prelim."

"Shit, that trail's cold. Wait a minute, if they killed Pender that long ago, what the hell were they doing watching his house?"

"Waiting for someone to come by?"

"You mean waiting for Shaw and Katie to come by. Just like the funeral in Wisbach. What the hell were they thinking going there?"

"The officers on the scene at Pender's home said it looked like a burglary gone bad."

"Burglary my ass. So what's the story on this Pender? Who is he?"

"He owns a firm called Pender & Associates based in northern Virginia. The picture isn't completely clear, but it seems to be some sort of PR firm."

Frank called Royce, filled him in, and arranged to meet the MI5 agent in the lobby in five minutes. He grabbed his gun, ripped open the door, and ran down the hall, pulling out his cell phone and punching in a number as he jogged along.

"Shaw and James are in serious trouble. Track him. Now!"

Frank hooked up with Royce in the lobby and the two agents raced to their car.

As they drove off Frank called the FBI agent.

"I want a strike team to hit Pender & Associates right now."

"We don't have the search warrants yet."

Frank yelled, "What are the odds of a guy on our list getting popped and Shaw and James getting snatched from the guy's house *not* being tied into this whole damn conspiracy?"

"About a billion to one," the agent admitted.

"So screw the warrants. Nail Pender & Associates. Now!"

Yet Frank's gut was telling him it was already too late. For Pender & Associates.

And too late for Shaw and Katie.

92

Shaw slowly rose from the mud and brush and steadied himself against a leaning, shallow-rooted pine. He stared down at the wreckage of the car; the flames started to burn down as the gas was used up. He had stopped yelling for Katie because he'd grown hoarse. He made his way down the hill, holding on to whatever he could. As he neared the burning car, he didn't want to even think about what was inside it. The charred fragments of Katie James.

The small groan caught him so off guard he nearly toppled forward and down into the flames. He whirled around, staring into the darkness to his left.

"Katie?" He was almost afraid to say the name for fear of hearing nothing back.

There was definite movement now. And it was too big for a rabbit or squirrel. He lunged forward, tripped, fell down, picked himself up, and raced to her side.

Katie was lying facedown next to an oak but struggling to rise. Shaw knelt beside her, gently turned her over.

"Damn, I thought you were dead."

Her face was bloody, her arm bent at an odd angle. She looked up at him, smiled weakly, but then grimaced in pain.

"So I'm *not* dead?"

He shook his head. "Not unless I am too. And I'm hurting too much to be anything except alive. Can you walk?"

With his help Katie got to her feet, holding her right forearm. "Think I might have busted my arm up."

He looked at it. Part of her bone was sticking out through the skin.

"Shit!" he exclaimed. "We need to get you to a hospital." He took off his jacket and fashioned a crude sling to keep the shattered bone as immobile as possible.

"Can you walk?"

She nodded. "If you can help me."

He put a big hand under her armpit and his other arm around her waist, and they slowly made their way up.

"What happened? You were holding on to me and then you were gone."

"Lost my grip and then I got snagged on the door handle."

"How did you get out of the car, then?"

"Pure luck. On the way down, the car hit something, probably another chunk of rock. The door popped open and I fell out." She looked back at the blackened mass of burned-out metal.

"A little close," she said.

"A little."

"Shaw, I think I'm going to be sick."

"It's okay, I've got you."

He held her while she emptied her stomach.

"Sorry," she said with an embarrassed look after she'd finished.

"Compound fractures always make me puke too," he said, attempting a smile.

As they neared the top they heard cars screeching to a stop on the road above and then running feet started coming their way.

"Get down, Katie."

"Shaw, Shaw, you down there?"

It was Frank.

"We both are," he called back. "And we need some help. Katie's arm is broken."

Five minutes later they were being driven off in an SUV. Frank and Royce rode with them.

"Pender's dead, but you already knew that because you went to his house tonight," Frank said accusingly.

"Can you wait at least until tomorrow until you jump all over my ass, Frank?" Shaw said.

"Why? It won't be any better tomorrow. Only worse."

Royce said, "Do you know who kidnapped you?"

"Never saw them. Whoever it was hit us fast and hard." He looked over at Katie. "She needs to get to a hospital."

"That's where we're headed," Frank said. "I already made the call."

"How did you know where Shaw and Katie were?" Royce asked.

Frank glanced at Shaw before answering. "Lucky guess."

Before Royce could say anything Frank's phone buzzed. He listened for about five minutes without saying anything other than curse words. He clicked off and tossed his phone on the floor.

"I take it that it's not good news," Royce said.

"They hit Pender & Associates."

"And?" Shaw said.

"And they got squat. Place was cleaned out."

"There has to be employees they can talk to."

"Oh sure. But after what happened to Pender, I doubt many of them will be real excited about talking."

Royce said, "But they have to interrogate them."

"They will, only don't hold your breath."

"I doubt anyone other than Pender knows the name of the third party," said Shaw.

"How do you reckon that?" Royce asked.

"Because he's dead," Shaw said bluntly. "What'd you find out about Pender & Associates?"

"FBI did a quick and dirty on them," said Frank. "They're sort of a specialized PR firm."

"No, they're a lot more than that. They're a *PM* firm," Katie suddenly exclaimed. "That's where I knew the name."

Everyone looked at her.

"What the hell is a PM firm?" Frank exclaimed.

"That's what we call our prime minister," Royce added helpfully.

Katie said, "Well, this PM stands for perception management. It's the way to manufacture the truth, on a large scale. The Department of Defense has it more precisely defined in some manual or other. The military really got into PM in a big way after the Vietnam War. There are a number of firms around the world that specialize in it. I did a story years ago on the subject. Or at least tried to do a story. A few people were speculating that PM firms were behind some of what happened in Persian Gulfs One and Two. WMDs, embedded reporters buying the company line, stuff like that. They have all sorts of methods and devices to do it. The best PM firms have taken it to a high art."

Frank snapped, "So if they specialize in this crap why didn't anyone suspect them of being behind the damn Red Menace?"

"Most people, including a lot of government leaders, have no idea they even exist. And like I said, I *tried* to do a story on them, but got nowhere.

There's not much information on them. They keep a low profile and don't talk in public about what they do. The firms I did manage to ferret out, including Pender & Associates, wouldn't talk to me. All shrouded in secrecy."

"And besides, the Russians are an easy 'bad guy' target," Shaw noted. "They're like North Korea. People will believe anything bad about them, and usually with good reason."

"Which is undoubtedly why they were selected," added Royce.

Katie said slowly, "So Pender & Associates might have also been hired to make the Chinese appear to be behind the Red Menace."

"You mean they killed twenty-eight people in London and blamed that on the Russians," Shaw added fiercely.

"But that's crazy. Why would anyone do that?" Frank said.

"Russia and China are just about to go to war. The rest of the world is rearming," Katie said.

"Okay, but who would want that?"

Shaw said, "Countries are all of a sudden spending hundreds of billions on weapons. And that money's going somewhere."

Frank scowled at him. "What, you're saying *defense contractors* are behind this? I really doubt Northrop Grumman, Ares Corp., or Lockheed are involved in this crap. They have boards of directors and shareholders and all that. There's no way they could keep that secret. And from what I can tell, they're all making plenty of bucks anyway."

"And really, Shaw, British Aerospace is doing quite nicely without resorting to inspiring possible Armageddon," Royce added.

"Maybe it's not about money," said Shaw.

"What else do big companies care about?" Frank countered.

Shaw sat back and closed his eyes.

"Shaw? Shaw, you better damn well answer me if you've got an idea about this."

But despite Frank's blistering broadsides as they drove along, Shaw did not break his silence.

At the hospital Katie was taken into surgery. Her broken bone was put back in her arm and reset and her forearm was placed in a cast. She stayed in the hospital overnight with Shaw sleeping next to her bed. When they got back to the hotel the next day she went with Shaw to his room. Katie sat on the bed with a pillow propped under her injured arm while Shaw made an impromptu snack for them from the contents of the minibar. Katie rubbed her cast. She was on pain meds but her arm still throbbed, and her entire body ached from her wild ride in the car down that slope.

As she munched on some organic chips and drank

a diet soda Katie said, "Okay, Frank's not here. Do you know why Pender would be pitting Russia and China against each other if not to make some fat defense contractors even richer?"

Shaw sat down in a chair and chewed on some nuts. "Think about what's really been happening."

She scowled at him. "Death, destruction, war? The plague? Or did I miss something?"

"Anna said something to me when she first started looking into the Red Menace."

"What was it?"

"She said it reminded her of something. Of attempts to create a new world order, or at least an old new world order, if that makes sense. The Russians wipe out a big part of the Taliban with one strike and tell the other Arab countries to back off or risk annihilation. Now the Middle East is going to hell and nobody cares because everyone's focused on Russia and China going toe to toe. And now the *major* countries are rearming for what looks to be a long-term standoff." He looked up at her. "Déjà vu."

"So you're saying whoever's behind this wants us to go back to what, the cold war?"

"By all accounts Russia and China scared the crap out of each other. They won't attack again. Just go into a long rearmament phase, along with all the other major powers; a mutual standoff. And now that Russia used cruise missiles against Afghanistan and got away with it, you think other countries might not try that

503

tactic against some of the other unruly nations, Muslim or otherwise?"

"You mean big boys exerting their muscle again? Like Russia and the U.S. used to do?"

"Something like that. Maybe somebody's tired of terrorists running the world's agenda. They want the old ways back."

"Yeah, great, the old ways that entailed the constant threat of *nuclear annihilation*."

"But the cold war also sparked the greatest military buildup in history. And aside from the Israel–Palestine equation nobody really gave a damn about what was happening in the Middle East for the most part back then except for oil. There were no murky moral questions about right and wrong or religious differences. It was simply a case of clearly defined good versus evil. People didn't have to think about it, it was what it was. Maybe some prefer that, even with the Armageddon possibility. Hell, maybe a lot of people do."

Katie finished her last potato chip. "You know, that asshole Pender never paid me my twenty million dollars."

"So?"

"So I said if he didn't I'd tell the world the truth."

Realization spread over Shaw's face. "Katie, you know that'll make you a target."

"I'm already a target."

"Then it'll make you a bigger one."

the whole truth

With difficulty she scooted to the edge of the bed
and put her feet on the floor. "Shaw, I've spent my
entire adult life trying to find the truth and I'm not
stopping now. And them coming after me is probably
the only way we're ever going to get to the truth."
She reached across and touched his arm. "Besides, I've
got you to protect me."

Shaw gripped her hand. "Okay, if we do this, we
have to do it my way. There'll be a lot of risk but
you have to trust me."

"I do. I actually always have."

93

At zero hours Universal Time, Katie James appeared on a video released on the same Web site as Konstantin had been. It was not a coincidence.

The footage had been shot by Shaw in her hotel room.

Katie had returned to her natural blonde hair, though it was still spiky. She spoke clearly and firmly using no notes. "My name is Katie James and everything I wrote in my earlier story was wrong. I told my newspaper not to publish it but they did anyway without telling me. But I can tell you the truth now. The Chinese are not behind the Red Menace. And the Russians did not commit the London Massacre. My source, Aron Lesnik, lied." She held up her injured arm. "I was almost killed by the people really responsible for all this." She paused. "And who are they? A man named Richard Pender was one person behind it. He ran Pender & Associates, based in Virginia. He is or was a perception manager. He's dead now, killed by whoever employed him to create the truth out of lies and make the world believe it.

Konstantin was a lie. The tens of thousands of people we thought had been slaughtered by the Russian government was a lie. The 'Tablet of Tragedies' was a lie.

"This was all done for one reason: to bring Russia and China to the brink of war. Why? So that the world would rearm. Who would want that? Who would possibly benefit? Well, over a dozen governments, including Russia, China, the U.S., England, France, and Japan have recently placed orders for trillions of dollars in weapons with a number of defense contractors because of the events put in motion by the Red Menace. Someone is trying to create a new cold war where we all live in fear of annihilation. But that's not going to happen because we won't let it. So whoever is behind all this, here's a little message from me." She paused, "The real truth will come out. And *trust* me, you won't like it when it does."

Along with Katie's statements on the video, leaks were made to all major news sources about Pender's involvement and subsequent murder with details designed to make her fellow journalists do all they could to find out the truth. A list of defense contractors benefiting from the new rearmament fervor was posted on the Internet. Details of how it was discovered that Lesnik was lying and his murder were released to two dozen major blogger sites. To say these facts spread like a California wildfire would have been a bit of an understatement.

The global reaction was swift. It was said that skies around the world were filled with smoke from the burning of "Remember Konstantin" T-shirts. The *Scribe* newspaper scrambled to put a positive spin on what had been done with Katie's story, found they really couldn't and Kevin Gallagher, Katie's editor, was sacked. The FBI started throwing thousands of assets at Richard Pender's murder. And in London the same was done with the massacre and Aron Lesnik's death.

All major defense contractors issued statements claiming they'd had no involvement in the Red Menace campaign. Much like the treatment of the Russians, few believed their denials.

Defense departments in every major country were ordered by their civilian leaders to suspend all contracts for new weaponry. Meanwhile, the Russian and Chinese governments ordered a stand-down in their near-war, and President Gorshkov and his counterpart in China agreed to meet at a neutral site to discuss their two countries' future relations.

Yet the world wanted more. Much more. They wanted to know who had lied to them. They wanted the person or persons really behind it all. And they wanted them yesterday.

94

Nicolas Creel sat all alone in his sumptuous conference room on the *Shiloh*. He'd heard from his executive teams at Ares. And the news was all bad. The contracts were all being suspended, every last one of them. There went several trillion dollars straight to oblivion. The idiot woman had guaranteed that the world would remain stranded in a hellish quagmire, where the weak and maniacal ruled the powerful and civilized. And she was anointed as a savior? Was he, Nicolas Creel, the only one who could see the truth? Under his vision the world would be a far safer place; now all that was ruined. And she had cost him his PM maestro. Pender could be replaced, but Creel knew he would never find anyone as good.

Because of Katie James, a legion of investigators would be delving into every detail of the origin of the Red Menace. And despite Creel's great pains to keep his involvement unknown, someone might get lucky enough to follow the trail to his doorstep. He would never go to prison, of course. The rich and powerful almost never did, despite whatever crimes they might have committed. His lawyers were too accomplished, his purse too deep, his reputation too good. He had built elaborate safeguards into the plan as part of his exit strategy in the case of a disaster. And his men had destroyed every single scrap of evidence at Pender's office. There was no direct proof anywhere. His fingerprints were on nothing. Pender was dead. No one else knew of his involvement except for a very few who had just as much to lose as he did.

No, it was not fear of prosecution that was crushing him now. It was the taste of a terrible injustice done to him. Instead of his triumph, instead of the world being put back into its natural balance, the earth was resonating with one name: Katie James. James had saved the world, people were saying. James had righted a great wrong. The woman was a true hero.

Yet the only thing James really had done was *screw* him, Creel concluded, and emasculate the part of the world that really counted. And for that she would have to pay. He was not a man who held grudges. At least not for very long. He was far too impatient when it came to that. The offending person must be dealt with quickly. Revenge was not best eaten cold. It was a dish that needed to be served with hatred still blazing hot.

He picked up his phone. He might not be getting his beloved cold war back. But there would be more casualties. Starting with one in particular.

He said into the phone, "I don't care if you have to take out an entire city with a dirty bomb. Either you bring me the lady within forty-eight hours, or our arrangement is ended *permanently*. And so are you."

Nicolas Creel left his beloved *Shiloh* and boarded a launch headed to shore. He spent the next several hours visiting with Italian officials regarding the construction of the new orphanage. After that he prayed in the chapel, the mother superior by his side. That evening he had dinner at a local restaurant and shared a bottle of Chianti with the mayor and his wife, trying to forget at least for a few hours the complete disintegration of his vision for the world.

Before returning to his yacht, Creel visited the construction site. He stood looking down into a pit that had been excavated a few days before. Very soon they would pour the foundation here. Hundreds of thousands of cubic yards of concrete would flow into this hole. The place would stand for a century, providing a worthy roof for many orphans.

But the foundation would not be poured until Creel gave the order. And he wasn't going to do it just yet. He had something very special he wanted to bless this place with. A gift that would lie here for all eternity.

He rode the launch back to the *Shiloh*.

And counted down the minutes until Katie James's death.

It wouldn't make everything all right, of course. For now, though, it would have to be enough.

95

Frank and Royce burst into the room where Katie was being kept under the watchful eye of two FBI vets. Frank said, "We just got another credible bomb threat. They must've found out where she was. There's an SUV waiting in front."

They hustled down the stairs. Royce pushed Katie into the SUV and then called out to Frank. "This is the third damn time. We better bloody well get her out of the country, Frank."

"I'm on it."

"Where do you want me to take her this time?"

"Location four. I'll meet you there in twenty minutes."

Royce nodded, shook his head wearily, and climbed into the seat next to Katie.

"Here we go again," he said kindly. "Sorry, Katie."

The driver sped off and the man next to him, big and burly, turned to face her, a large gun in hand.

Caesar smiled and said, "Glad to have you with us, Ms. James."

Katie looked startled, but then something jabbed her in the arm. She looked down at the syringe sticking out of her. And then at Royce who was pushing the plunger all the way down. As the meds hit her bloodstream, Katie slumped over in the seat.

Royce pulled the needle out and nodded at Caesar.

Caesar said, "Bugs?"

Royce expertly searched Katie for surveillance devices and shook his head.

Caesar handed Royce a battery-operated saw, which he used to cut off Katie's cast. Royce checked it over minutely and shook his head again.

The truck slowed to a stop, Royce got out, and tossed the split cast into a passing garbage truck. He climbed back in. "If the cast is bugged, they'll be on a jolly nice detour now. Hit it!"

The driver punched the gas and the Suburban shot forward, hung a left, and was gone.

Eight hours later the private plane touched down on a remote airfield in Italy. A truck pulled up next to the aircraft and a box was loaded onto it from the plane. Several men got in the truck and it rolled off. An hour after that it arrived at the Italian seaside, the Mediterranean moodily aglow under a setting sun. A launch carried the box, Caesar, Royce, and several other men out to the *Shiloh*.

The crew had been given the evening off. Only the captain remained on board, and he was sequestered on the upper bridge. Special visitors of a sensitive nature had been the only explanation given to the man. He didn't ask for another.

Nicolas Creel was sitting in the ship's library surrounded by first-edition books he'd purchased over the years, and unlike some collectors he'd actually read them. When the door opened and the box was brought in he didn't smile. He actually felt as though he would never smile again.

He nodded at Royce. "Good work. I never had any doubts your association would pay off for me."

"Pleasure, Mr. Creel. MI5 never saw my potential. And certainly never paid me fairly for it."

Creel looked at Caesar. "Shall we let the illustrious Ms. James join us?"

The big man opened the box and lifted Katie out. She was just coming to. Caesar laid her on a table. The men stood there until she sat up and looked around.

"Welcome, Katie," Creel said. "I may call you Katie? I feel like I know you so well even though we've never even met."

Katie slipped off the table and dropped into a chair. She rubbed her head and grimaced as she clutched her arm. "Where the hell's my cast?"

Royce said, "We thought it best to remove it. GPS devices can be embedded in such things."

"It was just a damn cast, you idiot." Katie held up her arm where the break in the skin was clearly visible.

"So you say."

She turned her attention back to Creel. "But I do know you," she said. "Nicolas Creel. Any journalist worth her salt would know you."

"I'm flattered. Yet you don't seem altogether surprised."

"Once I'd thought out a few things the list of suspects narrowed considerably." She glanced at Royce. "His involvement I didn't figure on, though."

Creel did smile now. "Of course not. But one must always have a safety valve. An inside source. And Mr. Royce shares my view of how the world should be. A view that you have now effectively destroyed. I can't even imagine how much you've cost mankind."

"What *I've* cost it? By stopping China and Russia from going to war?"

"There was never going to be a war, you fool!" Creel roared. "The cold war was the safest period humanity has ever lived through. My plan would have liberated the world. That's right, I was a *liberator*," he snapped, as Katie stared at him incredulously. "Now you've ensured that we will be ruled for eternity by savages who have no regard for human life. They have toppled all balance, crushed all possibility of diplomacy. We are as close to global annihilation as we have ever been, thanks to you, *Katie James*." He said her name as though it was the most repellent two words that had ever passed his lips.

515

"Yeah, I'm sure that has you bummed. But I'm thinking you're *really* pissed about losing out on all those weapon dollars."

"I have enough money, I can assure you. But Theodore Roosevelt had it right. Speak softly and carry a big stick. America's greatest presidents knew that military power was the key to everything. Everything!"

"Yeah, war is great, isn't it?"

"You built your career covering them, so you have no room to complain. Glory always goes to the victor."

"I didn't cover them by *choice*. And my reporting showed the horror of wars. I never found any glory in it."

"You obviously didn't look hard enough. Political history is defined by such confrontations."

"Didn't some famous general say it's a good thing war is so terrible or we'd grow too fond of it."

"That was Confederate general Robert E. Lee at the Battle of Fredericksburg. And, as history has shown, he was a *loser*. I only deal in winners."

"Have you ever been in the military, Mr. Creel? You ever been shot, or even shot at?" Creel didn't answer her. "Well I have. And let me tell you, with people who actually fight the damn wars there are no winners or losers. They're just survivors."

"Yes, well, I didn't bring you here for a lecture. I brought you here to die. But I wanted you to know why. And I want you to die knowing you have no one to blame but yourself."

She moved a bit closer to him. "Can I tell you something?"

"Every condemned person is granted a few last words."

"Go screw yourself."

"Brilliant, Ms. James. What a wordsmith you are."

The door opened and one of his men came in. "You have a visitor, Mr. Creel." His voice sank lower.

After he listened to him Creel said, "Get her off the ship right now."

The man said, "Sir, she mentioned something about seeing some computer files in your office."

Creel's eyes widened a bit. "I see. All right, I'll come out."

Out in the hall, Creel's wife was standing in high heels and a short skirt. Two of Creel's men stood next to her.

"My dear, what a pleasant surprise," Creel said.

Her response was to slap him. Creel's men grabbed and held her.

She screamed, "You think you can just leave me by the side of the road like a pile of crap? After all I did for you? And *to* you? You bastard! I'm Mrs. Nicolas Creel and that's the way it's going to stay."

"I can see you're upset. But all good things must end and the divorce payment is more than generous."

"You're *not* divorcing me. I know things," she said, a triumphant tone in her voice. As Creel eyed her stonily, she hurried on. "I know you think I'm just some dumb shit. But do you remember I told you I liked your office? Well, it wasn't for the reason you think. I've found it's always nice to have a little ammo in case people get too big for themselves. So I checked your computer. You know, Nick, when you divorced your last wife you should've stopped using her name as your freaking password. And from what I saw you've been a really bad boy."

"Well," Creel began pleasantly. "That does put a whole new spin on the matter. Come with me and we'll talk this out." He looked at his men. "Send her launch back in. She won't be needing it. She's staying with me."

Miss Hottie pulled away from the pair and sauntered after her husband.

When they entered the room and Creel shut the door behind them, Miss Hottie slowly looked around at the men in the room and then her gaze fell on Katie. "I know you, you're Katie James."

Creel stared in mock sadness at Miss Hottie. "I'm afraid your timing could not have been worse, my dear. And, by the way, you coming out here all alone and telling me what you know shows that you are indeed a *dumb shit*." He glanced at Royce and nodded. Royce pulled out his gun and fired a bullet right into Hottie's brain.

The dead woman toppled forward onto the table, slipped off, and crashed to the floor.

The phone buzzed. It was the captain. A boat was approaching the yacht.

"Who is it?"

"Looks to be the Italian police, sir. One of the boats patrolling the *Shiloh*'s perimeter."

Creel looked at Caesar. "Drug James. There's a body bag in the engine room. Put her in it and then take her and that"—he pointed to his dead wife—"to the sub. Quickly."

Royce held a struggling Katie down as Caesar stuck a needle in her. She fell limp again.

As the men dashed off with Katie and the murdered woman, Creel adjusted his jacket and went calmly abovedeck to greet his visitors.

96

Shaw emerged from the water after ditching his propulsion scooter and diving mask with a small oxygen tank built in, and scaled the port side of the *Shiloh* using magnetized grips against the steel hull. Even with the aid of the grips, it was tough going with his injured arm. He'd had a cortisone injection there because he knew things were probably going to get violent, but the limb was still weak. He looked at the transmitter device strapped to his wrist. Katie was on board somewhere in the bowels of the massive five-story-high ship.

Once Katie had been kidnapped Shaw's plan swung into action. They'd tracked her by satellite, followed the private jet here, and seen the launch heading out to the ship. Frank had been prepared for everything and had the necessary equipment flown over with them for Shaw to break into virtually anything. They'd agreed that he would go in first and then call them in at the critical time.

The *Shiloh* undoubtedly had first-class electronic security systems, which was why Shaw was wearing a jammer device around his middle; it would make him invisible to virtually anything the ship could throw at him.

Of utmost concern was Katie's survival. While she could've been killed at any time along the way, they'd concluded that whoever wanted her would want to do a face-to-face, which was the only way they could nail the person anyway. It was incredibly risky and yet Katie had never wavered from it, though they'd given her ample chances. His admiration for the woman's courage had never been higher. Now he just needed to get both of them out of here in one piece.

He took a gun from his waterproof bag, saw a door and slipped through it.

A minute later the police boat pulled up to the yacht.

Nicolas Creel graciously welcomed the uniformed officer onto the deck and spoke with him in the man's native tongue. The officer seemed embarrassed, apologetic to be bothering the rich man. Creel offered him a glass of wine and asked him how he could help.

The policeman said that it had been reported to them from shore that a very angry woman had boarded a launch to come out to the yacht. "We saw a launch pass, but we saw it was Mrs. Creel so we let it go. Then we got a description of the angry woman and it turned out it was your wife." The man looked embarrassed and said awkwardly, "So we came here to see if all . . . was all right, sir."

Creel laughed and thanked the man for his concern. "My wife is a bit tipsy, yes, but not remotely dangerous. In fact, I can say without reservation that she will never harm anyone."

"You are sure?"

"Quite. I'm only sorry you had to come all this way for nothing."

"No trouble at all, Mr. Creel."

As the man stepped back onto his boat, Creel gave him a little salute.

Shaw made his way down into the bowels of the ship and was surprised he didn't run into anyone along the way. The absence of crew didn't make him feel better, only more paranoid that he was being set up. That caution paid off because he hesitated for a split second before rounding a corner. An armed man walked past, and a second later collapsed to the floor with a cracked skull.

Shaw kept moving, eyeing the tracker on his wrist. He was getting closer to Katie. But the transmitter couldn't tell him if she was still alive. A pang of guilt hit him squarely in the chest. He never should have asked her to do this, even if she wanted to. There were so many ways for it to all go wrong.

He reached a set of double doors and opened one.

Staring back at him was a lavishly decorated theater. As he kept going down the hall he smelled chlorine. He opened a door, and the smell intensified.

The owner of this floating city had an indoor pool.

He felt the presence before he saw the person.

Shaw and the man collided, and the impact sent them both into the water. One of the man's arms encircled Shaw's neck. He grabbed his attacker's hand and his finger was nicked by the knife the man was holding.

Shaw bent the fellow's wrist back, breaking it. He seized the knife, swung it around, and felt it sink into the man's side. The grip around his neck loosened. Shaw made another stab to the man's chest and kicked free.

As he climbed out of the pool, he watched the body sink to the bottom, the water now clouded red.

Fortunately, he'd lost his gun before he'd gone into the pool. He snagged it, ripped open the door, and raced out.

And stopped dead.

Royce leveled his pistol at him. "That was too easy. I'm hardly impressed, Shaw. Now drop the gun."

Dripping wet Shaw did so and muttered, "How's it feel to be a dirty cop, Royce?"

"When I didn't show with James I guess you knew all you needed to know."

"No, I figured it out before."

Royce cocked his head, unease settling across his features. "How?"

"It won't matter to you."

"Why?"

"Because you'll be dead."

Royce waved his pistol, regaining his confidence. "You really are a damn fool. Well, I'm sure you want to see little Katie, so let's go. We'll do you together. She's in the submarine," he added jauntily. "How about that? The man's got his own bloody sub. Now that's real power."

Shaw brushed his hand against his belt, depressing a tiny dimple there that sent out a distress signal to Frank.

"But I will let you in on one thing, Royce."

"Really? What's that?" Royce said, sneering.

"Did you ever bother checking your watch? Because we put a bug on it."

Royce shot a glance at the timepiece on his wrist.

The next instant he was clutching his chest where the hilt of the knife stuck out, the blood from his burst heart already flooding the chest cavity. He looked back at Shaw.

"Impressed now?" said Shaw.

As Royce dropped to the floor, Shaw was already past him heading to the sub. And Katie.

The belly of the *Shiloh* was a series of huge hangars, the thirty-five-ton submarine parked in dry dock in the center of one of them. Shaw watched the men standing guard. There were three of them, one even larger than Shaw with long black curly hair. A radio buzzed in the hand of the big man. He listened, said something Shaw couldn't hear, and he and the two other men hurried off.

Shaw clambered on top of the sub, lifted the hatch, and dropped down inside. He searched as quickly as he could. When he saw the arm and legs of a woman sticking out from under a bench near the rear of the vessel, he felt his heart nearly stop. When he pulled the woman out and saw the blonde hair, he felt paralyzed. When he realized it wasn't Katie he started breathing again. Then he saw the body bag and it all hit him again. He unzipped it with shaky fingers.

Then he heard another sound. The men were coming back.

97

"Take her out of here now. And bury her in the excavation pit for the orphanage," Creel instructed the two men who held the body bag between them. "Put her in a box. I'll arrange everything at the construction site. I'll tell them it's a time capsule. Where's Royce?" he asked Caesar.

"Around here somewhere."

One of the men said, "Do you want us to kill her first, Mr. Creel?"

"No, I want her to wake up and realize she's been buried alive. They say there's no greater fear in humankind. I want her to feel that horror."

The body bag was loaded on the launch and the men set off.

Caesar said to Creel, "What now?"

"Now you disappear. Until the next time."

"I don't think so."

They slowly turned. Shaw was standing there pointing a gun at them.

Creel flinched as he saw who it was, but then quickly recovered. "They call you Shaw, don't they?"

Shaw said nothing. "I know of your connection to this matter so I doubt money will induce you to go away." Shaw still said nothing. "So it seems that we're at an impasse," Creel concluded.

He pointed his gun at Creel's head. "I don't see it that way."

"Mr. Creel?"

The captain was staring fearfully at them from the steps leading to the top deck.

Shaw took his gaze off the two men just for an instant. It was still too long.

The shot fired by Caesar burned a crease along the side of his head.

Shaw instantly rolled to his left and placed four compact shots of return fire.

Creel had already taken up hiding behind the bar area while Caesar was seeking higher ground to get a better shooting angle. Shaw sent those plans awry when he nailed the man in the foot. Caesar emptied his clip at Shaw. A moment later while Shaw was lining up his killing shot, his gun jammed.

Caesar dragged himself up the stairs with Shaw right behind. The two giants squared off on the top deck. After a few jabs to test the other's defenses, Caesar landed a shot to Shaw's injured but numbed arm and got a blow to the gut for his troubles. He next tried a headlong charge and his superior weight carried Shaw off his feet and the two men flew against the bridge console. Caesar grabbed hold of Shaw's shirt, nearly ripping it off. Shaw tried to take out the man's legs, but Caesar, showing considerable agility for a man his size and despite the wound in his foot, jumped out of reach and then attacked.

He gripped Shaw around the neck and started to squeeze. Shaw got a hand in under Caesar's chin and tried to lever his head back. But Caesar ducked under Shaw's grasp, spun behind him, and got him in a chokehold.

Shaw tried to break Caesar's grip but quickly realized that even if he'd been at full strength, Caesar was too powerful. His eyes started to bulge out and his knees buckled.

Caesar, obviously sensing victory, said, "First your lady and now you. Nice little pair. She died without making a sound when I pumped the round in her brain." He tightened his grip. "And I can see the same silent exit for you, asshole."

At the man's words, Shaw's mind went entirely blank, and then with a scream he broke Caesar's grip from around his throat. He bent the man's arm back so far and with such violence that he wrenched it completely from its socket.

"You," Shaw said.

Caesar dropped to his knees, vomiting from the pain. Shaw smashed him in the face with one of his size fourteens, toppling the man onto his back.

"Are."

A knife flashed in Caesar's good hand, but only for

a second before Shaw tore it free with a strength born of rage.

He plunged the blade straight into the man's gut and then slowly walked it up Caesar's torso, cleaving flesh and bone along the route until he stopped at the man's throat. Caesar was just about to die when Shaw pulled his pistol, cleared the jam, cycled in a fresh round, took aim, and fired it into the man's forehead.

"Dead," Shaw finished.

98

A large chopper circled the *Shiloh*. Over a PA system a man's voice said, "FBI, we are boarding this ship. This is the FBI, we are boarding this ship."

A hundred meters away the Italian police boat was skimming toward the ship. As the chopper landed on the helipad and the police boat tied up to the yacht Nicolas Creel stood imperturbably in the middle of it all.

The FBI and Frank wanted to arrest Creel on the spot. The Italian police insisted that this could not be done. They spent the next twenty minutes arguing, with neither side making any inroads.

"Mr. Creel is within Italian waters."

"And what does the FBI want with me anyway?" Creel said innocently. "It can't be tax evasion. I'm not a U.S. citizen."

Frank piped up, "Tax evasion! How about creating global mayhem? How does that grab you, asshole?"

Creel turned to the Italian police captain. "I have no idea what this man is raving about. They've invaded my yacht. Guns have been fired. Some of my men have been injured and even killed I believe. I'm the one who should be pressing charges. You were just out here, Officer. Did you see anything amiss?"

The policeman glowered at Frank. "Nothing at all, Mr. Creel. And now I will escort these men to shore."

"I'll be along to press charges against them."

"We're not going anywhere," an FBI agent said. "We have the full power of the United States behind us."

"Well, you are not in the United States," the policeman retorted. "You have no jurisdiction here."

"Actually they do."

All heads turned as Shaw came down the steps from the bridge.

Creel stared up at him. "I'm listening."

"The kidnapping of an American citizen," Shaw said.

"Who?" snapped the Italian police officer.

"Katie James!" Frank bellowed. "I suppose you've heard of her, Katie James?"

"She is here, you are saying this?" the officer exclaimed.

"She is not here," Creel said smugly.

"Really?"

They all turned again as Katie stepped onto the deck. Now Creel paled and he looked out to the water in bewilderment.

"Your guys took the woman who was killed, I guess your wife, in the body bag after Shaw made the switch," Katie said. "They didn't bother to check that it was me in there. We were about the same size and weight."

The Italian policeman looked at Creel. "Your wife is dead?"

"Of course she isn't. She's not here. I had her taken back to town. You must have seen the launch pass by."

"And then how did Katie get here?" Frank said.

"Same as he did," Creel said, pointing at Shaw. "Obviously, they're trespassing."

Katie held up her broken arm. "The tracking device wasn't in the cast. It was in me." She pointed to the wound on her arm. "They cut me open at the same spot as my compound fracture to put the transmitter inside me." She looked over at Shaw. "It was a technique I recently became acquainted with."

"That *is* how we followed her here," the FBI agent said. "And then we got a distress call from Shaw and came charging in."

"I am confused," the Italian policeman said. "What is all this about?"

"This man—" Katie started to say before Creel interrupted.

"She's been making these outlandish accusations on the Internet. Now I suppose she's going to say that

I'm some criminal mastermind, Officer. Which is absolutely preposterous."

"He kidnapped me," Katie said.

"And I'm saying I didn't. It's your word against mine. Hardly the stuff of a successful prosecution."

"Mr. Creel is building an orphanage in our town," the Italian said.

"I don't give a shit if he's gold-plating every road you got," Frank exclaimed. "We are taking his ass with us."

"I do not think so."

Creel said, "Officer, I will remain here, on my yacht. I'll call my lawyer and these things will be dealt with in an orderly, legal fashion."

"He also has a submarine on here," Shaw pointed out.

Creel rolled his eyes. "Oh, yes, let me escape in a submarine. Very James Bond." He studied Shaw closely. "But I believe the facts will show there *is* a violent criminal on board. This man murdered my personal bodyguard. Look at the blood on his hands and shirt."

Shaw was indeed covered in Caesar's blood.

Creel added, "Go up on the bridge and see for yourself."

One of the policemen ran up, then came right back down looking green and making the sign of the cross. 'My God, he has been mutilated."

The officer looked at Shaw. "Did you kill that man?"

"Yes."

Creel said triumphantly, "At last, a confession."

"I killed him in self-defense. I didn't exactly get this way all by myself." He indicated his bruised face and torn shirt.

"That's for an Italian court to decide. Officer, please take this murderer off my boat immediately."

The policeman drew his weapon, as did his men. Frank and the FBI agents did the same.

"No," said Shaw. "I'll go with them."

He looked at Creel. "This isn't over."

"Of course it isn't. You'll bring your ludicrous charges and my team of lawyers will fight them and by the time it's over I'll still be a free man loved by the world while you rot in prison. Now that's what I call justice."

Shaw launched himself at Creel before he was pulled off. No one saw Shaw's hand slip inside the man's pocket.

A breathless Creel said, "And now you can add assault charges to the list."

"Come on, Shaw," Frank said. "We'll get this all straightened out. And you," he said, pointing at Creel. "You try to get off the boat in a sub, a chopper, or a freaking spaceship, your ass is history."

"Good-bye, gentlemen. I look forward to addressing all of this in court and to seeing each of you suitably punished," Creel said coolly. He faced Shaw and smiled broadly. "And I'll think of you every time I'm on my yacht."

After the chopper and boat left, Nicolas Creel retired to his stateroom. He had numerous phone calls to make to deal with this mess, the first being to the men who were no doubt planting his fourth wife in Italian soil right now. Yet he would get it all worked out. He always did. It would just take a little time, a little money, and a little ingenuity mixed with nerve. That's all it ever took.

He slipped a cigar from his humidor and felt in his pocket for a lighter. His hand closed around a metal object, but it wasn't a lighter. He pulled it out. It was slender and flat. How the hell had that gotten in his pocket? He looked at it closely. Was that a smudge of blood? He could also smell something, something that seemed remotely familiar.

Creel had no way of knowing that at that moment Shaw was gripping a small remote control device. His hands manacled together as he rode in the police boat, he eyed Katie who was standing next to him. She looked at him—more specifically, at his torn shirt. Only Katie seemed to have noticed that the stitches Leona Bartaroma, the tour guide/retired gifted surgeon from Dublin, had sewn over Shaw's arm wound were missing. Then Katie eyed the small device in his hand before glancing up at him.

As their gazes locked, Shaw started to say something, but Katie shook her head. "It's okay, Shaw. You do what you have to do."

She squeezed his hand and looked away.

While the FBI chopper soared over them Shaw looked out to sea where the large steel floating footprint of the *Shiloh* sat like a great overstuffed whale on its back. Yet he wasn't thinking about billionaires' water toys bought with death money. Nor did he dwell on PM masters like the deceased Pender. Neither was he focused on going to an Italian jail for killing Caesar. And right now not even the truth concerned him all that much.

Against the dark sky he thought he could see Anna's face staring at him, perhaps beckoning to him, he wasn't sure. They were just two people trying to love one another in a world that didn't always allow that to happen. They had been caught up in a nightmare not of their making. And Shaw was so enraged by it all, so paralyzed by a loss that he would never be able to fully understand or overcome, that it was all he could do to merely press the button on the tiny remote he was holding. But staring at Anna's imagined face in the sky he found the strength. When he was done he tossed it over the side where it disappeared into the water leaving barely a ripple. The effects elsewhere would be far more lasting.

In his stateroom, Creel felt the metal object growing warm. It was the last thing he would ever notice.

When he heard the screams and smelled the smoke the captain raced down the stairs and entered the stateroom. Yet by the time he got there the spot where Creel had been sitting was now only a blackened mass of ash and bone lying on the floor. Later examination would show that it was the remains of the man even if it no longer resembled a human being. The captain would later testify that Creel had been completely alone when he died. And thus no one would ever be able to explain exactly what had happened. Or why Nicolas Creel had apparently committed suicide using a highly lethal phosphorus-based incendiary device.

99

Operating on a tip, the local police discovered the body of Mrs. Creel in a freshly dug hole at the bottom of the excavation pit the next morning. A few minutes after that, Shaw was released from an Italian jail. He walked out a free man with a fresh shirt on and his arm wound stitched up nicely courtesy of a local doctor called to the prison.

It would take a long time to uncover, catalog, and dissect what had happened with the Red Menace, Nicolas Creel, and Pender & Associates. But regardless, that truth could never be told to the public, decided the powers that be, including the United States, Russia, and China. Every scrap of information unearthed about Nicolas Creel's grand plot was immediately classified and buried forever. It might seem amazing that this was possible, but it was also true that such "burials" happened all the time all over the world.

Katie, Shaw, and Frank, among others privy to the details, were sworn to secrecy for the rest of their lives.

Katie had not taken this directive well. "Why keep it a secret? So we can make the same mistake again?"

She was told that if the world learned how close it had come to Armageddon and how governments around the globe had been deceived it would cause people to lose faith in their leaders.

"Well, maybe people should," Katie had shot back.

Yet when the president of the United States himself pleaded his case and appealed to her sense of patriotism, Katie had finally relented. But she had issued a caveat.

"Next time, why don't you people think about these things before rushing to judgment? How's that for a strategy?"

Eventually the world shrugged off this near-cataclysmic event and moved on, as it always seemed to do. It might not have been as safe as it was during the cold war, yet at least it wasn't a mere *perception* of security built on lies.

Shaw, Katie, and Frank traveled to London where there was a memorial service for the victims of the London Massacre. Anna's parents were in attendance, but Shaw kept his distance from them. Being attacked by Wolfgang Fischer in a London cathedral was not how he wanted to memorialize the woman he loved.

He did travel once more to Wisbach, to visit Anna's grave. On the second day he was there, and unknown to him, Katie and Frank arrived in the small town and knocked on the door of the Fischers' home.

Wolfgang, looking very old and tired, answered.

Katie said, "I'm Katie James. This is Frank Wells."

Wolfgang looked at them suspiciously. "What is it you want here?"

Frank said nervously, "I need to set the record straight, so to speak, about Shaw."

"I do not need the record set straight with *that* man," Wolfgang said, his face flushing.

"Yeah, I think you do," Katie said firmly.

"Why is that?"

"Because he deserves it. He deserves the truth. And you need to do it for Anna."

"For Anna? What do you mean!"

"Your daughter was brilliant and beautiful and accomplished and also head over heels in love with that man. And you need to understand why."

"Let them come in, Wolfgang."

They all looked at Natascha, who was standing behind her husband. "Let them come in and we listen. She is right. We must do this for Anna."

Frank and Katie swept past Wolfgang and for the next couple of hours the four of them discussed what had really happened.

"My God," Wolfgang exclaimed when it was over. "I would like to see Shaw. Tell him, tell him . . ." He looked helplessly at his wife.

"Tell him how we feel, that it is different now, how we feel," Natascha finished for him.

"Yes," said Wolfgang. "Different."

Katie said, "Get your coats."

100

Shaw sat on the ground next to Anna's grave. The leaves were just starting to turn and the wind had a bite. It felt good to be here, as though she were still alive. Her presence seemed very real. He believed he could stay here forever.

He heard them approaching long before he could see anyone. He rose and stared as the group came into view, Wolfgang leading the way. Shaw started to furtively back away from Anna's grave until he focused on Katie and Frank. Then he stopped, unsure of exactly what was going on, or what he should do.

Wolfgang walked directly up to him. "These people"—he motioned to Katie and Frank—"they have told us things about what happened."

"They have told us the *truth*, Shaw," Natascha said, taking his hand in hers. "And we are so sorry for how we treated you."

"Yes, so very sorry," Wolfgang added with a guilty glance at him.

Shaw looked sharply at Katie and Frank. Frank didn't meet his gaze, but kept his eyes pointed at the ground. Katie just gave him an encouraging smile.

Wolfgang slipped his arms around Shaw and hugged him, while Natascha embraced both men. Soon, tears were slipping down the Fischers' cheeks. Even Shaw's eyes moistened and his lips quivered from time to time as the three stood around Anna's final resting place with their arms interlocked, quietly talking.

Katie had to keep wiping bunches of tears from her eyes as she watched with Frank.

He finally whispered, "I can't take this anymore. I'm no good with the emotional stuff, Katie. Give me a nine-millimeter Glock stuffed down my throat over this crap any day." He turned and left, but not before Katie thought she heard a tiny sob escape his lips.

Nearly an hour later Wolfgang and Natascha took their leave.

Katie slowly walked over to Shaw as he stood by the grave.

"Thanks for what you did," he said, his gaze on the mound of dirt.

"How are you holding up?"

"Part of me knows that Anna is dead. The other part . . . just can't accept it."

"Grieving is an odd thing. They say it's a process with discrete phases. But it seems so different for everybody. And you feel so alone, that I don't see how they can call it anything other than a random sort of . . . personalized hell."

He turned to look at her. "You lost someone?"

She shrugged. "Anyone who's lived has lost somebody."

"I meant someone in particular."

Katie opened her mouth but just as quickly closed it.

"Is that why you drink too much?" he said slowly, his gaze now on the colorful trees.

Katie dug her hands in her coat pockets and stabbed at the earth with her toe. "His name was Behnam. He was a little boy who should have grown up to be a fine man, but he didn't. And it was my fault. I won my second Pulitzer and he ended up in a hole outside of Kandahar." She took a deep breath. "And, yeah, that's why I drink too much."

"You'll never forget him, will you?"

She shook her head. "Never. Can't." She choked back a sob.

"I know just how you feel," he said. He put a hand on her shoulder. "Good-bye, Katie. Take care of yourself."

He turned and walked off. In a few seconds, Katie could no longer see him.

She stood there by herself among the dead. Glancing at Anna's grave, she bent down and moved the flowers Shaw had placed there closer to the headstone. In the few words carved in granite Katie saw the life and memory of a remarkable woman, and the haunting image of the man who had loved her in life, and still clearly loved her in death.

She finally rose from the consecrated ground, turned, and slowly walked back into the world of the living.

And then Katie started to run.

The sounds of the footsteps approached him from the rear. He turned, his face registering surprise when she came into view.

Shaw said, "What is it? Are you okay?"

"I just realized I don't have a way out of here."

"I can give you a ride somewhere." He checked his watch. "We can be in Frankfurt in about ninety minutes. You can catch a flight to New York from there. Maybe be home in time for a midnight dinner at your favorite dive."

"I don't want to go to New York."

"It's where you live, isn't it?"

"I've lived out of a suitcase my entire adult life. And I don't have a job."

"You probably *could* get Amanpour's CNN gig now."

"Don't want it."

"So what *do* you want?"

"A ride from you."

"Okay, but where?"

"We'll talk about it on the way."

They stared at each other. Her eyes were glistening and Shaw's gaze drifted to the sidewalk. He said hesitantly, "Katie, I can't—"

She put a hand up to his mouth. "I know you can't, Shaw. And if you'd said anything else other than that, I would've already walked away. That's not what I want."

"So what *do* you want?"

She glanced off into the darkness of the Wisbach night before looking back at him. When she spoke her voice seemed to buckle with the weight of her words.

"I'm an alcoholic. I'm unemployed. I don't have many friends. In fact, I don't think I have *any* friends. And I'm terrified, Shaw. I'm scared to death that this is it for me. And if you tell me to go to hell, I'll tell you that we've *both* been there and it's just as bad as everyone thinks it is."

As the wind rustled the leaves on the trees and all around them the good folks of Wisbach settled in for a pleasant night's sleep, Shaw and Katie stared at each other in silence. It was as though neither had the courage, the breath, or the heart to speak.

Finally, Shaw murmured, "Let's go."

The two of them turned and walked down the quiet street.

Exactly to where, it was certain, neither of them knew.

AUTHOR'S NOTE

The term "perception management" has firmly entered the public lexicon. The Department of Defense even defines perception management in one of its manuals, so the military folks obviously take it very seriously. Many public relations firms now offer perception management, or "PM," as one of their services. However, it seems that not many of them do it very well. Apparently, if you want to be exceptional at creating the Big Lie, you really need to specialize in it.

PMs are not spin doctors because they don't spin facts. They *create* facts and then sell them to the world as the truth. And that, to quote the venerable Mark Twain (who would've had a field day with the PM guys), is the difference between the lightning bug and lightning.

Many of the techniques outlined in the story are standard operating procedures for these folks, even if I give them a different rubric. And by using these methods, a major untruth can be established so quickly and overwhelmingly across the world that no digging by anyone after the fact can make a dent in the public consciousness that it actually isn't true at all.

And that's precisely what makes it so dangerous.

ACKNOWLEDGMENTS

To Michelle, your early comments really paid off with this one. Without them I might have lost the readers at the first chapter.

To Mitch Hoffman, great editing job. Your advice and gentle prodding really helped the book realize its potential.

To Aaron Priest, Lucy Childs, Lisa Erbach Vance, and Nicole Kenealy, for allowing me to focus on the books.

To David Young, Jamie Raab, Emi Battaglia, Tom Maciag, Jennifer Romanello, Martha Otis, and all the folks at Grand Central Publishing, for helping to turbo-charge my career.

To David North, Maria Rejt, and Katie James at Pan Macmillan. David, you're a true visionary but, better still, a helluva guy to drink a pint with. Maria, your comments were rock solid as usual. Katie, I hope I did your name justice. Guys, it was cool to finally place a thriller across the pond.

To Steven Maat at Bruna, thanks for a great tour and for helping me polish the Dutch points.

To Stefan Lubbe, Helmut Pesch, and Barbara Fischer

at Lubbe. Stefan, thanks for being a book lover and a publisher who really understands both the business and writers. Helmut, thanks for the German insights and careful critique. Barbara, a long overdue thank you for all you've done for me over the years and for the use of your last name for a fabulous character.

To Luigi Bernado, for your help on the Italian piece.

To the Richter family, for the use of your names.

To Eliane Benisti, for the use of your name. I made you president of France! I hope you wanted the job.

To Leona Jennings, finally—finally—you made it in. It only took fifteen books, but I hope it was worth the wait.

To Bob Castillo and Roland Ottewell, for superb copyediting.

To Grace McQuade and Lynn Goldberg, for really getting my name out there.

To Deborah and Lynette, for somehow keeping me straight.

extracts reading groups
competitions books new
discounts extracts
competitions events
books
new
events books
extracts reading groups
new title reading groups
interviews
events extracts
discounts
new books events
events new events
discounts extracts discounts
www.panmacmillan.com
extracts events reading groups
competitions books extracts new